P9-DJB-041

JB

Forevermore

Forevermore

CATHY MARIE HAKE

BETHANYHOUSE
MINNEAPOLIS, MINNESOTA

Forevermore
Copyright © 2008
Cathy Marie Hake

Cover design by Jennifer Parker
Cover photography: Linda's Photography, Linda Motzko

All rights reserved. No part of this publication may be reproduced, stored in a retrieval system, or transmitted in any form or by any means—electronic, mechanical, photocopying, recording, or otherwise—without the prior written permission of the publisher. The only exception is brief quotations in printed reviews.

Published by Bethany House Publishers
11400 Hampshire Avenue South
Bloomington, Minnesota 55438

Bethany House Publishers is a division of
Baker Pubishing Group, Grand Rapids, Michigan.

Printed in the United States of America

Library of Congress Cataloging-in-Publication Data

Hake, Cathy Marie.
    Forevermore / Cathy Marie Hake.
        p.   cm.
    ISBN 978-0-7642-0318-3 (pbk.)
1. Women cooks—Fiction. 2. Texas—Fiction. I. Title.
    PS3608.A5454F67   2008
        813'.6—dc22

                                                    2007034141

To Cianna, Audrey, and Fiona—
three bright girls who see life's promises and
possibilities and embrace them with courage and joy.

CATHY MARIE HAKE is a nurse who specializes in teaching Lamaze, breastfeeding, and baby care. She loves reading, scrapbooking, and writing, and is the author or coauthor of more than twenty books. Cathy makes her home in Anaheim, California, with her husband, daughter, and son.

Forevermore

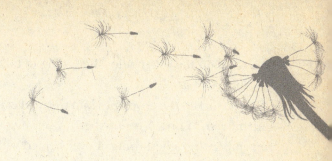

One

1891 Texas

The fields lay ripe for harvest; the house looked ready to collapse. A bounty of weeds fought vegetables in the garden for space, and a scraggly rosebush by the porch wouldn't last another week if someone didn't water it. Hope Ladley reckoned this was the right place to stop. God had a habit of sending her where folks needed a helping hand, and this farm practically shouted her name.

"Whoa." She didn't bother to pull back on the reins, for her mule never stepped lively enough to require more than a simple command. Hope jumped down from her two-wheel cart, gave Hattie an appreciative pat, and called out, "Anybody home?" She grabbed a sizable stack of envelopes and headed toward the house.

An obviously pregnant woman stepped out onto the front porch and shut the screen door with one hand while rubbing her lower back with the other. "You be a good girl," she said

9

to a child on the other side. "I'm going to talk to someone for a minute."

Hope tucked the envelopes into the pocket of her apron and murmured, "Lord, I do my best to serve you, but you gotta remember the onliest things I ever helped with a birthing had four legs."

The woman shuffled out from under the porch awning and lifted a hand to shade her eyes from the blazing sun. "Hello."

"Hello, yourself. I'm Hope Ladley." Hope headed toward her and belatedly remembered she'd shucked her shoes a few hours back. Oh well. No fixing that oversight now. "Ma'am, I'll come to you. Best you stay in the shade up there. Hotter than the hinges of Hades out here."

"It is terribly warm." The woman still wrapped her arms about herself as if she'd felt a chill. She looked past Hope. "Are you all by yourself?"

"I reckon you could say that, but God—He's always with me. And Hattie there—she's my mule—well, might hurt her feelin's if'n I didn't say she made for a fine travelin' companion."

Slowly, the woman nodded. She hadn't given her name and inched back up each of the four steps. Her tongue darted out and moistened her lips; then she cast a look at the tall, black yard pump. "Did you stop to get some water?"

"Hattie and me—well, we both had a long, cool drink a mile or so ago. Nice of you to offer, though."

"Annie?" A tall, broad-shouldered man in blue jeans came around the corner. He yanked off his straw work hat and cast a questioning look at his wife. Deep grooves bracketing his unsmiling mouth and scrunched brows bore testament to a man whose mind dwelled on more than his fair share of worries.

The lady on the top porch step said, "We have a visitor. Her name is—"

10

"Hope Ladley," Hope declared as she stepped up and shook the farmer's hand. It was big, sunburned, and callused—the kind of hand that bespoke someone who worked long and hard for everything he owned. He'd sweated and toiled to own this farm. Good, honest dirt under his nails—one of the best ways a woman could tell a man was a hard worker.

"Jakob Stauffer." His voice sounded as icy as his eyes looked.

Lord, I'm steppin' out in faith here. If this ain't where you're wantin' me to be, I reckon you'll send me away. Since the farmer didn't introduce his missus, Hope bridged the awkward silence. "I'm a plainspoken woman, Mr. Stauffer, so I'm gonna be up-front. Your ox's wallowin' beneath all that straw."

"There's nothing wrong with my team." The farmer scowled and dragged his hand from her grip. "Not a soul could say my livestock—"

"Now, hold it there for a minute. I'm just usin' a Bible sayin'." She leaned toward him a little and half whispered, "Aren't you God-fearin' folk?"

"Jakob, I think she meant the ox is in the ditch."

Hope perked up. "That's it! Then what critter gets all the straw?"

"A camel." The woman waddled down the stairs and stood real close to her man. "I'm Annie Erickson."

She's not his wife. Hope felt more than a bit confused. *Lord, I'm confounded. I must've been wrong about this bein' where you wanted me.* "So you already got yourself a housekeeper."

The woman twitched a pitiful excuse for a smile. "Jakob is my brother."

"You were talking to at least one young'un inside. Got a passel of 'em betwixt the both of you?"

"This—" Mrs. Erickson's voice caught. "This is my first."

"We'll be praying for you to have an easy time of it and for the babe to be healthy." Hope nodded and turned back to the farmer. *It's his turn to crow about his family.*

Sleet would look warm compared to his icy glare. "What do you want, Mrs. Ladley?"

"It's Miss. I'm free to follow wherever God takes me." She swept an arm toward his fields. "Harvest is nigh upon you. I don't mean to boast, but I can cook real fine. What, with all the men you'll have round to labor on your land, seems you could stand to keep me here to feed 'em."

"We were just talking about hiring two of the Richardson girls." Mrs. Erickson didn't sound very sure of herself.

Mr. Stauffer muttered something about the lesser of two evils.

"Tell you folks what. You don't know me from Eve."

"It's supposed to be Adam," Mr. Stauffer growled.

Hope shook her head. "Can't be. 'Course, you'd know me from him. Eve was the gal. Anyway, I reckon you oughtn't hire me right off without having some proof that I can turn out a decent meal. So tell me how many I'm to feed supper, what you have a notion to eat, and what time it's to be ready."

The farmer ran his hand through mud brown hair, but that didn't begin to remove the imprint from his hat. His grim expression didn't change one iota as he raised his chin toward his sister.

If he's leaving the decision to her, he's got to be a widower. Hope pulled the packet of letters from her apron and handed them to Mrs. Erickson. "Recommendations from other farmers. Some folks like that kind of stuff afore they make up their mind whether to keep me on."

Looking down at the thick stack in her hand, Mrs. Erickson sounded uncertain. "I suppose we could give her a try, Jakob."

"Dandy. I'll move my mule and cart outta the way. Mr. Stauffer, are you hankering after anything special to eat or is there any particular chore that needs doin'?"

He shook his head and took the porch steps two at a time. He paused at the doorstep and looked down at his dirty boots. "Emmy-Lou," he called before opening the door and hunkering down.

A little girl threw herself into his arms. "Daddy! Are you gonna take me to see the piglets again?"

"No." He cupped his big hand around his daughter's towhead and held her close.

Hope's heart did a little do-si-do. A man who cast aside his own troubles, knelt down, and loved on his child—there was a man to be admired.

He pressed a kiss on Emmy-Lou's head. "Milky snuck off and had her litter."

"She did?" Emmy-Lou pulled back. "I wanna see them! How many?"

"You be a good girl, and I'll show you where they are after supper."

"How many, Daddy?"

Mr. Stauffer rose. "I'm keeping that a secret right now. Since you're going to be a good girl, you'll be able to come out and count for yourself."

"It's always nice to have something to look forward to." Hope smiled at the girl. She had her father's blue eyes, but instead of being cool, they shone with innocence. Hope winked at her. "So is Milky a cat or a dog?"

"A cat." Emmy-Lou yanked on the side of her father's jeans. "Daddy, does that lady know how to bake cookies?"

"Shore do. You got a favorite kind?"

Curls bobbed as the little girl nodded. "Big ones!"

A smile flitted across Mr. Stauffer's face, then disappeared. "Miss Ladley, tie your mule to the sycamore. Shade's hard to come by."

Hope tromped back toward Hattie. Mr. Stauffer might seem all gruff, but he liked kids and animals. And his sister, too. With that many points in his favor, she knew he was a good man. A red bandana hung loosely around his neck, and a blue one had peeked out of his back pocket when he'd bent down to hug his little girl. That detail hinted that he was given to neatness. Well, then, he'd appreciate her helping things run smoothly.

As she walked Hattie right past the porch and toward the shade, Hope heard Emmy-Lou's high, little giggle. "Daddy, how come does that lady's mule wear a hat?"

"Her name's Hattie, and by wearin' one, she carries her shade 'long with her where're she goes," Hope called back. With her mule unhitched and roped to the tree, Hope stopped by the water pump with her stockings, shoes, and a towel. After washing her hands and face, she dampened half the towel and went to the porch. Mr. Stauffer had gone back to work, so Hope sat on the top step, swiped her ankles and feet clean, then pulled on her stockings and shoes.

"Are you," Emmy-Lou asked as she hopped and wiggled, "gonna make me cookies now?"

"Can't say for certain. Don't you worry none, though. I promise I'll bake up a batch."

"Big ones?"

"C'mere." Hope tugged Emmy-Lou close and inspected her hand. "My, you're a big girl!"

"Un-huh!"

Hope traced her finger around Emmy-Lou's palm. "Well, a girl your size would probably want a cookie so big it would barely fit in her hand."

Mrs. Erickson remained by the door. "Emmy-Lou, it's naptime. *Gehe zum Bett.*"

Go to bed, Hope translated in her mind. Emmy-Lou's lower lip poked out in a pout. Hope turned her and gave her a nudge. "*Ja*, Emmy-Lou." She searched for the German words for "sleep well." "*Schlaff gut.*"

"*Sprechen sie Deutsch?*" Mrs. Erickson gave her a startled look.

"Only a tad." Hope held open the screen door. "Just enough to get by in the kitchen. Don't much matter what the language, a rumbling belly sounds the same."

Once inside, Mrs. Erickson held Emmy-Lou's hand and looked a little uncertain.

Hope inhaled deeply. "Mmm-mm. You're bakin' bread. If'n you tell me how much longer it needs, I'll be happy to pull it outta the oven so's you can take a nap yourself."

Mrs. Erickson shook her head. "I need no nap. Have some coffee." She looked away and added, "I will be back with you in a minute."

While Mrs. Erickson tucked her niece into bed, Hope glanced around the downstairs of the farmhouse. Stairs divided the area in half. A large, sunny parlor with a piano lay to the left of the door. Just beyond it, a door to a small room stood open. Snooping would be wrong, so Hope satisfied her curiosity simply by standing on tiptoe and craning her neck. A rolltop desk and a shelf of books told her Mr. Stauffer must have a lot of book learning.

To her right, a set of matching maple furniture made her breath catch. The washstand, hutch, table and chairs looked so grand, Hope figured even a king would be proud to own them.

Shafts of wheat woven into pretty designs hung on either side of the washstand, and on the adjacent wall a sampler and a framed photograph decorated the wall to one side of the sunny window. The picture captured a blond woman, aglow with love, gazing up at Mr. Stauffer. In contrast to his present worry lines, in the picture he looked completely carefree. A clock hung on the other side of the window. The gleaming brass pendulum ticked the seconds while the hands momentarily clasped together to show the time of five minutes past one.

Beyond that were the kitchen and a door that undoubtedly led to a pantry tucked beneath the stairs. Blue-and-lavender-flowered feed-sack curtains swagged to either side of a window right over a big sink, and coffee stayed warm on a huge Sunshine stove.

Hope headed into the kitchen. Women could be mighty particular about their kitchens, and she'd learned to pay heed to what a lady said. Following directions on the first day invariably put everyone on a good footing. As it was, Mr. Stauffer acted downright unfriendly, and Mrs. Erickson seemed pretty standoffish. *If'n this is where God wants me, all's I need to provide is a good meal and a little time, and we'll all get along.*

"Mugs . . . mugs . . ." In the second cupboard she opened, Hope found dishes—white ones with a dainty ring of forget-me-nots along the edge. She took out two cups and went to the stove to fill them. Hearing Mrs. Erickson come down the stairs, she asked, "Should I get cream out of the icebox for you?"

"*Nein*. I can get it."

Hope slid the cups onto the table. "Ma'am, I'm here to help. All I did was sit in the mule cart all morning. I'd count it a favor if you'd let me stretch my legs again by fetching the cream before we have us a sit-down."

Mrs. Erickson nodded. Her gaze skittered away.

Poor woman was timid. Maybe embarrassed, too, at starting to slow down on account of her big belly.

A chuckle bubbled out of Hope as she lifted the whimsical porcelain creamer. "Never milked me a frog, but this'un's cute enough, it makes me think 'tis possible." She set it down on the table and scooted the sugar closer to Mrs. Erickson. "Reckon gettin' sugar and cream from a frog's loads better'n gettin' warts."

"I . . . I suppose so." A hesitant smile crossed Mrs. Erickson's face.

Hope slid into a chair and took a sip from her cup. "Oh, you make a fine cup of coffee. I like putting eggshells in with the grinds to take out the bitterness. What do *you* do?"

"Eggshells."

Hope smiled. "Now, how'd you like that? No wonder I thunk yours tasted so good. I noticed that stove there. Mighty fine one. Big reservoir shore must come in handy."

"It does not burn so hot as a wood stove, but I like it."

"Me too! Baking takes a few minutes longer, but the biscuits won't burn as quick if you get busy with something else." Hope took a sip of coffee. "I saw the coal bin. If'n you tell me where you keep your coal, I'll fill it up."

Mrs. Erickson glanced at the clock and started to rise.

"Betcha the bread's ready." Hope hopped up and motioned her to sit back down. "Ma'am, I don't mean to horn in, but it seems to me that there's gonna be plenty 'nuff for us to do.

Might as well have you save up your strength whilst I work out my wiggles."

Over the next fifteen minutes, Hope coaxed information from Mrs. Erickson. When they'd decided on what to make for supper, Hope asked, "How many do we cook for?"

"There will be Jakob, Phineas, Emmy-Lou, you, and me."

So that's her husband's name. I wondered where he was. Odd-sounding name. Hope repeated it to commit it to memory. "Phineas."

"My brother's farmhand." Mrs. Erickson stuck her spoon into her coffee cup and stirred, even though she'd already swallowed all but the last mouthful. "He sleeps in a room in the barn, but he eats with us here."

Something's a-goin' on and she don't want me to know. Well, I don't gotta know. She'll tell me when she's good and ready. Hope decided to change the topic. "That Emmy-Lou, she's a comely child. Her hair puts me in a mind of duck down. Is it just as soft?"

Relief flashed in Mrs. Erickson's eyes. She nodded.

"How old is she?"

"Four. Almost five." When Hope nodded encouragement, Mrs. Erickson hesitantly added, "They cut her hair when she had the fever."

"Long hair drains a sick gal's vital energy." Hope straightened her apron. "Lopping it off probably saved her life."

Mrs. Erickson bobbed her head—a tiny jerk of a movement.

Either this lady's painfully shy, or she don't want to get too friendly in case they decide not to keep me on. Well, won't be the first time I had to prove myself. "If'n you don't mind, I'd shorely like to bake up a batch of cookies for her. Young'uns have a habit of taking a thought and turnin' it into a promise."

"We can do that."

"Mrs. Erickson, ma'am, do you mind me askin' on whether you can read?"

"Yes." Hastily she tacked on, "I'm sorry. I don't mind you asking. Yes, I read."

"Dandy! Then, how about me gettin' the lay of the kitchen whilst you read them recommendin' letters?"

Hope refilled Mrs. Erickson's coffee cup, then mixed up a batch of oatmeal raisin cookies. As she dropped spoonfuls of cookie dough onto the baking sheet, she asked, "Do y'all have a springhouse?" *Blop*.

"What do you need?"

"That cream's about gone, and so's the butter." *Blop*. "Reckoned I'd go fetch some." *Blop*. "What with Emmy-Lou nappin' "—*blop*—"I'm shore you"—*blop*—"don't want her"—*blop*—"wakin' up to a stranger." *Blop*.

"You do that so fast!"

Hope grinned. "You know the sayin', 'Strike while the oven's hot.' "

"Iron." The woman barely mumbled the request and couldn't even look Hope in the eye as she made it.

"I'd be glad to iron." She popped the cookies into the oven, banged the flatiron on the stove, and asked again, "So where's that springhouse?"

Jakob's gait slowed as he walked past the garden. Dark pockmarks in the soil abounded where weeds once thrived—freshly tilled spots that accused him of not having seen to the garden as he ought. Oh, he'd had every intention of weeding the garden, but urgent things kept popping up. So had weeds.

A few items fluttered out on the clothesline—even though it wasn't laundry day.

Knocking some of the earth off his boots on the edge of the lowest porch step, Jakob wrinkled his nose. Vinegar. Odd. Unsettling, even. As he approached the door, the scent made sense. Someone had cleaned the windows. He corrected himself. Window. Only the one to the left of the door had been cleaned. Dust still coated the right one.

He spied Miss Ladley through the clean window. Standing in profile to him, she ironed Annie's Sunday-best dress. She'd been wearing a straw hat earlier—a battered one that hid her hair. In fact, if she hadn't cut holes for the mule's ears in the other hat, she should have traded the beast and worn the better one. At any rate, he could see her hair now. The color of ripe wheat and braided to resemble the same, her hair was pinned in a large circle around the back of her head, and dozens of small wisps coiled around her face and nape.

As women went, she was ordinary enough—neither tall nor short, fat nor thin, pretty nor homely. Upon meeting her, he'd absently noticed the sprinkling of freckles across her nose and the directness in her hazel gaze. The former made her look young; the latter lent an air of maturity. Jakob rubbed the back of his neck. He'd talk with his sister and ask how the day had gone. Annie needed help, but she didn't need anyone prodding her or prying into things.

Pulling his gaze from the woman, Jakob opened the door. The mouth-watering aroma of meat and potatoes filled the house. Miss Ladley glanced at him from the other side of the ironing board and motioned toward the washstand. "Do y'all like your water cool after a hot day, or warmed up a mite?"

"It's fine the way it is." He hung his hat on the peg by the door, then paused at the washstand and went through his usual ablutions—but it felt odd, having a strange woman in the kitchen while he did so.

"Your daughter's out on the back veranda with her auntie. Soon as your hired hand comes in, I'll put supper on the table."

"All right." He walked past her, through the kitchen. Ever since Naomi died, he'd stopped coming through the back door at suppertime. It grieved him too much to come in and not see her standing by the stove. She'd always stop her humming just long enough to welcome him. Eight jars sat back by the sink—each filled with string beans. Who bothered to can only eight jars? It made no more sense than only one clean window. Brooding, he shoved open the back door.

"Daddy!" Emmy-Lou sprang into his arms. "I've been good! Will you take me to see Milky and the kitties now?"

"After supper." He pressed a kiss on her forehead and turned toward his sister. "Annie?"

Annie continued to whirl the hand crank on the Daisy paddlewheel butter churn. It was a light chore, to be sure, but he still frowned. Annie was fragile, and he didn't want her working so much. She cast a glance toward the house and whispered, "Her letters—they all praise her. Lavishly praise her. Twenty-three of them, and I read them all. Do you remember Lionel Volkner?"

He nodded. "Leopold's oldest brother."

"One recommendation is from him. He said he's never seen a woman work harder."

"Is that so?" Lionel Volkner was a man of few words, and most of them were harsh.

"Daddy?" Completely oblivious to how her father and aunt had been whispering, Emmy-Lou said loudly, "She baked me big, big, big cookies. Do I getta eat one while we see the kitties?"

"Have you already eaten one?"

Emmy-Lou wrinkled her nose and turned to Annie. "I didn't. Did I?"

"We all shared one after you woke up from your nap."

The door opened. Miss Ladley laughed. "Milk and cookie then, and after supper, Emmy-Lou wants Milky and a cookie again."

Emmy-Lou giggled as she galloped to the door. "That was funny. You could see Milky with me and have your own cookie."

"We'll see. Your pa worked hard all day. First off, we've gotta feed him." She'd leaned down to talk to Emmy-Lou, but now Miss Ladley straightened up. "Lookee here, Emmy-Lou!" She took the butter churn from Annie. "Your auntie done went and churned butter, and she made you buttermilk to go with your supper. Wasn't that nice of her?"

"Uh-huh!"

Pulling herself out of the chair, Annie reached for the churn. "I'm sorry I took so long. I should have had that butter rinsed and pressed by now."

Before he could say anything, Miss Ladley responded. "Weren't no hurry. And cream can be stubborn. It takes a notion how long it wants you to churn afore it gives up the butter. What say I rinse and press this whilst you help your niece spruce up and get to the table?"

Jakob held the door open. Miss Ladley waited until Annie and Emmy-Lou entered, then slid past him and went directly to work. As he pulled the door shut, something caught his eye: Annie's dress, his white shirt, and Emmy-Lou's tiny dress—their Sunday-best clothes—freshly ironed and ready to be carried upstairs. Jakob's initial rush of gratitude changed to astonishment as he looked a little higher to see how she'd managed to hang the

22

clothes. That crazy woman created a peg by wedging a table knife between the top of the pantry door and lintel.

One hand barely closed around the hangers before the other yanked out the knife. Almost desperately, he studied the spot and reassured himself she hadn't damaged the wood or paint. Perfect. The knife hadn't marred it at all. He'd painted the kitchen one Thursday as a surprise when Naomi went to market. He'd worked like a madman to get it all done before she returned, and the memory of her delight washed over him in a bittersweet wave.

"Daddy's got the clothes."

"Ain't that nice of you to take the clothes upstairs, Mr. Stauffer?" The tin pitcher tinkled as Miss Ladley poured the buttermilk into it. " 'Tis always grand to see a family that pitches in and helps out."

Annie looked terror-stricken. "I'll do it, Jakob. I—I should have taken them up sooner."

Annie needs to see I'm willing to pitch in—that I'm not like Konrad and won't lose my temper. "You're helping Emmy-Lou. I'll take care of this."

"Mind your steps once you get to the upstairs hallway." Miss Ladley turned back toward the stove and said over her shoulder, "We threw a rug over a floorboard 'cuz the nail took a mind to pop up its head and look around. After supper, I'll take a skillet and pound it back in place."

Jakob's guilt, doubts, and worries mounted as he climbed the stairs. He'd seen that nail and forgotten about it. *I should have taken care of it.* But he feared Annie or Emmy-Lou could slip on the rug. Annie needed assistance since she'd grown heavy with child, and she certainly needed dawn-to-dark help during the harvesting and canning. Miss Ladley seemed busy enough, but she apparently didn't finish anything. His mind ticked off what chores he'd seen her abandon only partway through the job . . . laundry, window washing, ironing, and canning. *I'll bet her cookies are only half-baked, too.*

But the only alternative he could come up with was to hire two of the Richardson girls. They were capable farm gals who knew what to do, and they'd gotten better about not blurting out the first thing that crossed their minds—thanks to Tim Creighton's wife's lessons. But the Richardson girls were far more interested in catching a husband than in cooking and cleaning. Jakob hung the dresses in the armoire and suppressed a groan. He'd rather suffer an invasion of locusts than fend off those girls after they got the mistaken notion that this was a bridal interview instead of temporary help.

With twenty-three letters, this Hope Ladley has wanderlust. I won't have to trouble myself over her making matrimonial plots. He went to his bedchamber and strode past the bed without looking at it. Glimpses of the wedding-ring quilt Naomi had so lovingly made while they were courting brought memories he couldn't entertain right now. He hung his shirt on the knob to his armoire. Even a year and four months after he'd lost her, opening the armoire hurt—the empty space inside drove home that she was gone. No one could ever fill the void in his heart and life. No one. In that respect, Hope Ladley was probably the best candidate for the helping out around here. Unlike the Richardson girls, she'd wander on to the next town when her work was done.

Organization had been Naomi's gift. She could put anything into order and keep it that way, and their home had always been a haven. Since her death, the household had been chaotic, the inner turmoil Jakob suffered matching the disarray surrounding him. He craved the serenity he'd once known—but Naomi was gone. If the housekeeper could bring things back to order, that would help a little.

Phineas shouted, "I'm going to say grace and start eating all on my lonesome if you don't shake a leg!"

"Coming." As Jakob descended the stairs, he overheard Hope telling a story about somewhere else she'd been.

"No doubt about it," Miss Ladley said, "that Latimer boy ain't gonna try a crazy stunt like that again!"

Phineas belted out a laugh, but Jakob's blood ran cold. What if she left here and talked? One slip of her tongue, and all would be lost.

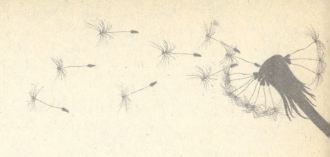

Two

"I can't decide whether supper smells better than it looks."
Phineas stared at the food.

"I reckon how it tastes is most important." Miss Ladley put a large pot of water on the stove.

Cucumber salad and watermelon on the table looked cool and refreshing. A steaming gravy boat sat near Jakob's place. Shepherd's pie with the mashed potatoes crust baked just the way he liked it—not pale golden brown, but deep, dark crispy brown . . . just the way Naomi always made it. Suddenly Jakob's appetite fled.

" 'Tis easier for me to hop up from the table, Mrs. Erickson. Do you mind if'n I take that seat there?"

"No . . . I . . . no, not at all."

Jakob seated his sister while Miss Ladley took the spot on the other side of his daughter, closest to the stove. Phineas scooted in her chair. "Thankee kindly," she said.

Multiple thoughts spun through Jakob's head—but if he prayed, he might speak them aloud and make matters worse.

"Phineas, go on and ask the blessing." Jakob folded his hands and bowed his head.

Phineas said grace. As soon as he said amen, Emmy-Lou drew in a breath and plunged into the prayer she'd been taught. *"Komm, Herr Jesu, sei unser Gast, und segne, was Du uns bescheret hast. Amen."*

"Nice to hear a young'un talkin' to the Almighty." Miss Ladley gently tucked one of Emmy-Lou's pale blond curls behind her ear. "That was the first prayer my mama taught me."

"Auf Deutsch?" Phineas looked as surprised as Jakob felt.

"Nope." Miss Ladley scooped a tiny serving of cucumber salad onto Emmy-Lou's plate. "I learnt it in English. It rhymes thataway, too. 'Come, Lord Jesus, be our guest and may these gifts to us be blest.' Ain't it something, how the love of God don't depend on the words of man? The feelin's the same, no matter whate'er tongue you use."

"I only got one." Emmy-Lou opened her mouth and stuck out her tongue.

"And you used it to thank Jesus. God loves a cheerful heart. I'm shore He must be a-sittin' on His throne in heaven, just a-smilin' down on you right this very minute."

Miss Ladley neither laughed at nor scolded his daughter for her action. Emmy-Lou befriended everyone, but it did Jakob's heart good to see how Miss Ladley took note of her pure intent. Emmy-Lou beamed back at her.

Miss Ladley lifted her chin toward Annie. "You got the server o'er by you, ma'am. The menfolk are lookin' hungry as can be."

Annie's gaze dropped along with her voice. "You prepared the meal."

"Nonsense! You peeled the 'tatoes and onion. Cut 'em up, too. The meat we used—I bet you put that up when one of them fine cows of yours got butchered."

"Ja, she did." Jakob picked up his plate, stuck it out, and waggled it a little at his sister. "Smells great. Let's eat." Even if Miss Ladley jumped from one chore to another like a mindless grasshopper, she treated his sister and daughter well. That counted for a lot. *I'll get Annie alone for a few minutes and see what she thinks. It's hard for her to make up her mind about things, so I'll have to be sure to let her know I can let Hope go anytime if Annie feels things aren't working out or if she feels too uncomfortable around the housekeeper.*

Assuming Annie says it's okay, I'll ask Miss Ladley to stay. But someone with her recommendations—she might charge more than I can afford. Money was tight. Jakob mentally juggled finances and tried to find ways to scrape together an offer she'd accept.

Emmy-Lou jabbered during the meal. Phineas teased her by saying a few things about Milky, yet he refused to answer her questions. Miss Ladley popped up from the table to grab the coffeepot and refill their mugs, and she subtly scooted Emmy-Lou's cup so it wouldn't get knocked over. Suddenly a trill of laughter flowed out of her. "Mr. Phineas, you got me ev'ry bit as curious as Emmy-Lou 'bout that litter."

"When your daddy was a boy," Annie said softly, "he had a gray striped cat that followed him like a dog."

Her comment took Jakob by surprise. Timid as she was, she didn't tend to say more than she had to. Was she talking because she was nervous around Miss Ladley, or because Miss Ladley made her feel . . . safer? More comfortable? Jakob gave his sister a smile and bobbed his head. "That is true. That cat—he got me into big trouble."

"He did?" Emmy-Lou's eyes grew huge.

"We had a big old cottonwood by our house. In the summer when it was hot, I'd leave my window open. Fleck—I named him that because he was gray with a black smear down his back and *Fleck* means smudge—Fleck climbed the tree, jumped to the house, and curled up at the foot of my bed. Mama or Dad would find him there." He shook his head. "They said even if he didn't know better, I did."

Phineas cleared his throat and eyed the shepherds' pie.

"I'm sorry. I should have offered you more. Here." Annie hurriedly gave him a third serving, then held the server over the last of the shepherd's pie. "Jakob?"

He accepted with alacrity.

Once he took the first bite, Emmy-Lou said in a tearful tone, "It's all gone and I wanted more."

"Here." He shoveled his fork under a hefty bite.

"Hold your horses." Miss Ladley tipped her head down and asked in a loud whisper, "Did you remember to save room for a cookie?"

"I forgot." Emmy-Lou sat up straighter. "Daddy, I'm almost all full-up."

Annie sighed softly. "I'll be sure to give you more next time."

"Okay." Emmy-Lou held up two fingers. "Daddy, they made two of those. I helped carry the other one out to the springhouse."

Knowing there'd be another of these fine dinners didn't disappoint him in the least. Jakob smiled at his daughter. "It is *gut,* you helping."

"Emmy-Lou's a good weeder, too." Miss Ladley picked up a wedge of watermelon. "Your daughter's a fine worker."

A few minutes later, Jakob looked about the table. Every last plate was clean—even Annie's, which didn't happen often. A small thread of relief darted through him. She didn't eat much at mealtime, and as far as he could tell, she didn't nibble all day long the way Naomi had when she was expecting. When Naomi had only a month to go, she'd needed to leave some of her buttons open beneath the cover of her apron; Annie's belly bulged, but not with the same abundance that bespoke a fat, healthy child. If he hired Miss Ladley, maybe she could coax Annie into eating more.

"Jakob?" Phineas gave him a questioning look.

Miss Ladley glanced over Emmy-Lou's head. "Some of the families I helped just say grace before the meal. Others, they go before and after. What about you?"

"Both." He bowed his head and mentally translated so Miss Ladley would be able to share the prayer in English. "Our hearts are grateful, you have satisfied us now. Let us in work, joy, and pains rest in your love! Amen."

Miss Ladley didn't raise her head. She kept her eyes closed and whispered, "If'n y'all don't mind, I'd feel better if you said it together the way you normally do."

"But Daddy said it funny. I don't know it that way," Emmy-Lou piped up.

Miss Ladley reached over and curled her hand about Emmy-Lou's. *"Dankbar sind Dir unsere Herzen . . ."*

They all joined in once she started. Afterward, Miss Ladley stacked the dishes. "I don't come to change things. I just come to help out."

Jakob shot his sister a questioning look. Annie chewed on her lip and said nothing. That action tattled, though. She was unsure.

"You surprised me." Phineas chuckled. "I've never heard German spoken in that accent, though."

"It's 'cuz she has two tongues. I only got one." Emmy-Lou stuck hers out again. Suddenly, her eyes lit up. "When I grow up, will I grow another one?"

"They don't mean what you have in your mouth, *Liebling*," Jakob explained. "Tongue also means speaking another language."

"Oh." Emmy-Lou looked disappointed.

"There's a hymn from a man what wisht he had a thousand tongues." Miss Ladley carried dishes to the sink. "He said he'd use 'em all to praise God."

"He'd look silly." Phineas grabbed a cookie.

"He'd sound grand, don't you think, Mrs. Erickson?"

Annie nodded. "I suppose so." She started toward the sink with more dishes.

Miss Ladley took them from her. "That niece of yours—she's been itching to go see them kitties. How 'bout you grabbing cookies and taggin' 'long? Emmy-Lou, you want your auntie to see Milky's litter, don't you?"

"Yeah!"

"The dishes—" Annie protested.

"I'd like a cookie, too, Annie." Jakob beckoned her. He wanted one last chance to make sure she'd be happy if this woman stayed—if she did, then he'd see if Miss Hope Ladley would agree to what he offered and with the conditions he set.

Hope slipped the last plate into the cupboard as she heard them returning, grateful she'd finished the dishes before Mrs. Erickson got back. The poor woman looked like a wrung-out mop. Throughout the day, Hope witnessed how little it took to tucker her out. Mr. Stauffer now wore the look of a man determined about something—only Hope couldn't be sure whether he intended to hire her or send her packing. Well, even if he sent her packing, then God had allowed her one day's worth of helping out a nice lady.

The door opened, and Mrs. Erickson gasped. "You've done all of the dishes!"

"There wasn't many. 'Member how we already done that bunch after we made the shepherd's pies? So what about them kitties?"

"There are five!" Emmy-Lou clapped her hands delightedly. "Milky is hiding with them."

"And you are to leave her alone." Mr. Stauffer tilted his daughter's shining face up toward his. "New mamas don't like everyone to bother their babies."

"So when Milky's babies get bigger, can I hold them?"

Mr. Stauffer cleared his throat. "We won't keep all of them. One. I'll let you keep one."

"Do I getta pick which one?"

Hope glanced out the window. She'd forgotten the few things fluttering on the line. "I'd best bring them things in. They oughtta be dry by now."

Emmy-Lou piped up, "I'll come with you."

Mr. Stauffer rested his hand on Emmy-Lou's shoulder. "*Nein.* You will stay in the house."

Guess that's my answer. If'n he wanted to keep me on, he wouldn't mind his little girl skippin' 'long. Well, Lord, I'll trust you to show me where to go next. Hope draped the dishcloth over a dowel to dry and walked out the back door.

She'd hung her own quilt out to air. First off, she'd fold it up and put it in her cart. Afterward she'd take down the other things, carry in the wicker laundry basket, and say good-bye. Leaving the crazy quilt on the line, she took one side and folded it toward the other. Once again, she folded it, then lifted and dragged the warm, thick piece off the line.

The textures of her quilt never ceased to bring pleasure. Feed-sack cotton took on a special softness, but it was different than the downy nap of the occasional patches of velvet. Twenty-five thumb-sized yellow silk stars dotted the willy-nilly kaleidoscope of colors. One more fold, and—

"Miss Ladley."

"Yes?" She finished her task.

"Your letters . . ."

"Oh. Hold on." She walked to her cart and tucked the quilt along one side.

Mr. Stauffer followed her, a frown plowing furrows across his forehead. She took the letters from him and tucked them beneath the quilt.

"Mr. Stauffer, you don't gotta say nothing. I understand." Staring him straight in the eye would be rude—like she was challenging his decision, so she focused on the shirt button playing peek-a-boo with his red bandana. "I gotta say, that sister of yours—she's dreadful tired. Them neighbors you mentioned, you'd best better fetch 'em straight off."

An odd sound curled out of him, forcing her to look up. The rows in his forehead deepened.

"Mrs. Erickson—well, she's hangin' on by the thread of her teeth."

"Hanging . . ." He looked bewildered.

"I was a-feared of that. What with you bein' out and doin' all your chores, you probably don't see how hard it is for Mrs. Erickson to get stuff done. Just a few minutes of workin', and she went white as a sheep."

"Don't you mean white as a sheet?"

"Nope. Sheep are white. You work with cattle so much, you forget what they look like? Okay, then, pale as a goat."

"I've seen plenty of sheep," he muttered. "It's supposed to be pale as a ghost."

"I've never seen a ghost. Hope I never do. How would I know how pale one is? Seems mighty wicked that a God-fearing body would truck with ghosts."

"It's just a saying!"

"Well, if it's just a saying, why are you carrying on so?" Hope drew in a deep breath and let it out. "I'm sorry. You're worried, and the last thing you need is to have to tippy-toe round the eggshells with me. I'll trot on into the kitchen, grab my hat, and tell your sis and little girl 'bye."

His jaw hardened, and he stared at her. "You're not staying."

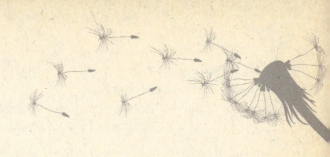

Three

When a mind's made up, it's set. The man of the house makes the decisions. If'n you took the notion that I'd try to get Mrs. Erickson to go against your say-so, you're wrong; but I'll just take the rest of the things from the clothesline whilst you get my hat. How's that?"

Mr. Stauffer folded his arms across his chest. "Do you, or do you not, want to stay?"

Leaning against the cart, Hope shook her head. "Onliest thing I want is to go where're God sends me and farmers need me."

"You just said Annie can't keep up. Do you think someone else needs you more? Or is it money? I can't—"

One hand shot up in the air. "Hold it right there. You and me—I get the funny feelin' I'm talking turkey and you're talking goose. Far as I can see, you folks could use my help—"

"Of course we can!"

"Then, why didn't you just say so? I thunk you was tryin' to send me off."

He jerked his gaze to the side, and his hands fisted, then opened. "What do you charge?"

"I don't bicker or dither. For all the work he does, a farmer don't earn much money. What he gets, he's gotta use for his family. God and them, that's where his loyalty lies. Me? My deal's straightforward and plain as can be: When the day comes that God sends me down the road, you give me whatever you feel you can afford. So there you are."

"Someone could cheat you."

"Never have." She shrugged. "God takes care of me. 'Tis Him I lean on."

Mr. Stauffer studied her face, then glanced at her cart. One step, and he dipped his head to see its contents. "Who keeps the rest of your belongings?"

"Nobody."

Eyes narrowed, he pushed her quilt and discovered nothing beneath or behind it. "Two cans? All you have are two cans of food?"

Hope smiled at him. "Two cans more than lotta folks got."

"You're staying—at least for a while. As long as Annie wants. She's the woman in my home, and the decision is hers to make."

"I'll do my best to help her out."

"Two cans," he muttered to himself. Raking his fingers through his hair in one savage move, he rasped, "I don't know who's saving whom."

"Jesus saved me. As for anybody else—well, He puts us together to help one another out. Suppose you tell me where you want Hattie to go. Pasture or stall—don't matter which. She don't mind bein' round any of God's other critters. Fact is, cows and horses and—" She caught herself just before mentioning sheep. Some folks held a strong dislike for them, and from what he'd said earlier, Mr. Stauffer was one of them. "—and goats all seem to take a shine to her. Hattie's got a way of calming other beasts."

He nodded. "Donkeys and mules—they're good at that. I have a mare that's trying to wean her foal. We'll put the foal and your Hattie in a stall together tonight."

"Fine. Fields look to be ripening right nice. When's harvest set to start?"

"Week and a half or so. Maybe two weeks." He took a breath and let it out.

Hope shoved a hand in her apron pocket. "Mr. Stauffer, you got the look of a man fixin' to say something, but the words don't taste none too good. Why don't you just go on ahead and say what you gotta?"

He grimaced. "My sister—she is . . . having a hard time. The heat and her being, umm . . . well, there are things she shouldn't do."

"Yep. I reckon you and me're gonna have to team up and set her to simple tasks so she feels she's useful. Don't want her to feel I'm shoving her outta her own kitchen, but I aim to be takin' charge of things and say I've gotta earn my keep."

His shoulders relaxed. "*Gut. Sehr g*—Good. Very good." He smacked his hand against the cart. "This can stay here, and I'll take Hattie to the barn."

She grinned at him. "*Sehr gut.*"

❦

Jakob paused a moment on the bottom step. "Good morning, Miss Ladley."

"*Guten morgen,* Mr. Stauffer." Her voice came out in a low, pleasant tone. She remained seated in the chair closest to the

39

oven and finished lacing her boot. "Is there something special you'd like for breakfast?"

"Anything, so long as there's a lot and it's hot." Since she'd yanked down her skirts and rose, he felt it acceptable to stride past her. With Annie not feeling her best, Jakob had grown accustomed to stoking the oven fire and setting the coffeepot over the heat. Instead, the first hint of the rich aroma of a pot just starting to brew wafted toward him. Last evening, he'd tried to find a way to tell this woman that she'd have to work harder than what might ordinarily be expected because allowances needed to be made for his sister. Instead, Miss Ladley pointed out the issue and volunteered to ease things for Annie. This was a good sign—the housekeeper had gotten up and come down to get the morning started.

A few minutes later, the sunrise silhouetted Miss Ladley in the barn's open doorway. Jakob quirked a brow. "Did you need something?"

"I came to milk the cow."

"We have two *milch* cows. Phineas and I trade—one day, I milk and he mucks; the next day, he milks and I muck."

"Two cows? So there are about forty gallons of milk each day?"

"Ja. Whatever we do not use or sell goes to the swine. I'm fattening them for slaughter."

"The butter yesterday—it came out very yellow. The color told me the pasture is good, so you aren't using much hay. Do you normally sell the milk, or has your sister skimmed the cream and made butter and cheese to sell?"

Pain lanced through him. "No one makes hard cheese." *Not anymore.* Naomi had been adept at making a fine cheddar. In fact, one year, when they were starting out, her egg and cheese money paid for the wheat seed.

"If'n you got any rennet, I don't mind makin' some cheese. Might be, it takes a few days ere I get to it, though."

"Other chores are essential."

"And I'd best better get to 'em." Her faded brown-checked skirts swirled as she turned and left.

Whirlwinds. Dust devils. Whatever a man called them, those gusts that came out of nowhere, whipped everything into a crazy spin, then disappeared just as rapidly—they matched Hope Ladley. By supper, she'd probably covered every inch of his house and barnyard twice—and some spots, three or four times for good measure. In a move that took him by surprise, she'd taken a broom to the outside of the house and swept off layers of dust. Why, he couldn't say for certain. Dust would blow it all right back on. And it coated the left front window she'd washed just yesterday.

Did I do the right thing, asking her to stay? I acted without praying first. He couldn't complain about the food, though. Eggs, biscuits, and gravy for breakfast. Cabbage and sausage rolls for lunch. Hearty black bean soup and corn bread for supper.

But who gathered eggs after lunchtime? And who bothered to do laundry when all they did were socks? Furthermore, what woman in her right mind made only two crocks of watermelon pickles at a time? His mouth watered. He loved them. Annie hadn't gotten around to making any. Perhaps he ought to fill the wheelbarrow with melons and leave it at the back steps. Surely she'd take that hint.

His cousin, Miriam, had planted the garden before she left to get married. Naomi had loved her garden, and neither Jakob nor Miriam had the heart to cut back on the size. Two-thirds of an acre now brimmed with vegetables. Loamy soil, an intangible sweet moistness of green leaves, tomato tanginess—aromas that mingled, testified to God's bounty, and promised his family wouldn't go hungry. Well, as long as Miss Ladley got busy. She'd watered the garden today—no small task, that. But canning only a few jars a day wouldn't meet the need, and most of the food would rot out in the sun.

In all fairness, what did she know of a family's requirements for a whole year? The woman lived from hand to mouth. Two cans. Two pathetic cans, and she considered it to be sufficient. Compared to two cans, it was no wonder she'd consider a half dozen to be gracious plenty. *If I say anything to Annie, she'll feel it's her fault for not seeing to everything. Another woman . . .* The Smiths were too busy, and the Richardson girls—well, he'd rather not do anything that might even vaguely be construed as an invitation. Velma! Yes, Velma over at Forsaken Ranch was due to come over any day now. The housekeeper from the neighboring property checked on Annie's pregnancy now and again. She could bring along Big Tim Creighton's bride, and the women could all see to matters.

"Daddy," Emmy-Lou's little voice called through the screen door, "will you tuck me in?"

Emmy-Lou's request took him by surprise. Normally she sought a good-night kiss from him, then Annie put her to bed. "Ja." He went into the house. Annie and Miss Ladley sat at the table, slicing fresh peaches. When Annie started pulling herself out of a chair, he motioned her to sit back down.

Emmy-Lou scampered over and gave her aunt a good-night kiss. *"Ich liebe dich."*

"I love you, too."

Leaning the other direction, Emmy-Lou stood on tiptoe and puckered her lips. Miss Ladley gave her a quick kiss. "If'n your dreams are half as sweet as these here peaches, you'll have to tell me all 'bout them in the mornin'."

" 'Kay." Emmy-Lou gawked around. "I don't 'member where I put my dolly."

"Right there," Annie said. "By the windowsill where you left her."

Emmy-Lou shuffled to the side and brightened. "Dolly!"

"*Komm*, Emmy-Lou." Jakob held his daughter's hand and took the stairs slowly so she could set both feet on each step. Her short legs didn't quite allow her to manage alternating feet on the steps yet.

She knelt at the edge of the trundle bed and folded her hands. "Daddy? Aren't you going to pray with me?"

"Of course I will." He tore his gaze away from Miss Ladley's quilt. Though folded neatly, it rested in the corner of the room. He knelt beside Emmy-Lou. She nestled closer. "Will you say it with me?"

"Ja."

"Ich bin ein kleines Kindelein,
Und meine Kraft ist schwach;
Ich moechte gerne Selig sein,
Und weis nicht wie ich's mach."

The innocent prayer hit him hard. *I'm a little child, and my strength is weak. I'd like to be holy, but don't know how . . .* The words resonated. Though a grown man, Jakob felt every bit as helpless as a child before the throne of the Almighty and under the heavy burdens he bore.

Emmy-Lou climbed into the trundle, but Jakob stopped her as she started to tug up her blanket. "Did you sleep here last night?"

She nodded.

He'd assumed Annie shared her bed with his daughter and gave the trundle to the housekeeper. Jakob frowned. "Then what about Miss Ladley?"

Emmy-Lou shrugged. "I don't know." A frown creased her brow. "Where's my dolly?"

"Right here." He'd distracted her, and she'd lost track of her beloved rag doll. She managed to lose track of it quite often, but each time she found her doll, the joy on her face kept him from chiding her for being forgetful. Soon enough, when she started school, she'd mature enough to keep track of things better. With the household in a dither, it wasn't always easy for him to find things either. Jakob picked up the doll from the edge of the bed and pressed it into Emmy-Lou's hands.

"*Danke*. I love you, Daddy. Night-night."

"Sweet dreams." He pressed a kiss on her forehead. "I love you." He made sure the curtain was pulled back so a slice of moonlight filtered into the room, then blew out the lamp and left. The housekeeper went to bed after his daughter—had she shared Annie's bed? Annie—Jakob halted. Annie wouldn't sleep well with someone in bed with her. They'd moved Emmy-Lou to the trundle because she squirmed and thrashed in her sleep.

Once he went downstairs, he watched as his sister reached for another peach to slice. Miss Ladley stood over by the sink. She dunked peaches into scalding water and peeled them. "Smells heavenly."

"Ja." Annie nodded.

"Purdy as these here are, you oughtta put a jar in the county fair."

Annie winced.

Unaware of that reaction, Miss Ladley scalded and skinned another peach. "Mr. Stauffer, do y'all like pie or tarts best?"

"Tarts." He cast a glance at his sister. "I like to take one in each hand when I go out to the fields. Isn't that right, Annie?"

"Ja, but you work hard, so you need to eat lots."

"Them peach trees you got—they're fine ones. I reckon the grocer begs you for the fruit to sell. Me and Mrs. Erickson—we can use up the bird-pecked ones and such. They taste just as good."

During supper, Annie had called her Hope, but she still addressed Annie by her married name. Was it merely a sign of respect, or had Annie left up that barrier because she wasn't sure she could trust Miss Ladley yet?

"Jakob?" Annie's knife paused halfway through the peach she was slicing. "If it's not too much trouble, would you please get the screens for us tomorrow? We need to dry some for later."

"They're out in the barn. I'll fetch them now." He reached over and grabbed a slice from her bowl. "And Annie? It is no trouble. I'm glad to get the screens. You know how much I like peaches."

He went out to the barn. Even though they'd been stored in canvas, dust coated the mesh screens. Phineas set aside a halter he'd been treating with saddle soap. "Those need a good scrubbing."

It was considered woman's work, but Jakob never minded pitching in. Ever since Annie came, Phineas had gotten good about seeing needs and helping out, too. More than once, Jakob found himself wishing their father had wanted Annie to marry Phineas instead of Konrad. Phineas wouldn't have . . .

"Are the frames weak?" Phineas gave him an odd look.

Jakob glanced down and realized he'd gripped the edges and begun to twist them. "They're strong enough to do the job. The women—they're doing peaches."

Phineas snatched up a bar of lye soap. "What are we waiting for? Let's scrub those now so they can put up more. No one makes a better dried peach pie than your sister."

A while later as they stacked the screens on the back porch, he heard Hope through the open window. "Ain't it something how menfolk have a clock in their heads that chimes when food comes outta the oven?"

"Oh?" Phineas crooked a brow at Jakob.

"I asked for tarts for the morning." He tried to ignore the mouth-watering aroma wafting toward them. It was Thursday. No one baked on Thursday. Saturdays, yes. And often on Tuesday. But never on Thursday.

"Mrs. Erickson, ma'am, seems to me we got some hungry men out there. Good thing you thought to put on another pot of coffee to go with these here tarts."

"That sounded like an invitation to me!" Phineas wrenched the doorknob and plowed inside. "Annie, I just told your brother that nobody makes a better peach pie than you."

"They're tarts, and Hope made them."

Jakob quelled his greed. "We can wait 'til tomorrow."

"Nonsense." Miss Ladley turned from him to his sister. "And nonsense to you, too. You and me—we done baked them tarts together. I peeled the peaches and made the crust, but you sliced and seasoned the peaches. Yep. We worked better'n a hand in love."

Hand in glove, Jakob silently corrected.

"And Mr. Stauffer, of anybody, I reckon you understand that the best—your name bein' Jakob. In the Good Book, Jacob didn't mind bein' a hand and workin' hard all them extry years on account of him lovin' Rachel so much."

The housekeeper had mangled another saying, but somehow, it made sense. Jakob nodded.

"Well, your sis is a real nice gal, and I have me such a good time in her company that I don't even notice how we're working. Lookee here." She waved at the counter. "Got us a full dozen tarts made, and I just popped 'nother half dozen into the stove."

"Did we really make eighteen?" Annie's eyes widened.

Jakob slapped Phineas on the shoulder. "I guess we can swipe one tonight."

Phineas took a big bite and chuffed air around it. "Hot. Hot, but ohhhh, *gut. Sehr gut.*"

"Betwixt Mr. Stauffer's fine peaches and his sister's special mix of spices, 'tis no wonder at all." Miss Ladley set a plate with a tart on the table in front of Annie and swept away the assortment of spice tins. "Betcha that little babe's gonna have a sweet disposition with you eatin' the likes of that."

Annie's hand went to her tummy, and her cheeks turned ruddy. Phineas cleared his throat and looked away.

Miss Ladley heaved a loud sigh. "Guess I spoke out of turn. When there's mixed company, some folks don't make any mention 'bout a woman bein' on the nest. Sorry I opened my big mouth. I won't say nothin' more."

"That would be best." Jakob decided to change the subject. "Tomorrow, I will build a cot for you, Miss Ladley. While you're here, we need to make you as comfortable as we can."

"No need to make a cot. My quilt's nice and thick. I'm used to a pallet." She licked a little speck of sugar from her lip. "You're decent men, and I'm a God-fearin' woman. That bein' the case, I reckon 'tis silly for you to waste your breath on fancy manners with plain old me. I wouldn't take offense if'n you men called me Hope."

Fifteen minutes later, out in the barn, Phineas chuckled. "I didn't say anything, but that new cook you hired is funny. She tangles her words up and still ends up making sense. I doubt there's another woman who could talk about her bed and in the next breath invite men to call her by her given name without it coming out as sinful."

Jakob shook his head. "She is different, but Annie needs her."

When he went to his bedroom that night, Jakob shut the door and unbuttoned his shirt before turning around. Every night he did the same thing—sliding down his suspenders and shrugging out of his shirt, sitting on the chair and peeling off his boots and socks, then finally shucking his britches before ever looking at the empty bed. Nights stretched long enough without facing the loneliness any sooner than he had to. When he finally faced the bed, Jakob froze. A flat expanse of sheet lay where Naomi's pillow belonged.

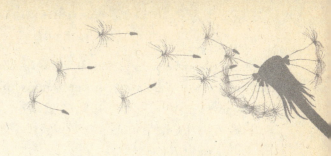

Four

Hope waited until Mrs. Erickson's breathing stretched into a slow, steady rhythm. Careful not to awaken her or little Emmy-Lou, Hope slipped back into her work dress. She tiptoed to the door, sneaked out, and went over to the room across the hall. Trying to stay as quiet as possible, she tapped lightly.

The door opened so savagely, Hope jerked back and tightened her hold of the pillow. Barefooted, bare-chested, and wearing jeans, her boss didn't say a word, but the wild look in his eyes made her catch her breath. "Mr. Stauffer, sir, I don't need this." She extended the fluffy pillow toward him. The moment she'd laid her head on it, the faint scent of roses had drifted up to her.

The muscles in his cheeks twitched, and his jaw remained just as clenched as his hands.

I was right. This here pillow belonged to his missus, and he counts it dear. He hadn't accepted it yet, so Hope took a small step closer and pressed it against his arm. The pink peonies embroidered along the hem and the matching pink tatted lace edge looked impossibly feminine against the tanned, ropy muscles of his

49

forearm. She whispered, "I didn't want to upset your sister. She was tryin' to follow your order to make me comfortable. A pillow never made a lick of difference to me, so you might as well put it back where it b'longs. G'night." She tiptoed back to her room and stopped.

Mr. Stauffer stood in his doorway. Backlit from the lamp in his room as he was, she could see he now clutched the pillow to his chest, but his features were cast into shadow.

Just as well. A man's entitled to the privacy of his grief. She lowered her gaze. "I'll wait 'til you shut your door so's the light in your chamber won't wake up your sis."

The door he'd practically torn from the hinges now shut with a silence that was every bit as unnerving.

"I'm sorry." Mrs. Erickson shuffled past Hope's pallet and climbed back into bed.

"Nothin' to be sorry over. You can't help it. Fact is, you oughtta sleep in a mite to make up for all the times that babe makes you get up durin' the night. It only takes one of us to make breakfast, and since I'm the hired cook, that means I'm gonna earn my keep."

"But—"

"Frettin' ain't no good for you nor that babe. There's plenty of work for us to share the rest of the day. You might as well rest while you can."

Emmy-Lou sat upright on the trundle and announced, "Chickens don't like butter."

"Shhh. *Schlaff.*" Annie coaxed the little girl to lie back down. After she had covered her niece, she murmured, "She talks in her sleep sometimes—crazy things."

"Well, you got her all tucked in real sweet-like. Not having a mama's hard on a gal—but she's blessed to have you here to dote on her. Of all the things you do, that's gotta be the most importantest of all."

"After Naomi died, a cousin—Miriam—came for a while. A terrible accident happened, and she tried hard to get past it, but she grew so afraid that she had to leave. Jakob came to get me so I could mind her. He is still very worried and doesn't allow Emmy-Lou to go where we cannot see her for even a minute."

"I don't abide gossip, so if'n answering would make a talebearer of you, don't feel obliged to answer. But can you tell me what happened so I can help you mind her?"

Only Emmy-Lou's sleepy breaths filled the room; then Mrs. Erickson said softly, "Jakob needed more water, so they were drilling. A test hole didn't yield water, so they started drilling a ways off. Emmy-Lou fell in the first hole."

Hope sucked in a sharp breath.

"Nobody talks of it. Poor Emmy-Lou is terrified of the dark now. It is why we leave the curtain open a little at nighttime." Annie yawned.

"If'n we switch your bed to that other wall, the light will fall across her trundle instead of slanting 'cross your mattress first. Would you sleep better if'n we did that?"

"I don't think Jakob would want things rearranged."

"Maybe. Maybe not." Hope pretended to yawn and snuggled under her quilt. "Much as he dotes on his baby girl, once we mention it, I bet he'll set the stairs afire, rushin' up here to move things."

Mrs. Erickson soon returned to her slumber, but Hope didn't fall back to sleep. Accepting the fact that she'd not doze off again, she went downstairs and rushed to skin, slice, and blanch more fruit. Seven jars wasn't a lot—but every little bit she could squirrel away without Annie knowing was just that much more work the poor woman would be spared. Tossing a peach cobbler into the oven would explain the heavy, sweet fragrance in the kitchen. Oatmeal and coffee topped two of the burners. The two largest pots held water she heated.

Hope stepped out onto the back porch and pulled her comb from her apron pocket. It didn't take long to unravel her bedtime plait, comb her waist-length hair, and braid it again. A few jabs with hairpins, and she'd seen to making herself decent. Well, almost. She curled her toes on the smooth planks for a moment before cramming them into her boots. Across the barnyard, the rooster started warming up.

G'morning, Lord. I shorely do love the way you start the day—with all them purdy gold and pink ribbons streamin' 'cross the sky as it turns lavender. 'Tis like you got yourself a paint box to fix up a new picture every mornin'. Takes my breath away, how each one is different from the last. I gotta praise you for that. And, God, 'tis plain to see why you sent me here. These folks—they need a helpin' hand. Ain't just a hand, neither—leastways, not just mine. They're sore in need of your touch. The Good Book says you walked in the garden with Adam and Eve. Ain't my farm, but I'm givin' you the invite to come walk this garden with me. Make my heart still so I can hear what you want me to say and do for these folks.

The door opened. "Miss Ladley? You are up early again."

Hope turned. "Dawn's my most favoritest time of the day. Sky's so beautiful, it makes me wanna reach up and touch each of them streaks." She stood and dusted off the back of her dress.

If he hadn't crooked his brow slightly, she might have thought he hadn't heard her.

"You didn't answer me last night 'bout the peaches. You gonna take most of 'em to town or ship 'em off by rail? Could earn yourself a purdy penny thataway."

"Monday." He strode past her and out to the barn.

Well, his plan made sense. By the time he picked and packed bushels of peaches today, he'd have to wait 'til early tomorrow to take them off—and shipping food on Saturday would be foolish.

"Oh!" Hope chased after him. "Mr. Stauffer!"

He turned.

She stopped a few feet away. "I wanted to ask—well, that office of yours is a wondrous place, and I don't mean you no insult, but that sis of yours . . ." She took a deep breath. "A woman in her last months uses the necessary a dreadful lot. Nighttime trips to the outhouse are wearin' her out. I'd be careful to empty out a chamber pot straightaway each mornin' if'n you wouldn't mind me tuckin' it in that study at bedtime each night for her."

A curt nod, then he turned and continued on.

Hope scanned the yard and scuffed her toe in irritation. "If'n I find the cat, I'll bet she got that man's tongue."

ॐ

"I've been thinkin' on what we can fix ahead for the menfolk to eat, come harvest." Hope settled the last screen of peaches atop the large stack and covered the whole affair with netting to keep out insects. "I reckoned we could make a big ol' mess of noodles and dry 'em. Whaddya think?"

"That would be smart."

"Dandy. We'll need eggs to make noodles, but that henhouse is brimming with 'em. Do y'all want Emmy-Lou to come with me whilst I feed the chickens and go work the garden, or do y'all want her to help you gather the eggs?"

"I can feed the chickens. They're good scratchers. We don't have to feed them as much as some of the new, fancy breeds." Mrs. Erickson took Emmy-Lou's hand.

"Uh-huh. Dominiques are fine chickens. Hearty and lay mighty tasty brown eggs. I always like the brown eggs better." Hope walked alongside them toward the coop. "You'll never imagine what I heard early in the spring this year."

Emmy-Lou continued to trot along. "What?"

"There's a feller named Wilson clear back in New Jersey. He built hisself an incubator that handles four hundred eggs at a time. Well, newborn chicks don't gotta eat or drink for a day and a half, so he's taken to shipping day-old chicks by rail express clear to Chicago!"

"You don't say!" Mrs. Erickson's face clouded over. "Those poor chickies."

"You've been to Chicago?" Emmy-Lou wrinkled her nose. "Is that way, way far away like Dallas?"

"I've been to Dallas, but not to Chicago. It's much, much farther away; but a farmer's wife came back after visitin' her kin, and she brought one of the crates he shipped them chicks in. She said them little chicks was parched. They had to tip those little critters' beaks into water to get 'em to drink up, but it worked. Can you imagine?" She laughed. "Lookee at me. I got so wound up in telling my tale, I follered you right out here. I might as well feed the hens. This is a fine brood you got."

"We gots a hundred." Emmy-Lou squatted down and trailed her fingers along the back of one of the black-and-white-feathered hens. "Nobody else's looks like ours. Mrs. Creighton's are mostly white. Their eggs are easy to find 'cuz they're white."

"But just think of all the fun they're a-missing!" Hope pressed an egg basket into Emmy-Lou's hands. "A hen works to lay her egg. When she takes the trouble to hide it, doesn't seem fair just to snatch it away. Searching a little—well, that's like a game you play. You look down low, and your auntie can look up high. Thataway, them hens will figure they done a good job. Betcha they're so happy, they'll lay another tomorrow. Plenty of hens don't lay eggs every day, you know."

"Ours do!"

Hope gave Mrs. Erickson a puzzled look. "Yesterday was Thursday, and you didn't go to market. Most ever'body goes to market on Thursday. When do all y'all go?"

"Phineas went on Wednesday. He takes the eggs, butter, and produce in so Mr. Clark has them for the women when they shop the next day. Sometimes Jakob goes. If I need anything, they get it for me."

"Stretches my imagination, tryin' to figger out anything you ain't got. This here farm is like a corner of paradise on earth. Suppose I ought to stop blitherin' and start workin'."

She headed to the garden, which was nearly exploding with ripe vegetables. If she stripped all the pods off the pole beans, they'd continue to produce more. Soon a whole bushel of beans rested at the end of a long row. Another of ripe tomatoes joined it.

"Miss Hope, I finded lotsa eggs!"

Hope turned around. "*Sehr gut,* Emmy-Lou. We'll use some of them to make noodles today. Do you want to help?"

"Can I roll them out?" Emmy-Lou galloped closer and tripped over a cabbage.

Hope caught her. "Careful there." The outer leaves of the cabbage were torn. "We'll make us some coleslaw. For what I have in mind for lunch, we're gonna need an onion. How about if you go find one and pull it?"

"Emmy-Lou!" Mrs. Erickson's voice carried a panicky edge. "Emmy-Lou!"

"Here! I'm over here!" Emmy-Lou waved. "Miss Hope said I can pick onions and make noodles!"

Her aunt hastened over, the basket of eggs swinging from her arm in time with the pregnant woman's waddle. "Do not go off on your own."

"I'm sorry." Emmy-Lou hung her head.

"A good girl only goes where she's told." Mrs. Erickson rested her hand on her niece's shoulder. "You must remember not to wander off on your own."

"Okay."

"Take these eggs into the house, then come back to pick the onion. I'll help pick vegetables."

Though she would have preferred to harvest more, Hope didn't want the pregnant woman stooping over. "Are you already done crating the rest of the eggs?"

"Ja. Jakob is taking them to the springhouse."

"How's about you holdin' out your apron?" Hope cut two more cabbages from their stems and placed all three into Annie's apron. "Now, if that wasn't good timin', I don't know what is. If'n you carry those in, I'll bring in the tomatoes."

As they walked to the house, Emmy-Lou came back out. Hope set down the bushel of tomatoes. "You go on ahead, Mrs. Erickson. I'll go on out and water a wee bit while Emmy-Lou's out here. Then she and I'll bring in the beans."

"I could start lunch. The cabbage would be good for *bierocks*. I have time to make the dough."

"Mmmm!" The thought of the meat-and-cabbage-filled rolls made Hope grin. "You got yourself a good plan." Mrs. Erickson trundled on into the farmhouse. Hope watered half the garden; she'd come back out later and finish the rest while Emmy-Lou napped and Mrs. Erickson cut the noodles. A woman that far gone with a child had no business hauling water.

Jakob sat at the supper table and surveyed the kitchen. He'd never seen such a mess. Bowl upon bowl—some covered with cloth and others heaping with string beans—were lined up along the counter on the pump side of the sink; a dozen jars of tomatoes stood in rows like pairs of soldiers on the other side. Small patches of flour dusted the floor, spools of thread and needles sat on the surface of the hutch, and he knew for a fact that only half of the garden got watered this morning. Though the shepherd's pie tasted wonderful, he knew Hope simply took it from the springhouse and popped it into the oven. It hadn't required any cooking.

Friday was housecleaning day. Naomi's embroidered dish towels even proclaimed that fact. But instead of creating order in his home, Hope caused chaos far beyond anything he'd ever witnessed. The fine layer of dust on the furniture and the smudged mirror on the washstand proved his new housekeeper didn't keep house.

"—more chicken feed." Annie ducked her head.

Jakob realized he hadn't been listening, but he didn't want his sister to feel ignored. "Mr. Vaughn mentioned he would get a big shipment of feed in this week. Perhaps you should go with me to buy the chicken feed, Annie. That way, you can choose the sacks you like best."

"What with all that butter you churned today, I reckon you'll have that storekeeper happy as a lamb," Hope chimed in.

"Happy as a clam," Phineas said.

"Never seen me a clam. Wouldn't know whether he was happy or not. Y'all don't seem none too fond of sheep."

Phineas frowned. "You don't understand."

Hope held up her hands. "Now, don't think I'm finding fault, 'cuz I'm not. I know plenty of folk don't cotton much to sheep, what with them range wars betwixt cattlemen and sheepherders.

I heard 'twas on account of the sheep eatin' clear down to the roots of the grass so's the land's spoilt for the cattle. Didn't think that'd bother you, you bein' a farmer. But anyways, you shore can tell when sheep are happy. 'Tis a joy to watch them gambol."

"Daddy." Emmy-Lou reached over and tugged on his sleeve. "You said gambling and beer are sinful. Why does she like lambs when they do sinful things?"

While Phineas hooted with merriment, Jakob patted his daughter. "The words sound alike, but they are written with different letters. One way means to dance and play. The other means to—" He caught himself just before he said "play" again. "It means to spend money on foolish guesses."

"How d'ya like that? I didn't know them words got writ with different letters." Hope didn't look the least bit embarrassed to confess her ignorance. "You got yourself a right clever pa, Emmy-Lou. I never seed me anyone who had more books, neither. You'll go to school and learn how to read and cipher, and one of these days, you'll be as smart as your pa and auntie."

Emmy-Lou beamed. "Aunt Annie read a Bible story to us today, Daddy. Then we taked our nap. Miss Hope tucked us in. She said Auntie has to teach the baby to take naps."

Jakob glanced at his sister. She blushed, but he didn't want her feeling awkward. So what if the kitchen needed to be straightened? Annie needed to rest, then—

His mind skidded to a halt. Suddenly it all made sense. Annie read aloud because Hope couldn't read. If Hope couldn't read, then the lettering on Naomi's dishcloths wouldn't make any sense to her. No wonder she wasn't doing the assigned chores on the correct days!

"If'n you go to town first thing in the mornin', you'd get the eggs and butter to the grocer so he could sell it off to women who wanna do their baking."

Well, at least she knows to do her baking on Saturday. "That's a fine plan. Annie, we'll leave after breakfast."

Hope cleared the dishes and set bowls of sliced peaches before each of them, then took a pitcher from the icebox. She poured cream from it onto Emmy-Lou's fruit. "The cream from your cows shore is rich and sweet. Anybody else want some cream on theirs?"

Phineas and Annie did. Jakob noticed how Hope managed to coax his sister into nibbling a little more. It had to be his imagination, but in the few days since Hope had come, Annie didn't look quite so thin and pale.

They said their after-supper prayer; then Jakob and Phineas went back out to take advantage of the longer, lighter evenings. Whenever he happened to be within sight of the yard, he'd glance over. Hope started watering the other half of the garden. If the weather weren't so hot, he'd worry that she would rot the roots. Surely, though, she hadn't finished watering when he saw her by the clothesline. Dishcloths, small clothes, and handkerchiefs— but not the sheets. After those items, his bandanas waved in a checkerboard of red-blue-red-blue.

Naomi always hung the reds together, then the blues.

Jakob shook his head to dislodge that memory and forced himself to focus on the problem. Even if the housekeeper didn't know Monday ought to be laundry day, it made no sense that she'd boil the water and do only a small portion of the job. And why in the evening? Things wouldn't dry before she had to take them down.

By the time he went back into the house for the night, Emmy-Lou had gone to bed. Annie sat at the table, sticking a threaded needle through string beans she pulled from a colander. She glanced up from her work. "The beans have come ripe."

He nodded. From his youngest days, he recalled his mother drying string beans this same way. Blanched, then strung up, the beans would dehydrate. The shriveled beans were nicknamed "leather pants." All through the winter, they'd be added to stews and casseroles where they'd plump up again and be tender and flavorful. This chore didn't take much effort, and tired as Annie looked, Jakob felt a flare of relief that Hope found something vital for his sister to do that wouldn't strain her.

"Where is Hope?"

"I'm not sure. She went outside. Maybe the garden or the springhouse. Oh—maybe to visit her mule. She loves Hattie." Annie set aside the beans and levered herself up. "Did you need something? I should have asked. I'm sorry—"

"Sit, Annie." As soon as the words left his mouth, Jakob regretted his sharp tone. He softened his voice. "You have nothing to apologize for. It is good—you making leather pants."

She twitched a poor excuse for a smile.

"How are things going with the new housekeeper?"

"Okay."

Jakob watched as his sister started to chew on her lower lip again. "Annie, I made a point of telling Hope that you're the woman of my home, and she'll stay only as long as you want or need her to. If there's a problem, you only need to tell me so. I'll take care of it."

Annie's eyes grew huge. "She works hard. It puts me to shame, how little I do. She does all her work and most of mine, too."

The way the house looked, Annie was sorely mistaken, but Jakob didn't dare disagree with her.

Annie snatched up the needle and frantically started stabbing beans onto the thread. "I'll try harder. I will. I'm sorry—"

"Annie, no." He reached to tilt her face toward him, but she flinched. That instinctive reflex cut him to the core, but he pretended nothing had happened. "Hope's here to help you, Annie. I'm glad she's a hard worker. Emmy-Lou sure has taken a shine to her."

Annie nodded. "Emmy-Lou loves and trusts as only a child can."

His sister's comment held an unspeakable sadness. Jakob couldn't reply without making the situation worse, so he cleared his throat. "I need to see to the books." He strode to the study and shut the door.

Once alone, he sank to his knees by his desk and rested his elbows on the chair. In despair, he folded his hands and bowed his head. "Lord, what am I to do? How am I to follow your will when I can't see it? Your Word says it is not good that man should be alone, yet you took my Naomi." Anguish tore at him. "Why didn't you take Konrad instead and rescue Annie from his cruelty?"

Five

"That preacher-man—he's gotta fine way of thumpin' his Bible." Hope curled her arm around Emmy-Lou and thought about how nice and smooth the road was. Most places, the roads bore ruts and holes and bumps. The Stauffers' buckboard hardly jostled at all. And just to be sure their Sunday-best clothes didn't get dirty, either her boss or the hired hand had spread a thick blanket in the bed of the buckboard, too.

"Reverend Bradle is a scholar," Mr. Stauffer said. "He went to seminary."

"Hmm. I s'pose a man could learn a lot there 'bout folks' souls." Hope reflected on it for a moment. "Yep. It never occurred to me before now, but it's the truth. I 'spect there ain't another place where folks go that makes 'em take stock of their doin's and shortcomings and decide to change their ways before it's too late."

"The Lord's Day is good for that." Phineas stretched his legs across the bed of the buckboard.

"If'n you stop up yonder, Mr. Stauffer, Emmy-Lou and me can hop down and gather up some posies. That'd be a right nice remembrance to leave, don't you think?"

Mr. Stauffer turned and shot her a confused look. "What are you talking about?"

"You're the one what brung it up. The preacher man went there, and since Phineas said the Lord's Day is a fine time to do it, I reckoned 'twould be nice to have flowers to leave." Hope scanned their surroundings and frowned. "I usually got me a good sense of direction, but I must be mixed up. I thought you was a-gonna turn to the east back at that fork."

"There's nothing there but the cemetery." Mr. Stauffer sounded like he'd just been forced to gargle kerosene.

"That's what I thunk." Hope wondered what was wrong with her boss. He'd been standoffish ever since Friday.

Mrs. Erickson tentatively rested her hand on her brother's arm. "You and Hope are talking about two entirely different things. You said seminary; I think she thought you said cemetery." Annie twisted as best she could. "Hope, seminary is a special Bible college to make men into pastors."

"Thankee for tellin' me." She let out a short laugh. "No wonder Mr. Stauffer didn't turn!"

"I still wanna stop and pick flowers." Emmy-Lou popped up onto her knees and stuck her head around the bend of her daddy's arm. "Can we?"

"No." Mr. Stauffer's abrupt tone closed the subject.

Mrs. Erickson cringed.

So it ain't just me who thinks he's gotten surly. Well, no use dwelling on that. "Can you 'magine being so lucky that you got to go to school to do nothin' all day but surround yourself with the things of God? That seminary must be a wondrous place. Just like when we was all a-singing the hymns this mornin'. Everybody lifting their hearts to Jesus. 'Magine how tickled God must be that folks go study at a fancy school just so they can preach better. It shorely worked for him. Ain't never heard me a finer sermon."

Nodding, Phineas said, "Parson Bradle has a way about him."

"I'd sure be tickled to hear that verse he used until I can recollect it on my own."

Phineas gave her the black leather book he'd brought to church. "You're welcome to borrow my Bible."

Reverently, she gave it back. "Can't read. Never learnt how. 'Twould give me a gladsome heart if'n you'd teach me the verse, though. There's a place in the Bible that says, 'Thy word have I hid in mine heart, that I might not sin against thee.' I like to tuck verses in my heart every chance I get."

"The hundred and nineteenth psalm," Mr. Stauffer said.

"You got yourself a fine memory. Me? I can't make head nor tales of numbers. I always wondered 'bout that sayin'. You can't make up a story out of numbers."

Mrs. Erickson gave Hope a shy smile over her shoulder. "It's like 'gambol' and 'gamble' the other night. The words sound alike, but they're spelled differently. In that saying, the spelling means 'an animal's tail.' "

Emmy-Lou giggled. "You can't make a story out of a horse's tail. Or a cow or a pig, either."

"Coins have two sides—a front and a back. They are called heads and tails." For having sounded so grouchy earlier, Mr. Stauffer seemed to have calmed down a mite. "When someone says they can't make head nor tail out of something, it means that no matter which way they look at it, it makes no sense."

"That's me all right." Hope paused a moment as a flock of birds startled and took flight. "Two years of schooling, and we all gave up on me. Teacher said I got stuff backwards, sidewise, and upside down. Couldn't make sense of it. A washtub's a washtub no matter what way you look at it, but them letters flip upside down or swap the stick to t'other side and they ain't themselves anymore."

65

Emmy-Lou's eyes were huge. "Don't you wanna read?"

"We don't always get what we want." Mr. Stauffer bit out the words as if they tasted mighty bad.

Hurt and confusion mingled on Emmy-Lou's face, and Hope hastened to soften the unintentional upset Mr. Stauffer's words caused. " 'Tis true we don't. But the Bible says God is our Father, and He always gives us what is best. So I can't read, but God brung me here to your house where your auntie reads to me and your parson tells me more 'bout the Bible. Ain't it something how my heavenly Father looks after me?"

"Daddy and Aunt Annie look after me."

"Well, I reckon that means you and me oughtta look after them. What say we fry up a chicken to feed 'em for Sunday supper?"

"Yummy!"

Once they reached the Stauffer home, Hope caught herself before hopping down on her own. She caught the worried glance Phineas shot toward Mrs. Erickson; then he reached up to Hope. "Miss Ladley."

A pregnant woman oughtn't hop down. Us setting an example is a good notion. "Thankee."

As he set her on the ground, Emmy-Lou giggled. "Phineas helped you 'cuz he wants fried chicken!"

"Is that so?" Hope held out her arms to catch the little girl.

"Uh-huh." Emmy-Lou jumped to her and wrapped her arms around Hope's neck in an exuberant hug. "I like fried chicken, too." Her little legs locked around Hope's waist. "Do I get the gizzard or the neck this time?"

"Ask your auntie."

"Aunt Annie?"

"Whichever you want." Annie glanced past the garden, toward the outhouse.

Hope gave Emmy-Lou a squeeze. "You and me need to go change outta our Sunday clothes. I surely am lookin' forward to eating some of your auntie's coleslaw with the chicken."

While Phineas drove the buckboard across the yard to the barn and Mrs. Erickson went to the necessary, Hope walked up the back porch steps. Emmy-Lou continued to cling to her, and Mr. Stauffer opened the door for them.

"Miss Hope, do you gotta change out of your Sunday-best dress? It's so pretty, and I like green. The other one's ugly."

"Emmy-Lou!" Mr. Stauffer's brows crunched into a stern V, and he pulled her off Hope and into his own arms. "That was rude."

"We all got our favorite colors. I reckon lotta folks don't cotton much to brown. Yeller's probably my favorite on account of it bein' so sunny. But brown—'tis a fine color, too. Why, I bet Emmy-Lou and me can name all sorts of grand things that're brown whilst we change our clothes. Dirt's brown, and ain't nothin' like rich, damp earth to cradle seeds. Now you tell me something that's brown."

Emmy-Lou didn't bother to look around at all. She looked up with complete adoration. "Daddy's hair."

Golden fried chicken. The last bite of a peach tart's crust. Tree trunks and lumber. Sturdy leather boots. By late afternoon, when the sun still gave light but heat no longer shimmered in the distance, Jakob marveled at how many things were brown and what a vast array of shades that color held. Never before had he scanned his farm and appreciated the fence posts or the smooth arch of the yokes. The supple look and feel of harnesses and saddles. To be sure, on occasions those thoughts had flitted through his mind, but today he'd seen his surroundings in a whole new light. Maybe it was because of Hope's little game. Maybe it was because of all the brown things Emmy-Lou might have named first. His daughter had said, "Daddy's hair." Nothing but pure, innocent love rang in her voice. Even now, hours later, the memory watered his parched heart.

Jakob now watched as Hope and Emmy-Lou walked hand in hand toward him. Their arms swung with exuberance back and forth in an exaggerated pendulum's arc.

"I don't believe my eyes!" Phineas gave Jakob's shoulder a shove. "You're smiling! I thought you'd forgotten how."

Jakob shrugged. "Look at my daughter. She's happy. A man wants his child to be happy."

"Daddy! Miss Hope says I gotta ask you. Can we go see Milky and her kitties?"

"Ja."

Emmy-Lou curled her fingers through the hammer loop on his overalls and gave it a tug, just as certainly as she'd tugged on his heartstrings earlier that day. "Daddy, I want you to take me."

"I'll go yonder and take a Sunday stroll." Hope gazed at him directly, making him know she'd ease away so he could have time alone with his girl. "Hattie's winking at me and her ears are a-twitchin' howdy, so I reckon I'll take her 'long."

Jakob rested his hand on Emmy-Lou's head and felt her soft curls coil about his fingers. "Would you like a saddle and halter?"

"Thankee, but no. Well, maybe a rope halter. Hattie follows me just like your cat Fleck used to tag after you."

She'd remembered that? Jakob covered his surprise by turning to fetch a length of rope. As she and her mule walked off, Jakob scooped up Emmy-Lou. "Let's go see the kittens."

Now that he'd taken a closer look, Hope's everyday dress was the only brown thing he'd seen that day that didn't carry a scrap of charm or beauty. Faded from repeated washings, the small checks looked drab as could be. A stingy one-inch ruffle made from the same fabric as the dress stood up to form a collar and V-eed down the bodice. Emmy-Lou was right—Hope's everyday dress went beyond ugly; it was hideous. Many years ago, his grandmother would have nodded and pronounced Hope's dress practical. It wouldn't show dirt. Dim praise indeed.

I'll talk to Annie. She can give Hope some feed sacks to make herself another dress. No . . . maybe I'd better not. So many other chores are in dire wont of doing. The last thing Hope needs is another project to distract her from the essentials. When she leaves—that's when I'll give her the sacks. It'll be a little something extra.

"Daddy, when I go to school, do I getta ride a horse?"

Jakob halted midstride and looked down at the precious child he held in his arms. He didn't want to let her out of his sight. The very thought of her going away each day made his blood run cold. She'd come close to being buried alive when she fell into the test hole for the new well. Going off to school . . . anything could happen, and he couldn't bear to lose her.

"I know how to ride a horse. You let me ride on Josephine sometimes."

Only when he was by her side or she rode in his lap—never alone. He resumed his path toward the cat. Keeping her home from school wasn't an option, but he'd do everything he could to assure her safe transit. "*Liebling,* you're too small to go such a long way all by yourself. The Smiths—they have so many children, they take a wagon to school. When the time comes, I'll walk you to the road, and you can go with them." As much for himself as for her, he added, "It'll be good for you to be with your friends, ja?"

"Miss Hope could go with me. We could learn to read together."

Jakob shook his head. "No."

Her little hand came up and patted his chest. "Daddy, you promised I getta keep one of Milky's kitties." When he nodded, she clenched her fingers, balling his shirt into her little fist. "I'm not gonna. I wanna keep Miss Hope instead of a kitty!"

Jakob set Emmy-Lou down and knelt beside her. "You can't keep Hope, but I will let you have a kitty."

Ignoring the playful, fluffy litter, Emmy-Lou leaned close and peered into his eyes. "Why can't I keep Hope?"

Pain burned in his chest. *How am I to explain this, Lord? She's too little to keep losing the ones she loves.* In her short life, his daughter had already lost her mother and brother; then her cousin Miriam left, as well. *She needs to know Hope won't be here long so her heart isn't broken again.* "We didn't keep Cousin Miriam. Remember? She just came to help for a while, then she left. It's that way with Hope, too—only her stay with us will be much shorter."

Distress streaked across her little features. "Auntie Annie isn't going to go away, is she?"

"*Nein.* She will stay with us. You can be sure of that."

The certainty of his tone erased only a portion of Emmy-Lou's upset. "But, Daddy, why can't we keep—"

"People aren't like kittens, to be kept or owned. You can't keep Hope." The forlorn look on his daughter's face tugged at his heart, but Jakob knew he had to be firm. He couldn't foster his daughter's fantasy; doing so would only hurt her more when Hope left.

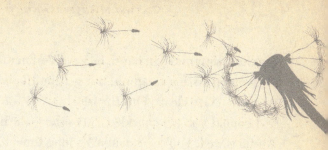

Six

I have something for you." Leopold Volkner didn't bother to dismount; he simply handed a gazette and an envelope to Konrad Erickson.

Konrad accepted the mail. Though he could have gone to town today, he'd stayed home specifically because he knew the letter would arrive. Jakob was like that—dependable. Stolid and predictable. There wouldn't be a letter inside. Only money. But no one else had to know that.

Invariably, a neighbor would bring by the envelope. It made everyone believe Annie was corresponding with him, and the envelope served as a not-so-subtle reminder to neighbors that Konrad sorely lacked a woman's assistance. Occasionally, someone would bring by a covered dish or a baked treat the day after the letter came. He'd send that person back with the most recent "news" Annie's letter supposedly contained.

He straightened his left arm and tucked the gazette into his left hand—a seemingly casual move. The last two fingers of his left hand were missing, and Konrad had perfected such moves so that no one would notice it. Pressing the envelope from Jakob to his chest with his right hand, he gave Volkner a sheepish smile. "It's embarrassing to admit, but getting these letters from my Annie . . ." He cleared his throat.

Leopold Volkner chuckled. "My sister—she'll be glad to know Annie is well. You've been apart a long time, haven't you?"

Forcing a smile, Konrad shrugged. "Not so long, really." Pride forced him to pretend all was well. "You know how softhearted my wife is. She's just what Jakob and his little girl need—their grief is horrible." He shook his head. "God forbid, but when we have a family, I'd be *vewustet* if Annie and our baby son died."

"Ja. It is terrible. You show great mercy to your brother-in-law, allowing your wife to help him."

Covering for Annie's absence grew harder all the time. At first, everyone called him kindhearted, but as the months passed, Konrad knew people were talking. As their sympathy for him waned, so had the invitations for meals. The thought of food made Konrad's stomach rumble. He rubbed it and smiled ruefully. "I change my mind. It's been forever since my Annie left. Of course, I started saying that the second day she was gone. I'm a horrible cook."

"Come next Sunday for supper."

"I will." His smile broadened. "I'll give you all the news Annie wrote."

Volkner nodded. He squinted at the fields around them and let out a sigh. "Your wheat—it looks good. I should have planted wheat this year. The greenbugs got all my sorghum."

"Mine too. Crop's ruined. If the weather holds good, the wheat might be enough to save me."

"I'm glad for you." Volkner took off his straw hat, raked his fingers through his wavy blond hair, and slapped the hat back on. "For me—the loss is too much. I'm going to go south and hire out to help with harvest. By the time the crops there are in, your field will be ripe. I wanted you to know so you can still rely on my help."

Konrad nodded curtly. "Thanks. If you go to Jakob Stauffer's farm, be sure to tell my Annie I miss her. When do you leave?"

"Day after tomorrow . . . but don't worry, I'll be sure to tell everyone at home that you're coming to Sunday supper."

Konrad watched Volkner ride off. The exchange went as well as it could, considering everything. It wouldn't be hard to make up a story or two about Annie and Jakob's kid. In fact, Konrad considered himself a skilled storyteller. So what if his words were lies?

He looked down at the envelope and opened it with one savage rip. Cash slid out. Five dollars. Five paltry dollars a month. That's what Jakob sent to keep him away. It wasn't enough, but Konrad couldn't leave now. He had no one to mind his crops.

Rage filled him as he strode toward the house. Konrad was the one who had worked the land these last six years, toiled under the scorching sun to bring in each crop. That, and he'd married Stauffer's mousy daughter. Everything had been going according to his plan until two years ago, when the old man died. Oh, Konrad planned on his dying. In fact, Annie babied the old goat and kept him alive far past what anyone expected. Konrad played his part well, too. More than once, the old man had said he was just like a son. In the end, it was all easy enough. He'd sent Annie to bed and done away with the old man by simply holding a pillow over his face. No one ever suspected anything, and Konrad knew all he'd ever wanted now belonged to him.

Or so he had thought.

A son ought to inherit—but after the funeral, at the reading of the will, Konrad learned he'd been cheated out of everything he'd planned on, sweated for, and expected. The house should have been willed to him, but Annie's father hadn't bothered to see the attorney and change the paper work. His will left the farm to be split evenly between his sons—but with Bartholomew dead, that meant Jakob inherited everything. Everything—the house, the barn, the animals, the land—all went to the sole surviving son.

Jakob didn't need it; he had a farm of his own. Even more, Jakob didn't deserve it. But Jakob wielded his ownership of the farm in a way Konrad never anticipated.

Jakob unexpectedly whisked Annie away one afternoon. Left on the table was a scrawled note. The words burned in Konrad's memory and soul: *Work the land. Keep the profit, but stay away from my sister.*

He'd dared to leave such an order—as if Konrad was still a hired hand instead of the man of the house and the one who ran things.

A wry smile twisted Konrad's mouth. He refused to stand for such an order. The money in his hand proved he'd fought back and won. He'd fired off a letter that resulted in Jakob sending funds each month.

Now Konrad wished he'd demanded more money. A farmer earned about twenty dollars a month, a hired hand got about ten. Women weren't worth as much as men, but Stauffer might have paid another dollar each month. Maybe even two.

Women tended the garden and put up food—but Annie wasn't here. That forced Konrad to buy expensive canned goods at the mercantile. If Annie were here like a good wife would be, he wouldn't be dealing with that problem. She had no business leaving him. Jakob shouldn't have taken her away. A woman belonged with her husband. Belonged *to* her husband. Yet for seven months now, Jakob had been benefiting from her labors.

The five dollars crinkled in Konrad's fist. Annie owed him her labor and care, yet she'd abandoned him. And why? He was a good husband to her. Far better than she deserved.

Her thoughtlessness provoked him. She'd deserved his irritation and earned his anger, but he was sorry for having been stern with her on occasion. To his credit, each time after he'd had to discipline her, he always went out of his way to be kind. Unfortunately, Annie was slow to learn, and she'd inevitably do things wrong and earn his wrath yet again.

Hadn't he told her repeatedly not to starch the collar of his Sunday-best shirt so much? And when they ran low on raisins, she'd put a stingy scoop of them in his oatmeal—then had some herself. Annie should have planned better and deserved to go without until she got to the mercantile to buy more. Well, she'd learned. After that episode, she always gave him plenty of raisins and ate her own oatmeal plain.

She'd gone to town without once asking permission. Even spent the egg money on buttons for a dress for herself. He'd made her take them back and give him the money. She'd vowed to honor and obey him the day she became his wife; she'd done neither. He'd had to train her, and after a year he still found her sadly lacking.

Nevertheless, he needed her. A few weeks more—then he'd get her. Once he brought in the wheat, Konrad decided, he'd go south and fetch his wife. He'd say whatever was needed to convince Jakob that Annie belonged alongside her husband.

Only Jakob was a stubborn man.

Konrad slowly fingered the bills as he considered the problem and concocted a plan. The best way would be to show up on Sunday and say something in the churchyard after the service about how he'd tried to be understanding all this time, but the

Bible said no man should pull asunder what God had joined together. Folks would side with him.

Of course, he'd also say that he'd missed his darling Annie, but they'd chosen to be apart this long because Jakob promised to sign over the deed so they'd be able to call the land their very own. Yes, that's what would happen. Annie was so mealymouthed and mousy, she wouldn't dare tell a single soul that it was all a lie. A smirk tilted Konrad's mouth. Jakob wouldn't like it, but he'd sign the deed—otherwise he'd be branded a liar and cheat.

The thought of that victory calmed Konrad. Annie would be a better wife, now that she missed him. She'd come home and behave. Even give him sons. Yes, several sons. Sons to work by his side and make him both rich and proud. Strapping ones who would inherit the land and take care of him in his old age. But first things first. He'd bring in the harvest. Then he'd get his wife and farm.

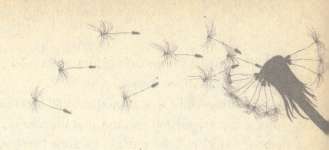

Seven

Hope cast a look at the bushel baskets she'd set at the end of every other row in the garden. Placed on the far side of the garden, those baskets weren't visible from the house or the path toward the outhouse. She made a habit of traversing a different row each time she went outside for something. As she passed through, she'd harvest the ripe vegetables into the skirt of her apron, then slip them into a basket. Mrs. Erickson didn't know, and Hope wanted it to stay that way.

Carrying a large crock to the back porch, she called out, "Emmy-Lou, please open the door."

Little feet pattered, and the door burst open. "What're we gonna do now?"

"We're gonna fill this here crock with watermelon pickles."

"My brother . . ." Mrs. Erickson sounded almost apologetic. "He likes the pickles made of the fruit itself and dill."

"So do I!" Hope grinned. "We'll pickle the fruit with dill and the rind with sugar, cinnamon, cloves and vinegar. That way, nothing goes to waste. Does that sound about right to you, Mrs. Erickson?"

"Ja." Mrs. Erickson gave her a timid smile. "I call you Hope. You should call me Annie."

Knowing Annie was as timid as could be, Hope acknowledged her act of friendship without making a to-do about it. "Well, then, Annie, we'll be gettin' a lot done here, won't we?"

Annie looked concerned as she set aside the sock she'd been darning. "I should have cleaned the crocks."

"Of course you could have, but them socks there would still need darnin'. I'm fixin' to tote in a passel of melons. If'n you finish the socks, might be good for you to slice up a few cabbages. We could salt the shreds and start up a batch of sauerkraut."

Much later, when the men came in for supper, Emmy-Lou galloped over to her father as he stopped at the washstand. Straddling the broom, she giggled. "Daddy, watch me! I'm riding a horsey, and my horsey is cleaning the floor."

"Too bad her horse can't pull a load." Phineas waited for his boss to use the pitcher and bowl first.

A grimace creased Mr. Stauffer's face.

Hope wiped her hands on the hem of her apron. "Something happen to one of your beasts?"

"Josephine is fine, but Nicodemus took exception to something and kicked in his stall. Didn't break anything, but I mudded and wrapped his leg. The last thing I need is a lame horse at harvest."

"What's the first thing you need, Daddy?"

He rinsed his hands, then knelt by Emmy-Lou as he dried them. "I got you, so I can't complain."

"Hattie and Josephine are of a size." Hope turned back to the stove and opened the warmer up top to take out a big bowl of macaroni and cheese. The sharp, creamy fragrance filled the air. "Wouldn't be the first time Hattie worked with a horse."

"You wouldn't mind?"

Hope gave her boss a startled look. "Why? That would make me like a dog with a stranger."

"I think you mean dog in a manger," Phineas said as he washed up.

"You got things turnt about. 'Twas Jesus in the manger. A dog with a stranger—there's a critter what ain't sure he wants to allow anyone near his property." She turned her focus on her boss. "Well, we ain't strangers, and I wouldn't mind a bit. Josephine's been weanin' her foal. Since he's been keepin' Hattie company out in the pasture, he's carried her scent back to his mama. I reckon all it'd take is bribin' them with half a peach in the mornin', and they'd stand for bein' harnessed together."

"I'm obliged." Mr. Stauffer inhaled appreciatively as he moved so she could set the hot bowl on the table. "Does Hattie prefer right or left side?"

"Left, but she'll do right if you need her to."

Mr. Stauffer's shoulders eased down a bit more. "Left is good. Josephine—she likes the right. Emmy-Lou, your hands are dirty."

"I'll see to her." Annie scurried over.

Emmy-Lou yanked on the broomstick and did a little sideways hop. "Whoa, horsey!" She lost her balance, and her father caught her, but the broom went the other way. The tip of the handle struck the sampler, which in turn jarred the photograph. Hope watched, helpless to stop the Stauffers' wedding picture as it slid down the wall and crashed, shattering glass all about.

Emmy-Lou let out a shriek; then only her sniffles broke the ominous silence.

"I'm sorry." Annie bowed her head and whispered, "I shouldn't have let her play like that." She tugged Emmy-Lou over and sidled in front of the child. Annie turned into a magpie all of a sudden. "I'll sweep this up. I will. Right away. You men go ahead and eat while supper's hot. Emmy-Lou—"

"I'll help her wash her hands." Phineas picked up the child.

Mr. Stauffer had gone pale beneath his tan. Glass crunched beneath his boots as he stepped forward. "It was an accident." His voice sounded just as brittle and gritty as the broken glass.

"I-I'll clean it up," Annie insisted.

"No." He cleared his throat, then said in a measured, almost soothing tone, "Sit down, Annie. Eat your supper."

"He's right, Annie. I'm cleanin' it, and that's that." Hope bustled over. "What's a housekeeper for? All ya'll go take the load off and dig in." She grabbed the broom and reached for the broken frame.

Mr. Stauffer's hand closed over it first. The corner of the picture bent inward, hiding the image of Mrs. Stauffer's face. With exacting care, Jakob's big thumb lifted the flap. A crease now marred the photograph—it angled right through his wife's hair.

Reverently, he grazed the likeness of his wife, almost as if the touch would erase the crease in the same way it would coax back an errant wisp of hair—but it didn't repair the damage. An impossibly long, utterly silent sigh slid from between his taut lips. Anguish turned his eyes the same shade as pewter. For just an instant, he closed them.

Lord, this man's a-hurtin' something fierce. Could you comfort him?

Mr. Stauffer opened his eyes. He said nothing, but straightened up and carried the picture upstairs. Each step he took echoed with grief; then his bedroom door shut. The oh-so-quiet click was the final, lonely sound she heard.

"Mr. Stauffer?"

Jakob didn't turn around. Instead, he stood by the barn stall and murmured under his breath to Josephine. He'd been silent at supper. What happened was an accident. That didn't change the pain wrenching his heart.

Jakob cherished that picture. On their wedding trip, they'd dressed up in their wedding finery and gone to a photographer. The photographer kept trying to get Naomi to face forward, but she'd insisted she couldn't take her eyes off her handsome husband.

Now the picture was ruined. A white line creased the corner, angling through Naomi's hair. Reason told him the photograph wasn't destroyed and anyone else would consider the damage inconsequential, but all the logic in the world didn't erase the savage stab of grief that blindsided him. Hoping to minimize the fold, Jakob had carefully placed the photograph between the pages of his Bible—but when he'd opened his Bible, it had fallen open to Proverbs Thirty-one. Of all the passages, why that one? It described the attributes of a good wife. No other passage could have left him feeling more desolate.

He'd come out here to be alone, to have a chance to grieve. Phineas was smart enough to leave him alone. The last thing Jakob wanted was to talk with Hope.

"Ain't that something?" Oblivious to the fact that he hadn't even turned to acknowledge her, Hope approached the stall. "You done a smart thing, puttin' Hattie and Jo as neighbors tonight. Let 'em get better acquainted."

He grunted.

Cocking her head to the side, Hope studied Nicodemus. "How's your gelding?"

Realizing she wasn't going away, Jakob grudgingly replied, "I expect he'll be better in a few days."

"Like you said the day I drove up, you take good care of your livestock. Been right nice to my mule, too. She's gotta memory long as her ears. Come mornin', you'll find her eager to show her appreciation."

He made no reply as he checked the bolt to be sure Josephine wouldn't get out of her stall. She seemed to have a talent for that. About once a week she'd be out of her stall and visiting one of the other beasts when Jakob opened the barn door. In times past, he'd thought Naomi or Phineas was playing a joke on him, but they weren't.

"That's some bolt you got on that stall. Never seen such a big 'un."

"Josephine's an escape artist. Even now, she lips this one until it slides free every so often."

"Spirit. That's a good quality. Whether it be in a critter or a child, it makes for a few headaches; but in the long run, 'tis the spirited ones what got the spark and the smarts that make 'em a cut above the best."

"A cut above the rest." As soon as he corrected her, Jakob wondered why he bothered. In a way, her mangled cliché held some truth. The best and brightest often required more of an investment, but they invariably paid dividends.

"Rest. Ain't gonna be much more of that round here. Not with harvest upon us. Maybe God's givin' Nicodemus a few days to store up all the oomph it'll take for him to pull his weight. Long as I'm here, though, you're welcome to Hattie's help."

"He'll be better." *He has to be. The timing couldn't be worse. Besides, Hope won't be here much longer at all—a week at most.* Annie had said Hope figured she'd move on and help at least five more families this season. Jakob moved toward Nicodemus's stall and looked at the huge bay gelding. Nicodemus allowed the hoof on his sore leg to still make full contact with the ground. That was a good sign. "Before I go to bed, I'll take off his mud wrap. Might rub on some liniment."

"I could mix you up a liniment if'n you don't have one."

"I've got McLeans Volcanic."

"Hoo-ooo-ie! If that don't cure it, nothin' will."

Her emphatic reaction made him finally look at her.

Hope wrinkled her freckled nose. "That stuff stinks so bad, the hurt runs off begging for mercy."

Even in his foul mood, her words forced Jakob to stop frowning. "It does smell bad."

"Bad?"

A recollection of the pungent odor forced him to admit, "Terrible. It smells terrible."

Hope crossed her arms and tapped her foot. "It rivals a skunk."

She had a point, but more than what she said, it was her tone of voice that transmitted her opinion. Jakob's lips twitched.

Hope's eyes twinkled. "In an outhouse."

The crazy woman had a way with words. When she didn't intend to be amusing, she was, but now when she was trying, her humor sparkled. Almost against his will, Jakob felt an unaccustomed grin stretch his sunburned face.

Her brows went up, and she leaned the slightest bit toward him and tacked on, "In a wind—a stiff wind."

A chuckle bubbled out of him.

Her laughter joined his. "I'm gonna be a stinker myself. If'n you decide to use the liniment, I'm gonna run t'other way and let Phineas help you out. 'Bout the onliest help I'll be is to offer you each a clothespin for your nose." She gave her head a sorrowful shake. "Not that a clothespin would do much good.

The fumes from that bottle of McLeans is still liable to make your eyes tear up and your nose run."

"It's strong."

Her hazel eyes looked almost golden in the lantern light. "I'm thinkin' on the way a simple bottle holds the powerful smell and fire of that liniment. Reminds me that it ain't the vessel that counts, but what fills it."

"The same can be said of man."

"You shore said a mouthful there." Rocking from heels to toes, Hope grinned at him. The hem of her skirt swayed back and forth, fanning bits of straw to flutter around her. "The abundance of the Lord God Almighty a-fillin' us spills over. 'Tis a blessing and a joy. But that bottle's somethin' else entirely. Knowin' what it holds makes me glad you're the sorta man who's mindful enough to check the lid to be sure it's on right snug."

"I'll be sure it's secure." Her confidence in him—even though it regarded something that paltry—still counted as a compliment.

Hope caressed Hattie's muzzle. "Jo ain't the kind to be jealous, is she?"

"Jealous of what?"

"Hattie's straw hat, of course." Hope continued to baby her animal.

"Her hat." The woman's mind skipped from one subject to the next, just as crazily as she jumped from one chore to another. It made no sense to him. "What made you think of her hat?"

"We're talkin' 'bout lids. Caps, hats, bonnets—"

No. Oh no. It was one thing for a woman to parade around with a decorated mule, but a man had his dignity. "Your mule won't be wearing that hat while I'm working her."

"You'll be wearin' your straw hat."

Incredulous, Jakob stared at Hope. "That's different."

Hope nodded. "Yep."

Relief flooded him. He'd made her see reason.

"Your ears don't stick outta the top."

⁊

A while later, Jakob sat at the dining table once again, only this time he'd read his Bible to Annie and Hope. He closed his Bible, taking care that the photograph stayed securely within the pages. "It is getting late."

As if to punctuate his assertion, the clock struck ten. Annie set aside the tiny gown she'd been sewing.

"Thankee for reading to us." Hope wiped the top of a jar. "Can't you just 'magine how Balaam felt when that ass of his started talkin'? If'n God ever started tellin' me things through Hattie, I'd be scairt outta my skin. Smart as she is, she still don't have nothin' to say to me."

If she could talk, she'd tell you to stop sticking that hat on her. Jakob's chair scraped the floor as he stood. "God had a purpose."

"Yup. Guess Balaam's partly to blame that God ended up making the donkey talk. Imagine that Balaam feller beatin' on that poor critter. Once the man saw the angel for himself, he understood, though. Reckon 'tis an important story, seein' as it's in the Bible, but it sorta settles poorly on me. Never could abide violence, though—not even in a story."

Jakob asserted, "It was a long time ago."

Annie took a lantern from the table and started toward the door. The room dimmed. "Ready, Hope?"

"You go on ahead, Annie. I got me a second breath of fresh air."

"Almost every night, you get a second wind." Annie sounded almost guilty.

"Hearing Mr. Stauffer read from the Good Book—well, it fills my heart so full, I gotta stay up and savor the words. Either that, or the story niggles at me, so I gotta figure out why it's weighin' on my mind. No use in me lying in bed, starin' at the ceiling."

"Mama was like that." Annie's voice held the softness of a treasured memory.

"If Mama were here, she'd shoo you off to bed." Jakob took the kerosene lamp from his sister. Her shadow on the wall outlined her maternal condition. "You don't need to go outside."

She blushed.

"Mercy sakes, no." Hope waggled her finger at Annie. "If Balaam's donkey were here, he'd tell you to exercise your horse sense. Yep, he would. No one rides a horse at night when he's got a roof over his head."

A smile flickered across Annie's face. "The man has the roof, or the horse?"

Jakob looked at his sister and marveled. He didn't know how Hope did it, but she had managed to make Annie comfortable—comfortable enough to indulge in that teasing question. He'd noticed a change in his sister—she'd warmed up to the housekeeper, and Hope now called Annie by her first name. Those things gave Jakob a glimmer of hope for his sister. With time and loving care, perhaps she could recover.

Laughter bubbled out of Hope. "This here farm's so fine, man and beasts all have roofs over their heads." Her brow knit. "That made it sound like y'all have a bunch of heads apiece. Well, don't make no never mind. Even with one head, you're smart enough not to risk fallin' and hurtin' yourself out there in the dark."

"Daddy?" Emmy-Lou whimpered from upstairs.

"Ja." Jakob hastily set the lamp on the table and bolted up the stairs two at a time. "Ja, I'm right here."

Emmy-Lou stood in the door to her room, afraid to step away from the shaft of moonlight and into the dark of the hallway. One hand curled around the doorframe, and she reached out for him. Small and shaking, her hand barely connected with his before she desperately curled her fingers around his.

Jakob scooped her up and clutched her to his chest. "See? I am here."

"I was all alone."

He wasn't sure whether she meant she'd been alone in the room or was referring to the time last year when she'd fallen into the wellhole. The memory still haunted them both. "You aren't alone. I'm here, and Aunt Annie is here."

"And Miss Hope?"

"Yes. And Jesus." She clung to him, as if she wanted to burrow into his shirt and stay buttoned against him forever. Jakob bent his head, kissed her temple, and murmured soft reassurances to her. The tension in her quivering muscles began to ease.

"How is she, Jakob?" Annie called up to him.

"It's been hot as can be. I bet lil' Emmy-Lou would like a nice, cool sip of water." Hope stood at the foot of the stairs. Jakob noticed how she'd wound her arm around his sister, as if to share Annie's concerns. "Would you like me to bring up a dipper, or do all y'all wanna come down here?"

"Daddy," Emmy-Lou whispered against his neck, "I gotta go."

Jakob carried her downstairs. Annie took her to the study where they now kept a chamber pot. When they came back out, Hope knelt down and swiped a cool dishrag over Emmy-Lou's face and hands. "Didja listen to the music all them crickets are a-makin'? Sounds to me like the Lord Jesus gave 'em all teeny-tiny, itty-bitty fiddles, and all of 'em are playing songs to tell Him how they love Him."

Emmy-Lou cocked her head to the side and listened. She whispered, "There's lots of them!"

"Yup. I reckon there's a star in the sky for every last one of them crickets. Betcha they start a-twinkling when the music gets a-goin' so they can shine out their glory just like they did the night Baby Jesus got borned. Don't you think so, Annie?"

"Ja. Bright and pretty."

He didn't know what the women discussed when he wasn't around, but Jakob knew Hope understood his daughter was afraid of the dark. Whether or not she knew why . . . that didn't matter at the moment. Her matter-of-fact approach and comforting thoughts erased some of the fear in Emmy-Lou's wide eyes.

Hope set aside the dishcloth and pressed a little tin cup into Emmy-Lou's hands. Emmy-Lou drank the water. "Thank you." She yawned.

Hope took back the cup. "Did you say your night-night prayer tonight?"

Emmy-Lou whispered, "Yes."

"No better way to end the day than to put yourself in God's hands." Hope gave her a hug. "You can snuggle up and listen to the crickets sing 'til you fall asleep."

"Aunt Annie is tired, too. She'll stay with you upstairs. Won't you, Annie?" Jakob looked at his sister.

"I am tired."

Annie and Emmy-Lou went upstairs. Jakob emptied the chamber pot and returned it to the corner of his office. When he came back out, he stopped cold and stared at the housekeeper. Anger pulsed through him. "What are you doing?"

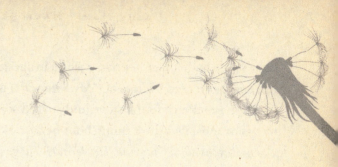

Eight

W hen you went to go fetch your daughter, your Bible slipped from the edge of the table. Didn't seem right, the Holy Bible layin' on the floor. That picture fell out, too. Though the glass from the frame busted all over creation, I tacked the wood back, good as new." Hope wandered to the far side of the dining table and hung the frame with the picture back inside it. "Come Wednesday, when you or Phineas take the butter, eggs, and milk to town, you can replace the glass."

Relief sprouted in him—a small seed that grew and flowered the longer he gazed at the picture. It wasn't ruined, after all. Throughout dinner, the empty spot on the wall where the picture had hung tore at him. Seeing Naomi there again felt right. Comforting.

"Your wife—you made her a powerful happy woman. That smile on her face glows with contentment. Makes me wanna grin myself."

For almost a year and a half, no one mentioned Naomi. Hope's words felt like rain after a ten-year drought. "Naomi—" His voice caught. He hadn't said her name aloud in ages. Emotion welled up, and he cleared his throat. "My wife was a good woman."

Hope went back to the stove and stirred something. "What was your most favoritest thing 'bout her?"

The way she always hummed. Her serenity. The gentleness of her kiss. But those all seemed so personal. "Her . . ." He paused. "She made everything better, brighter."

Nodding, the housekeeper continued to stir the pot. "Contentment. It fills a home and heart. Leaves memories to treasure. From the grand coop you have, I betcha Naomi loved chickens."

"She named the hens." The admission surprised him. He hadn't thought of that in years, not since he'd first heard her do it. The memory didn't hurt like he expected . . . or maybe it was simply that Hope was easy to talk to.

"People names, or animal names?" She fished jars from the stove's water reservoir.

"Names from the Bible to start with, but she ran out. There aren't that many women in the Bible."

"So what did she do next?"

Jakob drank the last of the coffee as Hope canned stewed tomatoes. He found himself telling her about Naomi. Nothing personal—but little things, recollections, bits and pieces of the life he'd once shared with the woman of his heart. Hope laughed at the right times and asked questions that led him down memory's path. He'd missed Naomi so, and sharing her with Hope allowed him to savor what he'd had.

Hope treated the cans in a water bath to seal them properly and washed the pot and ladle. When she pumped water into the coffeepot and ground coffee beans for tomorrow's breakfast, Jakob rinsed out his mug. "It's late."

"I didn't notice. Had me a good time, gettin' to know your missus. As the years pass, Emmy-Lou will love hearin' your stories. It'll mean the world to her, knowin' more about her mama."

When he went upstairs and shut his bedroom door, Jakob didn't follow his usual ritual. Instead, he tugged open the top drawer of his bureau. A picture lay there, facedown. Slowly, he turned it over. He'd hidden it there the day of the funeral. Naomi sat in a wicker chair with Emmy-Lou standing on the seat beside her. One of Naomi's arms wrapped around Emmy-Lou's waist; the other held Jakob Jr.

Emmy-Lou was too young to remember Naomi. Hope had pointed out the obvious: A daughter deserved to grow up knowing her mama loved her. Just as he cherished the love light in Naomi's face in the picture downstairs, Emmy-Lou would treasure this photograph. Like a wounded animal that curled up and hid away, he'd retreated in silence—but by doing so, he'd been stuck in his grief and robbing his daughter of the vital message that her mother adored her.

Jakob knelt by his bed and held the picture. He set it on the wedding-ring quilt and smoothed his rough hand over the tiny cotton pieces. In the years ahead, he'd find a little thing to tell Emmy-Lou each day about her mother—and as time passed, like the pieces of a quilt, a pattern of comfort and love would result. Tomorrow, he'd show the picture to Emmy-Lou.

Instead of folding his hands in prayer, Jakob laid them on either side of the picture. "Lord, I miss her. You know I do. There was so much about her to love. You were good to me, to give me such a wife. Help me be strong enough to look back with gratitude instead of grief, and let me share my memories of Naomi so our daughter will carry a piece of her mother in her heart."

The cool predawn air wafted through the wide open windows. Hope slipped the domed glass lid atop the Mason jar she'd filled with Crowder peas and slid the wire assembly clamp into the groove to fasten it. That jar joined the others in the stove's water reservoir.

A quick glance at the clock let her know she could do one more batch if she hurried. Adding more coal to the stove, she planned everything they'd do today.

A small creak on the stairs made her wheel around.

Mr. Stauffer stood there, his shirt unbuttoned and suspenders hanging down, feet bare. A small patch of hair stuck straight up at the back of his head, making him look like he'd suffered a huge shock. The protective intensity on his face changed to bewilderment. "It's you."

She nodded.

As if suddenly aware of his half-dressed state, he buttoned his faded blue shirt and drew closer. "What—" His voice came to an abrupt halt as he spied the jars cooling on the table.

Hope held a finger to her lips.

He glanced toward the stairs. "It's early yet."

"I'm countin' on that." She started fishing jars from the water reservoir. "I'd 'preciate it if 'n you'd not say anything 'bout this here batch."

He studied her for a long moment, his blue eyes unblinking. "You don't want Annie to know."

"You and me made a pact to make things easier on her." The water on the outside of the hot jars evaporated immediately. "You pickin' up the baskets in the garden and puttin' 'em on the back porch—that's been right kind of you."

"I thought . . ." He shook his head. That wild clump of hair still stood at attention, not daring to wobble or fall.

"I'll put the coffee on in two shakes of a short stick."

His brows rose. "A short stick?"

"Long sticks take longer to go back and forth." She wrinkled her nose. "Come to think on it, maybe not. If'n that was true, clocks with a longer pendulum would make time go slower, wouldn't they?"

"I'm sure the clockmaker knows how to adjust for that."

Hope nodded. For being a clever man, Mr. Stauffer didn't act all biggety. If he didn't know something, he didn't bluster or change the subject. Showed good sense and humility. Those were fine qualities. Since he was up, the least she could do was get the coffee on the stove. A blink later, the pot she'd prepared the night before sat over a burner.

"I saw all the butterbeans you gathered yesterday." He hitched his suspenders up onto his broad shoulders. "Do you need the drying screens on the porch again?"

"That'd be mighty nice of you." She set a tray on the table. Hot as the jars there were, she had to use potholders to pop them onto the tray. As soon as she'd filled the tray, Mr. Stauffer lifted it. "Are you putting these in the pantry?"

She nodded. Having him carry the tray would help. Once inside the pantry, she hastened up both planks of the stepstool and quickly moved jars from the middle shelf up to the highest one. That way, the hot jars would be easier for her to check later. She twisted to take the hot jars from the tray.

Mr. Stauffer stood just inside the door. Gawking at the shelves, he remained just out of reach.

"Could you please step a little closer?"

He closed the distance and held the tray higher.

Quickly as she could, Hope transferred the hot jars where they could continue cooling, yet be out of the way. As she took the last one, she smiled down at him. "Would you mind fetching the tray o'er by the pump?"

She hopped down and moved the stepstool so when he returned, she was ready to tuck away stewed tomatoes. "There."

Mr. Stauffer held the empty tray and stared up at the shelf. "Those jars—they were hot, too. They weren't the tomatoes you made late last night."

"That garden of yours—'tis bountiful. Come wintertime, you'll be glad them tomatoes didn't go to waste."

Blocking the doorway, he scanned each shelf. Finally, his gaze returned to her. "You've put up more than I thought."

She hitched her shoulder. "Little bit at a time adds up in the end."

His fingers curled around the tray until they turned white. "Is that what you tell my sister?"

"It's the truth."

His wide shoulders swiveled as he surveyed the pantry from one corner clear to the opposite one. He didn't just scan across, either. His gaze dropped and rose to take in the contents of every last shelf in the cramped quarters. "The truth," he paused and stared into her eyes, "is that you have done much in secret."

Hope tugged the tray from him. "I've done a little bit here and there. Your sister and me—we've been doin' plenty together. Them leather pant green beans—she strung 'em all herself. I'd best get back to the stove, else you won't be havin' anything but coffee for breakfast." He stepped aside, and she slipped past him.

It wasn't until then Hope realized she hadn't put up her hair yet, and the intimacy of it made her stomach flutter. It still hung down her back in a simple plait—like a schoolgirl. *Well,*

I'm barefoot like a schoolgirl, too. Don't make no never mind, anyhow. "Are y'all wantin' grits or oatmeal this mornin'?"

"Either." He leaned against the table and folded his arms across his chest.

"If'n 'tis all the same to you, I'll make oatmeal. Addin' in raisins—that's good for Annie. We need to build up her blood. Liver and raisins and blackstrap molasses—they all help. When all the workers are here, we'll fry up plenty of chickens, but I'm plannin' on holdin' back the livers and frying 'em with a mess of onions those nights for your sis."

"*Gut. Sehr gut.* Annie—I'm glad for her that you're here."

Hope smiled. "Thankee. But I'm glad for me that I'm here, too. Your sis and little daughter—they're sweet as sugar sandies."

"Sugar candy?"

"That, too, I reckon. But sugar sandies—they're my favorite. Dreadful expensive to bake, though, what with them having pecans in them and such."

"I have to go to town anyway. I'll get some pecans. What else do you need?"

Just the mention of pecans made her mouth water. Nothing tasted better than freshly-hulled pecans. Shoving aside the temptation, Hope set down the tray. "Pecans seem more suited to Thanksgivin' and Christmas than to harvesttime. 'Twould strike me as odd, bakin' with 'em at harvesttime. They wouldn't be quite so special over the holidays if'n I had 'em other times."

"What else do you need?" he repeated.

"Sugar, flour, vinegar, and paraffin wax." Relief flowed through her. She shouldn't have said anything about pecans in the first place. They were an extravagance, and she'd be embarrassed if her boss squandered money on them. "Yep. Sugar, flour, vinegar, and wax. Other than them things, you're sittin' real fine. Don't forget 'bout the glass for your picture frame. You can take nearly all them crated eggs 'long, but we'll be a-needin' 'bout two dozen of 'em and all of today's eggs to feed the harvest hands. After that, while you go help out at the other farms, I can take eggs to town for you."

"Hope?" Though he said her name, he looked away, through the window as if something out there demanded his concentration. His voice dropped. "Smith's got a big family and a small coop. They eat whatever their layers produce. We'll be here two days, then Sunday falls between our harvest and his. I'll tell him to send someone over for eggs."

"There'll be plenty enough for sharin'." She busied herself at the stove and glanced back over her shoulder. "Your sis said she doesn't know what we take to the other farms for harvest."

"Peaches, two loaves of bread, and a dessert—that is what Naomi always did." His voice started out sounding certain, but faded a touch.

"Mr. Stauffer, sir, rememberin' your dearly departed wife has gotta pain you somethin' fierce. I just can't tell at this moment whether 'tis your grief or you hesitating. I know the Bible says to give with the left hand in secret 'cuz 'tis right." His eyes widened, so she thought she'd guessed what he'd been thinking. "Bein' a God-fearin' man, that might be what's on your mind, so I'm gonna open my big mouth and ask. Do y'all want me to maybe dress up some chickens and send 'em over to the Smiths 'long with the eggs?"

He nodded.

Hope started oatmeal, then set to filling the next set of freshly boiled jars. She felt unaccountably flustered. *It's my fault he's up so early; he doesn't have to get to chores yet.* "Ain't put up any corn yet. That sweet corn is nigh unto ready. Coupla the Yankee farmers up north like succotash. Are you wanting me to put some up, or do you like your corn and butterbeans kept apart?"

"Apart." He hitched his shoulder as if to dismiss something. "Annie and Emmy-Lou—they don't like butterbeans. Miriam planted the butterbeans. Don't bother with them. I'll take them to town."

Hope tilted her head to the side. "What 'bout you? You like 'em?"

"Yes, but it's a waste of time to prepare something for just one person."

"Don't know as I agree. Just goin' along with that for a moment—does Phineas like butterbeans?"

"Don't know. He always eats whatever's on the table."

Hope shot him a saucy smile. "I'll be shore not to leave any laundry or mending on there."

Jakob opened the glass door on the front of the clock and wound it. The tightly sprung, metallic *zzzt-zzzt-zzzt* filled the kitchen. Carefully closing the door again, he made sure the clock still hung straight. While nudging it ever so slightly to one side, he commented, "Speaking of laundry—other women do it all on Monday. Ironing on Tuesday."

"True enough. Been known to do that myself sometimes."

"Then why—" His voice skidded to a halt. His eyes widened, then narrowed. "Because of Annie."

"Don't you go blamin' her," Hope whispered. " 'Twas my idea."

He glanced at the stairway, then leaned forward and spoke in a deep whisper, "It's more work for you to spread it out. You have to fill the kettle and boil it each time you do laundry."

"Only on the day when we do britches and such. The rest of the time, it's been easy enough to use the kettle to boil up jars and heat seal them. Then I shave in a tad of lye soap and wash

97

up a few things. Annie rinses them out and hangs 'em on the line. Your sis—she loves the feel of a breeze wafting through the damp clothes. The heat gets to her, and that's an easy way for me to cool her down a mite."

What's gotten into me? she thought as a small laugh bubbled out of her when she saw his brows rise. "That didn't come out quite right. Sounds like I'm comparin' her to a horse, but I'm not." Hope turned back to the stove.

Mr. Stauffer didn't say another word. Even if that one stair step didn't creak, she would have known he left. Odd, how the room felt different when he was in it. Smaller. She plunged a jar into the hot water. *Fanciful thinking. The steam must be gettin' to my brain, twistin' it like the pieces of a bentwood rocker.*

She had enough Crowder peas for only four more jars. With those done and oatmeal going, Hope scooped her boots from the floor and took them outside. As a rooster warmed up and the sun started to sneak a peep at the day, the screen door opened. She didn't cast a look over her shoulder but yanked the laces tight on her right boot. "Gonna be a scorcher today."

"While I'm in town, we'll decide on when to harvest. My fields are usually the first. Smiths' next, then Richardsons'. At church on Sunday, we talked about starting on Friday."

"I heard that." She grinned at him. "Heard y'all got two reapers. That's right smart. Hot as it gets here, you wanna cut the wheat before it scorches."

He cleared his throat. "Hot as it's gotten, I'd rather start the harvest tomorrow. I don't know that we'll get everything done here in two days. Some places say the ox is in the ditch and harvest on Sundays, but we don't do that in Gooding."

"Ain't for me to tell a man what to do on his land or what's right betwixt him and the Lord, but deep in my own heart, I agree with you. Don't seem to keep the day holy, and nobody gets any rest."

Hope continued. "I already planned on three days. Don't matter how hard the men and beasts work, a reaper can only go so fast. Twelve or thirteen acres a day. I reckon you got fifty, maybe sixty acres wavin' in the wind out there. By startin' tomorrow, you'll have it done by Saturday night."

"It's short notice. I should have told you last night."

Hope shook her head. "Wouldn't have changed nothin' for me, but it woulda put your sister in a dither. We'll get it all taken care of." Mentally she listed all the chores she needed to attend and details she ought to iron out. She tied her boot and shoved her left foot into the other, sighing as she tied it.

"Is your foot hurt? Don't your shoes fit?"

"They fit me just fine. Truth is, given my druthers, I'd go barefoot as a heathen." She smoothed down her hem and rose. "Ever notice in the Bible, how Adam and Eve wore leaves, then God made 'em clothes from animal skins?"

"Yes." He stared at her, waiting.

"Neither of 'em was a-wearin' shoes. Did y'all ever take note of that? I bet the devil was jealous of folks havin' feet. Snakes don't got 'em, so that old Lucifer probably decided to rob people of the joy of dew-soaked grass beneath their feet or the fun of squishin' mud 'twixt their toes. Shoes. That's how he done it. Once man got outta the Garden of Eden, he ended up wearin' shoes. It makes me wonder if that's where the sayin' came from—you know, bein' booted out of someplace."

"I don't know. The saying sure fits." A slow smile kicked up the corners of Mr. Stauffer's mouth. "The only thing better than wearing a pair of broken-in boots is taking them off."

"That's a fine way of thinkin' on it. Makes me grateful both ways."

᙭

Smiling pulled the muscles in Jakob's face contrary to where they wanted to go, and the tiny nick he'd gotten shaving twinged. Served him right. He'd been so busy looking for Hope to accomplish things a certain way, he'd been blind to the truth. Busy remonstrating with himself as he took care of his morning ablutions, Jakob managed to catch the angle of his jaw with the razor. The styptic pencil stopped the bleeding. If he hadn't already been wide awake, the sting from the pencil would have done the job.

Ever since her arrival, the chaos of his household had changed. The shift had been so subtle, he'd failed to notice what was right under his nose. Just because she approached tasks differently didn't mean they weren't accomplished. He'd mistaken her flexibility for disorganization.

"I don't come to change things. I just come to help out." The words she'd spoken after their first supper ran through his mind. She'd changed just about everything . . . but Jakob had to admit, for the good.

By Saturday, the reaping would be done . . . and Hope would leave. She'd agreed to stay through harvest. One taste of her cooking, and word would spread—other farmers would snap her up. Even if he convinced her to stay through threshing, Jakob knew that wouldn't be more than another week or so—not nearly long enough. He had to convince her to stay longer, but would she agree? She had her own livelihood to consider.

He'd come back downstairs, rehearsing what he wanted to say. Off-balance at not finding her in the house, he'd come out onto the porch and ended up talking about boots. That was all well and good, but—

"I'm needing to get back to the stove. Time to stir up the oatmeal."

"Wait." He couldn't risk letting her go without trying to secure her. "I wanted to—"

"Whoops! I hear your sis. 'Scuse me." She bustled past him and into the house. " 'Mornin', Annie! Looks like we all wanted worms today."

"Is Jakob going fishing? Today?"

Jakob opened the door. "Don't tempt me. I think Hope meant we all rose early."

"Yup. The early bird gets the worm." Hope washed her hands at the kitchen pump.

Jakob and Annie exchanged a stunned look. Hope hadn't mangled the cliché.

Oblivious to their astonishment, Hope finished washing up. "Reckon that's why roosters make a bunch of racket at the crack of sunrise. Ain't that just like a man—to go squawkin' if 'n he's hungry?" She laughed. "And truth be told, I'm just like all the hens that start a-cluckin' after his first notes. Only they lay the eggs and I just cook 'em."

"I'll make breakfast." Annie cast a glance at the stove, and her face fell. "You already started."

"Yup. But tell you what: If 'n y'all go on ahead and make shore the oatmeal don't burn and maybe set the milk and buttermilk on the table, I'll see to a few other chores."

"Hope is right. It's early yet. Do I have time to milk the cows before breakfast?"

"I can set the oatmeal aside and leave the lid on so it stays hot." Annie chewed on her lower lip for an instant—one of the habits she'd never had until she'd married Konrad. The action tattled on how uncertain and easily flustered she'd become.

"Better still, why don't Phineas and I each milk a cow? That way, everything should be done about the same time. He can muck the stable while I go to town."

101

"Aunt Annie? Miss Hope? Daddy?" Emmy-Lou's tone grew more shrill with each name.

Jakob called, "We're already downstairs, *Liebling*. Come down to us."

"Daddy?" Near panic still quavered in her tone.

"I'm comin' to fetch you." Hope sounded easygoing, yet she mounted the stairs with notable speed. "Fact is, I needed to come grab my hairpins. I clean forgot 'em." A second later, her voice drifted down the stairs to Jakob. "Now, lookee at that. See that purdy little wren out there?"

"It's too dark. I don't see him."

Jakob tensed, ready to go up and soothe his daughter's fears.

"He hopped behind that branch, but you can still hear him. Betcha he heard the rooster and decided to make up a mornin' song for hisself. You wanna sing a tune whilst we get you dressed and I pin up my hair?"

"I shouldn't have left her all by herself up there." Distress twisted Annie's features.

"What will we sing?" Emmy-Lou asked.

Jakob relaxed at how eagerness replaced the fearful tone in his daughter's voice. "Emmy-Lou is fine, Annie. Hope is good with her. Listen . . . she's already singing. It will take time, but she will get over her fears." Jakob wasn't sure whether he was trying to convince his sister or himself. His cousin Miriam had been minding Emmy-Lou when the accident happened. Though no one else blamed her, Miriam couldn't forgive herself or forget. She'd been every bit as anxious as Emmy-Lou—which was why she eventually left.

Snatches of a ditty drifted down to him. Hope didn't dwell on Emmy-Lou's fear, but instead diverted her attention toward something fun. *I should remember that trick.*

"She *is* singing." Annie's shoulders melted with relief.

Jakob smiled at his sister. "See? All is well. I'm going to do the milking." How many times had he reassured her about things since he'd brought her home? He'd smooth over whatever he thought concerned her, then let her know where he'd be. *Lord, my daughter and sister are so . . . scared. So fragile. Surely you sent us Hope. I don't know who needs her the most—Emmy-Lou or Annie. Almighty Father, help me now to keep Hope.*

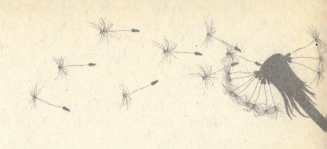

Nine

"Annie, the rosebush is gonna be bribin' the dog if'n it don't get watered today."

"I'll water it." Annie set down her spoon and started to rise from the breakfast table.

Hope motioned her to sit back down. "Thankee. I keep forgettin' it. I reckoned on getting a bunch of things done ahead of time. Your brother says he's hoping to hurry things up a bit and have harvest start tomorrow."

"So soon?" Annie looked horrified. "I'm not ready!"

Concern shot through Jakob as he detected the frightened edge in her voice.

Hope laughed. "Show me a woman who is! I ain't ever seen one. But you and me—we're a good team." She nodded her head. "Yup. We work right fine together, don'tcha think?"

"Yesss . . ." Annie stretched out the single syllable, testing what Hope asserted. "We do."

From the way a timid smile appeared on his sister's face, Jakob knew Hope's response was perfect. Gratitude filled him. "Hope, you're right. Annie, you and Mama used to run around like chickens without their heads when Dad said harvest was upon us."

Annie nodded.

"Women take care of their own farm and help out with the neighbors' harvests. Hope's probably done more harvest meals in one year than most women do in ten." Jakob had no trouble sounding confident of that fact.

"I've got a way of going about getting prepared and makin' shore things get done. Annie, do y'all mind too much if'n I get bossy and take over? I reckon I will anyway, but havin' you agree would make me feel better."

"I don't mind." In fact, Annie sounded relieved.

"Good. I wanna earn my keep. No use in your brother hirin' me if'n I don't do a bang-up good job. Ain't that right, Mr. Stauffer?"

His mouth full, he mumbled, "Uh-huh."

"Goin' from pillar to roast like I do—"

"It's from pillar to post," Phineas corrected.

Hope blinked at him, then threw back her head and laughed. "For true? I just always figured folks said it on account of women having to rush from the porch to the kitchen."

"Pillar to post is the cliché, but your version—it makes just as much sense." Annie smiled.

"Bless your heart, Annie, you gotta be one of the most kindest souls God ever made."

"She's right." Phineas stared over the rim of his mug at Annie.

Annie swallowed hard and dipped her head.

"I didn't mean to embarrass y'all with my words, Annie. 'Twas just that ya got a rare kindness in your heart, and I 'preciate it. Mr. Stauffer, how's about you givin' your sis them raisins for her oatmeal? She needs to build up her blood."

"No!" Annie went white, then flushed and stammered, "The men should have them."

"I already poured maple syrup on mine." Phineas dug into his bowl for another bite. "No raisins for me."

"I got raisins already." Emmy-Lou took a bite. "Mmmm-mmm!"

Though he didn't care whether he added anything other than a sizable plop of butter to his oatmeal, Jakob took a spoonful and passed the bowl to his sister. "Hope's right, Annie. You need to eat a lot of these. Is there anything else you think Annie should eat, Hope?"

"Liver, blackstrap molasses, and plenty of milk or cheese. Speaking of cheese, Annie, I thought we'd make farm cheese today. It'll keep in the springhouse just fine. And we can use it to make *kasenophla* or to stuff *bierocks*. I'll whip up a few batches of noodles today, and y'all can cut 'em. If'n we keep 'em in the springhouse, they'll still be nice and fresh so we can serve the men chicken and noodles. I like to measure all the dry ingredients for corn bread and cakes and drop biscuits, then store 'em in jars. Thataway, we can add the eggs and such and whip up gracious plenty real quick."

"Okay." Annie scooped three paltry raisins into her bowl.

"Lookee at what your auntie is doin'." Hope tapped Emmy-Lou's arm. "She made eyes and a nose. Do y'all think she'll make a smile or a frown to go with 'em?"

"Make a smile, please!"

"A big one," Jakob said. "Right, Hope?"

"No other kind. I used to do that when I was a girl."

"You still are a girl." Emmy-Lou wrinkled her nose and looked at Hope.

Phineas started to laugh.

Hope didn't. She dipped her face and rested her forehead against Emmy-Lou's. "Yup. But let me tell you a little secret: Deep inside of any grown-up is still a little piece of a child. Sometimes we get silly or scared, too."

"You do?" Emmy-Lou twisted to face him. "Do you, Daddy?"

What man wanted to admit he couldn't face life on his own— especially when his little daughter depended on him . . . and when his sister lived in such fear? A denial sprang to his lips, but his heart suddenly changed what came out of his mouth. "I have a heavenly Father. Just as you call for me when you are upset, I go to Him when I need help. In the Bible, David did that a lot."

"Now, there's a fact." Hope subtly scooted Emmy-Lou's cup so she wouldn't spill her milk. "All of them psalms are David goin' to God when he was happy or sad or ascairt."

Annie didn't say anything, but she carefully made a small mouth on her oatmeal.

Jakob plucked two raisins from the dish and poked them into her bowl. "Ears."

Annie gave him a startled look.

Hope stood up, grabbed more, and leaned across the table. "I'm fixin' to add dimples."

Phineas added eyebrows, and Emmy-Lou decided the mouth wasn't big enough. Jakob couldn't recall the last time they'd had such fun at the table. Annie laughed. Laughed! And she ate, too.

The conversation drifted back to plans for the day. Hope announced, "Whilst you water the rose and Emmy-Lou helps you collect the eggs, I figured on picking vegetables and watering the garden."

"The hens hide their eggs in hard places. I can't find a lot of them." Emmy-Lou swirled her spoon in her oatmeal.

"That's why Aunt Annie and you work as a team." It hadn't escaped Jakob's notice that Hope assigned the easy chores to his sister and kept the physically demanding ones for herself.

"Them raisins—they make me think we could whip up a few pies. Raisin sour cream. Shoofly pie. Golden carrot pie. What else do all y'all like?"

"Annie's peach pie." As soon as he spoke, Phineas cleared his throat and grabbed his coffee.

"Along with cool water to drink, Naomi always brought a bushel basket of fresh peaches out to the field at midmorning." Much to Jakob's surprise, the memory didn't bring pain this time. "I would like you to bring peaches, too."

"Emmy-Lou, you'll remind us." Hope smiled at his daughter. "That should be your job."

"I can do that!"

Hope mentioned a few more tasks—assigning the easy ones to Annie again. She also got Phineas to pledge that he'd bring out the sawhorses and planks so they'd have several makeshift tables.

Annie set down her spoon. "I'm not doing my fair share."

"That's where you're dead wrong." Hope stretched far across the table and pressed her fingers down on Annie's fingertips. The contact looked strangely intimate—strong, yet gentle. Tenderness whispered in Hope's voice. "Every minute of every hour of every day, you're a-weavin' a miracle inside you. Ain't no more important work than that. Ain't nothin' more sacred. Any of us could do these chores, but you—God's trustin' you to cradle that babe. Don't get so caught up in the gotta-do-it-now's that you forget you're workin' on something timeless."

Tears filled Annie's eyes. "You're too good to me."

Hope patted her hand. "Tell me that tonight, after I've bossed you around and worked you silly."

A sense of longing rushed through Jakob as he watched the exchange. What Hope did for his daughter, alone, was wonderful; but she was magnificent with his downtrodden sister. What would it take to get Hope to stay? And how long would she be willing to remain here instead of living her rootless existence, chasing employment from one place to the next? Jakob opened his mouth to ask Hope to stay, but he thought better of it. Hope's contentment with her wandering life could lead her to refuse his offer. If she turned him down, his sister and daughter would be crushed.

"I think Hope wants to get rid of us so they can start working." Phineas wiped his mouth.

They recited their after-meal prayer; then Jakob went out to hitch up the buckboard for his trip to town. He didn't know when the right opportunity would emerge for him to ask Hope to stay after the harvest. *But I must. Annie and Emmy-Lou need her so.*

$\approx$

"Someone's coming." Annie tried to brush a powdery clump of flour from her cuff as a buckboard drove up. She didn't sound excited in the least. In fact, from the look in her eyes, Annie didn't want anyone dropping in.

"I'll answer the door." Hope dried her hands off on the hem of her apron. Never once had Annie mentioned her husband, yet she wasn't wearing mourning attire. If her husband had passed on more than a year ago, she wouldn't be with child. Nothing added up. Most of all, Annie seemed uncertain, jumpy . . . fearful.

Hope opened the door and spied Phineas jogging over to the buckboard. He called to her, "It's the ladies from Forsaken!"

Hope turned back. "Didja hear that, Annie? It's Velma and that English lady. I don't recollect her name."

"Sydney." Relief colored Annie's voice. "Sydney Creighton."

Emmy-Lou let out a squeal. "She's the one who saved me from the dark wellhole!"

The two women came in, and the older one planted her hands on her ample hips. "We ran into Jakob in town. Had we known they'd be starting the harvest tomorrow, we would have been here yesterday!"

"Hope is doing so much already, but it is nice to see you."

"Hmpf. You need to be an octopus to get everything done." Velma shook her finger at Annie. "And I ordered you to rest more. Well, while I'm here, let's go on upstairs and have a look at you."

Sydney Creighton walked through the kitchen and took an apron off a peg. "I'll help with the pies while you're doing that."

"I'm baking, too!" Emmy-Lou proudly showed the scraps of pie crust that she'd rolled out and dusted with cinnamon sugar.

"Ohhh," Sydney said. "Do you think maybe I could cut that into strips and we could bake them so we ladies could have tea together?"

"Can we? Please?"

"I think so, don't you, Hope?" Annie looked to her.

" 'Tis a dandy notion. I reckon Miss Velma should go on up and check you out, Annie. Miss Velma, I'd take it kindly if'n y'all would come back down and tell me what Annie needs. We wanna make shore to do all we can to help her out. Gotta tell you, it does my heart good, knowin' you're round to call upon when our Annie's time of need arrives."

Velma and Annie went upstairs. Velma called over her shoulder, "We're not going to have tea and leave. We're staying through lunch and most of the afternoon."

"Indeed." Mrs. Creighton straightened her apron. "The first thing I ever learned to bake was pie."

Velma's snickers reverberated in the stairwell.

Sydney's eyes twinkled. "To everyone's relief, I've gotten much better at it. What kind are we making today?"

Hours later, when they stood on the porch and waved goodbye, Hope wrapped her arm around Annie's shoulders and squeezed. "Wasn't it just like God to send them ladies here? Velma knew just what all the other ladies'll be bringin', so that saved us a bunch of time."

Annie scanned the kitchen and nodded.

I've got 'til Saturday to get her through the harvest. Sunday at church, could be someone else'll wanna hire me to help at their place. Leavin' here'll be hard, though.

"I worry. There's so much to be done, and I'll probably forget something important."

Hope crossed her eyes and huffed. "That's why I'm here. I'll take care of things, and when I forget something, you'll remind me. We work together right good—like a hand in love."

Concern painted Annie's face. "Do you truly think we're ready for tomorrow?"

"Yep. This is gonna be a fine harvest dinner the farm'll lay out. We got more done today than a whole army of ants."

"We would have gotten more done if I hadn't taken a nap."

Hope giggled. "We woulda gotten less done, on account of me and Velma woulda taken turns sittin' on you to make you stay put."

Emmy-Lou gasped. "Would you really sit on her?"

"If'n I did, it would be her fault." Hope felt Annie go stiff. Immediately regretting her comment, she tacked on, "But your auntie is a very good woman. We won't ever have to worry 'bout that. Annie, you shore got some fine neighbors, don'tcha?"

Annie stammered, "I'm glad you thought to offer them some peaches."

"That made Velma happy 'nuff, but Sydney's tickled pink you gave her that peach pie. She claims her man's got a fearsome sweet tooth."

"I should get back to work." Annie scanned the kitchen. "What do you want me to do?"

Hope played with Emmy-Lou's curls. " 'Member how you helped sweep the floor the other day? After all our work today, that floor shore could use it. How 'bout you bein' a big girl and seein' to that?"

"Okay!" Emmy-Lou dashed inside.

When Annie turned to follow, Hope stopped her. "I know Velma says you're doin' fine, but that don't mean you gotta work 'til you pop." She glanced meaningfully at Annie's tummy. "And since 'tis just you an' me out here, I'll tell you, it looks like you'll pop right soon."

Annie's features tightened. "No. Not for a while. I can still work. Really. What do you want me to do? Just tell me, and I'll do it."

Hope tried to think of something minor. Simple. Easy. "We've been real busy with all the cookin'. Seein' as we'll have neighbor women droppin' in to help at noon tomorrow, maybe someone will play the piano. Rubbin' them ivory keys with a cloth you dampen with milk sure makes them shine. Little things like that are good finishin' touches, don'tcha think?"

Annie nodded. "I'll do it. Right away." Only she wouldn't meet Hope's gaze.

Some folks were timid. Shy and unsure of themselves. It was the temperament God gave them. It could be that Annie Erickson fell into that category. Hope tried to tell herself Annie was just hot and tired. Then, too, most women grew anxious about feeding all the harvesters. They wanted to put on an ample, tasty spread to thank the men and entice them back again the next season.

None of those facts explained everything, though. *Annie apologizes for every little thing. When Emmy-Lou spilled her milk, and when the picture frame fell and broke, Annie got jumpy and looked ready to burst into tears. Women who are with child tend to be emotional but . . .* Hope shook her head.

Annie rasped, "What's wrong?"

Hope grabbed her hand and squeezed it. "Do y'all mind if 'n I go out to check on Hattie and make shore she's workin' real good for your brother? I shoulda asked him at lunch, but it slipped my mind."

"Go ahead."

Hope walked down the porch steps and out to a nearby field. All about her, wheat rippled in a golden sea. She gawked about, reassured herself that Phineas wasn't in earshot, and tromped over to her boss. Shouldering her way past dense stalks that released their unique scent of sunshine, earth, and ready-to-bake bread, Hope found no comfort in the surroundings that usually filled her with contentment. "Mr. Stauffer, I'm fixin' to say something."

He stopped working and turned to face her while mopping his forehead and neck with a rumpled red bandana.

"You're a-waving that red bandana like a cape, so I'm chargin' ahead."

He dipped his head in assent.

"Time was, I had me a friend. We was both in pigtails. Well, her pa brung her a puppy dog one day. Rescued it from a feller what was sore mean to it. Well, that pup never was quite right. Took him nigh unto a year before he didn't slink wherever he went. Sorta ducked when someone took a mind to pet him." She watched Mr. Stauffer's tanned features. He said nothing.

"Now, your sister is a right nice lady, and I'd never say a word against her. But I've been round enough to know some men are wicked bad clear down to the feet of their souls. Them men—they use their words or their might to beat down the ones they're supposed to love."

Tell me I'm wrong, Hope pleaded silently. *Tell me Annie's just timid and ascairt of havin' her babe.*

Only the soft brush of wheat stalks in the wind sounded.

"Annie ain't said nothin', but I got a sad feelin' deep inside me that she's been hurt."

Hope longed for a denial and reassurances to spring from his lips. Only that didn't happen. Mr. Stauffer's hold on his bandana tightened. Then, he stared off over her shoulder. Always before, he met her eyes squarely. His jaw hardened, and a small muscle twitched there. The anguish in his eyes and a convulsive swallow confirmed Hope's worst fears.

She held up her hand and swished it back and forth—just like the schoolmarm used to, to erase the chalkboard. "You ain't gotta figure out what to say. I don't want you to break a pledge. Your silence done said more'n any words ever could. If'n my suspicions was nothin' more than a tale spun by a fanciful mind, you woulda rushed to say so."

Hope felt sick to the depths of her heart. She steeled herself with a deep, shaky breath. "I'll pray real hard for Annie. If'n y'all know of something—anything—I can do to help her, you just tell me."

He drew in a slow, deep breath and let it out. Finally, he met her gaze. His blue eyes held an intensity she'd not yet seen. Hope repeated, "All you gotta do is tell me how I can help her out. I ain't known her long, but I count your sis as my friend."

"I want you to stay after the harvest—not just 'til the threshing is done, but until Annie has her baby and another two weeks afterward so she's on her feet again."

The words came from the farmer's mouth, but they rang true in her soul, filling her with the sense she had when she knew the Lord's will for her. The concerns she held about how Annie would struggle with chores dissipated.

"I know what I ask isn't what we agreed upon, but it's what my sister needs."

"It's not what I usually do." Hope wrinkled her nose. "But it's sorta what we decided. You told me Annie's the woman in your home and I'm to help her. So I reckon we could say that's part of the bargain. Between now and when I go, I'll be able to set up your household so's Annie won't have to do too much for a good long time."

He stared at her intently. "You would do this?"

"I told you I go where God sends me and where men need me. Well, in this case, it's where the woman needs me. I'll stay on 'til Annie's had her babe and is back on her feet."

"*Gut. Sehr gut.*"

Good? It was dreadful, that Annie hadn't been cherished by her man. But God gave her a strong, good-hearted brother who'd taken care of her. "Mr. Stauffer? About your sister—I won't never say nothing to nobody. You got my word on it." Hope looked at the blue bandana he fished out of his back pocket and extended toward her. It wasn't until then she realized she'd been crying.

"There is something more you should know."

Hope clutched the bandana and couldn't imagine anything worse.

Jakob cleared his throat. "Konrad—my sister's husband—he didn't know she was with child when I brought her away from him."

᷒

Dozens of hard-boiled eggs filled the bowls, and large pots of strong coffee fragranced the predawn air. Rashers of crisp bacon and pans of coffee cake were all ready. Jakob gulped down the last of his second mug, hoping it would help wake him up. Sleep had eluded him most of the night.

Until now, he'd kept busy with the farm and in easing Annie's fright. Living day-to-day took all he had. With Hope there, helping, he'd started to feel life might somehow regain balance and order. Now, though, the future loomed ominously. How long could he keep Konrad ignorant of the baby? What would Konrad do? Jakob barely balanced the finances with what he now paid to keep Konrad away.

"God shore is generous. Lookit the bountiful field out there, with ever' single stalk of wheat standin' tall and proud on its last mornin'. The sight's so beautiful, it makes me wanna lift my hands toward heaven and holler out a million hallelujahs." Up on tiptoe, Hope peered out the window and started singing, "Oh, for a Thousand Tongues to Sing."

Over by the table, Annie softly joined in.

Lord, keeping my eyes on you—that's what I should be doing instead of worrying.

"My gracious Master and my God," the duet filled the kitchen. "Assist me to proclaim . . ."

The phrase hit him hard. Asking God to assist him . . . yes, that is what he needed to do. Over and over, that needed to be his prayer.

"Jesus, the name that charms our fears," Annie's voice wavered and cracked.

Jakob immediately joined in, "and bids our sorrows cease; 'Tis music in the sinner's ears, 'Tis life, and health, and peace."

Hope turned around. "Thankee for singing that with me. My heart was full and the onliest thing better than singing to the Lord was having the both of you raise up your hearts and voices, too. No better way to start a day than giving Him our praise and trustin' Him with whatever's on our hearts and minds."

"Hope has a good voice, doesn't she, Annie?"

"Yes."

"Thankee. I think God gave that to me on account of Him knowin' I wouldn't be one to draw close to Him in readin' His Word. Well, I'd best start totin' stuff out to the tables. Ain't gonna be long now before the crowd depends."

Descends. The crowd descends. Jakob couldn't correct her. He didn't have it in him to spoil the morning by nitpicking. *Besides, the crowd will depend—on all the food she's serving.*

"You've done well." Jakob opened the door to allow Hope to carry out the coffee. She'd already taken out the dishes, silverware, and mugs. Most of the men would arrive in the next hour, but a few had begun to wander or ride up the road.

"Looks like you got some laborers comin' to offer themselves to hire for the day."

"Ja. Every year, there are a few. Five, I will take. The rest, I will ask you to feed before I send them away."

Hope was halfway down the steps. She turned back. "If'n you didn't hire me, how many men would you take on?"

"Five. I have good, strong neighbors. Five additional men—that is how many are needed. Last year, there was a man with his son—a small son, far too young to sit on the lead horse pulling the reaper. I should have asked you before, but I forgot about the boy until now. If he comes again, do you mind watching him so the father can work?"

"I'd mind if you turned him away." Hope hastened away, her lively step taking her to whatever chore she had in mind.

Annie came close. She murmured, "Do you think maybe years ago, a farmer's wife watched Hope so her father could work?"

The question brought him up short. He'd been so busy with his own thoughts and concerns that he'd never found out anything about this strange woman under his roof!

After propping open the screen door, Jakob went to the barn to check on his gelding. Nicodemus stood still in his stall—a poor sign. He usually greeted Jakob by tossing his head and letting out a whinny. Jakob murmured to him softly, unlatched the gate, and let himself in. After rubbing the horse's neck and withers, he bent and ran the backs of his fingers down the gelding's long leg. His father taught him that trick—that callused fingers don't detect heat well. *If I have a nephew, I'll teach him the same thing.* Heat registered—nothing extreme, but enough to let Jakob know Nicodemus wasn't fit for work.

Phineas was mucking out another stall. He called over, "What do you think?"

Jakob straightened up and swallowed his disappointment. "The leg—it's still hot."

"I thought so, too. There'll be plenty of horses here today. We'll rest Nicodemus and let him heal."

He went back outside and noticed a few men starting toward the food. Four so far. Two he recognized as hard workers from years past. He saw Hope pouring coffee for another man, then glanced up to see his sister. She halted at the base of the porch steps, her face frozen in terror.

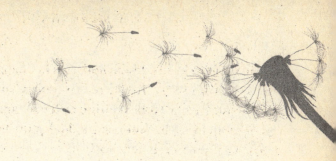

Ten

"Here you go. There's plenty more coffee, so don't be shy." Hope's cheery voice sounded a tad too loud. Jakob tore his gaze away from his sister for a split second. Hope grabbed the man's arm and wheeled him away from the house, toward the barn. "Yoo-hoo! Mr. Stauffer, this here buck says you was neighbors once upon a time! How's about me goin' to fetch more eggs whilst you natter a moment or so before all y'all set to work?"

"Leopold Volkner! You're a long way from home." Jakob strode over. As long as he kept Volkner's attention diverted, Hope could sweep Annie into the safety of the house.

Never once had he thought someone from back home would come this far south to help with the harvest. Sending Leopold Volkner off instead of hiring him for the day would only attract scrutiny. Though it would cause some awkwardness for Annie, Hope would smooth that over. She'd immediately comprehended the danger and taken measures to distract Leopold and alert Jakob.

If Hope hadn't come to me last evening with her suspicions, this would have been a disaster. It still could be. Disciplining his features so his concerns wouldn't show, Jakob asked, "What brings you so far from home?"

"Greenbugs." Leopold grimaced. "They destroyed my sorghum entirely. I put in very little wheat this year."

"Such a shame. It's hard to imagine how something so small can do so much damage."

"Ja. Your brother-in-law's crops have done better than mine. I'm sure he wrote to you about the greenbugs and his sorghum, but his wheat's in fine shape. He might not have much of a profit this year, but . . ." Leopold shrugged.

"Any year where a farmer holds even is a success." Jakob nodded sagely.

"Me? I hope to earn enough, hiring out for the harvest to make up for the loss and keep our heads above water. Where is Annie?" Leopold craned his neck and scanned the barnyard. "My sister wants to know how she is."

"You know how it is for a woman on harvest day." Jakob strove to sound casual. "Annie's going to spend most of her day at the stove or searching for something in the pantry."

Leopold chuckled ruefully. "And woe to the man who's foolish enough to interrupt that woman!"

Jakob forced out a laugh.

"Volkner!" Phineas motioned to Leopold. *"Komst!"*

"He's going to want me to help him harness the horses." Leopold smacked Jakob on the back. "It's good—seeing you. Working alongside you will be like old times."

As soon as Leopold headed toward the barn, Jakob strode to the house. With every step, he prayed for wisdom and guidance. The minute he stepped into the kitchen, the sight of Annie tore at him. She braced herself against the cabinet with one arm, and the other hand covered her mouth to choke back her sobs.

"What's wrong, Aunt Annie?"

Hope knelt down by Emmy-Lou and took her by the shoulders. "I'm fixin' to do the outside work today, and your auntie's a-gonna do the inside work. I reckon with all them fellers out there, we're in sore need of a helper. What about if'n we give you a special job? Y'all be a big girl and go fetch one of your daddy's red bandanas. Anytime your auntie needs to tell me something, you stand on the porch and wave it at me."

"I can do that!"

"Dandy! Now one other thing: Your dolly is very special, and today's a dreadful busy day. I'm thinkin' perhaps you ought to take her upstairs and tuck her into bed so's she don't get bumped."

Eyes wide, Emmy-Lou clutched her doll and went upstairs.

Hope rose and oh-so-casually swiped a speck of something off the bib of her apron. "Annie, since you know all the ladies hereabouts, it only makes sense you stay indoors. I'll handle the outside half of things. That'd be good organizing." She looked at him. "Don't you think so, Mr. Stauffer?"

"Absolutely."

Annie whispered in a raw tone, "What am I to do? What is to become of me?"

"Stay in the house. That is best." Jakob glanced at Hope, then tilted his sister's face up to his. "I have prayed much, asking God to protect you. Just as He sent Jonathan to be David's friend, He has sent Hope here to help me safeguard you."

"That's right. We ain't got time to pussyfoot round, so I'm gonna be plainspoken." Hope crowded close beside Annie and slipped her arms about Annie's bulging middle.

Annie slumped against her, almost as if seeking shelter from her fears.

"Annie, I got me an uneasy feelin' bout things yesterday. 'Member on how I went out to talk to your brother? Well, 'twas because the Lord revealed to me that you had a special burden."

A small sound curled in Annie's throat.

Hope continued to hold her with one arm and cupped Annie's head to her shoulder with her other hand. "Shhhh," she murmured. When Hope looked at Jakob, the liquid gold centers of her warm hazel eyes transmitted a promise to help him shield and care for his fragile sister.

Hope dipped her head and half whispered, "That knowledge our heavenly Father placed in my heart, Annie—'twas timely. God was makin' shore that you'd be protected. Ain't nothin' to be done but for us to love one another and lean on the Lord. I reckon that's why He brung me here—just like your brother said, a friend to safeguard you."

"But what can you do?"

Jakob didn't wait for Hope to answer. "Just as Jonathan hid David from Saul, Hope is hiding you." As he spoke the words, Jakob strove to draw reassurance from them for himself, too. "Hope's plan is sound."

"Speakin' of plans . . ." Hope jerked her chin up ever so slightly—a subtle gesture, to be sure, but it told him to take courage. Her tone went brisk. "I usually use my cart to haul water and food out to the hands about midmorning."

Jakob understood at once. Hope changed the topic so Annie would focus on tasks to be done. "Hattie's a fine mule, but I won't need her today. Plenty of my neighbors will ride here. There'll be more than enough draft horses. I'll hitch Hattie to your cart."

"Nah. You got plenty to do, and Hattie—she cooperates just fine for me." Hope gave Annie a reassuring smile. "I reckon we'd best better put on another pot of coffee and get some corn bread in the oven. If'n y'all do that, Annie, I'll go out to the springhouse and fetch them chickens we cut up last night."

Emmy-Lou came back down the stairs. "Dolly's taking a nap, and I got a danbana." A red bandana fluttered from her hand.

Hope's hazel eyes sparkled, and she whispered, "I ain't got the heart to tell her she says that wrong. Fact is, them words she gets tangled make her all the more dear to me."

ॐ

Men streamed in. Harvest always carried with it this sense of energy and excitement. The low hum of men talking, the full-throated laughs, a gathering of well-worn overalls and jeans represented a brotherhood where each man knew he'd receive the best work of all who came, just as he would give in return.

Vim—that's what his grandmother called it. The robust energy of men with an important task ahead of them. Some came from barely started farms, most had places about the same size as Jakob's, and two owned spreads twice the size of his. It didn't matter. Every last man would labor until the work was done. Mornings like this, Jakob felt this was a little foretaste of heaven—of everyone being of one mind and hearts raised in praise for God's goodness.

Though most had eaten at home, that didn't stop them from grabbing something more. The work ahead would demand much of them. Hope raced in and out of the house, bringing out more coffee, another bucket of hard-boiled eggs, and calling greetings to the newcomers. She'd been to church only once, yet she recalled the names of many of the men. How she managed that flummoxed him—and from the surprised look many of the men wore, they couldn't imagine how she knew who they were, either.

"Mr. Smith!" Hope waved at him. "Lookit them fine sons you brung. You young'uns—I got milk and buttermilk in the springhouse."

Smith brought his oldest sons—schoolboys who were of a size that they could ride the lead horse in the team of three that pulled the older model of the McCormick thresher the community owned. The elder of the boys had proven himself capable a few years back; the younger was eager to show he'd grown old enough to have a turn at the job. Even though the newer thresher didn't require a third horse or a small rider, traditions were important. A boy who rode this year would walk behind and make windrows with the men in another few years. It was a rite of passage.

Asa Bunce arrived with his sons, too. The hopeful looks on their fresh-scrubbed faces made it clear they wanted to become "men" today instead of "helper boys." Helper boys ran errands and brought water—but most telling, they arrived later in the morning, alongside their mamas.

Phineas frowned. "We've got too many boys."

"They can take turns." Asa hooked his thumbs into the bib of his overalls. "Smith's boys can take one thresher. Mine will do the other."

Moments like this were bittersweet. Jakob knew he ought to feel blessed to have a fine crop and neighbors to help, but deep inside a void yawned. He had no sons. Whenever that thought troubled him, he tried to reassure himself that Annie just might give him a nephew. That would be a fine thing—having a boy to rear to respect and tend the land.

"What is that?" One of the men shaded his eyes, then let out a whoop.

Mr. Richardson made a grand appearance. The last man to arrive, he'd taken his time—but for good cause. His horse trotted at a dignified pace, and behind him a team of three horses dragged another reaper!

"A man with daughters needs help." He dismounted as everyone chuckled. Mr. Richardson was well-known for making jokes about the fact that he had several daughters. He loved every last one of them, but a farmer still hoped for strapping sons. "I have a . . . sort of a cousin . . . who has sons. He sent two to help, and they brought their reaper. No use in it sitting unused."

"I'm obliged." Jakob couldn't imagine this blessing. He'd planted more wheat this year than ever before. He'd not been sure they'd bring the harvest in by Saturday night.

"Not that we aren't glad for the help," someone shouted, "but how do you come by a cousin?"

Richardson shrugged. "He was a good friend on the orphan train. He got adopted three stops back, but we kept in touch. He sent his older boys."

"Three," one of Asa Bunce's boys said in wonder. "You'll be running three teams."

Jakob turned and gave Smith's eldest son, Lloyd, a restrained slap on the back. "You've grown big this year. Huge." He made a point of looking the boy up and down, then nodded somberly. "Perhaps it is time for you keep your feet on the ground and let the young boys ride the leads."

Manly grunts of approval and agreement filled the air. Every one of those men recalled the day they'd been promoted—it was never a father's place to do. Someone else in the community always made the gesture. It meant more that way.

Lloyd stood so straight, Jakob marveled his spine didn't crack. "I'll work hard."

The three other boys stood awestruck for a moment, then one yelled, "Then we all getta have our own rig the whole day!"

Jakob rested his hands on his hips. "Psalm one-forty-five, verse fifteen, says, 'The eyes of all look to you, and you give them their food at the proper time. You open your hand and satisfy the desires of every living thing.' The Lord has been generous, not only with my crops, but also with my friends and neighbors. I give Him—and each of you—my thanks." He then said a prayer, and they all went to the fields.

Work had a rhythm to it. Soon the reaper went through the field, whirring and cutting. Tiny particles flew up, filling the air with a distinct aroma and giving a golden-tan shimmer to the world. Looking like bank robbers, men wore bandanas over the lower half of their faces to keep from choking. The more they accomplished in the early morning, the better off they'd be. Texas midday heat was rough on man and beast. All of them knew it, and they pushed hard.

Out of the corner of his eye, Jakob saw a dishcloth wave in the air. He turned, smiled, and waved back to Hope. Inserting two fingers into his mouth, he let out a piercing whistle. It took a few repetitions, but the work ceased.

The men flocked to the edge of the field. Hope stood by her two-wheeled cart. Each of the four corners of her cart held a bucket of cool well water and dippers. She'd remembered his request to bring out peaches—a bushel of them rested in the center of the cart—but in addition to that, two trays heaped with cookies invited the men to help themselves.

"Stauffer—next year, you should plant more so we have to come help for more time!"

"Hope—do you hear them?" Phineas grabbed a peach. "You will come back next year, won't you?"

Hope hitched a shoulder. "I can't rightly say. I go where God sends me. I don't plan or promise; I obey. But I can't take credit for them cookies. Annie's the one what baked 'em. Mr.

Toomel, you'd best not wave that cookie—" She halted and burst out laughing.

Mr. Toomel looked sheepish, wiggling his empty fingers. "Serves me right for holding a sweet by a mule. I didn't think she could see it, with her wearing that hat." He accepted another cookie.

"All y'all shore are workin' at a good pace. Reckon you'll be starvin' at midday. I'll take care to tie Hattie outta the way so's she won't take a mind to sample all the food we set out."

Toomel took another bite of a cookie and looked at Hope. "When the harvest is done here, I'll hire you. I need help—I don't have a wife."

"I can help you get a wife," Richardson declared.

Uneasy chuckles sounded, so Jakob announced, "Hope's agreed to stay here awhile."

Hope looked at Toomel. "Sir, Mr. Stauffer's right. I already gave him my word to stick around for a few weeks. Don't you worry none, though. I'll represent the Stauffer farm and help all the other ladies what come to feed all you men, no matter which spread you're harvestin'."

Jakob noticed how she refrained from mentioning the baby. Though she admitted to being plainspoken, Hope exercised admirable tact. Pledging that she'd help out at the other farms was good, too.

Toomel looked longingly at the empty cookie trays. "No one else bakes cookies for us men."

"Linette's good at cookies," Richardson started in.

"Betcha you could hire Mrs. Orion at the boardin' house to bake you some," Hope cut in. "Her bein' a widow woman, she could probably use a little cash money."

"Widow O'Toole could bake something, too." Mr. Peterson's eyes crinkled and his voice lilted with humor. "But with her bein' a rabid teetotaler, it won't be rum balls or beer bread!"

After hooting with laughter, the men turned back to work. They did a quick inspection of the reapers. The knotters on the binders usually required a little attention, and the man in charge of each machine made a point of announcing the binder still had sufficient steel wire to get the job done.

Jakob recalled how he'd grown up with everyone having to gather and bind the wheat shocks by hand. McCormack's 1885 light steel binder accomplished that task along with the reaping—an improvement that sped up and simplified harvest. The first year, inspecting the wire supply was done out of worry. Since then, the announcement hadn't been necessary—but it was a tradition that stuck.

Work started up again. Shocks of bound wheat dropped behind the machine, and men hefted them into windrows. Muscles strained, the air grew thick again with particles, and the sun beat down upon them.

℘

Hope skipped up the porch steps. "Them cookies of yours shore did get snapped up. Tonight, we'll have to make more for tomorrow."

"Okay."

Hope took Annie's hand in hers and gave it a reassuring squeeze. "How's about us singin' that verse from the hymn we started this mornin'? From 'Oh, for a Thousand.' I've been thinkin' on those words today. You know . . . 'Jesus, the name that charms our fears.' "

"Fears aren't charming," Annie whispered.

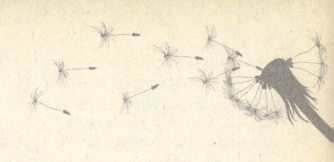

Eleven

Lord of Mercy, this gal's hurting so bad on the inside. Whisper to me what you'd have me say to her.

Her voice shaking in terror, Annie repeated, "Fears aren't charming."

" 'Course they ain't." Hope gave her hands a gentle squeeze. "But the Savior, He's the One what gots all the power. I reckon it would take a fool not to choose up sides with Him. God's on your side, Annie. You know that, right?"

Annie swallowed hard and managed a tiny, jerky nod.

"Your brother talked about David. Ever notice how everybody else got all scairt of that giant Goliath? They all quaked in their boots. Well, I don't reckon they wore boots— probably sandals. But that ain't the point. All the shields and swords they had didn't make 'em feel ready to do battle. But Davy didn't fret over that stuff. Nope. Not him. He weren't nothin' more'n a little boy, but he teamed up with God. Them three little pebbles wasn't what done Goliath in. 'Twas the power God added. Davy just gave over his fear and trusted God to do His part."

"Aren't you ever afraid?"

"Shore am. Being ascairt is natural. 'Tis what we do with them fears that matters. The song—it says Jesus charms our fears. When my knees get to knockin', I gotta get down on 'em. I betcha Davy didn't bend over and pluck up the first three rocks he spied. I suspect he done went down on his knees and asked God's guidance and got mighty choosy until he was shore them was the right rocks for the job."

Annie wet her lips nervously.

Hope figured she'd said enough. "I saw some dust clouds in the distance. I reckon the neighbor ladies finished their mornin' chores and are bringin' their covered dishes. How's about me makin' a quick trip to the springhouse? I'll fetch butter and more milk. Was there anything else you want me to grab?"

"I've run out of eggs for the corn bread."

"I'll be shore to grab us some. We ain't gathered eggs yet today. I know you and Mr. Stauffer want Emmy-Lou close by. How's about if'n she and some of the other young'uns gather the eggs whilst we have some of the others pick green peas and snap beans?"

Upon hearing her name, Emmy-Lou galloped over. "Can I? Please?"

Annie nodded. "Emmy-Lou, first go to the springhouse with Miss Hope and bring back more milk so you children will have plenty to drink."

The springhouse sat only a stone's throw away. Water from the windmill ran through a channel in the cement floor, keeping the windowless building cool and dank—a welcome change from the bright sunlight or the heat radiating from the kitchen stove. Hope stepped inside, then turned in puzzlement. "Why're you just a-standin' there, sugar pie?"

Emmy-Lou clung to the doorframe. "It's dark in there."

"Yup, it sorta is. Since I know where I put everything, it don't bother me none. How's about if'n you stand there and hold the door open just a crack? I'll pretend I'm a fishy. 'Tis cool and wet in here just like it must be for a lazy old trout in a shady creek. He knows where all the rocks are, so he just sorta floats and swishes along." Quickly gathering the necessities while she spoke, Hope rejoined Emmy-Lou. "There we are."

"You don't look like a fish."

"I'm glad of that." Hope laughed. "I'm even more gladder that I don't smell like one!"

Emmy-Lou giggled. "You're funny."

"Well, fish probably don't carry butter, but I'm fixin' to. How's 'bout totin' these here eggs back to the house for your auntie?"

In the short time they'd been gone, neighbors had arrived. Bowls and dishes of all kinds covered the table. The yeasty scent of breads vied with the sugary sweet aroma of cakes and pies. Older girls sat on the porch peeling potatoes while Mrs. Richardson organized a few of the boys to take pails of cold water out to the fields. "Gramma," a woman somehow related to the Smiths, took charge of other children and went out to garden and gather eggs.

Delighted squeals came from the front porch. Sydney Creighton came in laughing. "I brought the latest *Godey's Lady's Book*. The older lasses have asked to look at it as soon as they're done with the potatoes."

Tilting her head toward her sewing basket, Lena Patterson laughed. "I sneaked the new *Peterson's Magazine* in past the girls. I thought it might be fun for us to all bring our feed sacks to the last harvest and have a swap so we can match up the patterns. Then, a week or so later, we could have a sewing circle."

"You can hatch your plans later." Velma elbowed her way in and set a large roasting pan on the seat of the nearest empty chair. "Someone taller than I am needs to put this on top of the warming box. I'm too short."

" 'Twas mighty nice of y'all to bring all this here food. Annie and me—we'll be shore to pitch in and help when 'tis your farms the men are harvesting."

"Ja, we will." Annie reached for the roasting pan.

Hope smoothly swiped it first. "This is heavy."

Velma shrugged. "We butchered a cow a couple days ago. No use in trying to preserve much in this heat, so I made a roast."

"My husband has a sweet tooth," Sydney said with a smile. "That peach pie you sent home with us yesterday captured his attention. He insisted on sending over the roast so I can get your recipe."

"Oh, Annie's the one what seasoned up them peaches." Hope stood on tiptoe and balanced the roasting pan on top of the almost-full warming box. "Annie, we're a-runnin' outta table space. How's about you sittin' on the piano stool and using a bench to work on? Slice up some watermelon and put it in a washtub. Ain't nothin' more refreshin' than a big old chunk of melon." Hope turned toward the other women. "Y'all, I wanna make shore I do my job. Mr. Stauffer, he hired me to do the cookin' and such."

Her announcement took care of several details—the women came to her with their suggestions or questions, and they also took the cue to make sure Annie only did light chores.

Hope added more coal to the stove, plunked down the largest skillets, and started frying chicken. Buckets of water, soap, and towels were set out on two benches so the men could wash up before eating. Everything hummed with the same industry as a beehive.

"Mmm, that chicken smells delicious!" Lena finished mixing flour and water so she could make the gravy.

"Thankee." Hope scooted to the side of the stove and kept turning the chicken breasts. "You got enough room here?"

"Goodness, yes. Jakob bought the largest stove available for Naomi. Cooking for harvest here is always a pleasure because there's so much room!"

"No doubt about it," Mrs. Smith said. "He doted on his wife. Took losing her and his son mighty hard. I didn't think he could look worse—but he did the day he left to take Emmy-Lou off to your place, Annie. You coming here's been a sacrifice on your part, but your mercy and compassion made it so Jakob didn't have to give up his daughter."

Annie bit her lip and blinked back tears.

"Oh no." Hope forced out a little laugh. "There she goes. Annie has the most tenderest heart of anyone in the whole, wide world. Velma, you're the granny woman round here. Do you find gals you're minding seem built close to the water?"

"Heavens, yes!" Velma nodded. "And they weep a fair bit for weeks after the babe comes."

"I used up every last hanky I owned one morning a couple of days after Mandy was born." Daisy Smith shook her head at the memory. "My mama told me she'd done the same thing."

Hope pounced on the opportunity and announced, "Mr. Stauffer—he done asked me if'n I'd be willin' to stay on for two weeks after the baby comes." She dredged more chicken in the breading and slid it into the sizzling skillet. She shot a smile over her shoulder at Annie. "It's a pleasure to be asked."

"You'll stay?" A tear streaked down Annie's cheek.

"Well, I dunno. If'n the thought makes you wanna cry, maybe I—"

"I want you to stay! I do!"

"I hoped you'd say so." Hope waggled her brows. "Is this a good time for me to beg you for your peach pie recipe? Ain't just your brother and Phineas and Sydney's husband who love it!"

☙

"Dinner!" A trio of little boys shouted from the end of the wheat field. They waved feed sacks in the air to signal the men—just in case they hadn't heard them.

Hard work sharpened a man's appetite, and Jakob's mouth started to water as he thought of the meal that awaited him. He let out a piercing whistle, and work halted.

Volkner slapped him on the back. "If dinner's half as good as those cookies and peaches we had earlier, I might decide to sell my place and hire on here."

"You'd never sell." Jakob gave him a wry smile to cover for his concern. Leopold's farm seemed to experience more than its share of woes. In fact, the fields there managed to sprout more rocks and lower yield each year. Water—the lifeblood of any farm—managed to make itself scarce. In the unexplainable vagaries of weather, storms would drop their rain on the neighboring farms and cease when passing over the Volkners'.

Leopold didn't crack a smile. "I don't know. My brother—he went on to better land. I cannot provide for my mother and sister if I can't bring in the crops. This year, I had high hopes, but the greenbugs . . ." He shook his head.

Mr. Richardson started to approach. Jakob murmured, "The man coming—Mr. Richardson—he has several unmarried daughters."

"No sons?" Leopold quirked a brow.

"He'd gladly settle for sons-in-law."

"So that's why he sent for those so-called nephews to help with the harvest."

"Ja. It is only fair that I . . ." Jakob halted before he said, *warn*. He didn't want to be unkind. "It is only right that you know his oldest daughters will help serve us today."

The men all stopped in the barnyard and lined up at the washtubs on the benches. Groans of pleasure vibrated in the air as the water refreshed and cooled the men down. Even so, the men didn't linger. Hunger led them to the tables. They jostled into places as the women scurried out with the last platters and bowls to set on the tables.

Jakob remained standing. He raised his arm high, and silence fell. "I want to thank you all for your hard work. Among God's blessings to me, I count my friends and neighbors." He prayed.

As soon as he finished, Hope called out, "Eat up! The women have been a-cookin' plenty!"

Reasoning it was better for him to sit near Volkner than to have him elsewhere and overhear something he oughtn't, Jakob elbowed in. Eating was serious business. The men didn't say much more than grunting for more potatoes or complimenting Hope on the chicken.

"I still haven't seen your sister," Leopold said between bites.

"No doubt she's at the stove."

Hope slid another basket of rolls on the table, then straightened up and cupped her hands around her mouth. "Annie! Annie— stick your head out the window and say howdy."

Admiration streaked through Jakob. Clever as could be, Hope devised a way to satisfy Leopold's interest in Annie's welfare without revealing her secret. The sensitivity that led Hope to suspect Annie's problem now gifted her with the ability to creatively handle the situation. He looked at the window, hoping his sister would comply.

Sure enough, Annie appeared in the window. Leaning forward as she did, her apron fell away from her body, effectively hiding the baby. She smiled and waved.

"Ain't that just like our Annie?" Hope dusted off her hands. "Me out here a-hollerin' like a fool and her bein' ladylike. The Good Book says the trumpet's gonna sound when the Lord Jesus comes back, and I can't help thinkin' 'tis on account of bellowin' folks like me. God's gotta do something mighty loud to be heard over us." She flashed a smile. "Reckon I'd best better make sure all the desserts come out. The neighbor ladies brung so many fine things, makes me think how lucky cows are."

"How can you say a cow is lucky," Leopold asked, "when we are eating roast beef?"

Hope flashed a sassy grin. "A cow don't care none that he gave his all for the meal—he can't, bein' as he's dead. But all them days and months he was alive—he got hisself four stomachs. Four! Just think on how much food he got to savor."

As she bustled off, Leopold grabbed another piece of chicken. "That woman—she's spirited."

Jakob robbed him of the chicken thigh and bit into it as he nodded. "Great cook, too."

"Your sister—"

"Look there," Jakob interrupted. "See that girl? The one carrying the pie? And the one just coming down the porch steps with a cake? They're two of Richardson's daughters. I've heard they bake good."

"Is that so?" Leopold's eyes narrowed. "The second one—she's pretty."

Jakob shrugged. He'd spent his time avoiding the Richardson girls.

"Has she dedicated her heart to the Lord?"

His brows furrowed, Jakob asked slowly, "What does it matter to you?"

"It matters."

"I recall her going to the altar and being baptized."

Leopold elbowed him. "Introduce me."

"I can't."

"Why not?" Outrage vibrated in Volkner's hot whisper.

Shrugging again, Jakob confessed, "I never bothered to figure out which sister is which."

After letting out a disgusted sound, Volkner wiped his mouth. He motioned toward the Richardson girl. Her eyes widened, and for an instant her jaw dropped, but she quickly shut her mouth and came over. Leopold made a show of studying the cake, then smiled up at her. "Did you bake this yourself?"

"Y-yes."

"What kind is it?"

"Prune cake."

Leopold elbowed Jakob again. "Prune cake! Did you hear her? My favorite!"

The Richardson girl blushed and said in a soft tone, "Then you should have the biggest slice."

Jakob could scarcely believe it. He'd heard Tim Creighton's wife was teaching the Richardson hoydens civilized ways; he'd chalked it up to idle gossip. It would take far more than months of the proper English lady's training to tame Richardson's daughters—or so he'd thought.

"Marcella, I'll take a slice, too." Mr. Patterson motioned to her.

"Marcella." Leopold grinned like a love-struck fool. "A pretty name for a pretty girl."

Her face clouded up, just like Emmy-Lou's did right before . . . Jakob muffled a groan.

Richardson's daughter bit her lip and thrust the cake plate into Leopold's direction. His hands closed around it, but as a sob shook her, Volkner shoved aside the cake and reached for her instead.

Marcella evaded him, wheeled around, and dashed back toward the house.

"Wait!" Leopold jumped up and headed after her.

For an instant, Jakob discounted it as utter silliness—until he realized Marcella had gone into the kitchen. If Leopold followed her—"Volkner!" Leopold ignored him.

Jakob raced toward the back porch. Mr. Richardson matched him stride for stride. "What did he do to my girl?"

"He called her pretty."

Richardson stopped dead in his tracks.

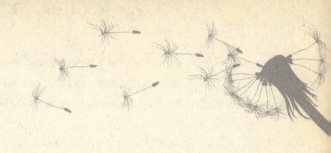

Twelve

O h, mercy." Hope yanked Annie to the table and shoved her into a chair. Thumping a bowl of snap beans in front of her, she hissed, "Trouble's a-comin'. Tug the tablecloth over yourself and stay put."

A second later, Marcella burst in and let out a loud cry.

"Whatever is the matter?" Sydney Creighton embraced Marcella.

Jakob's old neighbor stormed in. "Where—" He spotted Marcella and shouldered past Mrs. Richardson.

Unaware she'd been followed, Marcella wailed into Sydney's shoulder, "He made fun of me."

The man roared, "I did not!"

His brow furrowed with worry, Jakob stomped in. Hope stood in such a way as to block Volkner's view of Annie. Jakob scanned the room, and though the tension in his broad shoulders remained, the set of his jaw changed once he saw how Hope shielded Annie. Ice blue eyes met hers, and in that instant, Hope inclined her head ever so slightly. From the rise and fall of his chest as he took and released a large, silent breath, Hope knew the truth: They'd made a pact, and he trusted her.

Sydney held Marcella and patted her as Jakob crossed the kitchen.

Hope cleared her throat loudly. "How's about all of you gals totin' out the rest of the sweets?"

"But my sister . . . " Linette began.

"She can stay. You go on and help out." Hope pushed the closest dish into Linette's hands.

"Pickles? Those aren't sweets."

"Shore are." Hope nodded, as if to lend gravity to her assertion. "Them are sweet pickles. Out you go now."

Though many of the women clearly wanted to stay and watch, Gramma clapped her hands. "You all heard Hope. She's right. We got hungry men to feed."

Hope waved her hand toward Annie. "You stay put. Marcella oughtta have us here. It's only proper."

Mrs. Richardson scowled at Volkner. "This isn't my house, but that's my daughter, and I'm not leaving. What did you do to her?"

He raked his fingers through his hair, leaving it to stand up like a startled jaybird's crest. "You are her mother." He nodded. "*Ja.* I can tell."

"Work's waiting." Jakob folded his arms across his chest.

It didn't escape Hope's notice that he, too, positioned himself between Volkner and Annie.

Mr. Richardson came to the door. "Mama, come on out here."

"But, Jeb—"

"He called our Marcella pretty." Mr. Richardson motioned to her.

Sydney Creighton whispered something to Marcella, then wiggled free of her hold. "Hope, shall I take out this bowl?"

"Thankee." Hope didn't mention that the bowl was empty. Neither did Sydney. Those fancy English lady manners of hers came in handy.

Marcella hadn't turned to face anyone. Burying her face in her hands, she wept.

Utterly perplexed, Volkner tentatively rested his hands on Marcella's shuddering shoulders and turned her around. "I meant what I said. Prune cake is my favorite."

Hope burst out laughing. Everyone glared at her. "Y'all are more mixed up than flapjack batter. Volkner, she don't care what you think of prune cake."

"I do like it. And Jakob says she's a good cook."

Giving up on Volkner, Hope turned to Jakob. "Did I hear right? He called Marcella purdy?"

"I did. I still do." Volkner cast a quick grin at Mrs. Richardson, then nodded at Mr. Richardson. "Your daughter—she takes after her mama."

"I'm fat!" The words tore through Marcella.

"Fat?" Volkner repeated in shock. "*Nein.* You are healthy." His gaze swept down her just fast enough to assure everyone he liked what he saw, but not long enough to be rude. His hands stayed on her shoulders, and he jostled her just once to emphasize his assertion. "Sturdy."

"Sturdy." The word whooshed out of Marcella—half moan, half sob.

"Ja." Volkner bobbed his head and looked downright proud.

The man's got wheat chaff for brains if he reckons sayin' such a thing will win him a gal's undying love. May as well step up and help him out. "What Mr. Volkner means," Hope moved next to him, "is that he's a man who likes his girl to look womanly. 'Stead of a beanpole or one of them cinched-in-to-silliness gals, he appreciates a woman who won't break when he gives her a hug. Ain't that right?" Hope nudged his foot.

Leopold barely spared her an exasperated look, then went back to staring at Marcella. "That's what I said. Sturdy."

The oaf. "Can't blame a man for wantin' to hug a young lady he finds pretty." Hope nudged Volkner's boot again.

Marcella sniffled.

Volkner didn't say a thing.

Her toes already hurt, but Hope reckoned she had two good reasons to suffer a little discomfort. If she could keep Leopold Volkner busy, he'd ignore Annie; and if she could prod some sense into him, he and Marcella just might get along. *Thump.*

"Ouch." Volkner turned sharply and glared. "Why are you kicking me?"

"Hope wouldn't ever hurt anyone." Annie sucked in a deep breath. "Maybe there's a little flour on the floor and it's slippery."

"No doubt there's that. I'll sweep the floor right quick, if 'n y'all shoo on outta here. Marcella, you mop up them tears and give this here buck a nice smile. Ain't every day a handsome stranger happens along and chases after a gal what caught his eye."

Jakob said something in German to his friend.

Volkner nodded and wheeled around. "So you are Mr. Richardson. Jakob reminded me I should speak first with you." Volkner took a deep breath. "Herr Richardson, your daughter—she is comely." He slapped Jakob on the back. "My friend—his name should be mine today, for like Jacob in the Bible, I have set my gaze upon the woman I will love. I tell you now: I want your daughter for my wife."

Marcella let out a small squeak.

Mr. Richardson reached over and threaded his hand through his wife's arm. "See what I told you? Marcella favors you. It's no wonder this man wants her."

"Oh, Jeb." Mrs. Richardson leaned into her husband's side.

Jakob folded his arms across his chest. Hope watched how he continued to shield his sister. "Richardson, Volkner is a good man."

"You're his friend—that tells me some of what I need to know." Mr. Richardson squinted at Volkner. "But I won't let a man near any of my daughters if he won't love her with all his heart 'til his dying day. You know nothing of Marcella other than that she's pretty."

"She's not vain and she has a tender heart." Volkner's voice managed to sound both gruff and kind. "And she has family and friends who love her. Most of all, Jakob tells me Marcella is a believer. That tells me all I need to know—well, almost all I need to know."

He turned to Marcella. "You should know of me. The most important thing is Jesus in my life. Greenbugs ruined my sorghum crops, so this year, I've hired myself out in order to provide for my mother and sister. I cannot offer much to you of worldly things, but I would give you my heart. Now that you know these things, I ask: If your father gives his consent, would you consider my hand in marriage?"

"I . . .I . . .um . . ." Marcella turned the same shade as freshly canned beets and blurted out, "I don't know your name!"

Male laughter filled the kitchen.

"Honest to Pete!" Hope burst out.

"Peter?" Marcella flickering a smile at Volkner and jerked her head up and down. "I'm honored."

Annie started crying—hushed, deep sounds.

Anguish tightened Jakob's features.

Hope gave him a playful shove and immediately plopped down next to Annie—effectively blocking all but Annie's shoulders and head from view. "Honey, you done got your brother all horrified. Men don't tolerate tears none too good. He don't know they're happy tears on account of you bein' touched that Volkner's being all romantic-like with your friend Marcella."

Laughter boomed out of Mr. Richardson. "Mama's boo-hooing, too."

"I reckon you men oughtta skedaddle before we all drown in here." Hope waggled her finger at Marcella. "Best you take your beau by the hand and see if there's any of that prune cake left out there."

"Ja!" Volkner grabbed Marcella's hand and the new couple dashed past. Marcella's parents followed behind them.

Hope wrapped her arm around Annie and passed her a hanky.

Jakob shifted his weight from one boot to the other. "Is there something I should do?"

Hope nodded. "Better get on out there and take care of things. That gal don't even know her intended's name!"

Knowing the women would flood back any minute, Hope gave Annie a tight squeeze and whispered, "God's watchin' out for you. I'm a-tellin' you, He is."

"What will I do if Leopold finds out about the baby? He'll tell Konrad."

"We're gonna trust God. That's what we're gonna do."

Annie bit her lip and swiped at her tears. After cramming the hanky into her pocket, she started snapping beans again. "I'll try."

"Locust." Velma's raised voice gave warning. "I declare, those men descend like a swarm of locust and eat everything in sight."

"You're right," someone else agreed. The screen door opened, and a tide of women washed in, all carrying empty bowls, cups, and plates. Older children bore buckets of silverware and small stacks of plates.

"Gramma," Hope said, "what say you wrangle all these kids outside again? Them strong boys can tote out a few clean washtubs and put 'em on the benches, and the big girls can wash up the plates and forks and such."

"And the younger ones can set the table so they can eat." Gramma started motioning the kids toward the door.

"Thankee! Us women'll see to the rest. Powerful hungry as we are, that'll let us eat right quick."

Sydney whisked the bowl of snap beans from Annie. "I'm so glad you prepared more! Wouldn't you just know the men ate every last bean, and they're my favorite?"

The women chattered as they gathered whatever food was left into some of the bowls while washing the rest of the platters and bowls. Finally they sat on the porch to eat while the children ate at the tables in the yard. As they finished up, Sydney Creighton said, "Tim bought me the most wonderful invention. It's a sewing machine! It's far too heavy to cart anywhere, but Velma and I came up with a plan."

Marcella sighed dreamily. "I'll do whatever you want. I owe you dearly for all those courtin' lessons you gave me. Peter loves me."

Hope and Annie traded a glance.

"He couldn't help himself." Sydney smoothed her skirts. "Anyways, back to my plan. Having the older children here for harvest is a help—but the wee tots, well, that's not quite so easy.

Our ranch is central to most of the farms. Velma and I decided to ask Annie and Daisy to come there each day for the next week and a half. The rest of you—you're welcome to drop off your busy little babies and we'll mind them whilst you go help feed the men wherever they're harvesting."

Everything went quiet for a moment.

Lord, you done it. You gave Annie a safe place to be. Thankee. Hope glanced at Annie. Nervous as always, Annie cast doubtful looks around the porch. Though it wasn't her place to speak, Hope figured her place as an outsider was nothing compared to Annie's need. "Annie, don't that sound wondrous fine? Gentle and lovin' as you are, them babies are gonna be happy as lambs."

"Hmmm." Gramma tapped her foot. "I recollect we sometimes did that when I was young. Mamas whose babies were suckling took on the smallest ones. If we do that, I'd still like to mind the older children at whichever farm we're at. It's important for them to help out with chores wherever they go."

Hope rubbed her hands together. "Grand! Annie, you can tuck yourself away on Forsaken Ranch, and I'll go represent the Stauffer farm whilst the other places harvest."

"You wouldn't mind?"

"Mind? I reckon I probably skipped holdin' a rattle and went straight for a skillet."

Velma set down a chicken bone. "Hope's cooking is every bit as tasty as my own. She'll fill in for you nicely, Annie, and I'm glad to have you and Daisy away from the heat."

Daisy chewed on her lip. "I'll do it the rest of the time, but when the harvest is at my farm—"

"Daisy," Linda scolded in a loving tone, "of course you can stay there, but your baby's only two months old. None of us expects you to run all over and stand at the stove! The rocking chair is where you belong."

While the women murmured agreement, Hope leaned toward Annie. "You got the nicest neighbors I ever seen. Maybe them aren't really wheat fields out yonder. Maybe they're really streets of gold, 'cuz I can picture God a-walkin' up and bein' in our midst here."

"So you all agree to my plan?" Sydney beamed.

"Do you realize how many babies you're taking on?" Mrs. Richardson cast a meaningful look toward the house. "There must be a dozen of them sleeping in the parlor right now."

Sydney Creighton's cheeks went pink.

Hope gave her an assessing look. *I wonder if . . .*

The young woman drew in a deep breath. "That's all part of my plan, too. Or rather, God's plan. Tim and I are going to welcome a little one of our own. I could learn more about caring for babies."

Sounds of delight and congratulations swelled.

"To my reckoning, it'll come in mid–November." Velma looked more like a proud grandma than a housekeeper. "Sydney's right. She needs to practice up on taking care of diapers and such."

Sydney reached over and took hold of Annie's hand. "And I thought while we were watching the babies, you and I can use my sewing machine to make dozens of nappies and gowns."

"If you don't mind, I'd like to help with the babies, too." Etta Sanders pushed back an errant lock of hair.

Lena's brow puckered. "I thought you said you were done weaning your daughter."

Etta nodded. "I don't mean to take away from your news, Sydney, but I'm expecting again. To be honest, the smell of all that food today . . ."

"That settles it!" Velma stopped by the door. "I've tended most every one of you while you've been with child, and each year at harvest, I've fretted about you overdoing. No more. I'm taking matters into my own hands. Hope said she was bossy, but I'm a dictator—and I'm dictating. Etta, Daisy, and Annie are reporting for baby duty at Forsaken this year."

Hope lifted her hands to the heavens. "Well, praise ye the Lord!"

⁊

"Hallelujah!" Mr. Patterson pointed to the edge of the field. *More water,* Jakob thought as he turned. He could taste the salt of his sweat and the dust of the earth. Only it wasn't a cadre of little boys with water buckets again. Instead, Hope drove her mule cart into view.

Jakob let out a piercing whistle, and work ground to a halt.

The men thronged to her cart. She sat on the seat—which kept her at eye level. "Y'all probably already figured out I'm odd as a unihorn."

"Corn," someone muttered.

"Corn ain't odd. 'Tis a right fine food if'n you ask me. Anyhow"—Hope pressed a crock into Jakob's hands—"first things first. You're all sweatin' hard. I halved them pickles, and once you all chomp one down, the salt in it'll help you hold the water you drink."

"Pickles?" Leopold said in disbelief. Tradition was for the men to get something more substantial in the late afternoon— sandwiches were most common.

"Yep. Pickles. But be shore to drink a big cup of water after so's it won't make the food taste off." She whipped a lavender checkered tablecloth off the center of her cart to reveal trays stacked high with sandwiches and . . .

"Tarts." Jakob wasn't sure whether he'd said the word or thought it. He didn't have time to wonder. All around him, hands shot toward the mouth of the crock. *Good thing she didn't have any brine in this thing.*

Hope raised her hand to shield her eyes as she looked toward the west. "You men shore are gettin' a powerful lot of work done. Makes me think on how God created all the plants, but He made Adam the gardener. What all y'all are doin'—'tis a work of the hand that honors God's plan."

"True." Asa Bunce ruffled his younger son's hair.

Hope leaned forward. "Hey, there, lil' man. Didja get a pickle?"

"Yes'm."

While he ate, Jakob started wondering about Hope. She had a knack for dealing with kids. Kind and loving as she was, why hadn't she married? She'd make some man happy. The breath froze in his lungs. *She figured out about Annie. Did she know because she's endured the same? Is she moving around, trying to survive because she had to run away from a husband who was a bully?*

"At this rate," Richardson said, cutting in on Jakob's thoughts, "we'll be done with this farm by midday tomorrow. Smith, did you want us to move on to your place and get it started, or do you want to wait 'til Monday?"

"With the extra reaper, my place will take about a day and a half."

"Ain't that convenient?" Hope passed a tart to each of the boys. "I'll fix breakfast and serve lunch here, then Daisy will fix up your afternoon snack."

Smith scratched his head. "Guess that'd work."

Hope smiled. "What with Daisy havin' that bitty baby of hers, I bet havin' the Lord's Day of rest falling betwixt the reapin' days on your place will turn out right nice."

The men wolfed down the thick sandwiches and tarts. Not a single crumb remained on any of the trays. Hungry as they became with their labor, men would eat anything; but the gusto they put into eating made it clear the Stauffer farm provided above and beyond the usual.

"Mr. Stauffer, sir, how many of these fellers is gonna be stayin' the night in the barn? I'm fixin' to start on supper, so I'd like to know."

To her credit, Hope didn't single out Leopold, but Jakob knew she was alerting him to an upcoming hurdle. He shrugged and reached for the water dipper. "Volkner might—"

"Be our guest," Mr. Richardson inserted. "He needs to taste my Marcella's cooking."

"Your Marcella?" Volkner folded his arms across his chest. "Soon, God willing, she will be my Marcella."

"You can have Marcella," one of the out-of-town "cousins" said. "As long as you leave Katherine to me."

Mr. Richardson grinned. "Men, Linette is up for grabs."

"Time to get back to work!" Mr. Toomel wheeled around. The other local bachelors beat a hasty retreat, too. The married men followed just to escape the awkwardness.

Hope compressed her lips. It made her freckles seem more prominent. Tilting her head to the side, she said in a gentle tone, "Mr. Richardson, sir, your daughters are each special in her own right. God's pourin' out His blessings to match up two of them in one day."

"Linette is the oldest." He smiled sadly. "I don't mean to sound ungrateful. I'm thankful for both of the men, but Linette . . ." He shrugged.

"Better to be an old maid than to be married to the wrong man, that's what I say." Hope turned to check the cart.

Jakob eyed her carefully. *Which are you, Hope? The old maid, or the woman with regrets?*

Thirteen

The question nagged at Jakob. He knew nothing about his housekeeper's past. She had no one and nothing other than a quilt, a cart, and a mule. A woman who had to sneak away might have done so with only that. And she kept on the move. Her letters of recommendation proved she'd been all over. Like Annie, did she need safe harbor?

After supper, when the hired men went back to the barn for the night, Hope was too busy to pull away from her chores. She had Annie and Emmy-Lou out on the back porch plucking chickens while she stood at the hot stove. Cookies by the score, boiled potatoes to turn into potato salad, more bread, and heaven only knew what else kept her occupied.

The screen door banged behind Emmy-Lou. "I got another chicken for you. Auntie Annie says I need to go to bed now."

"All right, sugar pie. Can you please put the chicken on the tray like a big girl? Then we'll—"

"I'll take care of her." Jakob waited a moment while Emmy-Lou dumped off the chicken.

Emmy-Lou slid her slimy hand into his—a potent reminder that he needed to wash her before tucking her in. As he held Emmy-Lou to rinse off the soap into the washbasin, she asked, "Daddy will you sing me the night-night song?"

"What song is that?"

Emmy-Lou started, "Twinkle, twinkle . . ."

He and Hope sang along, only Hope continued to sing lyrics he didn't know. Emmy-Lou chimed in with about half of them.

"When the blazing sun is gone,
When he nothing shines upon,
Then you show your little light,
Twinkle, Twinkle, all the night . . ."

Finished, Emmy-Lou scampered over to Hope. "Night-night. *Ich liebe dich.*"

"Night-night. I love you, too." Hope knelt and gave her a hug and kiss. "Auntie Annie and me—we'll be up in a little while. But 'til then, what did I tell you?"

"Jesus is in my heart and room. And I got my own special angel and the twinkly star with me, too."

Jakob swept Emmy-Lou into his arms and carried her upstairs. He made sure the curtains were open, then knelt with her so she could say her prayer. One last kiss, and she snuggled in with her doll. Closing her eyes, she started singing to herself.

Jakob stood in the doorway for a moment to savor the sweetness. For the first time since she'd fallen into the well, Emmy-Lou was going to bed without fear.

By the time he got back downstairs, Annie sat at the table, slicing cabbage. "Where's Hope?"

"She cut up the chicken and took some pieces out to the springhouse. Should I get her for you?"

"No, no. You stay put. What are you making?"

"Coleslaw." As the knife shaved thin slivers from the cabbage head, Annie murmured, "I want you to talk to Hope."

Annie never asked for anything. Startled, Jakob asked, "About what?"

"She does too much and I don't do enough. So many things need to be done for tomorrow, yet she wanted me to go to bed."

"You worked hard today."

"Not nearly as much as Hope." Embarrassment tinged her voice and cheeks as Annie scooped the cabbage into her hands and dumped it into a large bowl.

Jakob laughed in hopes of easing his sister's worries. But tears filled Annie's eyes.

She's crying? Hope laughs, and Annie smiles. Why didn't it work for me? He moaned, wishing Hope would come back in and rescue him.

"Konrad was right. I'm useless."

"You are not! We need you—Emmy-Lou and me. Hope is here just to help for the harvest. She'll move on, but you—you'll stay. I couldn't manage without you. You know this. And Emmy-Lou—she needs you. She loves you."

Jakob reached for one of his bandanas to dry her tears but realized a full day's grime caked both of them. He grabbed the nearest cloth, then scowled at it. A potholder. What good was that?

Hope came inside. He shot her a helpless look.

A single sweeping glance, then Hope rested her hands on her hips. "Mr. Stauffer, sir, I told you I'm bossy. On account of that, it shouldn't come as a surprise that I'm gonna get het up if'n you don't put down that potholder. Annie, swipe it from that brother of yours." She made a silly face, and laughter tinted her voice. "Imagine, a man tryin' to cook!"

The funny face did the trick. Annie blinked away her tears.

"Who says I can't cook?" Jakob tried to sound outraged. "Annie, tell her I can cook."

Dutifully, Annie murmured, "He can cook."

"Badly!" Hope tacked on. Wiggling her nose, she reached out a hand. "If 'n you don't give up that potholder, the bread's gonna get singed. That would spoil everything Annie and me are doin'."

He set the pad in her work-chapped hand. "One burned loaf wouldn't change anyone's opinion. The men always expect hearty food—but the spread you women put out today surpassed anything we've ever had."

"See, Annie? I told you, your tarts were the bestest thing that'd happen all day. You shoulda seen them men out there in the field when they clapped their eyes on your tarts. They nigh unto turned handsprings." Hope headed to the oven.

"She's right, Annie."

Annie dipped her head and concentrated on slicing more slaw. "Hope and Velma made all the crusts. And all the other women brought food—good food."

" 'Course they did. You know the sayin': 'Put your best food forward.' "

"Food?" Annie's head shot up.

Jakob cleared his throat. "Put your best *foot* forward."

Glancing down at the toes of her scuffed boots, Hope shook her head. "One ain't any better than the other. I'm grateful to have 'em both and wouldn't want to favor one and leave the other slighted."

"Yes, but the saying is for foot, not food." Jakob didn't want to be unkind, but he figured Hope deserved to know the right word—as a cook, she probably made the mistake often.

Shaking her head, Hope opened the oven door. "Gotta feel sorry for that feller what come up with that sayin'. The bad foot must be painin' him something fierce." She pulled the bread out of the oven, magnifying the already warm, yeasty smell of the kitchen and inhaled deeply. "Maybe it's just me, but ain't nothin' more welcome than the smell of fresh-baked bread. Do all y'all think maybe Jesus thought so? He prayed for us to have daily bread."

"It always smells wonderful." Annie dumped several ingredients into the bowl and started to mix it.

"Didja tell your brother 'bout how God come through for you today?"

Jakob looked from Hope to Annie.

"If it's okay with you, Sydney and Velma invited me to go to Forsaken and help with everyone's babies while their mothers go to the farms to cook each day. If . . . if it's all right."

Relief flashed through him. Volkner was going to be hovering around the area for the entire town's harvest. With Annie tucked safely elsewhere, any number of catastrophic encounters would be averted. "Thanks be to God for His goodness. Ja, Annie. This is *sehr gut!*"

Worry still creased her features.

Hope robbed Annie of the bowl. "This looks delicious. I'll take it out to the springhouse in a little while. Suppose you tell us what's a-wrong, Annie?"

Annie chewed on her lower lip, then blurted out, "Sunday. Volkner—he will see me."

Jakob had thought about that, too. So far, he hadn't come up with a solution. He looked to Hope.

"I've been prayin' on that. Bible tells us to keep the Lord's Day holy. Two things would work. On the one hand, you could stay home and read the Bible. I'd be happy to stay with you and listen. You got a fine voice for readin'. On the other hand, we could be the first to get to church and take a pew straight up front. Then we'd wait and be the very last to leave. On the other hand, that Leopold Volkner feller is so moon-eyed over Marcella, I reckon he wouldn't see a snake if it kicked him in the knee."

Jakob and Annie exchanged a look.

Hope burst out laughing. "Oh, the both of you are dreadful nice not to ask me how I sprouted a third hand. Some days, it would come in right handy. Handy!" She lifted her palm and laughed harder.

A tense giggle shivered out of Annie.

Like a strong breeze that made a whole field of wheat wave and shimmer, Hope's presence filled the kitchen. Jakob couldn't help but bask in the warmth of her glow.

　　　　　　　　　　　　🙢

Mornin', Lord Jesus. Your world shore is purdy today. All them birds are a-raisin' their peeps to you, and the trees are a-wavin' their limbs like they wanna shout hallelujah. Lots to be done today, Father. Strengthen—

"Hope."

"Mr. Stauffer."

He glanced back toward the house, then approached her. He looked like a man set on doing something. She reckoned she might as well meet him halfway and save him some time. They ended up between the springhouse and the barnyard.

Brows furrowed, he cleared his throat. "I need to ask you something."

"Shore."

His eyes locked with hers. Resolve and something else rested in those blue depths. "Are you . . . um . . . were you ever married?"

"Me? Married? Mercy sakes, no."

Some of the strain left his features. He nodded.

"Why'd you pop up with that odd question?"

He half shrugged and motioned as if to wave off the thought. "I realized I hired you and knew nothing about you. Like where you came from or the like."

"I was born in Kansas, but most of my girlhood was here in Texas." She set down the pails she held and plucked a dandelion. Holding it up, she smiled. "But I'm like this here dandelion. God plants me someplace for a while, then He uproots me. By the breath of His will, He sends me on." All it took was one steady blow on the puffball, and the soft, white little stars caught in the wind.

Both watched a moment as they drifted away. "Back when I was knee-high to a grasshopper, we called them things wishies. Don't y'all like that? Now that I'm grown up, I still think it's a right purdy handle. The almighty, all-lovin' Father carries me along."

"Don't you have any family?"

"Yes and no. I don't have any blood kin, but I got me a whole family in Christ."

He rubbed the back of his neck. "How can you live like this— not knowing security or what tomorrow will bring?"

"Nobody knows what tomorrow will bring, and my security— well, if'n anybody take a mind to do me harm, God's on my side."

"God didn't help Annie."

Hope heard the anguish in his voice. She waited a moment. *Lord, I made a mistake. I thunk all his pain was from mourning his wife and son.* Looking at him, Hope shook her head. "I gotta disagree with you, Mr. Stauffer. God sent you to carry Annie away to safety. You brung her back here. From the mornin' when Hattie pulled me to your barnyard 'til now, I've seen how you are with her. God gave Annie a guardian angel, but He gave her an earthly warrior, too. You and me—we grieve that her man done her bad. Ain't a woman alive who deserves to bear the brunt of a man's temper."

"Part of me wants to track down that feller and serve him a wallop upside his head with the heaviest skillet I can find. I reckon you've felt the same—well, not the skillet part." She glanced down and noted how he'd balled his hands into fists. "But vengeance ain't ours."

"Vengeance, no; but justice is. If it wouldn't jeopardize Annie and the baby, I would do something." Slowly, he eased his hands open. "I didn't come to discuss my sister. I needed to know . . ."

Hope gasped as his words died out and his gaze roamed her face. "You was worried 'bout me? That maybe I was runnin' from a bad husband? Mr. Stauffer, you gotta be the most nicest man I ever met. Put your worries to rest, though. I ain't ever been hitched."

He cocked a brow. "Don't you want to be married?"

"Not yet. God ain't brung the right man along. King Solomon said there's a season and purpose to everything. Right now, my calling is to do what I'm a-doin'. If God takes a mind to changing my callin', I reckon He'll let me know. For now, I'm like the wheat in the field."

"That's hardly reassuring. We're reaping it."

She bent to pick up the pails again. "I was talkin' on the Bible verse about the wheat in the field. It doesn't toil or spin, but God dresses it up in a cloak of gold."

"It's in Matthew. I don't recall the chapter. 'Consider the lilies of the field, how they grow; they toil not, neither do they spin: and yet I say unto you, that even Solomon in all his glory was not arrayed like one of these.' "

"Oh, ain't that a grand way to start off the day? Hearin' the Word of the Lord." *And wasn't it nice of you just to say the verse and not make fun of me for remembering the verse wrong?* Hope glanced down at the dandelion stem between them, then looked back at him. "Your sis and all them ladies what come yesterday—they're all lilies, puttin' down roots and raisin' their faces to praise God. And your Emmy-Lou? I think she's like a bouquet of bachelor buttons—cheerful and fresh. Me? I'm a dandelion what blows along to serve God. Ain't it a kick to belong to a Creator who got such an imagination?"

"God's not the only one with an imagination."

Hope turned to go to the springhouse. She called over her shoulder. "We're made in His image. We're supposed to have imaginations!"

Hope stored the food and headed back toward the house, where Emmy-Lou sat waiting on the porch steps. Hope gave her a little hug. "Sugar pie, your auntie is going to go help with the babies at another house today. I don't know whether you'll go along or stay here with me."

A stricken expression streaked across Emmy-Lou's face, and her little hand clenched Hope's sleeve. "Auntie Annie isn't going away like Aunt Miriam, is she?"

"No, no, no." Hope stopped. "Your daddy told me he wants your auntie to stay here with you forever."

Emmy-Lou's hold of her sleeve didn't slacken. "And you too!"

Hope scanned the ground. Dandelions on a farm were a nuisance—but it was a fool's hope to think they'd ever be completely banished. She found one for the second time that morning. Kneeling down, she kept Emmy-Lou on her lap. For all the children she'd ever cared for, Hope had always known she'd breeze in and out of their lives—so she'd delighted in the transient joy of their company. In the past, when a little one clung to her as the time came for her to move on, she'd had a peace and managed to coax a giggle out of each one before Hattie pulled her away.

Now, for the first time ever, Hope's heart ached at the thought of leaving Emmy-Lou and Annie. Mr. Stauffer, too. Even weighed low by his own grief, he possessed a gentleness she admired. Leaving him and his kin would be different. Normally she looked ahead as she left a farm; when she left here, she'd be looking back.

I'm bein' silly and stupid.

With resolve she was far from feeling, she plucked the dandelion. "This here's a dandelion. Ain't it a purdy sight?"

Turning halfway to face her, Emmy-Lou corrected, "It's a wishie."

"Yep. That's what I call it most of the time, too. See all these here pieces?"

Emmy-Lou's face puckered. "No."

"Look closer. See all them teensy, bitty little pieces stickin' out? Sorta like umbrellas all around to make the ball. You and me—we're like them umbrellas, comin' together for a while, then we'll drift apart." Hope's voice caught, and she took a second before whispering in Emmy-Lou's ear, "Now, you and me're gonna blow and watch what happens."

They blew, and the seeds dispersed.

Emmy-Lou dipped her head and patted the front of her nightdress. "Where did it go?"

"Here's a little piece." Hope pinched it between her fingers and tickled the back of Emmy-Lou's hand. "See, this part stayed here with you. Another part blew away. Someday I'll drift off, but whenever I see a dandelion, I'll think of you; and when you spy a dandelion, you can 'member me."

"Hope!" Mr. Stauffer's call wasn't loud at all, but something in his tone made Hope snatch Emmy-Lou close and bolt to her feet.

Fourteen

Hope came in the kitchen door just as Marcella and Leopold entered the front door. Annie sat at the table as she had the day before. This time, she chopped cucumbers for a salad. Jakob pretended not to see how the knife shook in her trembling hand.

"Good morning!" Marcella singsonged. "Since Annie is going to go help with the babies and toddlers today, Mama sent me to help Hope with breakfast."

"My gracious! You're bright and early." Hope set Emmy-Lou down and turned to Annie. "Aren't they, Annie?"

"Y-yes, they are."

Giving Emmy-Lou a gentle nudge, Hope ordered, "Sugar pie, you run on upstairs and get dressed."

"What can I do to help?" Marcella didn't bother to take her eyes off of Mr. Volkner.

At least he's staring back at her. I've got to get him out of here. "Leopold, let's go hitch up the first team."

"Sure. After—"

"Who's Leopold?" Marcella's brows formed a small *V*.

"I am."

Blushing to the roots of her hair, the girl shook her head. "Hope called you Peter yesterday."

"It was all a mistake." Hope shoved an apron into Marcella's hands. "The real mistake," Hope continued, "would be for us not to have enough coffee for all the fellers. I reckon we'll have the rest of the men here faster than a whole army of ants can swarm a picnic."

Briskly rubbing his hands, Jakob moved away from Annie. "Since we're going outside, what do you want Volkner and me to carry?"

"Whaddya say, Annie?" Hope looked at her. "The crate with the mugs and two of the coffeepots?"

"Ja. And as soon as Marcella drains off the water, she can take out the hard-boiled eggs."

Antsy, Jakob didn't breathe freely until he had Volkner out of the house—only Volkner had no more than set the coffeepots on the table than he turned back toward the house.

"Have some coffee." Jakob shoved a mug into his hands.

Volkner set it down. "We have a minute. I'll help . . . the ladies carry out the rest."

Gritting his teeth, Jakob knew if he objected, it would be odd. If matters seemed out of the ordinary in any way, Volkner might well start looking for what was wrong. He groused, "Okay. One more trip. Then we'll hitch up that team."

They had barely stepped into the kitchen when Hope shook a big ladle at them. "Marcella, give your beau them eggs to carry out. And you"—she pointed the ladle at Jakob—"you can tote two of them coffee cakes out there. But I don't cotton to havin' to bump into big men and trip over their boots whilst I cook. If'n either of you sets foot in this here kitchen again today, I'm gonna splavocate."

Volkner echoed in a confused tone, "Splavo—"

"Pitch a fit." Jakob shoved him toward the door and forced a chuckle. "Believe me, you don't want to set her off."

As they descended the back porch steps, Hope's lilting, laughter-tinged voice followed them. "Them plowboys smartened up, didn't they?"

Volkner chuckled and called back, "No use riling the cook."

It wasn't long before all the men were in the field again. Midmorning, Hope drove out to them with peaches and water. She managed to give Jakob a sly wink and murmur, "Annie's over at your neighbors'."

Relief flooded Jakob. He wouldn't have to worry through the remainder of the day about Volkner's discovering Annie's secret.

At lunch, more food than he'd ever seen made the tables groan. Men commented on it. Hope happened to overhear Mr. Toomel's comment as she set a platter of ham on a table. "Well, we was plannin' on havin' to cook for a full two days—maybe even half of the third. With that extra reaper and team goin', you men're way ahead of schedule."

"Ja, we are," Jakob agreed with a great sense of relief.

Hope bobbed her head. "So me and the gals, we pulled out all the slops."

"Slops?" Patterson said in disbelief.

"Stops," someone else said.

Hope held up both hands. "I'll stop. I didn't mean for all y'all to think I was callin' you hogs. 'Tis just a sayin'."

Jakob didn't want anyone to humiliate her just because she'd slaughtered yet another cliché. In a slightly too-loud voice he said, "Truth is the truth. We're eating like swine. I, for one, won't apologize, either. You and the rest of the women—you've put on a fine spread."

Men grunted agreement as they ate their fill.

"Many hands make the work right." Hope straightened out her apron. "Holds true in the kitchen and in the fields."

She'd done it again. Mangled the old axiom, yet in such a way that it made sense. Jakob watched as Patterson's brow furrowed and he silently mouthed the saying as if to figure out where things took a detour. The whole situation struck Jakob as amusing. Then again, with the harvest brought in, he'd already been in a good mood. He scanned everyone and said loudly, "Our neighbors have been generous with their help. I'm grateful for all your help. Together, we were faster than ever before."

After lunch, it wasn't until he reached the Smiths' farm that Jakob realized he and Annie had left Emmy-Lou in Hope's care. Oddly, that didn't trouble him in the least. Hope was capable and loving. His daughter would be perfectly safe in her care. *Just as she charmed Emmy-Lou out of her fear of the dark, she's given me peace of mind about my daughter. Surely the Lord sent Hope my way.*

In the quiet that followed the noon meal, a passel of children sat on the parlor carpet, heads tilted upward like baby chicks waiting for food. Katherine Richardson sat in a chair with a storybook. "The name of this story is *Cinderella.*"

"And it's my brand-new book," her little sister Lottie boasted.

"I can't see," Emmy-Lou complained. Jakob's daughter normally had a sweet temperament, but she'd been a mite cranky today.

While Mrs. Richardson, Lena, and Gramma chattered about what flowers made the prettiest bridal bouquets, Hope set aside the platter she'd finished drying and stepped over to the edge of the parlor.

Emmy-Lou bumped shoulders with Mandy. "Move over." Even as Mandy scooched to the side, Emmy-Lou rubbed her eyes and whined again, "I can't see."

Without Annie here, it fell to Hope to handle Jakob's daughter. "It's your naptime."

"But I want to see the pictures and hear the story."

This was the first time Emmy-Lou had been quarrelsome instead of obedient. Hope gave the little girl a stern look.

Emmy-Lou responded by poking out her lower lip in a pout.

"It's not a very long story," Lottie Richardson said. She wiggled closer to Emmy-Lou.

"We need to go home." Mrs. Richardson motioned to her daughters.

"Me too." Lena folded a damp dish towel and set it on the counter.

"All y'all have been so kind and helpful. Annie and Mr. Stauffer and me—we appreciate all you done. In the comin' days, you can be shore I'll work every bit as hard at your places."

"We'll see you at church tomorrow." Mrs. Richardson claimed her cake plate from the array of dishes on the table.

Emmy-Lou let out an excited squeal and gave Lottie a hug. "Miss Hope, she says I can read her book today and bring it back to her at church!"

"Ain't that sweet?"

Prompted by the necessity of all of the regular chores waiting at home as well as the extra ones women did on Saturday so Sunday would be the day of rest, everyone left. Hope tucked Emmy-Lou into bed for her nap, then surveyed the downstairs. Doing just as she'd said, Gramma had marshaled all of the school-age children into doing all sorts of tasks. With the eggs gathered, chickens fed, vegetables picked, the garden both weeded and watered, butter churned, and the porches swept, Hope took a moment to drink the rest of her glass of sweet tea.

The book captured her attention. She'd never seen such a thing. Shaped like an arched stained-glass window, the book opened from the middle toward both sides. The colored artwork made it look as if the center portion was a stage in some fancy theater, and the black-and-white pictures on the side pages depicted the audience watching the play from fancy balcony seats. *Cinderella.* Hope knew the fairy tale, so she carefully turned the pages and enjoyed the story—even if the words all jumbled into indecipherable rows of circles and sticks and bumps. When Annie got home and Emmy-Lou woke up, they'd all sit together, and Annie could read to them.

In the meantime, Hope took some of the day's milking and set it to boil. It took little time to add vinegar, then line the colander with cheesecloth. The resulting ricotta cheese would be refreshing for lunch tomorrow. She made a second batch, but after straining it, she tightened the cloth to push out more whey, then compressed the still-hot ricotta between two plates to force out the moisture. Farm cheese—she remembered her mother making it and spreading it on bread or crumbling it on salads and vegetables.

Carrying a lumpy flour sack, Annie returned from minding the babies over at Forsaken Ranch. She emptied it on the table. "You wouldn't believe it. Sydney's sewing machine is a marvel. Just look!"

Hope picked up a soft flannel blanket. "Mercy's sake, these stitches are small and tight and even. How long did it take you to hem?"

"I made four of them in fifteen minutes!"

Gawking at the other three on the table, Hope said, "I didn't notice you'd hemmed 'em all. What, with all the babies you was watchin', gettin' one blanket done was all I expected. We'll have to cut some diapers and a few more blankets so you can get a bunch done next week."

Dropping both her gaze and her voice, Annie confessed, "I've made very little for the baby. It was foolish of me."

"I sorta reckoned you'd borrow whatever Emmy-Lou used when she was born. Them things gotta be round here somewhere."

Annie nodded, but she still didn't meet Hope's eyes. "A good mother should make things for her own child."

"You've been busy, bringin' in the harvest. Besides, you still have a coupla weeks."

Toying with another of the little blankets, Annie murmured, "Velma says babies come whenever they please, even if the mother's not ready."

"If your babe takes a mind to come before everything's prepared, it wouldn't be a problem. Hot as it is, if all he has on is a diaper, it'll be plenty." Hope pretended not to see the worry in Annie's half-shielded features and pretended to study the edge of the blanket. "I'm thinkin', what if we was to cut out a mess of gowns? You could use Sydney's machine to whip up the side seams and hems, and in the evenings, you and me—we could pop sleeves on 'em."

Annie finally looked at her. Several emotions shimmered in her eyes. "You'd help me?"

"Just you try to stop me." Hope set aside the blanket and patted Annie's arm. "You and me together can fix up plenty in no time at all."

"Especially if I do what you said—get the gowns started so we just add the sleeves." Annie's shoulders finally eased down into a relaxed posture.

"Bitty as baby gowns are, it wouldn't take but a few minutes to tat or crochet a purdy edge on some of 'em."

"You should see the beautiful gowns Sydney made. She put in lace insets and has rows of pin tucks and ribbons. With the machine, she said it didn't take much time at all."

"I wouldn't mind none if you stayed a few hours extra to sew after the mamas pick up their young'uns. Truth is, with the harvest done here, things oughtta settle down."

A self-conscious look stole across Annie's face. "I'm not sure. Taking care of that many babies left me—"

"You poor gal! Neither of us is gonna say another word. Y'all just go on upstairs and have a lay-down." Annie opened her mouth, and Hope shook her finger. "Ahh-ahh-ahh. No talkin'."

As Annie started toward the stairs, Hope said, "That's more like it."

"You talked," Annie whispered.

"So did you, just now. We're even, so you go rest." Deciding to add the hambone to the beans she planned to serve for supper, Hope headed out to the springhouse. It would still be a few hours before Jakob and Phineas returned home from the Smiths'. They'd reap until the last rays of sunlight died from the sky.

When she returned, she spied Emmy-Lou lying on her tummy on the parlor rug, engrossed in the book. Emmy-Lou drew back in order to open the pages to the next theater scene, then dipped her head again to study the picture. Her cheeks were still sleep flushed, and her curls looked as if someone had stirred them with a fork until they formed a froth.

"Sugar pie, if'n you get any closer to the pages, one of Cinderella's mice might run up your nose."

"I don't see no mice."

Setting aside the hambone, Hope went to the parlor. She sat down next to Emmy-Lou. "I looked at the book and saw lots of mice. What 'bout this'un here? He's fixin' to—"

"Where?"

Cold terror streaked through Hope as she pushed several wisps of hair from the little girl's forehead. *Lord Jesus, don't let it be what I'm a-thinkin'.*

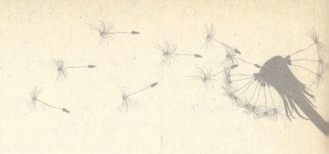

Fifteen

Jakob spied his house ahead and waited for the pain to hit. The place hadn't felt like home since the day Naomi died. Only the grief didn't come this time. Instead, the warm glow of a lamp near the window beckoned him home. For the first time, he wanted to urge Josephine into a trot to take him there more quickly—but he didn't. Only a fool would push a horse to do more than walk at night.

Phineas rode alongside him. "I hope we didn't pass up supper at the Smiths' only to go without. Don't suppose Hope thought she'd have to fix a meal, not with us staying so late."

Shrugging, Jakob said, "There'll be enough leftovers to tide us through."

"The way the men gobbled up everything in sight, I'd be surprised if there's a bite left." Phineas took off his hat and wiped his forehead with his sleeve. "Good thing we all ate such a hearty lunch."

"Ja." Neither of them mentioned the skimpy sandwiches "Gramma" served them late in the afternoon. She'd served them the best she could. Everyone knew the Smith larder was low. Because of that, the men proclaimed supper would be waiting back at their own homes.

Phineas chuckled softly. "Did you see Leopold's face when you told Gramma not to feed us supper?"

"No," Jakob said wryly, "but I heard him ask Richardson if Marcella was cooking tonight."

"For Marcella's sake, I hope she's as good a cook as Sydney Creighton claims."

Jakob guided his mount to the side a little to avoid a gopher hole. "Mrs. Creighton was a godsend—not just for Big Tim, but for Richardson's daughters. I don't know what she's been teaching them, but it's obviously working. Who would have thought one of his daughters would catch a beau, let alone two of them?"

"Whoa!" Phineas stopped dead in his tracks. "You? You want Marcella, too?"

"Nein!" Jakob halted his mount and gaped at Phineas. "What gave you that cockeyed notion?"

"You said Marcella had caught two beaux."

Emphatically shaking his head, Jakob hurried to correct his hired hand's misconception. "I meant two of the daughters had each caught her own beau."

"Phew." Phineas jostled the reins to start back into motion. "You had me scared there."

"I don't figure I'll marry again. There was only woman for me."

Silence hovered between them as the shadows deepened. For a moment, the light ahead of them went out, then shone again. Phineas cleared his throat. "Konrad—does he know? About the baby?"

"No."

"So." Phineas said the single syllable only as a German male could—with finality. It carried no question, no challenge—only acknowledgment.

"Annie's staying here. Forever." As far as Jakob was concerned, all that needed to be said was said. He continued to stare straight ahead at the beacon shining from the dining room window.

"I saw the bruises, and the fear in her eyes. . . ." Phineas let out a tortured sound. "The day you brought her home, I saw her."

They'd never spoken of it. Such a matter was intensely private. Surprised that his hired hand broached the subject now, Jakob remained silent.

Phineas drew in a deep breath. His voice shook. "When Annie was a girl, I held a special place in my heart for her. Now she is another man's wife—but I would lay down my life before I let Konrad take her back."

It was not a boastful proclamation; it was a promise of protection. Jakob appreciated the vow, but he also owed it to Phineas to reassure him the matter was settled.

"He can't take her back. I still own the family farm. I allow him to use the land and keep the profit, but only so long as he stays away from Annie."

"Annie is worth more than the land, but Konrad—he is a greedy man, Jakob. The time will come when he won't be satisfied." When Jakob made no reply, Phineas growled, "He's already wanting more, isn't he?"

"The harvest—it was good. I can pay him a little once I sell the wheat." Until then, Jakob would barely eke by. Clark at the mercantile and Vaughn at the feedstore would extend him credit, but he'd managed to remain debt-free until now. Phineas was right, though. Konrad's greed had already surfaced and strained matters.

"Pay him; don't pay me."

Jakob shot him a startled look. "It shouldn't come to that. The laborer is worthy of his hire. You—"

"I have food in my belly, a roof over my head, and clothes on my back. What kind of man would I be, what kind of friend or Christian brother, if I took money I don't need and put a woman in jeopardy?"

"Annie is here. Safe."

"But for how long?" Phineas halted his horse. "Konrad will push for more. Use my pay to help buy your sister's freedom."

"It shouldn't come to that. I've been careful." Jakob jostled the reins to make his horse move forward again. They rode in complete silence until reaching the barnyard. Jakob ordered in an undertone, "We're done—understand?"

The moon cast a bluish tone over the earth, leaving half of Phineas's face in shadow. The other half showed icy resolve as the hired hand curtly nodded once.

Hope sat out on the front porch in a wicker chair, crocheting. Beyond a shadow of doubt, Jakob knew this was the first time in days she'd rested. Her everyday dress looked like a damp brown dishcloth, and a plethora of tiny curls sprung free from her coiled braid. A lamp next to her illuminated them into a nimbus. It reminded him of the dandelion she'd held up to the first rays of sunlight and gently blown upon.

Imbedded in that memory was the understanding that once Annie had the baby and was back on her feet, Hope would leave. The thought hit hard—harder than it ought. Maybe it was because under Hope's tender care, his sister seemed less timid, less frightened. Hope built up his sister with honest praise. This morning, she'd come running when he called and protected his sister with her own unique brand of humor and bossiness.

The same hand that shook a ladle at him this morning now wielded a tiny steel hook and a filament of the stringy stuff women used to crochet. A delicate, lacy little pair of rows didn't give a hint as to what she'd started to make. She didn't pause working, but jutted her chin to their left. "Saw you men a-comin'. Wash bucket's yonder. Annie's takin' her Saturday bath, so I reckoned you'd appreciate a quick cool down to spruce up 'til you get your turn and before you eat." Her voice didn't carry its usual lilt of happiness, but tired as she was, that seemed understandable.

"Reckon you men are hungry 'nuff to eat the north end of a possum headin' south, so I fixed y'all plates. They're under the towel on that other bench."

The door opened a crack. "Hope?"

Hope set aside her handiwork. "I'm a-comin'." As she rose, she said, "Hot as it got and hard as you worked, you gotta be miserable. I'll be stayin' inside now to help Annie rinse out her hair, so if'n the both of you wanna strip off your shirts ain't no reason you can't."

The soft, indistinguishable sounds of the women talking in the house drove home how Hope had brought serenity with her—an odd variety of peace, to be sure. Instead of it being a thick wool blanket, it was a crazy quilt that still enveloped them all. *My thinking—it is fanciful. Just because she's eased Annie's life is no reason to start imagining things that aren't to be.*

"Are you thinking what I am?" Phineas shrugged out of his shirt.

Jakob gave him a wary look. "What are you thinking?"

"Hope—she twisted another saying around. It's supposed to be the south end of an animal going north. She mixed it up, but . . ." He grinned. "It still made sense. I don't know how she does it."

179

"She has her own ways." After sluicing the water over himself, Jakob briskly tumbled the bar of Pears soap round and round in his hands to work up a suds. In no time at all, he and Phineas sank down onto the chairs and whisked back the covering to get to the food.

"Mmmm." Phineas grabbed for a plate.

Jakob stared at his. Slices of melon ringed the edge, then four drumsticks formed a box around a small bowl of ricotta cheese. Only Hope would take the time and trouble to serve food in a pretty arrangement. It all looked appealing and refreshing and generous. Ten short minutes later, the food had more than fulfilled its promise to sate his hunger. Something didn't feel right, though. Maybe it was because he and Phineas had discussed Annie's predicament.

"It's odd, the cows not bawling." Phineas set down his plate and tilted his head to the side. "Do you think—"

"Hope must have milked them." *There's no telling what else she's done.* There she was again, doing, solving, making all his worries easier.

Phineas rose. "I'll go unsaddle and stable the horses."

"I'm so filthy, I could shake off an acre of dirt." Jakob stretched. "It's a good thing we have Sunday tomorrow. If it weren't normal time for a bath, I'd still shove you into a tub. You smell worse than a sick billy goat."

"And you"—Phineas headed down the steps—"smell like a dead billy goat. Hurry up in the tub so I'll still have warm water, will you?"

"Ja." He knocked on the door.

"The coach is clear," Hope called out.

A smile tugged at his mouth. Hope and her slaughtered sayings. Jakob grabbed the plates and went inside. He set them down by the sink and looked at the enormous aluminum washtub in the center of the kitchen. Big pots of water sat on the stove, promising the luxury of a hot soak for his tired muscles. For the first time, Hope didn't meet his gaze.

"Hope, Phineas and I—we're filthy. You should bathe first."

She looked up and swallowed hard. Instead of the joy that normally sparkled in her warm hazel eyes, aching misery shimmered there.

"What is it?"

"We gotta talk. I'm not shore, but I'm pretty shore—well, I ain't a doctor or nothin', so what I think ain't really—"

"What is it?" he repeated, his voice sharp.

"It's Emmy-Lou. I think you need to take her to a doctor right away. First thing tomorrow."

The acrid taste of fear filled his mouth. "Why?"

"It's her eyes. She can't hardly see nothin' at all."

"What makes you think there's something the matter with her eyes?"

"Lotta things. She's ascairt of the dark."

Relief started to trickle through him. "All children are. She's doing much better—especially since you taught her that song."

Sadly shaking her head, Hope sagged against the cupboard. "Ain't just that. She's always losin' her dolly, even when it's close by."

"Carelessness."

"When she's outside the house, she always stays beside someone."

"Because I've admonished her to." He gave her a reassuring smile. "See? It's nothing."

"I thought so, too. And I thought when she tripped or bumped into things and when she banged into your weddin'

181

picture and broke it—them was all accidents or clumsiness. But it's more. I wish with all my heart it wasn't nothin' more, Mr. Stauffer, but wishin' don't make things true."

"You're tired." Every woman was after feeding all the harvest hands. *And Hope's been getting up extra early and going to bed late ever since she arrived, just to get more done. When I got home, I saw she was tired, but I didn't realize just how exhausted she's become. A weary woman's liable to notice something minor and let her fears grow rampant.* Naomi had been that way, and he'd learned to listen and calmly point out that matters weren't so bad after all. A few reassurances, some sleep, and Naomi did fine. Hope was every bit as resilient. Jakob felt sure he knew how to handle her. "A good night's sleep, and everything will look different in the morning."

Hope rubbed her forehead and made a small sound. When her hand dropped, tears turned her eyes into molten gold. "I wisht all this would be a bad dream and a little sleep would make it go away, but it won't."

Compassion filled him. She'd worked herself silly and wouldn't rest until she let out her worries. He'd listen and let her speak her piece, then soothe her fears. "What makes you so sure something's wrong, Hope? Annie and I haven't noticed anything."

"Neither did I. Not really. Not 'til today. This mornin', she couldn't see dandelion fluff."

When he'd called to Hope this morning, he'd seen her showing his daughter the "wishy." How could Emmy-Lou have missed seeing the white flecks glowing and glittering in the morning light? He'd spotted them even from the porch.

Distress grew in Hope's tone. "This afternoon, she couldn't see the pictures in the big storybook, even though all the other kids saw 'em without any trouble."

"Maybe someone was in her way." Jakob searched for a simple explanation, only now he was trying not only to reassure Hope, but also himself. Each thing she'd said was minor, but put together, the facts became unsettling. Very unsettling. "My Emmy-Lou—she's small."

"When Emmy-Lou woke up from her nap, she couldn't even see the mice in the book, and her little nose—it was practically touchin' the page. Somethin's sore wrong, Mr. Stauffer."

Alarm poured through him. "Show me the book. Maybe the picture was blurry or something else was bigger. Or more interesting."

With leaden steps, Hope went to the parlor. She picked up a large, thin book. "I'll show you the page." Fingers made awkward by worry, Hope fumbled to open the middle of the front of the book, then leafed past a few pages before flopping the storybook wide for him to inspect the whole scene. "Do y'all see any mice, Mr. Stauffer?"

He barely heard her question. The illustration showed several mice. They weren't faintly sketched in or hidden among several other objects where an unobservant or distracted child would miss them. Taking the book into his own hands, Jakob stared at the picture. "My Emmy-Lou—you say she did not see these mice?"

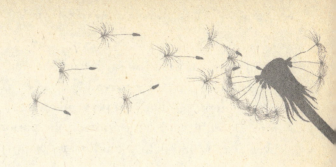

Sixteen

ary a one." Hope's voice trembled. "I didn't say nothin' to Annie. Your sister—she's got plenty enough to worry over without me addin' to the burden on her mind. Besides, you bein' Emmy-Lou's pa, I reckoned it was best to talk to you first."

He nodded somberly.

"But once I started a-watchin' close-like, so many little things walloped me in the eye. Didja know Emmy-Lou says 'tis hard to find eggs here and 'tis easier at the other places? Your Dominiques lay brown eggs. Most everybody else's hens lay white eggs. And ever notice how the toes of her shoes are scuffed dead straight on? She bumps into the first step on the stairs before she picks up her foot."

She's right. Emmy-Lou does that. Jakob felt as if he'd been kicked in the chest by Hattie. All he could do was stare at the book. The mice in the picture seemed to mock him. His daughter couldn't see well enough to enjoy the simple pleasure of the illustration. His gaze dropped—and the words of the story enclosed in scroll-like boxes toward the bottom of the page drove home another awful truth. "If what you say is true, she won't see the letters. My daughter can't learn to read."

"I thought on that." Hope gently tugged the book from him, closed it, and set it aside on the parlor table. "Maybe eyeglasses would help. Could be, a doctor could fix her up with spectacles."

Grasping at that possibility, he nodded once, emphatically. "Yes. Spectacles."

"But if 'n the doctor says eyeglasses won't help, 'twon't be the end of the world." Hope lifted her chin and finally met his gaze. "You been a-readin' to me, and so has Annie. Emmy-Lou will have y'all to read 'loud to her. She won't lack because you'll meet her need."

Denial sprang to his lips, but Jakob caught himself just before speaking. Hope couldn't read, and if he bemoaned the horrid void illiteracy would cause, Hope might think he was ridiculing her.

"I reckoned you oughtta be told, but I figured a man should eat his supper in peace first." Regret filled Hope's eyes and voice. "Ain't right for me to keep anything back from you—'specially 'bout your loved ones. I got to thinkin' on how Jesus didn't mind healin' folks on the Sabbath and knew you'd wanna carry Emmy-Lou to the doctor soon as the rooster rose."

Raking his hand through his hair, Jakob grimaced. "I wouldn't let the doctor here treat a hangnail."

"Velma said somethin' 'bout him bein' a quack. I hoped 'twas just about birthin' and not 'bout other things."

"I try to give a man a chance. Doctors—they can't fix everything. Even their best isn't always going to make things better. The Tyson kid—Doc set his broken leg."

Hope winced. "The one what hobbles, and his foot goes out cockeyed?"

Jakob nodded. "It was a bad break. At the time, the doc boasted he'd done well not to amputate. But then he rubbed goose grease and ashes into Slim Garner's burned arm, and the whole thing putrified. Velma barely kept Slim alive. Since then, he's done other things that prove he doesn't know what he's doing. I won't trust Doc with my daughter."

"Where'll you take her?"

He searched his mind for someplace that might have a decent physician. "Abilene. Fuller over on Forsaken went to Abilene to take a cure for his rheumatism. He said the doctor there was good."

Hope crammed her fists into the pockets of her apron. "Good." She cast a quick glance at the tub. "I'll go on out and crochet more. You take yourself a nice hot soak."

"After you."

She shook her head. "Mr. Stauffer, sir, you need to get yourself to bed so's you can head out first thing in the mornin'. I've got some deep thinkin' and prayin' that'll keep me up."

"Pray hard."

Later, Jakob lay in bed and peered through the dark. He couldn't imagine anything worse than his beloved, motherless daughter going blind. Terrified of the dark, how would Emmy-Lou ever survive without her sight? *Lord, please don't rob Emmy-Lou of her sight.*

Dozens of memories surfaced where Emmy-Lou had bumped into something, spilled her milk, or rubbed her eyes. *I should have realized it. What if it's too late to save what vision she has left because I didn't pay attention?*

He heard rustling downstairs. It was long past the time that Hope had taken her bath, so he knew it was safe to descend the stairs. Needing to escape his jumbled thoughts, Jakob headed for the kitchen.

187

"Mr. Stauffer, sir. Guess you're unsettled. Can't much blame you, seein' as I'm itchy myself. No use lying abed and wrestling with thoughts." Hope punched down some dough.

Words were useless. He didn't want to discuss his fears. Instead, he pulled open a drawer and withdrew the whetstone. One after the other, he sharpened the knives. Hope stayed busy baking. Every now and then, she'd refill the mug of coffee she'd set beside him. Put a sandwich in front of him. Slid a pair of big oatmeal cookies straight off the oven-hot sheet onto the table for him.

As he slowly wiped the last knife blade clean, Hope said, "You and me—we made a pact to make things easy on Annie. I'll do my best for your daughter, too."

Jakob looked at her tenderly. "I know you will."

She took off her apron and laid it across the counter. Naomi always hung hers on the hook, and so did Annie. *Hope gets up so early and goes to bed so late, I never noticed she didn't hang up hers.* To his astonishment, Hope took the tin of cinnamon, sprinkled a little on one apron string, and proceeded to rub it in. She must have seen his puzzled look, because she explained, "Emmy-Lou likes the scent of cinnamon. Most gals wear toilet water or perfume. Me? I reckon I'll do this so's she'll find comfort by me."

Jakob nodded curtly, abruptly pushed his way out of the house, and strode out into the darkness.

⁂

"We're going on a special trip!" Emmy-Lou scampered up to Hope. "Wanna come along?"

"Why don't you tell me all about it while I put this here milk in the icebox?"

"I'm thirsty. Please, can I have some first?"

She's just a short little thing. Maybe she's not tall enough to see. But even as Hope said that to herself, she knew deep down inside that wasn't why Emmy-Lou asked. "I poured some in a cup for you already. It's on the table." Hope turned and stooped—more to hide her reaction than to put away the milk bottle.

"Thank you. So me and Daddy and Auntie Annie are going on a trip! I'm gonna be a traveler just like in our song you were teaching me yesterday! Daddy says if we go right away, we can get there and come home all in one day."

Hope caught sight of her boss speaking in a low tone to Phineas. Both men looked somber.

No use in scarin' the child. Could be all she needs is eyeglasses. "Sounds like you're in for a fine adventure!" Hope interjected more confidence in her voice than she felt.

"Lottie and Bethany went to Abilene with their daddy on the train, but I'm going in the wagon."

"I ain't never been on a train myself. Dreadful noisy things, if'n you ask me." Hope straightened up, holding a dishcloth-wrapped bundle. "Your daddy tole me 'bout the trip last night, so I made up some sandwiches for you to take. Chicken salad. How's that sound?"

Hopping like a little cricket, Emmy-Lou proclaimed, "I loooove chicken salad!"

"Wonderful! I bet you like cookies, too."

"Big cookies!"

"Then it's a good thing I put some in the satchel. You're gonna have a dandy picnic today, aren't you?"

"A picnic!" She spun around. "Daddy, we getta have a picnic!"

"Ja, we will." The worry lines in his face deepened as he watched Annie descend the stairs.

"I told you, it isn't a good idea," Phineas said in a low, forceful tone.

Watching how Annie held the banister with one hand and rubbed the small of her back with the other, Hope gasped. "Are y'all okay, Annie? You're not—"

"No, no. I'm not in labor. My back—it's just cranky today."

Mr. Stauffer's eyes narrowed. "Are you sure?"

"Ja, Jakob. Did I hear Emmy-Lou say we're going on a picnic?"

"Emmy-Lou!" Phineas stuck out his arm and wiggled his fingers to beckon her. Suddenly he stared at his fingers, stopped, and started to swing his arm in a wide arc. "Let's go check on Milky and her kittens."

"Okay!"

Mr. Stauffer waited until they left. "Annie, Hope thinks Emmy-Lou's having trouble seeing well. I'm going to take her to a doctor in Abilene today."

Hope noticed how carefully he'd chosen his words.

"Emmy-Lou? What's wrong with her eyes?"

"We don't know. Perhaps she just needs spectacles. Isn't that right, Hope?"

Hope hitched her shoulders in an oh-so-casual shrug. "Probably. I'm no doctor, so I'm glad you're taking her to someone smart to check things out."

Annie frowned. "Abilene is a long way."

"Best better wolf down some breakfast so y'all can hit the road." Hope pulled a loaf of cinnamon bread from the oven.

"I suppose you're going today because the Smiths need you for tomorrow's harvest." Annie tried to smile, but she failed miserably.

Better for her to think that than to get all het up, thinkin' Emmy-Lou's problem is sore bad. Ain't good for a woman in the family way to get upset. "Your brother's a hard worker. I don't doubt that all them other farmers are glad to have his help."

Annie pulled on her apron. "It's a long trip without the train. Hope's right. You'll want to leave right away. As soon as Phineas brings Emmy-Lou back, I'll comb her hair."

Annie didn't understand that her brother counted on her going along. Hope glanced at Jakob, and the oh-so-slight movement of his head and flare in his eyes let Hope know he wouldn't ask his sister to accompany him.

"Phineas thinks it would be a bad idea for you to go with me," Jakob said. "He says it would be too hard on you."

Wariness flickered across Annie's features as she blurted out, "I'll go if you want me to. You just tell me, and whatever you want—"

"What I want," Jakob interrupted in a gentle tone, "is for you to stop worrying. If your back hurts now, jostling in the wagon all day would become unbearable."

Annie ducked her head. "I'm sorry."

"You don't have to apologize." Hope poured coffee into the mugs. "Your brother loves you. He and Phineas don't want you to get all wore out from a long trip. Isn't that right, Mr. Stauffer?"

"Yes, it is a long trip." Mr. Stauffer watched Annie as she trundled across the floor. "Are you sure you are all right?"

"Ja. I'm just big and clumsy."

"You're beautiful, and that's a blessin' you got hidden 'neath your apron." Hope pulled bacon out of the warmer. "Betcha God hisself looks down from His glorious throne room and smiles at the miracle you and Him are makin'."

"But what about the trip?" Annie chewed on her lower lip.

"I could make it quicker if I rode Josephine." A curt nod lent assurance to Jakob's assertion. "Ja. We could get there and back more quickly than if I drive the wagon. It's a good plan."

"Yup. With Annie's back naggin' at her, maybe she and me can stay home. She can read outta the Bible to me, and we'll have our very own worship."

"*Sehr gut.* We'd better get started, then."

A short while later, Hope tucked a pillow behind the small of Annie's back and sat next to her on the parlor settee. "There. How's that?"

"I'm worried. Perhaps I should have gone with Jakob."

"Piddle." When Annie gave her a shocked look, Hope laughed. "Did I get the wrong word again? What's the one what means it ain't nothin' but nonsense?"

"Piffle?"

"Piffle!" Hope chortled softly. "That's it! Well, I tell you here and now, Annie—that brother of yours ain't gonna do bad at all with his li'l girl. It'll do 'em both good to have a day away, just the both of them together alone. And Emmy-Lou's gonna be mighty happy to share the extra cookie with her daddy."

Annie clasped her hands tightly in her lap. "I wish I could be like you. I worry all the time."

"You got some mighty big things weighing heavy on your heart and mind. I reckon you'd be dumber than a bag of hammers if'n your mind didn't drift toward the difficulties. 'Tisn't that you think on 'em what matters. To my way of reasonin', 'tis what you do with them burdens that counts."

Annie's knuckles turned white as she held her hands tighter still. She rasped, "Konrad—he said I was stupid and brought on all my problems."

The pain tainting her friend's voice made Hope's heart ache. "I don't know Konrad. Truth be told, I'd live a happy life going to my grave not meetin' him. It nigh unto breaks my heart seein' how that man hurt you."

"For seven months now, I've been away. He hasn't hurt me since Jakob got me."

"We'll praise the merciful Lord that He delivered you. But, Annie, words can hurt every bit as bad as a fist. They tear a body down from the inside. Them wounds are every bit as tender, and their pain lives on far longer than bruises on your skin."

Tears slid down Annie's face. "If I had been a better wife—"

"He would have found something to fault. Some folk are just plain wicked to the core. The meanness festers inside them and the onliest way they feel good is to tear others down. When you got married, Konrad vowed to love, honor, and cherish you. He broke them holy vows. Ain't no pleasin' a man like that."

"I should have tried harder."

Hope tilted Annie's face toward hers. "Love ain't supposed to hurt."

"He'd say he was sorry."

"When I was a girl, my daddy told me sayin' I was sorry didn't just mean I regretted what I done. It meant I'd be mindful not to do that bad thing again. If'n your husband truly meant his apology, he woulda been real careful not to raise his hand or his voice to you again."

Annie let out a slow, shaky sigh.

"Ever notice how kids copy their mamas and daddies? If'n you got a son, would you want him to grow up beatin' his woman and lashing her with his words? Or if'n you got a daughter, would you want her to live in fear?"

"*Nein!*" Horror painted her features.

"Didn't think so." Hope paused. Annie's expression hadn't faded. *Pity never did anybody any good. Best I encourage her.* "Now

193

you got a child to protect. The thing we gotta keep in mind is that you don't have to do it all on your own."

"Jakob," Annie said in a leaden tone. "I know he will help me, but I worry that Konrad might harm him."

"That brother of yours—he's a good man. Strong. Smart too. Phineas ain't no slouch, neither. But most of all, God's gonna help you. We gotta put our trust in Him. He'll never let you down."

Slowly, Annie's hands unknotted. "It is the Lord's Day. We should read the Bible."

"I'd like that. Think you could read that psalm the parson read last Sunday? I been tryin' to recollect how it went. If'n it ain't too much of a bother, maybe we could say it a heap of times 'til I get all the words stored up in my mind and heart."

"Psalm one-twenty-one?"

Hope handed her the Bible. "Couldn't rightly say. Numbers just go in one ear and out the door. It was the one what talked about liftin' our eyes unto the hills for help and how God's with us forevermore."

Annie opened the Bible and carefully turned the incredibly thin pages. "Here. 'I will lift mine eyes to the hills . . .' "

"Well, glory hallelujah! You done 'membered the 'zact right spot!"

A timid smile chased across Annie's face. She continued to read.

"Hold it. That there verse. How's about you readin' it again?"

"The Lord shall preserve thee from all evil: he shall preserve thy soul."

Hope rubbed her hands with glee. "Oh, that's the bestest thing I heard all week. Ain't it grand to read our Father's Holy Word and get walloped upside the head with that promise?

Annie, you and me—we gotta commit that verse to memory and claim that as a promise for you. Konrad is one sorely wicked cuss, but the Bible there promises God'll preserve you."

A small line formed between Annie's brows. She dipped her head and her lips moved as she silently reread the verse.

"Well? Whaddya say we memberize that'un? You read it out loud, then we'll chop it halfwise and work on the piece."

In a few moments, they quoted the verse in unison. Hope let out a satisfied sigh. "That shorely blessed me. That verse, I'm always gonna think of it as bein' your special verse on account of how it's the most perfectest brace of words to fit your needs."

"I can't lie and say it makes me all at peace, but I don't feel quite so . . ." Annie shrugged tensely. "Anyway, there's still one more verse in this chapter. 'The Lord shall preserve thy going out and thy coming in from this time forth, and even for evermore.' "

"Them words nigh unto sing, don't they?"

"The other verse is mine, but this one—I believe it is yours. For you traveling everywhere, that God will look out for you."

Rubbing the center of her apron bib, Hope smiled. "Oh, that touches my heart. The forevermore sounds like a fairy tale, but God's better'n all them magic fairies in the made-up stories. 'Tis as if He's sayin' He'll be with me whenever and wherever I go."

"When I was a girl, I dreamed of marrying my prince and living happily ever after." Annie's voice shook. "Everything went wrong."

"I can't blame you for feelin' thataway. You got good cause for feeling things went bad. But that verse ain't talkin' about how a man's gonna carry us through the future. It says God'll be with us. He's all we need."

"Here you go." The doctor polished the lenses of the tiny silver eyeglasses, then carefully put them on Emmy-Lou. "Isn't that much better?"

Wrinkling her nose, Emmy-Lou made the spectacles ride up. "It feels funny."

"But you can see more now, can't you?" The doctor pointed at the calendar hanging on the wall. "What is the picture over there?"

Jakob held his breath and willed her to be all right. A simple pair of eyeglasses? Maybe a dollar and a half—and she'd be right as rain. Hopefulness thrummed through him.

They'd made good time to Abilene, and church had just let out. The doctor graciously agreed to see to Emmy-Lou right away. Good thing, too. Jakob wasn't feeling patient in the least. His precious little girl needed help.

Emmy-Lou tilted her head a bit to the right and blinked. The lenses magnified her eyes. Pointing at the calendar, she asked, "Is that the picture you want me to see?"

"Yes," Jakob and the doctor said in unison.

Emmy-Lou blinked again and leaned forward. "A birdie?"

Doubt and disappointment assailed Jakob. Emmy-Lou hadn't been able to see the calendar at all earlier. Even with the glasses, she couldn't make out the picture well. The doctor seemed young—maybe too young to have enough learning and experience.

"You know your colors and shapes," the doctor said. "Tell your papa how many red squares you see on the shelf by me."

Emmy-Lou turned. Her lips moved as she counted the brick-sized crimson tins that bore Latin inscriptions. "Four. I see four!"

"Excellent. Now why don't you go through the door and talk to my nurse?" The doctor pulled Emmy-Lou from the examination table and set her on the newfangled linoleum floor. He gave her a gentle nudge. "Tell her I said you've been a very good patient, and you may have a candy."

"Oh! Thank you!" Emmy-Lou galloped toward the door.

Once she was gone, the doctor turned to Jakob. "The glasses will help her some. Based on the examination, there's an abnormality inside your daughter's eyes, in the part called the retina."

"Both eyes?" Jakob grabbed at the possibility that it was only one—after all, Emmy-Lou tilted her head. One eye might still be okay. Even if not okay, then not as bad.

"Both." The doctor's stark answer hung in the air.

Grim, Jakob clarified, "So it is bad. But the glasses will fix her vision?"

"No." The doctor met his gaze unflinchingly. "The glasses are so she can maximize what vision is left. This isn't a common problem, so I can't predict what the future holds for her. My hope is that she will stabilize at this point so she doesn't lose whatever vision she currently enjoys."

Jakob rasped, "What do we do to stabilize her? The glasses? Medicine?"

"As I said"—compassion rumbled in the doctor's quiet voice—"the eyeglasses will maximize the vision she currently has. At this time, medical science has nothing to offer that will stop or reverse the damage she's already suffered. As you saw when I tested her vision before giving her the spectacles, Emmy-Lou's vision is severely limited."

Pressing his palm to his forehead, as if to push back the horrible truth, Jakob moaned. "How could this be?"

"Medical science has yet to determine the cause of some maladies. Since no one else in your family history has suffered eye problems, I doubt it is an inherited weakness. You spoke of her suffering a terrible fever last year. I can't be certain, but it might have burned away cells within the eye or robbed those cells of vital nutrients."

"But if that's so, why didn't she change right away? I never noticed my daughter struggling. Neither did my sister. Emmy-Lou does so well."

"I don't doubt that." The doctor picked up the odd contraption he'd used to examine her eyes. "The degeneration has undoubtedly been progressive. Indeed, that is why I believe it might be damage wrought by her illness that took hold and continued to do damage. Instead of a huge overnight change, I suspect the distance and width of her vision field have very slowly diminished. She knows where everything is at home, so she is able to navigate independently."

"But the glasses—they'll keep her from becoming blind." Fear forced Jakob to make it as a statement of fact instead of a question that might garner an unwanted answer.

Setting the medical instrument inside a velvet-lined case, the doctor said in a ponderous tone, "I cannot say whether she'll go completely blind or if she'll stay just as she is."

"You're saying my little Emmy-Lou could become blind?"

"Only the good Lord above knows what the years will bring. But from what I've ascertained, I would be remiss not to inform you that complete blindness is possible. As I've told you, her visual acuity without correction shows significant impairment."

"Is there someone else who should examine her? Maybe one of those specializing doctors?"

"At the risk of sounding like a braggart, you'll not find anyone in the region who is more skilled regarding eye problems. I studied in St. Louis under the nation's leading eye doctor."

"I'll take Emmy-Lou to St. Louis, to him." Desperation mingled with resolve in his voice. He'd mortgage the farm if necessary.

The doctor heaved a heavy sigh. "He's no longer with us. The instruments I used to diagnose your daughter—they belonged to him. His widow gave them to me.

"As for eyeglasses—the Mermod & Jaccard Jewelers in St. Louis ground the lenses to the most exacting of standards. It was quite fortuitous that I had the correct prescription at all, let alone in a child's size."

The idea that any part of this was "fortuitous" struck Jakob as obscene. He gritted his teeth to keep from saying so.

Folding his arms across his chest, the doctor met Jakob's stare. "Your daughter is a happy child. I know the news I've given you is a terrible blow; but for her sake, I recommend you keep a cheerful attitude. In my experience, whatever medical malady befalls a patient is never as crippling as the pity others show in response."

Jakob thrust his hand in his pocket. If it allowed his daughter to see even a little more for a little while, he'd part with every last cent he owned. It didn't mean he had to stand here and listen to such twaddle. "How much—"

The doctor picked up the deep green leather-covered-metal eyeglass case. The entire case didn't even traverse the span of his palm. He opened it, and a small tag inside the black velvet lining showed the exorbitant price of five dollars.

Heavier than iron, Jakob's heart fell clear to his boots. He'd brought all he had—but it wasn't enough.

199

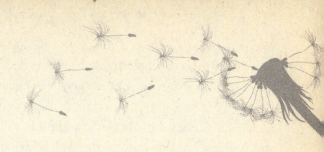

Seventeen

D addy?" Emmy-Lou came back in. The eyeglasses on her looked so foreign. All at once, Jakob both fiercely wanted them for her and hated them. Unaware of his turmoil, she held up her hand. A pair of red candies drooped in the air. "Daddy, the nurse said you can have a piece of licorlish, too!"

"You need to eat your lunch first."

Emmy-Lou's precious little face scrunched. The eyeglasses tilted upward with the action. "But do I still getta eat my cookie, too? I loooove Miss Hope's cookies."

"We'll s—" He caught himself before saying "see." It would be cruel to use that saying around her. "We'll talk about it later."

The doctor bent forward and rested his hands on his knees. "What kind of cookies does Miss Hope bake?"

"Big ones! Great, great, great big ones! We got a extra one 'cuz Auntie Annie didn't come with us. You wanna eat it? Daddy, can he have it?"

"Ja. The satchel is by the door."

"I see it!" Emmy-Lou pointed and hopped about enthusiastically. "I see it. It's right there! I'll get the cookies!"

While she was occupied, Jakob swallowed his pride. In a low tone, he said to the doctor, "About the eyeglasses—"

"After we've eaten." The doctor motioned to Emmy-Lou. "I have a swing on my back veranda. Let's all go there to eat the cookies." As they passed through the doorway, the doctor motioned toward the nurse. "Betty Jo, we're all done here. Why don't you run on home? Betty Jo got married last month."

Jakob mumbled a congratulations.

"Daddy and Phineas and Miss Hope aren't married. Auntie Annie is married, but she takes care of me." Emmy-Lou tugged on the doctor's coat. "Are you married?"

He chuckled. "No, but someday maybe I will be."

"You can wait for me. I'm getting bigger. I'll go to school soon, won't I, Daddy? Then I'll be smart and old enough to get married."

I don't know if she'll go to school. And what man would marry a blind woman? Emmy-Lou will always need someone to help her. Sick at heart, Jakob managed to grunt as a response.

Completely oblivious to anything, Emmy-Lou continued to be her perky self. "You can eat Auntie Annie's sandwich and peach, too. I helped pick the peaches."

"Did you, now?"

"Uh-huh. We gotta lotta peach trees."

"This," the doctor said, "sounds like a fine meal indeed."

"It's a picnic. Miss Hope said it's a picnic."

"Why, yes, we're eating outside. To be sure, that makes it a picnic, and I thank you for inviting me. I was going to make do by opening up a can of something. I'm a terrible cook, so I just eat out of cans."

Emmy-Lou giggled. "You can't do that. Your mouth won't fit! Our horses sometimes eat out of bags. The bags are great big, so—"

"Emmy-Lou." Jakob turned to the physician. "She meant you no insult."

The doctor chuckled. "As hungry as I get sometimes, it's a good thing the cans are small. Otherwise, I might forget my dignity. As it is, I've been known to eat directly from them with a fork."

Sick at heart, Jakob barely tasted his food. Emmy-Lou chattered on about the harvest and her friends and how she helped Annie and Hope.

"So Miss Hope is your housekeeper?"

Only rich people could afford such a luxury. Jakob rasped, "No. She's an itinerant harvest cook."

"Miss Hope's my wishy friend. She'll blow away, but we'll always look at wishies and 'member each other."

The doctor focused his attention on Jakob. "Judging from the bread and chicken salad, she's quite talented. Do you know if she'd like to stop traveling and assume a stable position?"

"Couldn't say."

The doctor took a bite of the oatmeal-raisin cookie. For a second, he stopped chewing, then savored that mouthful. He swallowed. "Send her my way."

Emmy-Lou shook her head. "Miss Hope's gonna stay with us 'til the baby comes. She's gotta, doesn't she, Daddy?"

"Miss Hope's going to have a baby, is she?"

Emmy-Lou giggled. "No. Aunt—"

"We need to settle up and get going." Angry that he'd let the conversation drift to a dangerous topic, Jakob bolted to his feet. "It'll be dark when we get back home."

"I'm not done yet." Emmy-Lou frowned at the peach and cookie nestled in the skirts of her dress.

"You only eat half a sandwich. Give the doctor your other half."

Emmy-Lou promptly handed off the other portion. "I only eat part of my peach, too. They're too big for me to eat all by myself."

Jakob grabbed her peach and thrust it at the doctor while shoving the other half of his own peach into Emmy-Lou's hands. "There."

A smile lit her upturned face. "Now I'll have enough room for my cookie *and* my licorlish!"

"Yes, well, you stay here and nibble on them while I set this food in the kitchen and your papa washes the juice off his hands."

Jakob followed the doctor back inside. As soon as he was sure Emmy-Lou wouldn't hear him, he cleared his throat. "About the glasses. I have two dollars and fifty-three cents with me. I will need to send you the rest."

The doctor shook his head.

Jakob's mouth went dry. "You can trust me."

"I don't doubt that in the least. But the glasses cost two dollars and twenty-five cents."

Desperation and pride warred within Jakob's chest. "I saw the price in the case."

The doctor shrugged. "The tags must have been switched. You'll recall I mentioned the Mermod & Jaccard Jewelers are the manufacturer. In my opinion, no one grinds better optical lenses, but as you might imagine, they also make some embellished spectacles for the fashionable crowd. The marquesite-studded bifocals for a grown woman run five dollars. Simple frames like Emmy-Lou's—especially small ones with such tiny lenses— couldn't possibly cost that much."

Unsure whether the doctor was showing mercy and generosity or if he was making a statement of fact, Jakob decided to be thankful and settle up. "And how much for your examination?"

"Let's see . . ." The doctor grinned. "A picnic lunch. Yes, definitely. And leftovers."

Jakob's eyes narrowed.

The doctor gestured toward the array of canned foods sitting on his kitchen shelf. "Clearly, you've never eaten a can of tomato and beefsteak. We're more than even. I'd appreciate it if you'd tell Miss Hope about me. I'd consider offering her a job."

Jakob paid the doctor. "I can mention you to Hope, but don't anticipate her coming. She's a here-today-gone-next-week kind of woman." Even as he spoke that truth, Jakob wished it wasn't so.

❧

"Welcome home!" Hope hastened down the steps and out into the barnyard. Night was falling fast, and she'd lit lamps in both the kitchen and parlor windows to light Jakob's way home.

Annie trundled after her slowly. "You made it home."

" 'Course we did. Daddy used the great big star in the sky." Emmy-Lou pointed heavenward. "Do you think it's the same star for when Jesus was born? And my special twinkle star?"

"That's the moon." Jakob's tone sounded leaden as he slid Emmy-Lou from his lap into Hope's arms.

"Uh-huh." Emmy-Lou grinned.

Annie came up beside them. "Emmy-Lou, you're wearing glasses."

"Uh-huh." She nodded. "Daddy buyed them from the doctor."

"She's to wear them at all times." Jakob dismounted.

" 'Cept when I'm sleeping."

Hope squeezed Emmy-Lou and gave her a playful shake. "You don't need no glasses when you're asleep on account of your eyes bein' closed, silly. Let's go on in the house so's I can see 'em better. Mr. Stauffer, I got supper waitin' in the warmer. You look like a man in sore need of a hot meal."

"I'm not very hungry," Emmy-Lou said. "Daddy let me eat both pieces of licorlish."

"Then I'll pour you a nice glass of your auntie's wonderful buttermilk and feed you apples and cheese. Soon as you're done, I'll get you all washed up and tucked in."

Phineas strode over, whistling. His gaze met Jakob's, and the tune halted abruptly. He took the reins. "I've got Josephine." As he led the horse toward the barn, he didn't resume whistling.

So it ain't just me thinkin' Mr. Stauffer's lookin' mighty upset.

They went into the house, and Hope set Emmy-Lou on her feet. "Now, let me have a gander at you! Oh my! Them spectacles of yours are a sight for shore eyes."

"Sore eyes," Jakob grated from over by the washstand.

"Her eyes won't be sore, what with her a-wearin' these. Know what, Emmy-Lou? Those glasses of yours look like jewelry for your purdy little face."

"They do," Annie said slowly. She smiled and ran her fingers through Emmy-Lou's mussed curls. "I like them on you. Can you see better now?"

"On the way home I spied all sorts of things. Daddy didn't make me take off my glasses when I napped 'cuz the case was in the satchel, and Daddy watched me and my glasses. When I waked up, I saw his shirt. Daddy forgot to do one of his buttons today. I helped him do it up."

While Annie swiped a damp rag over the little girl, Hope put food on the table. For all of his daughter's chatter, Jakob was notably silent. A long trip would make a body weary—but that didn't account for the strain in his jaw or the way he avoided meeting her gaze. Feeling unsettled, Hope quickly cut and cored an apple. "Y'all come have a bite."

"I gotta go potty."

"I'll take you." Hope reached for her. Taking her out of the house would permit Jakob to tell Annie what was wrong. When she came back, Hope's step faltered.

Holding Annie as she sobbed all over his shirt, Jakob looked up at Hope; then his gaze skidded to his daughter and jerked away.

Emmy-Lou clutched Hope's hand and quavered, "What's a-wrong?"

"Aunt Annie knows you don't like the dark. She's been worried about us riding home at nighttime."

To his credit, Mr. Stauffer hadn't lied. Then again, deep down inside Hope knew that he hadn't completely answered his daughter's innocent question.

"Don't worry." Emmy-Lou left Hope, went over, and wound her arms around Annie's skirts. "I got Jesus in my heart and a special angel to watch over me, and the twinkle moon." Emmy-Lou drew in a deep breath and started singing the verse Hope taught her yesterday, after she'd made the terrible realization something was wrong.

Her childish soprano filled the kitchen.

"Then the traveler in the dark,
Thanks you for your tiny spark,
He could not see which way to go,
If you did not twinkle so,
Twinkle, twinkle, little star . . ."

Hope joined in, "How I wonder what you are."

Jakob rasped, "Emmy-Lou's been singing that on the way home."

Blessedly oblivious, Emmy-Lou piped up, "Uh-huh. I did. And Daddy and me didn't worry—did we, Daddy?"

Jakob eased away from Annie and knelt on the floor. Gathering his daughter close, he pressed his cheek against her hair and held her. "We're home safely."

He hadn't lied. He hadn't said he didn't worry, but his response satisfied Emmy-Lou. She yawned. "I'm tired."

"Then you can just drink some milk, and I'll tuck you in." Annie wiped her eyes and scurried toward the table.

Burrowing close to her father, Emmy-Lou sighed. "Daddy, your tummy is growling like a bear."

"Then maybe he ought to pull up a chair and have hisself some supper."

While Annie put her niece to bed, Jakob silently shoveled his supper into his mouth. Boots grated up the back steps, and Phineas's voice whispered through the open window. "It's me."

"Come in," Jakob rumbled back in a subdued tone.

Hope quickly poured him a cup of coffee and refilled her boss's mug. Phineas slouched down at his usual place at the table, and Hope wavered between sitting down and standing at the stove just so she'd have an excuse to keep moving. Jakob focused on her chair and nodded toward it, so she did as he wished.

The clock ticked.

Upstairs, Annie's murmurings and Emmy-Lou's sleep-slurred words blended into a lull.

Jakob set down his fork. "The glasses will help some, but we don't know how long. Something's wrong. My Emmy-Lou . . ." His Adam's apple bobbed with the swallow he took to steel himself. "She could stay as she is, but in the future, she may be blind."

"So," Phineas said.

"No," Hope moaned at the same time.

"The doctor said nothing can be done." Jakob raked his hand through his hair. "I should have noticed it before now."

"If nothing can be done," Hope looked at him, "then why would it make any difference?"

"I would have been more careful with her. If I had known, she wouldn't have been outside and fallen into that wellhole!"

"You cannot believe that." Phineas drummed his fingers on the tabletop. "How many times have we praised the Lord for delivering her? Would you blame yourself now for something God used for His glory?"

Ignoring that, Jakob stared at the lantern. "My daughter doesn't know the moon isn't a star. She thinks there's just one. She hasn't seen the handiwork of heaven, and she never will. That's just the beginning. She'll miss out on countless things."

"Hold on a second here." Hope propped her elbows on the table and leaned forward. "Your little girl's smart as a quip. She'll catch on to plenty. As for the moon and stars—well, I can understand why that happened. Think on it. You're Mr. Stauffer to me and Jakob to Phineas here and brother to Annie and Daddy to Emmy-Lou. I reckon if one person can have that many handles, it makes sense that she'd think *star* was just a different word for moon. Why, her song is 'bout a star. The Bible tells 'bout that one Christmas star. Plain as can be, she's reasoned things out right smart."

"What does that matter?" Mr. Stauffer shoved his plate away, the scraping sound amazingly loud in the otherwise silent room. "She can't see them. She never will. How could God do this to my little girl? He took her mother and her baby brother. Now He takes her eyesight?"

"You said she might stay the way she is." Phineas continued to drum his fingers on the table. "That is what we'll pray for.

God could let her stay like this. She does fine, and with the glasses—"

"I cannot count on that. Even with the eyeglasses, she still doesn't see everything we do. Why? Why would God do this?"

Hope dared to reach across the table and curled her fingers around her boss's thick wrist. "It's dreadful hard to wrap my mind around this sorrowful thing. I don't much understand it, but if'n I have my druthers, it would be God understanding what's goin' on and me not know rather than the other way around."

He jerked free and bolted to his feet. "I don't want it either way."

"None of us does." Phineas rose. "Did you tell Annie yet?"

"Ja." Jakob bit out the word. "Already her heart was so heavy. This broke her heart."

Slow, heavy footsteps warned them Annie had started down the stairs. Hope cast a glance in that direction and squared her shoulders. "Mr. Stauffer, sir, we're all gonna work together and pray real hard. There's always hope."

His ice blue eyes bore through her. "Is there?"

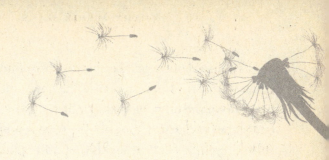

Eighteen

H ow many stars do you see?"

Jakob stopped midstride and stared through the open window at Hope. What was she thinking, to ask Emmy-Lou such a question?

"One, two, three. I see three."

"Yes, there are three." Hope paused a moment, then asked again, "How many stars do you see now?"

"One, two, three. Three."

"Them new eyeglasses of yours are helping you so much. Now tell me. Are they the same stars you counted a minute ago?"

Jakob leaned closer and held his breath. What odd game was Hope playing with his little girl?

"No. These are different stars. The other ones were on red and green. These are on blue."

"You're such a clever little girl! Just 'cuz you can't see them first stars, does that mean they ain't there on the red and green pieces?"

Giggles spilled out of Emmy-Lou. The sound warmed Jakob's heart, but so did her answer. "They are still on the blanket. They're on the other side, that's all."

"You're right. Just 'cuz we don't see something, that don't mean it isn't there. Now lookee here. I'm fixin' to open up my quilt real big. You can find lots of stars on it, and we'll count 'em later today."

When he went inside, Jakob disciplined himself not to look toward the parlor. He didn't want to notice the quilt he'd eavesdropped about. He corrected himself. He didn't want to see Emmy-Lou struggle to see the stars. Instead he looked at Hope. "Phineas and I are leaving now."

"Bound for the Smiths' farm." Hope lowered her voice. "Yesternoon, whilst Annie was taking a catnap, I carried all the eggs over to the Smiths' like you told me. Took 'em a few chickens, too."

"Very good." *In the middle of everything, Hope remembered that detail and saw to it.*

Hope raised her voice slightly. "Before you and Phineas hie off, I made something for you to eat. It'll stick to your ribs 'til lunchtime rolls around." She lifted the overturned mixing bowl on the table to reveal food. "Fried ham 'n egg sandwiches."

"Fine. About today. Emmy-Lou—" He cast a quick glance toward the parlor, where Emmy-Lou had one of her stubby fingers over a star on Hope's quilt. "She should go to Forsaken with her aunt. It would be best."

"But, Daddy, the babies go to Forsaken." Emmy-Lou scrambled over and tugged on his pants leg. "I'm a big girl. Big girls go—"

"Where their father tells them to." The lenses of her glasses magnified the tears filling Emmy-Lou's eyes. He couldn't give in. He had to keep her safe. Things would change now. She was different and had to be protected. *Resilience. Children have resilience. She'll learn to get used to things being different.*

Hope hunkered down—not a feminine pose in the least, but she balanced easily on her scuffed boots and tapped Emmy-Lou's shoulder. "That daddy of yours is doin' you a mighty big favor. Why, he's lettin' you go with your auntie. This way, you'll know all about what's gotta be done for a baby. You and me are gonna share the job of helpin' your auntie when the time comes for her to have hers."

"Yeah! I'm gonna be a big helper."

"You shore are." Hope stood up. "But for now, we need to let your daddy get goin'. Him and Phineas are gonna go do a bunch of man work."

As he headed toward his neighbor's farm, Jakob kept thinking of how Hope smoothed things over for Emmy-Lou. She'd twisted Emmy-Lou's disappointment into delight. But Hope wouldn't always be there to distract Emmy-Lou. The time would come—and soon—when they'd watch Hope leave.

He wouldn't be able to shield his daughter from the sadness to come. Today was just the first of countless times and things she would have to give up.

Why, God? Why?

Men milled about the Smith barnyard, eating hard-boiled eggs and coffee cake. The good-natured conversation came to an abrupt halt when Jakob rode in. Daisy grabbed her husband's hand, and Gramma called out, "Phineas asked us to pray for Emmy-Lou at church yesterday. How is she?"

Myriad answers shot through his mind. Jakob hadn't yet thought about what to tell others. Emmy-Lou would need their help at times. He couldn't let his pride stand in the way of that. But the doctor warned about the crippling effects of pity. Jakob cleared his throat. "There's a problem with her eyes. I bought her glasses, but my Emmy-Lou—she still cannot see as well as we do."

Mr. Toomel tapped the arm of his own spectacles. "If it weren't for these, I'd be blind as a bat."

The chuckles lashed Jakob. "Blindness is not funny." His voice shook with anger.

Gramma broke the uneasy silence. "Jakob, is Emmy-Lou going blind?"

"The doctor couldn't say."

"We'll all keep an eye on your little girl today"—compassion filled Daisy's voice—"and always."

"I'm obliged, but Emmy-Lou is going to Forsaken with her aunt. It is best that way."

As the day started out, and again at lunch, Smith prayed. He mentioned Emmy-Lou in his prayers. As lunch ended and the men headed back to the wheat field, a gaggle of little girls dashed up. Flipping a braid over her shoulder, Lottie Richardson said, "Will you bring Emmy-Lou to play with us tomorrow at my house?"

Before he could answer, Gramma sauntered by with an empty cake plate. "Of course he will. You girls let Mr. Stauffer get back to work and come help me. I baked a little cake special just for you, so you can all have a tea party."

Jakob watched them all skip away. Gramma overstepped herself by determining where Emmy-Lou would go tomorrow. Emmy-Lou needed to be watched carefully. But Jakob couldn't help but ask himself, *Then why am I upset that Emmy-Lou isn't here to enjoy the tea party?*

❧

Chattering like a magpie, Emmy-Lou wiggled into her chair at the supper table. "Babies cry lots and lots. Mrs. Sanderson's little girl crawls really fast. I chased her today, Daddy. I did. I caught her before she went up the stairs, didn't I, Auntie?"

"Ja. It was a good thing you did."

"I take it things went well?" Jakob looked at his sister but tilted his head toward Emmy-Lou.

"Ja." Annie slid her napkin in her lap as if the question and answer were nothing more than mere polite conversation.

Frustrated, Jakob didn't feel like praying. "Phineas, ask the blessing."

As Annie passed the platter with the bierocks to him, Phineas told her, "Marcella made her prune cake today again, and I hope she does every day. Volkner used to take a big wedge of your peach pie, but now he's eating Marcella's cake and leaving more for me."

"Does she remember his name is Leopold now instead of Peter?" Annie took a meager spoonful of peas.

"Merciful heavens, yes." Hope served Emmy-Lou, then herself before passing the platter to Jakob. "Everything she says starts with 'Leopold.' If it weren't so much fun to see them courtin', it might grate on a body's nerves. Can't hold it against her, though. The gal's pert near aglow with love."

"She'd better get her fill of him now." Jakob cut into the meat-filled cabbage leaves. "Tomorrow and Wednesday, we'll harvest her father's wheat, then Leopold will have to move on. His family needs the money."

"Betcha he stays with the Richardsons as long as folks in this township are harvestin'." Hope moved Emmy-Lou's cup.

Jakob stared at the cup. How many times had Hope moved it? Almost every single meal since she'd come. And before then, if no one else was fast enough to catch it, she spilled her milk. *I was such an idiot not to determine she couldn't see.*

Phineas raised his fork but stopped short of taking the bite. "Patterson was wondering if Richardson's so-called nephews will stay awhile longer, or if we'll be back down to two reapers when we go on to his spread."

"Lena asked while us gals were eatin' lunch. One of the boys'll go back to his pa's farm, and the other one's gonna finish up this township. I'm a-feared that poor Linette's gonna get her heart broke. She was hoping the one who ain't spoken for Kathleen would ask for her. I spied him smilin' at one of the other gals, though."

"Life doesn't always give you what you want."

Ignoring the surly edge in his tone and Annie's gasp, Hope said, "Well, I'm wantin' a dash of salt. Do y'all think I can get that?"

Embarrassed by his outburst, Jakob reached for the saltshaker. "Here."

As Hope sprinkled salt on her rice, she changed the subject. "Annie did some sewin' today on Sydney Creighton's newfangled sewing machine. It bottles the mind to think anyone can get that much stitchin' done in such short order."

"Boggles, not bottles." As soon as he said that, Jakob regretted correcting Hope. *I oughtta keep my mouth shut.*

"When you bottle somethin', you seal it up tight so nothin' more can get in. What happens when you boggle something?"

"Ja, Daddy. What happens?"

It would be rude not to answer—even if he'd just decided to stay silent. "Boggle is another word for confuse or jumble something up." *Messing up sayings isn't just a quirk Hope has. If Emmy-Lou can't read, she'll probably mess up on sayings.*

"Boggle. Shore sounds close to gobble. Only I wouldn't want anythin' to gobble my mind, so I reckon I'll 'member me the difference. Emmy-Lou, lemme show you a trick." Hope covered Emmy-Lou's hand and pressed the fork down on the rice. "This'll make the rice stick together better. Now use your bread like a wall so's the fork will scoop up the rice and make it to your mouth. There."

"I did it!"

"Yup."

Emmy-Lou finished that bite and started pressing down the rest of her rice. "Phineas, I'm learning to count up-up-up high. Hope's special quilt has lotsa stars. Me and her and Auntie Annie didn't unfold all of it yet, so I don't know how many more there are. I found eighteen so far."

"Eighteen." Phineas nodded gravely.

"God made lotsa stars in the sky. We can't see all of them, either. I counted the blankets for Aunt Annie's baby. She gots seven now, only she won't use all of them on the baby at the same time."

"Then she'll have plenty, won't she, Jakob? Naomi made a mountain of clothes for the babies. They have to be around here somewhere."

"No." Jakob glared straight through his farmhand. "None of them remain." In his grief, he'd gotten rid of all of Naomi's clothing and all of the baby gowns and blankets. Having them there mocked him, drove home the fact that he'd never again have his beloved wife by his side, his namesake, or any more children. He shoved away from his half-eaten supper. "I have chores to see to."

⁊ↄ

Hope drove to town on Wednesday to deliver the eggs and milk to the general store. With that chore accomplished, she turned Hattie down the road toward the Richardson farm.

Emmy-Lou sprawled on the mule cart seat beside Hope. "I see a birdie."

"It's a hawk. If'n you listen, you'll find every bird talks different from all the other kinds. Hear that purdy song? That's a lark. That hawk's up in the sky a-screamin' so's he can scare a little mouse into running. Then he'll swoop on down and catch that mouse for his supper."

Hope stopped the cart at Forsaken Ranch just long enough to hand off some fabric to Annie. "Your brother asked me to get this for you to make baby clothes. Don't forget that I'll help you stitch 'em."

As she helped serve lunch at the Richardsons', Hope murmured to Jakob, "I got that cloth you wanted for your sis. Whilst I was in town, the mercantile man gave me this letter what come for you."

Jakob accepted the envelope, took one glance at it, and shoved it in his pocket. "Fine."

He looked anything but fine. Hope didn't ask him why, though. He'd been in a foul mood ever since Sunday. The past few days, he'd grunted and growled instead of talked. It was a good thing they were in the middle of harvest, just so Annie wouldn't have to be around him. As it was, she'd suddenly reverted to being timid—at least when her brother was around. Well, no use letting his dark mood spoil the day. Hope picked up an empty bowl and headed back toward the Richardson kitchen.

Linette practically pounced on her when she entered the house. Dragging her toward the pantry, Linette squeaked, "We have to talk!"

"What's a-wrong with us talkin' in the kitchen?"

Cheeks flushed, Linette shook her head. "Papa asked if Phineas can stay over tonight. He's good with machinery, and one of the reapers needs some sort of work!"

"He's good with that sorta stuff."

"I saw Phineas watching me today. Maybe he's *the one*." Linette pressed her hands to her bosom. "You have to tell me all about him!"

"I don't wanna hurt your feelings none, but I gotta be dead honest with you. Phineas might be the one what fixes the reaper, but he ain't a man set on romance. More likely, he was hungry and lookin' at whatever you was totin' out for lunch. That man shorely does like to eat."

"But don't you see? That's all the better! I'm a good cook. I don't want to sound haughty, but truly, I know my way around a kitchen. We'll make such a good couple!"

Hope sighed.

"Mama says the way to a man's heart is through his stomach, and she's right—look at Marcella and Leo. What's Phineas's favorite dish? I'll fix it for him!"

The pantry door whispered open.

Hope wheeled around, ready to escape from the awkward situation. Instead, Mrs. Richardson pressed in and leaned on the door to shut it. "Linette? Did you ask her?"

"She was just going to tell me, Mama."

"Mrs. Richardson, ma'am, I was just tellin' your daughter here that Phineas is a man what knows his own mind."

A giddy laugh bubbled out of Mrs. Richardson.

This ain't goin' none too good.

"We'll make sure Linette gives him exactly what he likes. So if he were a dying man, what would he want for his last meal?"

He might wish he was dead if'n Linette chases after him. Hope tamped down that uncharitable thought. "If'n he was passin' on, eatin' probably wouldn't be much on his mind. You gotta 'scuse me, but—"

"Oh, just a minute." Linette grabbed her arm. "What does he like?"

"Whatever you was a-totin's probably a safe guess."

"Peach pie." Linette's hold on her arm tightened. "It was peach pie. Can I come home with you and pick some peaches? Then I can bake Phineas—"

Hope let out a desperate laugh. "Bein' out in the sun all day, I reckon all them men feel baked clear through."

"Then nothing would be more refreshing . . ." Mrs. Richardson started.

"Than fresh peach pie!" Linette said exultantly.

"I need to get outta here. Gotta keep an eye on Emmy-Lou." The words had no more left her mouth than a child started crying.

"That's my girl!" Desperate to get to Emmy-Lou, Hope wrestled out of the pantry and into the kitchen. Marcella was coming up the back steps, holding Emmy-Lou in her arms. "What happened?"

"Miss Hope!" Emmy-Lou pushed away from Marcella, clung to Hope, and wailed.

"It's her knee," Marcella said in a stricken tone. "I let Lottie and Mandy hold her hands, so I thought it would be okay if she jumped rope."

"Merciful heavens."

"There were only jumping 'Blue Bells.' " Marcella's explanation sounded more like a plea for absolution.

Hope didn't bother to reassure her at the moment. Right now, Emmy-Lou needed help. Hope twisted toward the sink, only to recall the Richardsons didn't have a kitchen pump. They carried water in from the yard pump. She plopped down in a chair, cuddled Emmy-Lou, and ordered, "Somebody, get me a stack of nice, clean cloths and a bucket of water."

Emmy-Lou nestled close and clung to her. "Owwwweeee!"

"Lemme have a look-see." She flipped up the hem of Emmy-Lou's dress and forced a laugh. "Goodness, Emmy-Lou, you got enough dirt on you to plant a whole row of 'tatoes."

"Owwwiieee!"

"Owww. Owww. Ooowwooo!" Hope repeated the sounds again. Looking at her with huge eyes, Emmy-Lou gasped and panted.

"Wait a second here." Hope pretended to be scandalized. "Y'all start howlin' like a coyote, and when I join in, you quiet down?"

"Emmy-Lou wasn't being a coyote; she sounded more like a wolf to me." Linda brought over a bucket of water.

"Onliest wolf I ever heard makin' that kind of racket done it 'cuz a skunk sprayed him." Hope accepted a clean cloth from someone and dipped it in the water. Emmy-Lou shuddered in her arms. "Lookee here, Emmy-Lou. Now that we got all the dirt off, it ain't hardly nothin'. You got scared is all, didn't you?"

Emmy-Lou bit her lip and doubled over to look.

"My knee is like yours." Mandy hiked up her skirt to display a scab and tacked on, "Mine is bigger."

While Hope dabbed witch hazel on the scrape, she listened to Emmy-Lou and Mandy assure Lottie that when she scraped her knee, she'd get to howl like a wolf too. An hour later, as they took their leave, Emmy-Lou hugged Lottie and again promised her someday she'd have a chance to howl. Hope smothered her smile and lifted Emmy-Lou into the mule cart.

She'd only been back on the Stauffer farm long enough to tuck Emmy-Lou in for a nap when Annie got home. "You oughtta go take a nap yourself, Annie."

"Actually, I'd like to work outside for a while. I spent most of my time at Forsaken, rocking babies. If I don't move around a bit, I won't be able to fall asleep tonight."

Hope steadied herself with a deep breath and confessed, "I oughtta tell you, your niece skinned her knee today."

"Is she okay?"

"Other than a spot about yea big"—Hope pinched her forefinger to her thumb to form a dime-sized space—"on her little knee, she's fine. I feel bad about it."

"I would too." A timid smile flickered across Annie's face. "But I'm glad she got to go play with her friends today. She doesn't have many chances to be with them."

"They all dote on her."

Emmy-Lou took a longer-than-usual afternoon nap while Annie picked pole beans and Hope weeded. Annie paused a moment and straightened up.

"You okay?" Hope stared at her large belly. Velma said the baby could come anytime, but Hope thought it would be nice for the child to wait another week or two, though she figured Annie was hot and tired and wishin' that babe would just come.

"I am . . ." Annie's voice died out. Her hand went up to shade her eyes. "Why is my brother home so early?"

Hope rose and turned to see Jakob dismount.

He normally had a powerful, long stride—but the barnyard dirt kicked up in small puffs around his boots as he stormed toward them. Yanking off his straw work hat, he revealed a clenched jaw and flashing eyes. His jaw unhinged just long enough for him to bark, "Hope!"

"Yes?"

"Where's my Emmy-Lou?"

"Takin' her nap." Hope dusted off her hands.

"She gets hurt so much that her friend tells me she howled like a wolf, and you don't get me? You don't even tell me?" He stopped glowering at her just long enough to cast a fleeting look at the upstairs bedroom window, then locked his focus on her again. "You were supposed to keep her safe."

"She got a scraped knee—"

"And whose fault is that? You were to watch her."

Hope tore her attention from him just long enough to take in how white Annie had gone. She fixed her gaze back on her boss and narrowed her eyes, then flashed a sideways glance at his sister.

He didn't respond to her cue but kept right on. "Emmy-Lou and Annie—you are to watch them and do the cooking. If it is too much, say so and leave."

Annie gasped.

"Don't you worry none, Annie." Hope pinched the inside elbow of her own sleeves and savagely yanked them to pull the cuffs higher. "Onliest place I aim to go is to the pump to wash my hands afore I take the linens off the line. Think you could go punch down the bread dough? I'd shorely appreciate it." Hope didn't wait for an answer. She walked off.

A moment later, her hands dripping dry as she headed for the clothesline, she heard Mr. Stauffer's distinctive step. Instead of pivoting toward him, she veered to the far side of the clothesline. *What is it about that man? Well, whatever it is, I won't have to figure it out. He's gettin' rid of me.*

All too soon, he came around the sheets to stand mere feet away.

Plucking a clothespin from the first pillowcase, she hissed, "You go on and vent your spleen, but don't you go bellowin' at me. Your sis don't need that."

"Don't you think I know that?"

Hope cocked a brow.

"You gave your word to watch my daughter." Fury vibrated in his words.

"All children get scrapes. I—"

"All *normal* children. Emmy-Lou—she can't see."

He'd already said she was leaving, so she might as well speak her piece. Hope yanked the pillowcase from the line. "She *can* see. Not as good as other kids, but Emmy-Lou can still see. You're the one who was moanin' over how she can't see and do all the things everybody else did. Best thing for her is to let her do as much as she can." Hope stared at him, meeting his heated gaze with resolve. "She was playin' with her friends and havin' a good time. You can't take that from her."

"She—"

"Got a scraped knee, nothin' more. When she wakes up, you can check her out for yourself. It ain't even a big scrape. 'Tis hardly anything at all." Three savage folds, and the pillowcase lay in the wicker basket at her feet. Hope reached for the next one. "The day I got here, I told you I didn't stay when the man of the house wanted different. That ain't changed. I reckon I spouted off too quick tellin' Annie that I wasn't goin' anywhere."

"So just like that, you'll leave?"

Thickheaded man! Hope didn't answer. She didn't trust herself to answer. She grabbed one end of a sheet and lifted it over itself. By walking along the line, she managed to fold it in half before pulling it free.

"You made a pact. That was your word—a pact. To take care of Emmy-Lou and Annie. You would break your word?"

"I'm not breakin' my word, and I don't like you callin' me a liar." She turned to the side so the breeze would stop working against her. Though sorely tempted to turn a little more so she'd give him her back, Hope resisted the urge. He had a lot of nerve trying to toss her promises back at her when he was shoving her out the door.

"If you leave, you've broken your word."

"Our pact was to work *together*, Mr. Stauffer. You're the one what just told me to leave, and I will. But afore I do, I'm fixin' to finish up with this here laundry and make shore supper's ready to be put on the table. Just in case you didn't notice, Annie's more tireder than a wound-down clock."

He made an odd sound.

Hope didn't look at him. Couldn't look at him. She'd worked hard for him and his kin. Even with him getting grouchy, he didn't have grounds to accuse her of having slacked or been a sluggard—but he had. That was bad enough. But his implying that she'd neglected Emmy-Lou and Annie—that hurt worse. Her work-chapped hands snagged on the delicately tatted edge of the next pillowcase. Of all things, the embroidery on it depicted a dove carrying an olive branch—the symbol for peace. *Now, there's a joke.*

Mr. Stauffer heaved a deep tested-to-the-limits sigh.

Hope practically tore the pillowcase off the line. "You ain't the onliest one round here who's worried or hot or tired. I'd take it kindly if'n you'd just keep your distance 'til I tell your sis and Emmy-Lou good-bye."

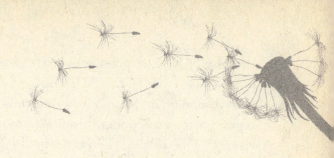

Nineteen

Grit. The grit embedded at the rim of his jagged nails dug into his palms, making him aware he'd fisted his hands. Slowly, Jakob forced his fingers to unfurl. He didn't budge, though.

He stared at Hope. Wild wisps of hair spun about her face and neck. Other than her green Sunday-best dress, she owned none other than the ugly brown one she now wore. Faded, limp, and damp, it bespoke a woman who'd labored hard and rested little, if at all. A fair breeze made the sheets puff. *She did all this laundry this morning, then took the milk and eggs to town before coming to the Smiths' to help feed the men. She's started bread and has supper planned and was weeding.*

Hope shoved the just-folded pillowcase into the basket and jerked the clothespins off the next sun-bleached sheet. Though she didn't spare him a glance, the set of her jaw made her feelings abundantly clear.

"I'm mad as a bold wet hen, but the Good Book says to be angry and sin not. Well, if'n y'all don't step away, I'm gonna have to, else I'll have to spend hours on my knees beggin' God for forgiveness."

Jakob turned on his heel and strode away.

Stopping at the water pump, he unbuttoned his shirt. Particles of wheat filled the air about him as he shook it out. After hastily washing up, he yanked on the shirt and fastened up the buttons as he headed back toward the housekeeper.

With things as tense as they'd gotten, it didn't seem right to address her by her given name. "Miss Ladley."

Her arms froze in midair. She dipped her head for a moment, sucked in a deep breath, then resolutely went back to her task.

He reached up and pinched the top of a clothespin. Instead of being smooth, the wood was weathered and brittle. *I need to buy new ones. There are so many little things I haven't noticed.* He copied how Hope folded the sheet over itself on the line. She made it look easy; his came out lopsided. "About the work you've done—"

"You don't gotta say nothin' more. I ain't never been pushed off a job afore, but you know what they say. There's a worst time for everything."

His hands stilled for a moment. She'd done it again. Distracted him with her zany sayings—but if ever one fit the situation, this was it. "Miss Ladley, you're right. There's a worst time for everything. I can't think of a worse time for you to leave than now."

She shook her head. "Timin' works out purdy good for you. I 'magine you can get Katherine and Marcella Richardson over here to help now. With them both bespoken, they'd be the best choice."

"I spoke in haste."

"Yeah, you did."

Any other woman would have demurred or cried. Not Hope. Her directness was refreshing. Even so, he didn't try to make light about her recommending the Richardson girls. Hope's sense of humor was arguably one of her best traits, but this wasn't a time to test that opinion. Jakob watched as she capably folded, flipped, and disciplined her sheet into a tidy block. He tried the same moves with his sheet and almost dropped it. Seconds later, it ended up a bundled mess against his chest.

Hope's well-disciplined sheet went into the basket. She still didn't look him in the eye but focused on the mess he held and gingerly took it away. Even though he'd shaken out his shirt, it was still dirty—and now the freshly washed sheet bore smudges.

He winced. "I'm making a mess of everything."

"Then that's two of us." She flipped that sheet over the line to get it out of the way and went after the next one. "You and me don't see eye to eye, but Emmy-Lou's your daughter. You got the responsibility and right to decide what's best for her."

"I'm worried about her."

"Yup."

He reached for another clothespin. The housekeeper gave him a stern look, and he backed away. He'd already made more than enough mistakes.

"You've a right to know what happened. Emmy-Lou's got herself a skinned-up knee. I reckon you're right 'bout it bein' my fault. Linette dragged me in the pantry. She and her mama cornered me there. Mr. Stauffer, I don't wanna be a gossipmonster, but they was pestering me about Phineas. Linette's got it in her mind that he's anglin' for her, and she's plannin' to chase him 'til he catches her. Emmy-Lou—she fell and hurt herself whilst them Richardson women was plannin' Phineas's last supper as a bachelor."

"You were in the pantry."

Hope's head dipped. "If'n I was bein' dead-level honest, I'd have to say the guilt's ridin' me hard. 'Tis likely why your words bother me so much. If'n I'd gotten outta there, I woulda known what Emmy-Lou was up to."

"You shouldn't feel guilty; I should. Once they are set on something, the Richardsons are immovable. I gave you no chance to explain."

"But I wasn't doin' my most importantest job."

"Lionel Volkner—Leopold's brother—wrote in his letter of recommendation that he'd never seen a woman work harder. I agree with him. The industry you've shown has been outstanding." Apologizing didn't come easy, but Jakob knew he had to. He owed her at least that much. "Anger made me say things I shouldn't have."

"You was angry. I probably deserve that anger, but 'twasn't anger behind most of what happened. At least, to my mind, it wasn't. You cherish your daughter and sis. From the time you heard Emmy-Lou got hurt 'til you got home, you must've been thinkin' all sorts of dreadful bad things that could be a-wrong with her. Since I didn't talk to you 'bout the problem whilst I was still over at the Smiths', you couldn't know 'twasn't nothin' more than a scrape. But even so, I ain't proved up to be trustworthy."

"That isn't true." Jakob shoved his hands in his pockets to keep from doing something stupid. Like putting a hand over her mouth so he could finish his apology instead of her yammering on. Or grabbing her and shaking some sense into her. Only he knew better. He'd never manhandle anyone. If he grabbed her, he'd—

In that second, he stared at her in shock. *I was ready to take hold and kiss her.*

The realization stunned him. His whole life, there'd only been Naomi. He'd never so much as asked another gal out for a Sunday stroll, but here he was, practically nose to nose with a woman whose spontaneity brought him to the brink of insanity. *What's so insane about me having feelings for her? She's all I could ever want for in a woman.* Mute with wonderment, Jakob drank in the golden fire in her beautiful hazel eyes and the smattering of freckles that he suddenly had the urge to trace, count, and even kiss.

Her gaze dropped as the corners of her mouth turned downward. "You don't gotta search so hard to try to find somethin' to say. More words won't change what happened." Leaden steps carried her away from him to one last sheet.

"Listen to me!" Once he bellowed the words, Jakob stomped toward her.

Hope spun around. Eyes alight with fire and body tensed like a lioness ready to pounce, she growled, "You hush your tone! Annie's already scared half silly."

I was a fool to think for even an instant she wouldn't protect Emmy-Lou and Annie. This woman has such fire and spirit! She's been under my roof and by my side at the table for days, yet I never noticed . . .

"Hold whatever opinion you want about me, but think about your sis."

Hope, if you knew what I was thinking . . .

A slow, deep breath forced his housekeeper's shoulders up, then they settled back into her usual take-on-the-world posture—not the round, stoop-shouldered stance of a weary woman.

Just as surely as she's kept Annie from the burden of too much work, she's shielded me from knowing how tired she's become from doing it all.

"Your sis—it's bad for her to see folks that can't get along. In the end, you was right." Hope turned back toward the laundry. "It's all for the best, me goin' my way."

"What is it about you and me and this clothesline?" In utter frustration, he reached up and yanked on it. "The other time we were out here, you thought I was trying to send you off and I wanted to hire you. Now I want you to stay and you're—"

She wheeled around. "Don't. Don't go decidin' to keep me on 'til your sis is back on her feet after havin' her baby unless you know I'm a-gonna mess up again, because sure as shootin' I will."

A slow smile tugged at his mouth, making his sunburned cheeks sting. "Don't you agree to stay unless you realize I'm going to mess up again, too."

Her eyes widened. The fiery glint in the hazel turned to a humorous sparkle as a smile very slowly bowed her lips and made all her freckles dance. "Oh, we are a pair, aren't we?"

"Ja." *In more ways than you know.*

⚭

Jakob strode across his bedroom, over to the oak dresser. Just before Naomi and the children contracted the fever, he'd splurged on a dress length of fabric at the mercantile. All of Naomi's gowns had been made of feed sacks, and he'd wanted her to have something extra-special—only he hadn't had the opportunity to give her the material.

Jakob knelt, opened the bottom drawer, and reached for the fabric. He'd never seen a plaid like it—the stripes going both directions couldn't be wider than Emmy-Lou's smallest finger. Women probably had fancy names for the colors—they always seemed to; but the two shades of blue, the green, and the gold crisscrossed together and created a wealth of tiny squares in countless rich shades.

Hope would look lovely in a dress made from it. The door slid shut, and Jakob rose. Instead of avoiding looking at the wedding-ring quilt on his bed, he laid the material on it and lifted the picture of Naomi he treasured so. "I'll always love you," he whispered gruffly. He studied her features and recalled how the serenity he saw etched there came from deep within her.

The turmoil he felt at having discovered his feelings for Hope ought to intensify now, but they didn't. Instead, everything shifted into place. God's Word said it wasn't good for a man to be alone. Having once known the blessings of a happy marriage, Jakob realized that instead of the memories holding him back, they nudged him forward.

"You would like her, Naomi. I know you would." As he lifted the fabric, he remembered the evening when Hope asked him questions about Naomi and listened as he shared about what a fine wife he'd had.

Hope won't ever replace Naomi. No one could. But life has changed. So have I. There's room in my heart for love again because there's Hope.

When he went back downstairs, Jakob found his sister in the parlor. Though she held a needle and a tiny white gown in her lap, she wasn't sewing. *I was a fool. She was starting to feel safe, and I scared her.* Jakob knew just what to do. A simple gesture would reassure his sister. He laid the fabric in her lap. "This is for Hope. For a dress."

Annie shoved it off her lap onto the floor. "No! I won't do it. I won't give it to her!" Then she burst into tears.

Perplexed, Jakob stared at his sister. "Annie! *Was ist los?*"

"What's the matter? You ask me what's the matter?" She sucked in a choppy breath. "Do you think I don't recognize what you're doing? Konrad did the same thing. He got angry. He'd shout. Oh—I heard you shout at Hope. Only soon, it wasn't just his voice that he'd raise at me—it was his fist."

Her stark words horrified him. Until now, Annie hadn't been forthcoming about anything other than that Konrad struck her on multiple occasions. Knowing it was too painful for her to talk about and wanting to let her put it all in her past, Jakob hadn't prodded her to say anything more than she chose to volunteer. In those few sentences, she confirmed what he'd suspected. "Annie," he groaned.

Cringing into the back of the settee, Annie stared at him with tear-drenched eyes. "Afterward, Konrad would be sorry. He'd give me a gift. The present was to prove he was sorry—only his sorrow never lasted. I won't give Hope your present. I don't want her to stay. I want her to go!"

Jakob groaned again, pushed aside the material, and took his sister's hands in his. "I'm not like that. It's not that way between Hope and me."

When he finally managed to allay her fears, Jakob said, "You're tired."

Nodding heavily, Annie wiped her face with her soggy hanky.

"Go up and nap." He thought for a moment. "Emmy-Lou is still sleeping. You can lie down on my bed." He rose and helped her to her feet.

Then suddenly, he stiffened.

૨૦

Hope carried the laundry into the house. Through the window, she could see Jakob streaking off on his horse like the devil was after him. Then she heard crying. Heart thundering and mouth dry, Hope dropped the laundry basket and raced up the stairs.

Annie lay curled on her side on Jakob's bed. A whole stack of Jakob's handkerchiefs lay on the pillow beside her.

Please, God, don't let her be having the baby yet. Everything's not ready. I'm not ready. Hope dampened the towel on Jakob's washstand and gingerly blotted Annie's face. "Are you okay?"

Annie shook her head.

Desperate to know Annie wasn't in labor, Hope grasped at the one other possible reason her friend would be crying. "Your brother and me—we ain't mad at each other. We got everything worked out. You know that?"

Annie nodded; then a strangled sound vibrated in her chest as she curled up tighter.

Sweat broke out on Hope's brow. Wiping Annie's, she searched for something to say or do. *God, please help me here.*

"I want to be alone."

"You shore?"

Annie nodded.

Uncertain as she felt, Hope reckoned she couldn't do any good just standing there. "I'll . . ." She looked around, but nothing triggered any helpful action or suggestion. Trying to instill more confidence than she felt, Hope started again. "I'll leave the door open."

Hope peeped in on Emmy-Lou. Blessedly ignorant of any of the goings-on, the little girl still napped. Assured of that, Hope dashed downstairs.

Boiling water. Folks always needed boiling water and towels for when a baby came. Everyone knew that. Hope hastily dumped more coal into the oven. Black dust covered the floor by the scuttle, but she didn't worry over that. Other matters

235

were more pressing. With the reservoir on the stove full, Hope pumped the largest kettles in the house full of water and set them on, too. That done, she set about gathering towels.

The stack of towels on the dining table looked meager. Hope added all the clean dishcloths. Annie would need fresh sheets on the bed after the birthing, and they were all sitting in the laundry basket—wrinkled as an old woman's face. Hope weaseled the iron onto the stove, too.

Whenever she paused for a moment, she could hear Annie's soft crying.

Lord, please get Jakob to Forsaken real fast and have Velma ready so she can hurry back. I don't know what to do. I probably shoulda asked her before now. I'm so stupid. How can I help Annie when I don't know what to do?

Every few seconds, Hope glanced out the window. Each time, she told herself it was too soon for Jakob to be back, but she wanted his help. His wife had given him two babies. Surely he had to know something about birth!

Suddenly so much needed to be done. Annie would need a hearty meal after her ordeal. But a loaf of bread would take longer to bake, and Hope wasn't sure they'd have time. She whacked the dough into pieces and stuck them in the oven.

"Now supper!" Focusing on something she could accomplish easily, she pulled out a roasting pan. Quickly dumping in several things, Hope knew it could stew in the oven for hours without burning. Her mind was awhirl with more fears than thoughts.

She looked down in dismay at the unappetizing mess in the pan. She'd dumped a cup of farmer cheese atop the chunks of canned roasted beef. "No use cryin' over spilt milk," she muttered as she reached for some spices. Trying to figure out how to rescue supper, Hope kept adding something more to the roasting pan.

Hope sniffed. Something was starting to smell. . . . "The buns!"

She ripped open the oven door and yanked out the cookie sheet. With towels all over the table, she couldn't cool the buns there. She had no more carried the buns toward the counter than the floorboard above her creaked.

"Annie?!" Hope dropped the cookie sheet and ran upstairs.

Bracing one hand on Jakob's dresser and the other against her belly, Annie looked more miserable than anyone Hope had ever seen. As Hope crossed the bedchamber, Annie turned away, stilled, then let out a wail.

The hair stood up on the back of Hope's neck. *Lord, she ain't ready for this. I ain't ready, neither, God.*

A small hand slid into Hope's. "Auntie Annie, what's a-wrong?"

Stifling a cry, Annie straightened up. "I need to . . . g-go."

"Oh!" Relief flooded Hope. Then another thought hit her. *The last thing we need is Annie birthin' her babe in the outhouse.* "Emmy-Lou, you be a big helper. Go fetch the chamber pot."

" 'Kay." Emmy-Lou gave Hope a hug about her thighs and left.

Look at me, bein' a coward. My friend needs help. But what in thunderation can I do? "Maybe we ought to tuck you back in bed." *Now that was dumb. She's gotta stay up so's she can use the—*

Shaking her head, Annie whispered, "I have my shoes on."

"I'll help you take 'em off." Hope steered Annie back toward the bed. Suddenly Annie halted and pressed her hand to her belly. She sucked in a loud breath and held it.

Even the light breeze blowing through the window did nothing to cool the streak of hot terror Hope felt. Unable to see around Annie, Hope strained to hear the sound of an approaching horse. Surely, Jakob had to be back with Velma soon!

A wobbly smile chased across Annie's pale features. "The baby—he's strong."

"Good. Good. You want a healthy one." Hope nudged her onto the edge of the bed and flopped onto the floor. It took half of forever to loosen the laces twining up the black boots to above Annie's ankles.

"I got it!" Emmy-Lou carried in the chamber pot as if it she was presenting a magnificent trophy.

"Thank you." Annie's voice sounded strained.

She ain't having another pang. She can't. It's too soon. It's just her working to wriggle and yank her foot free from this here boot.

"Emmy-Lou, go get your spectacles," Annie said.

With a laugh, Emmy-Lou set down the chamber pot. "I forgot about my glasses!"

As she scampered across the hall, Annie suddenly curled forward and let out a garbled cry.

"Whaddy'all want me to do?" Hope pushed aside the now-empty boots and shot to her feet.

Teeth gritted and air chuffing between them, Annie said, "Leg. Cramp."

After rubbing out the cramp, Hope helped Annie to her feet. "I'm gonna turn down this here bed for you."

"We haven't started supper yet."

"Don't you worry none over that. I've got something started." *Just don't ask what it is.*

Emmy-Lou tugged on Hope's apron. "Could we have noodles?"

"Ohhh. Noodles sound good." Right after speaking those words, Annie leaned against the dresser again. "You help Hope make supper, Emmy-Lou."

"I'm a good helper!"

Annie nodded and made a shooing gesture. Emmy-Lou left, and Hope wavered in the doorway. "Are you sure—"

Biting her lower lip, Annie looked her in the eye and nodded.

"I don't wanna leave you on your lonesome. It don't seem right."

Annie knew her mind, so Hope lagged back down the stairs. Every other step, she wanted to turn around and run back upstairs to help her friend. On the alternate steps, she fought the urge to pick up her skirts to dash out of the house and get as far away as possible.

Standing in the kitchen, Emmy-Lou held up a sugar bag. "I got noodles from the pantry."

"Aren't you smart! You 'membered we put the dried noodles in them bags, didn't you?"

"Uh-huh. Which pot are we gonna boil the noodles in?"

Hope glanced at the stove. How much water would Velma need for the birth? Afraid to spare any, Hope looked about. Her gaze fell on the roasting pan. *Why not? Everything else is in it.* "We're cookin' up a special supper tonight, Emmy-Lou. Them there noodles are gonna go in the roastin' pan with a bunch of other good things."

Emmy-Lou did a little jig. "Do I getta put 'em in?"

"You shore do."

After Emmy added them, she scrunched her nose. "Should I stir it?"

After it was stirred, Hope worried the noodles would absorb the moisture and everything would be too dry. She added a jar of stewed tomatoes. The result made Hope wince. *Looks like someone puked in the pan.*

"It smells yummy!"

"Good thing." Hope slapped on the lid and shoved it in the oven.

Ten minutes later, after having ironed two sheets and a pair of pillowcases, Hope glanced at Emmy-Lou. She'd been happy to sit in the doorway and eat a peach for a snack. Secretly, Hope thought maybe the little girl would see her daddy—but that was a futile hope. Jakob hadn't come, and even if he had, she realized Emmy-Lou's glasses couldn't enable her to see that well.

"Sugar pie, I put a stool by the washstand. Why don't you rinse off your hands, then you could . . ."

Annie's crying made it hard to think.

"Play with my dolly?"

"That's a dandy idea."

Emmy-Lou dawdled toward the washstand. "Is Auntie Annie sad again? She used to cry all the time. I don't like it when she cries."

No matter how scairt I am, I oughtta be strong for Annie and Emmy-Lou. Hope wracked her brain for some way of reassuring the little girl. The cradle! Last night, Jakob had brought it down from the attic, and Hope had polished it to a soft sheen. "If'n you're real careful, I'll let you rock your dolly in the cradle, and I'll go check in on your auntie."

The closer Hope drew to the room, the quieter Annie's weeping grew. Then the floorboards started to creak again. Hope hastened to the door. "Annie, what're y'all up to?"

Both hands braced at the small of her back, Annie paced the length of the room and back. "Is my brother back yet?"

"Not yet." *But I shore wish he was.*

Annie's face puckered up again. "I didn't think so."

"Now, don't be gettin' in a dither. Maybe y'all better lie back down. Rest up."

Annie sent her away again. Hope went directly into Jakob's office. "Lord," she whispered urgently, "you gotta help me help that gal. Every animal I've seen got fussy and paced just afore she got down to havin' her babe. I reckon it ain't no different for people. Two legs or four, it probably don't make any difference. But the other particulars—those gotta be special-like for people."

Hope stared at the spines of the books and ran her finger across them. Red, blue, brown, or green leather covered some. Others were covered in durable, heavyweight cotton, and a few with all the pictures were catalogs. Which one would hold the medical information?

She went through more than a dozen. The illustrations in some made it clear they weren't what she needed. The lack of illustrations ruled out others. Finally, she opened a book. Air *wooshed* out of her lungs. "Okay, God. This here's a start. Now could you help me read what I gotta know?"

જી

Something's wrong. The minute he entered the house, Jakob spied Hope. She sat next to a mountain of towels, poring over a book. So pale her freckles stood out in stark relief, she bit her lip and slowly dragged her forefinger along the page.

"Daddy!"

"Praise God!" Hope bolted to her feet. Just as quickly, confusion wrinkled her forehead. "Where's Velma?"

"Velma?" The book and towels took on special significance. "Is Annie having the baby?"

"Y'all don't know? Then where did you go?" Pressing her hand against her chest, Hope whispered, "Merciful heavens, you didn't go off to fetch Velma? What're we gonna do?"

Jakob took the stairs two at a time. Hope chased right after him. Annie lay on the bed in a nest of pillows, her eyes closed. He went to his sister's side and stared down at her.

Hope gawked and stammered in the barest of whispers, "She's sleepin'? *Sleepin'*?"

Jakob nodded slowly. He ushered Hope back out into the hallway. The door shut, and Hope wilted against the wall. "She was cryin' and cryin' and I thought—"

"Annie was upset about how I treated you." Admitting it tore at him—not only because of Annie's fragility, but because of the additional distress it caused Hope.

"I told her everything's okay betwixt us, but she kept on." Deep lines furrowed Hope's brow. "You shore she's not laborin'? Maybe she swooned."

"*Nein*. She cried herself to sleep. Annie's that way. When something troubles her, she cries."

The door downstairs opened.

"Hi, Phineas! Wanna see my dolly? I wrapped her up in a beautiful, beautiful new blanket, and Miss Hope said I could use the cradle."

Hope gawked at him. "You went and brung Phineas home." Jakob smiled slyly and she continued in realization, "To save him from the attentions of Miss Linette."

He noted the relief in Hope's voice. "Ja. He was thankful— very thankful. By the time I got there, Linette was pestering him. She even got the sash of her dress caught in the binder on the reaper."

He and Hope descended the stairs. Wearing a quizzical expression, Phineas stood by the table. "Hope, I thought you washed the towels a few days ago."

"I did." Hope scooped up an armload. "Mr. Stauffer, next time we go to town, we'd best better get more. You know—for when your sis has need of them."

"More?" Phineas gawked at her. "There are so many, I thought there was a snowdrift on the—" His voice skidded to a halt. "Annie? Is Annie—?"

"No."

Before Jakob could say anything more, Emmy-Lou piped up from the parlor, "Auntie was crying a lot. Like she used to. But she told me to put on my glasses and pretty soon, she stopped. Doesn't my dolly look pretty in her cradle?"

Twisting so she could see around all the towels, Hope said, "You done a fine job, Emmy-Lou. That baby doll of yours looks—"

"Happy as a lamb!" Emmy-Lou beamed.

While Hope put away the towels, Phineas muttered, "Boss, I was afraid of that. Emmy-Lou's picking up Hope's crazy sayings."

Jakob moved the stack of dish towels from the table. "Don't you like lambs?"

"Ja, but—What's that book doing out?" Phineas turned the medical text around. "I thought Hope couldn't read." His brows furrowed at the illustrated anatomy chart. "Is there something wrong with her foot?"

After a moment's reflection, Jakob shook his head. "I don't think so. She's walking just fine." Hope reappeared, so he asked, "Hope, do your feet hurt? Do you need new boots or something?"

"Whatever made you ask that cockeyed question?"

"The medical book—you had it opened to the picture of a foot."

Resolve straightened her weary shoulders. "Nobody was here to read to me, and I worried Annie was 'bout to—well, you know.

243

So I got the book and asked God to help me." She grinned. "He answered my prayers far and above what I asked. He made it so we got more time. I know it ain't exactly proper, but I'm still gonna ask: Will you read to me what to do if 'n your sister's time comes and I gotta tend to her?"

"Ja, Hope. I'll do that."

Tapping his forefinger on the illustration, Phineas asked, "But why were you looking at this page?"

As she took the roasting pan from the oven, Hope's cheeks went red. Jakob suspected the oven's heat wasn't the cause of her flush. "Far as I could tell, there wasn't a rhyme or reason to what was where in that book. I know baby starts with a B, but they didn't have nothin' there. Then I remembered hearin' someone usin' a high-falutin' handle for a newborn baby: Feet-us. So I looked thataway."

She'd been desperate and done her best. Admiration swept over Jakob. "I'll read to you, Hope."

"You already read to Miss Hope, Daddy. You read the Bible to her every day." Emmy-Lou wandered over, carrying the fabric he wanted to give to Hope. A tiny cloth hand stuck out of the middle of the bundle.

Jakob picked up his daughter. "Hope is right. Your dolly looks good in that. Maybe, if you ask real nice, after Miss Hope makes herself a dress from this material, she'll make one for your dolly, too."

Hope set the roasting pan on a trivet in the center of the table. "Annie'd look right fine in that dress length. How's about I make her and the dolly a dress outta it, and I'll use feed sacks—"

"This material is for you." Jakob watched her eyes widen. "I want you to have it."

"Thankee, but bolt goods are silly for the likes of me. It's like stitchin' a silk purse for a sow's rear."

Emmy-Lou cuddled the material and looked up at him. "But this is pretty, Daddy. Miss Hope's brown dress is ugly, and I can't find her very good until she wears the green one."

Clunk. Hope dropped the lid back down on the roasting pan. "I changed my mind, Mr. Stauffer. Thankee for that purdy dress length. I'll start in making it up straightaway."

"*Sehr gut.*" He smiled at her. "Speaking of *gut*—supper smells *sehr gut.* I'm hungry."

Phineas sat down at the table. "What is it?"

"Uhhh . . . mishmash." Hope wheeled around and grabbed plates. "I've been in such a dither, I didn't set the table yet."

"I helped make the mishmash!"

Phineas gave Jakob a wary look and silently mouthed, "Mishmash?"

"Ja, that mishmash smells delicious." He'd told the truth—the dish carried a rich aroma, but the name sounded unappetizing at best. After setting his daughter into her seat, Jakob turned toward the stove. "I'll get the c—" For the first time since Hope had arrived, there wasn't a pot of coffee on the stove. "Cups. I hope we still have some sweet tea around here."

"In the springhouse." Hope set the plates and silverware on the table. "Not many things more refreshing than sweet tea. All y'all can start eatin', and I'll run off and fetch a pitcher."

"I'll get it." Phineas rose.

Hope glanced at Emmy-Lou. "Sugar pie, you can't hold your dolly at the table. Go put her down someplace." With Phineas and Emmy-Lou both away from the table, Hope pressed the medical text into Jakob's hands. "Mr. Stauffer, sir, I'm gonna ask y'all to start readin' to me tonight. I took a powerful fright today thinkin' Annie was havin' the baby. We ought to be grateful the Almighty spared Annie from my bunglin'."

"You have my word; I'll read it to you tonight."

"Tomorrow, too?"

The urgency in her voice touched him. Hope loved his sister and wanted to do the best she could for her. Of all the ways God might work, Hope was the most unlikely way Jakob could imagine—but the very best. *And not just for Emmy-Lou and Annie, but for me, too.*

Her hazel eyes didn't waver, but her voice dropped to a hushed whisper. "Other gals—it wouldn't be fittin' for you to read such things to them. But you and me—we got ourselves a pact to do what's best for Annie."

Dear, sweet Hope. She set aside her own embarrassment for Annie's sake. She was right—the subject matter wasn't considered decent. *Can it be that it's not just for Annie? Could it be that Hope understands deep down inside that she can trust me?*

Unaware of his thoughts, she continued on, "After taking a gander at that book, I think it'd scare her silly to have to read 'bout what's to come."

Jakob nodded. He'd thought the same thing. "When the time comes, I'll fetch Velma, but it would be good for you to know what to do, just in case."

The darling little curlies surrounding her face all wobbled as she bobbed her head. "I'd best better get all the particulars set in my mind, just in case that pickled finger of fate points at me."

Pickled finger. Well, pigs' feet could be pickled. Hope's mangled version held a thread of logic. Figuring out how she'd reasoned her way into her crazy clichés was fun.

Jakob enjoyed supper and waited out on the porch as Hope tucked in his daughter. The open bedroom window allowed him to hear Emmy-Lou's sweet, high voice as she said her bedtime prayer. Hope insisted on them still praying in German. Fact was, Hope seemed to be picking up more German as the days went by. That first night, she said she hadn't come to change things—but she'd been wrong. She'd taken his battered family under her wing and given them the healing shelter of her love.

"Miss Hope? It's really dark tonight."

"Yup. Shore is. But 'member on what I showed you? Even when you can't see the stars on my quilt, they're still there. And the moon and stars are still up in the sky. And God is still watchin' over you."

"Even"—Emmy-Lou's voice went thready—"when it's dark?"

"Especially when it's dark. Didja know, in the Bible it tells us God made the light and the dark? I reckon He wanted it dark part of the time for a reason. I gotta 'nother verse for our Twinkle song. Wanna learn it?"

Jakob's heart warmed. As badly as Hope wanted for him to read to her tonight, she didn't rush his daughter. Her song drifted through the window and down to him.

"In the dark blue sky you keep,
And often through my curtains peep,
For you never shut your eye,
Till the sun is in the sky . . ."

"Twinkle, twinkle, little—" Jakob caught himself singing under his breath and grinned. Life had become so sweet again. He sat on one of the porch seats, but something crackled softly in his pocket. The letter. He leaned forward, pulled it out, and opened it.

Twelve dollars a month now. Konrad.

Jakob's mouth went dry. The paper crumpled as his hand clenched into a fist. Twelve. It might as well have been twelve thousand.

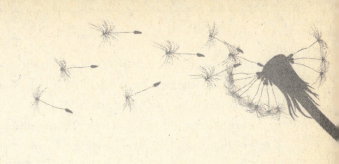

Twenty

Konrad's sweat-soaked shirt stuck to his body and hunger clawed at him. Sweat trickled from his brow and stung his eyes as he plopped down in the dirt and dragged the two pails closer. Not wasting time on the dipper, he took the first and gulped water from the rim. Instead of refreshing, cool well water brought by his wife, he had to settle for what he'd pumped and carried here himself—and the sun had heated it. Every swallow fired his anger.

The second pail contained the same thing day after day—eggs he'd hard-boiled, stale bread he'd bought in town and rationed out during the week, and jerked beef or fried bacon. Today, he had a runty tomato he'd yanked off one of the scraggly volunteer plants. What in years past had been an impressive garden lay as a weed-choked wasteland next to the house—a testament to a woman's neglect of her man and his land.

Starting next week, he'd be going to his neighbors' to help with reaping. At least then he'd eat decently. Thoughts of crispy-fried chicken, vats of potato salad, and succulent roasted beef flooded his mind. He'd pile his plate high with those and thick slices of fresh-baked bread slathered with just-churned sweet butter. Onion-and-vinegar soaked cucumbers would cool him. So would fat wedges of melon. Then he'd eat his fill of pies.

But for now, he ate like a pauper.

Every bite tasted of bitterness. How could a man sit on the edge of his wheat field and be starved for bread? The very staff of life rustled and rippled on all sides, mocking him.

The sound of a wagon trundling by pulled Konrad from his thoughts. He stood but didn't bother to dust off the seat of his britches. They hadn't been washed in . . . well, weeks. No use wasting the effort. Instead, he walked toward the road and doffed his hat to the two women. As always, he used his left hand so the brim would block the sight of his missing fingers. "*Guten Tag*, Frau Volkner. Fraulein Volkner."

"Herr Erickson." Leopold's mother looked like a fat old crow, sitting on the buckboard bench and tipping her head down at him. Her beaklike nose always made her look as if she smelled something bad, and her daughter inherited the same look.

It's probably why no man wants her. But I'm going to need them to cook for me. Pasting on a suave smile, Konrad waited a moment. "So what brings you ladies out today?"

"We went to town. Leopold sent us a letter. My son—he's always been so good to me." She didn't pause to take a breath and continued on as if she'd rehearsed everything she needed to say and was afraid she'd forget something. "Leopold asked for us to tell you he'd be home in time to help with harvest. He's sent money and says the farmers have all been fair to pay him for his labor."

Leopold's sister folded her hands in her lap like a prim schoolmarm. "*Ja*, and it is right. As Jesus said in the tenth chapter of Luke, 'The labourer is worthy of his hire.' "

"*Ja.*" The old crow continued to bob her head. "And in the same it says that the harvest is great, but the laborers are few.

I'm thinking you will need a lot of help here in your fields and maybe in the kitchen, too."

Not crow. Buzzard. Sitting there, ready to feast even if it costs me everything. They probably spent the whole way from town to make up this sanctimonious speech. Well, I'll take their help. After everything is over and they ask for their pay, I'll pretend it was a misunderstanding. After all, neighbors help one another.

"I don't suppose you have a letter for me, too? I hoped my Annie would write and tell me she's coming home in time for the harvest. She's been gone so long. I've missed her." *Her cooking, her cleaning, her gardening, and having her in my bed.*

"*Nein.*" Volkner's sister sighed. "There was no mail for you. I asked, too. They told me you'd just sent a letter last week."

Jakob got my letter. He's delaying. He doesn't want to give me more money—but he will. And it won't make a difference, because I'll still go fetch Annie. Jakob owes me. He owes me for the cost of the expensive food I must buy. He owes me for the comfort I've been denied. If he wants to act as if I'm merely a farmhand, he owes me monthly wages. Even so, I still will keep the profit from the crops. He did nothing at all—he deserves nothing in return.

Unaware of his thoughts, the young woman prattled on. "Maybe it's too soon for your wife to have replied. Annie's always been so conscientious. I miss her dreadfully."

"Nothing is right with her gone." He didn't have to act. Every fiber of his being cried that to be true. "It has been too long. I'd go fetch her now, but I'd be a fool to leave my crop just before the harvest. As soon as the reaping is over, before the threshing, I plan to go get her."

"The timing would be good." Frau Volkner graced him with a sly smile. "At least, it will be good for you as the wheat shocks dry. But you'll still be in wont of help to feed the men."

Why should I only get help when the reapers come? I should make it so I am fed better now. Konrad shrugged and held his arms wide. "You think it's only then that I'm in wont of help? I've taken to wearing suspenders because I couldn't punch any more holes in my belt. Ja, I have lost that much weight."

The women made sympathetic sounds, and he knew his calculated comments had hit the mark.

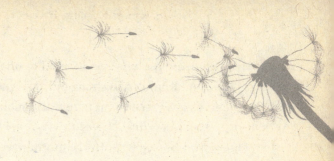

Twenty-One

"Phineas." Jakob swallowed his pride as he latched Josephine in her stall. "I got a letter."

Phineas straightened up and set aside the milk pail. "From the dark mood you've been in the past week, it was from Konrad."

"Yes." Jakob cleared his throat. He'd tried to set aside his worries as they'd completed the threshing. Evidently, he'd not succeeded in hiding his feelings. Had Hope noticed? Had Annie?

"I told you already, send him what you'd pay me."

"He wants more than that. Twelve." Merely saying the figure aloud made Jakob's mouth feel dirty. "He wants twelve dollars a month now."

Phineas didn't hesitate for a second. "Annie's worth it."

"My sister is worth a hundred times that, but she's not a woman to be bought or sold."

Phineas shot him an exasperated look. "Of course she isn't, but Konrad isn't smart enough to know that. I've saved some money. Not much, but you're welcome to it all."

"*Nein*, Phineas. You're a good friend to offer, but no matter what I give him, Konrad will always grasp for more. I've decided I'll pretend I didn't receive his letter. I'll mail him the same five dollars I've been sending."

"That could get you through another week or so. Then what?"

"That's my hope. By then, it'll be harvesttime for him. He'll be honor bound to help his neighbors." The plan he'd devised went contrary to Jakob's nature. A man ought to stand and fight for what he believed in and loved. Only in this situation, fighting wouldn't resolve the problem. He'd battled with himself, examined every possibility, and settled on the only course of action that stood any chance of working. Jakob lifted his chin. "Once Annie has the baby, I plan to send her away. Surely there is somewhere she could be safe."

Phineas grimaced. "What about Emmy-Lou?"

He'd thought it over countless times. There wasn't anyone else to whom he'd entrust Emmy-Lou. Hope. Hope would take her with them. "Konrad is not to be trusted. I can't have Hope or Emmy-Lou here. They'll go with Annie and the baby. I'm asking you to find a place, but don't tell me where. That way, I won't be lying when I say I don't know where Annie is."

"How long do you expect that to work?"

Jakob inhaled deeply, then slowly let out his breath. "Until I can sell this place. I'll take the money and move."

"Move?!"

"I have no choice. I'm telling you first because if you want the farm, I'll sell it to you cheaper. You could go to the bank and see about a mortgage."

Phineas stared at him. Slowly, he shook his head. "*Nein*. I couldn't buy your land. I would, for a time, sharecrop it. When it's safe, you can return."

"I can't ask that of you."

"You didn't ask. I offered. What do Hope and Annie say about this plan of yours?"

"I haven't told them. We have a few weeks before I'll need to do anything. Annie's already nervous about having the baby. I'll speak to Hope soon, but first I wanted to ask you to find a place. As long as she goes, I know Emmy-Lou and Annie will be okay."

"Hope will agree?"

Jakob didn't hesitate a second. "Ja. She loves my daughter and my sister. I wouldn't consider this plan if it weren't for her. I trust her completely."

Phineas nodded sagely. "A man does what he must to protect the women he loves."

"Ja."

Phineas smacked Jakob on the shoulder. "It's about time!"

Jakob raised a brow in silent inquiry.

"I said 'women,' and you agreed. I've wondered for days how much longer it would take for you to admit you love Hope."

"The time's not right." Jakob's jaw thrust forward. "I'm torn between wanting to keep Hope by my side and wanting to send her away. Until I can shelter and protect her, I have no right to say anything."

❧

"C'mere, sugar pie." Hope reached out and took Emmy-Lou's hand. "I got a grand idea. Whilst your auntie sits here and sews, how's about you and me havin' a little fun?"

"Okay! What're we gonna do?"

"I'm fixin' to show you some stars." For the past several evenings, Hope had plotted this. Before she hadn't had the time, but now with the reaping and threshing over, she grabbed the opportunity. In the twilight, beneath the sycamore, she and Jakob's daughter chased fireflies. Try as she might, Emmy-Lou couldn't capture any, but Hope caught some in a canning jar. Satisfied with what she had, she used the spring mechanism to seal the jar, then knelt down. "Emmy-Lou, lemme show you what I got."

Emmy-Lou twisted and tripped. She lay on the ground, her eyeglasses up on her forehead and her lower lip trembling.

It took everything within Hope to keep from springing up and running to her. Emmy-Lou hadn't hit anything hard enough to get hurt, and giving her pity would only make her cry. Instead, Hope asked, "Is the ground okay?"

"The ground?" Emmy-Lou pushed herself upright.

"Yup. I bet that patch of dirt didn't expect you to go floppin' on it. You'd best dust yourself off so's the dirt gets to go back to where it belongs. But first put your spectacles on your nose. You ain't got eyes up there on your forehead."

Pulling her glasses back into place, she giggled. "Daddy has eyes in the back of his head."

"I knew there was somethin' special 'bout him." *Actually, lots of special things. He's a good man. Best I ever met. Emmy-Lou and Annie are lucky to be his.*

"Did I put enough dirt back?" Emmy-Lou spread out her skirts.

"Almost. Yeah. You got that last spot real good. Now c'mere." Emmy-Lou came over and nestled close. Hope held up the jar. "What do you see?"

A small finger ventured to touch the glass. "Sparkles."

"Twinkles, like a star?"

Face bright with glee, Emmy-Lou couldn't take her gaze from the jar. "Is that how stars twinkle?"

"They look the same to me. Watch and see how there's a twinkle, then a couple, then it all goes dark."

"And then there's lotsa twinkles all at the same time! I saw it. I did! Did you see it, too?"

They sat beneath the tree, in the shade-cooled patch of grass, admiring the fireflies and chattering. Hope wasn't sure how much time had passed, but she heard footsteps. She recognized the sure, steady stride at once. The last few days, his steps had changed—become ponderous or sad. She wasn't sure which, or why. But Mr. Stauffer's approach carried with it the self-assured pace that normally characterized him. "I hear your pa a-comin'."

"Daddy! Miss Hope got me a whole jar of twinkle stars!"

"Did she now?" Mr. Stauffer lowered himself to the ground and sat cross-legged. He reached over and lifted Emmy-Lou into his lap. "Let's see."

He dipped his head so his cheek rested against his daughter's temple and listened to Emmy-Lou as she repeated the things Hope had told her. At all the right times, he hummed appreciatively or made comments.

Hope watched and listened, relishing the way Jakob lavished attention on his little girl. How could a man be so very strong, yet unspeakably tender? Whatever had been weighing heavy on his heart must be over, a fact that delighted her.

When little Emmy-Lou's chatter finally wound down, he tapped the side of the jar. "What made you catch these?"

"I dunno. Miss Hope, why did we catch the sparkle-fireflies?"

Hope thought for a moment. She'd made plans, but with Mr. Stauffer here, she suddenly felt self-conscious. *I'm bein' silly. Don't make no never mind what he thinks of me. I never bothered to worry what any other man thought. It's different with him, though. Don't know why that is. Well, yeah, I guess I do. A feller who's this devoted to his family—he's a man to be admired. It's natural to care what somebody thinks when you admire them.*

"Miss Hope?"

Hope shook her head to clear away her thoughts. *I'll leave here and he'll forget me, but I want Emmy-Lou to remember what we done tonight.* "Emmy-Lou, 'member how you went to Abilene and your pa used the light in the sky to help you get home?"

"Uh-huh! Like in our song—'bout the traveler in the dark."

Pleasure trickled through Hope. This would have been a delightful time, just playing—but Emmy-Lou's bright mind allowed this to be a time to learn, too. "When you hear in the Bible about the stars in the heavens, I want you to 'member all these twinkles. Right now, it's like you're holding stars in your hands."

Mr. Stauffer's head shot up. It was too dim to see his eyes well enough to tell what he was thinking. His lips parted, but he said nothing.

Emmy-Lou tilted her head back until it thumped against her father's chest, then craned her neck. "I see the tree. I don't see stars."

"Just 'cuz you can't see 'em, does it mean they're not there?"

Emmy-Lou giggled. "That's silly." She turned her attention back to the jar. "I can't count how many there are. They blink and go away. How many stars are there in the sky?"

"Only God knows how many, Liebling, but they shine like the little dots in your jar. Miss Hope is right." His voice dropped to a lower, softer tone that had the odd effect of making her yearn to lean closer to him. "It's like you have a piece of the sky in your hands."

Hugging the jar tightly, Emmy-Lou let out a blissful sigh. "I getta keep it in my room and have my very own stars every night now."

I shoulda thought about that. Well, it ain't fair to let her go on thinkin' she can keep 'em forever. Hope looked at her boss, and a lazy smile slanted across his face. Clearly, he'd left the explanation to her. "Sugar pie, the fireflies have families they wanna get back to. When they're where they belong, they'll twinkle better. When you open the jar, they'll fly up, up, and away to the ones what love 'em."

Emmy-Lou's lower lip poked out. "Don't they wanna stay and be my friend?"

"Just like you got to play with your friends and then come home to your daddy, them fireflies played with us and now they wanna go back home. Friends come and go. Family's what you keep."

"You don't got any family. We'll keep you!"

Hope leaned close in order to make sure Emmy-Lou saw her clearly. "We done talked 'bout that a while back. I'm like a dandelion wishy. I'll blow on down the road so's I can help someone else." An unexpected and unexplainable heaviness settled in her heart as she spoke those words. In spite of her own feelings, she put Emmy-Lou's welfare first. "Your auntie will have the baby, and after that, I'll be here for . . ." She thought for a moment. "I'll be here for two more Sunday church services. Then I'll leave."

"Let's not borrow the future. Let's enjoy this minute." Mr. Stauffer settled his arms loosely about his daughter. "I used to catch lightning bugs when I was a boy."

"Did Aunt Annie help you?"

A rich chuckle rippled out of him. *"Nein.* She and my brother and I would have a contest to see who could catch the most.

The only problem is, it's hard to count them because they move in the jar!"

"You got yourself a brother?" As soon as she asked, Hope wished she hadn't.

"I did, but now Annie and I are the only ones left."

He sounded so matter-of-fact, Hope wondered if his brother had died in his youth. But then why didn't Jakob stay on the family farm?

"Emmy-Lou, it's about bedtime for you." His hold on her tightened the slightest bit. "You'd best let out those little bugs now."

Emmy-Lou balked for a moment. Slumping back into her father's chest she asked in a tiny, sad voice, "Can we sing?"

"Shore. Your daddy can undo the latch, and when you're ready, you can lift off the lid."

Mr. Stauffer turned his attention on her. "Hope, come over closer. Help us."

How had he known that just minutes ago she'd yearned to lean closer? Hope felt her cheeks go warm.

"Yeah, Miss Hope. C'mon. I need your help, too."

As soon as Hope scooted closer, her boss surprised her by giving the waistband of her apron an almost playful tug. "I could drive a team of horses in the space between us. Get on over here."

An odd feeling shot through her. Hope couldn't quite figure out what it was. Part of her wanted to laugh at his outrageous comment. Mr. Stauffer wasn't given to speaking so glibly. But a strange longing also assailed her. For a moment, Hope wondered what it would be like to squeeze alongside him so she and Emmy-Lou would share his shelter and security. She compromised by wiggling a hairsbreadth closer. "There."

A large, incredibly warm hand suddenly curled around her shoulder and tugged her a mere inch away from him. "No." A grin creased his face and made the corners of his eyes crinkle. *"There."* Before Hope could react, Jakob began singing. "Twinkle, twinkle—"

Though Emmy-Lou immediately joined in, her sweet soprano blending with her father's rich baritone, Hope remained silent. Many, many years ago, her mother sang this same song with her. A wealth of bittersweet memories swept through her, leaving in its wake a heaviness. *This ain't like me, broodin'. Emmy-Lou ain't got herself a mama, but she has her auntie and her daddy—a first-rate daddy. Ain't never seen a man father his kid the way he does. I oughtta count myself lucky that Mr. Stauffer don't mind me bein' here and that God let me share this moment.*

Emmy-Lou started to open the jar and Hope began to sing as the fireflies flitted free. Mr. Stauffer didn't know the third verse, so she and Emmy-Lou sang a duet. Hope missed the rich tone of his voice. *I set out to make Jakob's daughter a memory tonight, but he done turned it around. I'll be leavin' here, and I'll always carry the recollection of us sittin' side by side in the dark, him cuddlin' her and singing. Emmy-Lou's gonna make it through life just fine because of him.*

Afterward, Mr. Stauffer gave his daughter a kiss. "I'll come listen to your prayers." He set Emmy-Lou on her feet.

Hope started to rise, but as she got to her knees, Emmy-Lou's arms wound around her neck. "Thank you, Miss Hope. I liked holding the bug jar. The sparkles were so pretty. I'm glad the sky has lotsa stars that twinkle like that."

"You're welcome." Hope squeezed her tight. The delicate wire frame of Emmy-Lou's glasses felt cool against Hope's cheek. Tilting her head ever so slightly to keep from bending the metal,

Hope whispered, "When you're in bed, you can close your eyes and still see all them twinkles."

"I'm sure she will." Mr. Stauffer extended his hand to her to help her up. "Hope?"

He's always such a gentleman. Ain't been a single time since I been here that he ain't pitched in, helped out, or shown fine manners. She accepted his assistance and rose. "Thankee."

When he let go of her hand, Hope felt odd. Lost. *I'm tired. That's all. It just ain't like me to be emotional.* Then Emmy-Lou slipped her small hand into Hope's. *I didn't realize how big Mr. Stauffer's hands are.*

Holding hands, the three of them walked to the house together. Every so often, Emmy-Lou lifted both feet so she'd hang suspended. Hope glanced at her boss as they approached the porch. Annie sat there, her needle poised over a bitsy white gown. Hope glanced at her boss and murmured, "You got yourself a mighty nice family, Mr. Stauffer."

"Call me Jakob, Hope."

His invitation took her by surprise. "You bein' my boss and all, it don't seem quite right. You deserve my respect."

"I respect you deeply, and I use your given name. For as long as you stay here, call me Jakob."

For as long as I stay here. But it won't be long now. Annie'll have her babe any day, and soon after that Mr. Stauffer will hitch Hattie to my cart and send me on my way.

"Say it. Jakob."

Hope scrunched her nose. "It'll feel odd to me, calling you by your given name." *Personal. Like we're friends. But we are. I don't know how it happened, me making a man my friend. But ain't a finer man on the face of the earth.*

"You'll get used to it." His voice sounded pleasant. "So?"

"Jakob," she said. Her voice sounded breathless. Embarrassed, she repeated, "Yep. You got yourself a mighty fine family."

"Thanks. I do have a 'mighty nice family.' What about yours, Hope? What happened to them?"

As if by some prearranged plan, they both turned loose of Emmy-Lou. She scampered up the porch steps, leaving them behind. Hope called out to her, "I left milk and a cookie on the table for your bedtime snack."

Annie pried herself out of the chair. "I ate the cookie. I'll get her another."

Hope started to do it herself, but her boss held her back. "You were going to tell me about what happened to your family."

Just to have something to do with her empty hands, Hope crammed them into her apron pockets. "I lost 'em all at the same time in eighty-two." She hitched her shoulders in a tense little jerk. "Smallpox."

He drew in a sharp breath. "You must have been so young."

"Fourteen."

"Hope"—compassion resonated in his voice—"how terrible. You were no more than a girl."

"I ain't gonna pretend it was easy." Most of the time she kept busy enough, and the past was a mere blur. Even now, a decade later, she felt the loss of all whom she'd loved. She dared to look into his steady blue gaze and confessed, "Even lookin' back sometimes pains me. I take refuge in knowin' they're resting in the bosom of Christ Jesus."

"Even knowing we'll be reunited in heaven—that doesn't make the grief go away." The glow of the kerosene lantern on the porch illuminated the understanding on his face.

He knows the ache. His is fresh, too, yet he's still strong for his daughter and sis. Hope looked away.

A rough finger gently turned her face back to his. "How did you survive?"

"An old lady took me in. Eudora Gray. She dragged me outta the swamp of my poor-pitiful-me's and got my feet firmly planted on the Solid Rock. Filled my heart and mind with God's truth." A small laugh bubbled out of Hope. "Nobody could be grumpy around her for long. Always struck me as odd, how a woman by the last name of Gray could always be so sunny. If 'n I close my eyes, I can still see her sittin' in her rockin' chair a-wagglin' her gnarly old finger at me."

Perching his hands on his lean hips, Mr. Stauffer drawled, "Is that so? Stretches my imagination that she'd ever have to ask you to do anything. You pitch right in and are a hard worker. What did she scold you about?"

"My attitude." Hope lifted her forefinger and imitated the action. " 'The Bible tells us in everything give thanks. It doesn't say *for* everything; it says *in* everything. Don't lie and tell God thanks when you're not grateful. He wants you to look past the problem and find the scrap of good that's there. God isn't a fairy-tale genie who gives us everything we want; we have to lean hard on Him and trust He'll work things out.' " Hope tucked her hand back in her apron pocket and smiled. "Them words of advice shore have sung in my heart over the years."

"In everything give thanks," he quoted slowly, thoughtfully. Brows shooting high on his forehead, Mr. Stauffer let out a disbelieving laugh. "I never noticed that. It really doesn't say to give thanks for everything."

"Neither did I—'til then. So Mrs. Gray set me to tryin' to find something good in the midst of every little thing. It shore did turn my attitude round."

"I'll have to meditate on that verse."

Annie came back outside, sat down, and picked up her sewing. They walked up the steps. Hope went to Annie's side. "Oooh, Annie, that's gotta be the most purdiest baby gown yet."

Annie knotted the thread and snipped it. "It's done. If it weren't for Sydney's sewing machine and all of your help, my baby would have to go naked."

"We've had us some wonderful hours." Hope turned to her boss. "Whilst we've been sewin', Annie and me—we been workin' on memorizing that psalm the parson preached on that first Sunday I came here. Annie's got the sweetest readin' voice."

Annie fingered the tatted-edged sleeve so it laid straight. "We each have special verses in that psalm."

"What are they?" Mr. Stauffer picked up the teensy gown and grinned at it.

Hope motioned for Annie to speak. Annie needed folks to put her first in line.

"I like verses two, three, and seven. 'My help cometh from the Lord, which made heaven and earth, He will not suffer thy foot to be moved: he that keepeth thee will not slumber.' And, 'The Lord shall preserve thee from all evil: he shall preserve thy soul.' "

Jakob slowly laid the gown across what little remained of his sister's lap. He tended to move slowly and deliberately around her, a point that won Hope's admiration. Annie needed men who made her feel secure. Looking at his sister, he nodded. "Those verses are fitting indeed. I'll learn them, too." He turned. "Hope, what's your verse?"

Annie set aside the gown and murmured, "Excuse me." She went into the house. "Emmy-Lou, why don't you come make a trip with me?" A moment later, the back screen door shut.

"What's your verse?" Mr. Stauffer repeated.

"The last one in the chapter. 'The Lord shall preserve thy going out and thy coming in from this time forth, and even for evermore.' What with me blowing along from pillar to post"— she flashed him a grin to let him know she'd remembered to say the old saw correctly—"it's good to know He'll be with me no matter where I go."

Mr. Stauffer pondered a moment. "Ja, Hope, it is true. God will go with you. Thinking on that should give us both peace."

The patter of little feet pounded up the back steps, the porch slammed shut, and Emmy-Lou came to the front door. "Daddy!"

"I'll come tuck you in, in a minute."

"But Auntie Annie said she needs you right now."

Twenty-Two

"Wait here." Jakob set his daughter off to the side and ran through the house. Hope hadn't hesitated. She was a few yards ahead, but by the time they reached the back door, he'd pulled up alongside her.

Manners dictated he open the door for her. Hope didn't stand on propriety. She grabbed for the knob, too. Their fingers jammed into a knot. She yanked back, but the minute the screen door started to open, Hope pushed it wide open and ran to Annie.

Annie leaned against the garden fence. In the moonlight, a patch of moisture darkened the earth by her hem. Hope skidded to a stop, propped her hands on her hips, and stared at that patch. "Annie, you shore got an odd way of waterin' the tomatoes."

Hysterics. That's what it had to be. No other explanation could cover why the women giggled.

"Phineas!" The moment he bellowed the hand's name, Jakob wished he hadn't. He should have urged Hope to take care of his sister and gone to the barn. Then he could have ridden off to Forsaken and gotten Velma. Instead, now he'd have to stay here. Unless Phineas didn't hear—

"Honest to Pete, Annie, this brother of yours missed his calling. Why, he shoulda been marchin' round Jericho with—" She laced her arm with Annie's and started to escort her toward the house. "I can't recollect which feller hollered and the walls come a-tumblin' down. Who was that?"

"Joshua." Annie made it up the back porch steps.

"Yeah. That's the one! Jakob could holler again, and Velma would probably hear him, don'tcha think?" Jakob stared in amazement. Hope's tone sounded playful, yet as she followed Annie inside, she feverishly swished her hand at him behind her back—an unmistakable gesture to hurry up.

Phineas came running. "What?"

"Annie's in labor."

Phineas shoved past him. "What are you standing there for? Go fetch Velma! Hope, move. Here, Annie. Let me help you."

Jakob stood in the doorway and watched as Phineas gently lifted Annie into his arms and started carrying her up the stairs.

"Daddy"—Emmy-Lou stood on tiptoe over at the edge of the parlor where he'd told her to stay—"can I come with you?"

Hope clapped her hands. "That's a dandy notion. You wait just a jiffy. I'll go grab your nightgown and dolly, and you can trade. Velma will stay here tonight, and you can sleep in one of Mrs. Creighton's purdy rooms. Tomorrow, you'll come home, and your auntie will show you your new cousin!"

"Ja. That is how we'll work it." To Jakob's relief, Big Tim Creighton and his wife were delighted to keep Emmy-Lou. Better still, Velma already had her doctoring bag packed— "Just in case."

Riding home in the dark took half of forever.

"God blessed us with a bright moon. We made good time." Velma dismounted and didn't bother to tether her mount.

Jakob looked at her—she didn't look as if she were teasing. If she couldn't tell time any better than that, would she be able to keep track of Annie's contractions?

Phineas came down from the porch. "I'll see to the horses."

"Just hers." Jakob led Nicodemus to the barn. As they tended the horses, he asked, "How's Annie doing?"

"Laughing." Phineas sounded as if he couldn't decide whether to be disgusted or relieved.

"Laughing?"

"Hope thought it was taking too long for you to get home. She got out that medical book and wanted me to read it."

"Why didn't she ask Annie?"

Phineas hefted the saddle and dumped it onto the stand. "She said the pictures would scare Annie. I told her Annie could look at the words, not the pictures."

Hope's big eyes probably shot fire at him. It wasn't right to make fun of Phineas, though. If Jakob hadn't been reading to Hope these last few days, in the moment of impending crisis he might well have had the same reaction. "What was Annie doing?"

"Sitting on the top step, bundled in her robe, laughing. Laughing!"

Oh no. I was hoping they'd gotten beyond the shock by now. If they're still having hysterics and it's early on, how will they cope toward the end of the ordeal? Jakob cleared his throat. "Does Hope have all the towels and dishcloths ready?"

"And water boiling. So there I am, holding that fat book, and Hope tells me where to find the information."

"Gut. Sehr gut." So it's not so bad after all. Hope is seeing to the essentials. I should have had more faith in her. She's level-headed. "It

makes sense that she asked you to read. I've been reading to her."

Finally, a smile chased across Phineas's face. "Ja. She told me childbirth went by a crazy name and I'd find it under 'part-you're-wishin'.'"

"Part . . . " Incredulous, Jakob shouted out a laugh. "Parturition. Only Hope. Only Hope could—"

"Mangle it. Annie figured it out right away. She and Hope started giggling over it."

"Better she laugh than cry." Jakob scooped a few oats for the horses. "The day she arrived, Hope told Annie she'd pray for an easy birthing."

"I've been praying for that, too." All humor fled Phineas's expression and voice. Clenching his fists at his side, he rasped, "A child should come to a home with loving parents."

He'd had that same thought many times over. Jakob instilled every scrap of certainty into his voice that he'd used when he'd assured his sister, "The baby will not want for love."

"I've been thinking." Phineas leaned forward, his eyes half-wild and cheeks flushed. "To protect Annie and the baby—I could say the baby is mine. Konrad would denounce her, divorce her. She could stay here and—"

"*Nein.*" Yet even after he gave the denial, Jakob felt tempted to accept Phineas's plan. If it worked, Annie would be free of Konrad—but at what cost? "I cannot allow this. I won't allow it." Jakob shook his head. "You mean well, but it isn't right."

"Better Annie is freed from him and—"

"Be branded as an adulteress and divorcée?"

"I'd marry her." Phineas half barked the words.

Jakob locked eyes with him. "You cannot right a wrong by committing another wrong act. In your mind, you think to rescue my sister; in your soul, you know this is wrong."

"Why would God allow His daughter to marry such a bad man?"

"I don't know. Just as I don't understand why He took my son and wife."

Phineas looked away. He dipped his head and let out a gusty sigh. "I won't ever say anything around Annie. You won't have to worry."

"I have your word on this?" If he didn't, Jakob knew he'd have to let his farmhand go. As badly as he needed Phineas's help, he'd still sacrifice it.

"You have my oath." Phineas spoke the words heavily. "Annie already bears an impossible burden. If you think it would make it harder on her, I won't say anything."

"That is the way it is."

Phineas squared his shoulders. "So."

"Ja," Jakob echoed the single word that settled the matter and closed it forever. "So."

They stayed in the barn and worked in silence. Myriad things wanted doing—another nail to reinforce a few places, a hook to hold a few odds and ends. They refilled the oat bin, filed and rasped rough edges on wooden surfaces, and oiled hinges. Phineas got out saddle soap, and they conditioned all of the leather.

Buffing his saddle, Jakob recalled when Naomi bore his children. Her mother had come to help, as had Velma. Naomi's cries had filled the night; he had yet to hear Annie make a peep. After the baby came, he'd cradled Naomi and their newborn in his arms and blessed the Lord. The memory would have brought anguish a few months ago; now it was a cherished moment of his past. *I'll make sure to do the same with my sister—to assure her that I see having her and her baby as blessings from the Lord.*

His stomach rumbled loudly.

"I'm hungry, too." The men walked to the house. To Jakob's surprise, Hope stood at the sink.

"Would you believe it?" Wisps of hair going every direction, the bib of her apron askew, she pumped water into a glass—well, she tried to. Her nervousness had the glass skittering all over. "I'm boiling all that water, and what does Annie want, but a glass of cool water!"

She's scared. A rush of gentleness sent Jakob to Hope's side. He wrapped his hand around hers and stabilized the glass. "If we fill a bowl, you can dip a cloth in it to wipe her. Naomi liked that when her time came."

"That's a fine idea!" Together, they filled a turquoise earthenware bowl. Jakob had to steady her hands the whole while. As soon as they finished that simple task, Hope promptly went upstairs and forgot it.

"Are you going to take that water up to them?" Phineas opened the icebox and inspected the contents.

"No."

"No?"

"It'll give Hope an excuse to come back out. She's rattled."

Phineas shut the icebox without taking out a morsel of food. "Hope's never rattled. Something must be wrong."

Hope's not the only one who's rattled. "Stop fretting like an old hen. If anything were wrong, Velma would be hollering for help."

Someone scurried down the stairs. Hope muttered, "Four legs, God. I thought you and me had a deal. I only help birthings when—" Her eyes widened and her words halted when she spotted the men.

"You came back for the bowl of water." Jakob handed it to her.

"If'n I was dead-level honest, I'd admit I'm sorely tempted to dash out the back door and keep on a-runnin'. If'n Annie and Velma didn't need me so much, I'd do just that, and don't think I wouldn't!"

"Hope—"

"I'm lily-livered." She hung her head in shame. "You'll never again in all your days see such a green-bellied coward."

"Yellow-bellied," Phineas corrected her.

Hope gasped as her head shot up. "Only drunken sots turn yellow, and I'm no sot, Phineas. If my friend didn't need me so badly right now, I'd give you a piece of my mind." She heaved a gigantic sigh. "But that wasn't very nice of me. You'll have to forgive me, and I'll forgive you. We're both worried sick about our Annie. When a body's sick, they go green. Just you look in the mirror yonder, and you'll see what I mean." Hope whirled around and disappeared with the water bowl.

Studying Phineas, Jakob drawled slowly, "You are a little green around the gills."

"As long as I'm not yellow." Phineas opened the cookie jar.

They sat out on the porch and ate every last cookie. The hours passed, but neither man budged. Finally, a squall echoed in the crisp predawn air. Jakob and Phineas exchanged big grins. "Whatever it is, it's loud. Healthy." Jakob leaned back in the chair and finally relaxed.

Phineas continued to rock. He'd done so all night. Jakob secretly marveled that the runners on the rocking chair hadn't formed big ruts in the planks by now. He hadn't said anything about it—Annie was a married woman, and any feelings Phineas held needed to be ignored.

"Your sister never said whether she wanted a boy or a girl."

Jakob shrugged. "It's God's decision, not ours. A boy would be good—one to teach about the land. A girl would be sweet—to play with Emmy-Lou."

"Timewise, I reckon this is good. Annie will have time to recover from the birth before—" Phineas stopped abruptly.

"Ja." He'd had the same thought. But after the enchanting moments he'd spent with Hope and Emmy-Lou under the sycamore, Jakob knew he never wanted to be apart. How could he send Hope away? But how could he not? Protecting her and Annie and the baby—that had to come before any other consideration.

Drumming his fingers on the arm of the rocker, Phineas said, "What's taking so long? Why don't they tell us what's going on? Do you think something went wrong?"

"Velma will have Hope bathe the baby; then it will need to be fed. These things take time." Jakob acted calm, but deep inside he worried, too. To keep his mind occupied, he mused, "I haven't decided what song to sing to the baby. You know I sang to Emmy-Lou and to Jakob, Jr. after Naomi had them."

Phineas paced across the porch and wheeled back around. "What difference does it make? The baby won't remember."

"But the mother—she will. So what do you think? 'Gracious Savior, Gentle Shepherd,' or maybe 'This Child We Dedicate to Thee'?"

Half singing, half murmuring the lyrics of the former, Phineas reached a part he spoke aloud. " 'Sweetly, gently, safely tended, from all want and danger free.' No, no. That's a bad choice. You don't want to remind Annie her baby might be in danger."

"So what about 'This Child'?"

The farmhand rubbed the back of his neck. "How does that one go?"

" 'This child we dedicate to Thee, O God of grace and purity!' "

Phineas hummed the tune and suddenly halted. Serving Jakob a withering look, he snapped, "It says, 'shield it from sin and threatening wrong.' Are you trying to scare her? Think of something else."

"You're the one who isn't happy with my choices. What do you recommend?"

They got into a rousing debate. It took a few minutes of Velma tapping her foot on the floorboards to make them stop. "It's about time! You can go up and see Annie and the baby, but make it a quick visit. She's weary."

"Is she—" Jakob began.

"Okay?" Phineas finished.

"Right as rain. That had to be the easiest birthing I ever tended. Baby's a tad on the scrawny side, but that often happens when the mother's heart is heavy."

"Boy or girl?" Jakob asked.

"Boy. Annie's frettin' over what to name him. You go on up now." Velma picked up a bundle of messy sheets and sauntered off.

Jakob blocked Phineas's path to the door. "I'll give Annie your best wishes. You're not going up to see her."

Phineas opened his mouth, then snapped it shut. Grim determination lined his face. Without a word, he turned and headed toward the barn. The very intensity of his reaction told Jakob he'd made the right choice, but that knowledge didn't make it any easier. Nonetheless, Annie's welfare came first.

Hope would understand; they had a pact.

⁊

Annie sprang back with miraculous speed. "You can stop pampering me. I'm fine." She hung on to Johnny instead of handing him to Hope. "I'll change him."

"Then the both of you can go nap."

Emmy-Lou pushed her glasses up her nose. "Do you mean Auntie Annie and me, or Auntie Annie and baby Johnny?"

"Actually, it's naptime for all three of you." Hope wanted to get them all bedded down so she could see to a bunch of trifling chores. With Annie recovering so quickly, Hope knew she'd soon be hitching Hattie to the cart and going on her way.

Within the next week, Hope would cut a small star from the scrap of yellow satin she kept in her sewing bag. Stitching the star on her quilt had become a ritual for her—she did it the last night she spent at a place. Stars were tricky things to sew. All the points on them required attention, or they'd fray. By the time she'd appliquéd the star in place, Hope would have finished praying for each member of the family she'd stayed to help. For a while, the Almighty Creator who hung the stars in the heavens had entrusted that family to her—it was her way of giving them back into His keeping and care.

Only she didn't feel ready to do that just yet. Her head told her the time was drawing nigh; her heart didn't.

"I ought to stay up and help you with chores."

Hope reached over and gently fingered Johnny's scant strands of sand-colored hair. "Today's a scorcher. No use in you staying up—anything important that needs doing can be done closer to sundown. Go have yourself a nice little lay-down."

Emmy-Lou nestled next to Hope and copied how she'd caressed the baby. "I'll help you sing and rock the baby to sleep."

"Just one verse." Annie winked at Hope. Emmy-Lou adored her cousin. Given the opportunity, she'd sing every verse of every song she knew.

Pursing her little lips, Emmy-Lou thought for a moment. "I already sang the first part of 'Jesus Loves Me' for his morning naptime. I should sing the next verse."

"Okay, but shuck your shoes so's I can polish 'em up for church tomorrow. You, too, Annie. I'll hold the little feller for you whilst you unlace them."

Minutes later, as Annie held Emmy-Lou's hand and carried Johnny upstairs, Hope bit her lip and turned away. *I'm being silly, God. You sent me here to set this family back on its feet. I ought to be a-praisin' you for all you done here. Ain't been a place yet where you sent me that I didn't enjoy myself. Lotsa folks out there need help, and I promised you I'd go wherever you took a mind to send me. It's gonna be different leavin' this time—maybe 'cuz of little Emmy-Lou's eyesight or on account of how I helped out when Johnny was born. Then too, I ain't never made a pact with none of my bosses. Jakob and me—we worked together. We worked real good together. Annie don't jump at shadows no more. She's gettin' to the point where she can run Jakob's home. He don't need my help no more.*

She pulled the laces from the shoes. No use polishing shoes and having dirty laces.

Emmy-Lou started singing, *"Jesus loves me! This I know . . ."*
Hope found herself singing along,
"As He loved so long ago,
Taking children on His knee,
Saying, 'Let them come to Me.' "

Let them come to me. The lyrics hit her. "You're trying to pound somethin' into my thick head, aren't you, God? Them kids belong to you. I'm supposed to let go of 'em and trust you."

The lyrics echoed in her mind again and again. She'd never known that little song had another verse—not until Jakob sat on the edge of Annie's bed after she'd had the baby. Radiating kindness, he'd assured himself that his sister was fine and admired her newborn son. Hope was on her way out the door to give them some private time—but Jakob called to her and patted the mattress.

"We have a custom. Come join us."

As the dawn of a new day broke, he'd blessed the Lord for the gift of the baby, then sang those tender words of Jesus' love to the child.

The memory sent chills up and down Hope's back. With the Lord's provision and Jakob's constancy, Annie and the children would thrive here. *Let them come to me.*

She looked around. The house was in order. Jar upon jar of food filled the pantry to overflowing. Through gleaming windows, Hope could see Sunday-best clothes hanging on the line, ready to be ironed. A bouquet of roses on the table proved even the once-scraggly bush out front now flourished.

"It don't make sense, God. Everything's in order. Why don't it all seem right to me?"

No answer came.

Hope washed the shoelaces, polished the shoes, and started to iron the clothes for church. Her dress came last—the new one. So Emmy-Lou could see her better, Hope had taken to wearing her green dress every day. The breathtakingly beautiful material Jakob gave her had become her Sunday-best.

Annie came downstairs. "I thought we were going to wait until sundown to do the hot chores."

Hope slid the iron back and forth. "I got to talkin' to God and just kept busy."

"I'll start supper. I thought maybe *kasenophla*. What do you think?"

Cheese buttons. Normally, Hope's mouth would water at the suggestion. She shrugged. "I'm not hungry for much of anything. Emmy-Lou and Phineas love 'em, so it'll make them happy."

Annie slanted her a funny look. "Are you okay?"

"Yeah. Just porcupined."

"Porcupined?"

"Yup." Hope clunked the iron back onto the stove. "You know—busy with a bunch of prickly thoughts."

"Preoccupied." Annie immediately pressed her fingers to her mouth. "I'm sorry. I didn't mean to correct you."

At times like this, Annie's confidence evaporated and she went back to looking scared. Hope waved her hand dismissively. "You're my friend. You wouldn't never make fun of me. Your word sounds right, but mine makes more sense to me."

Annie dropped her hand and relief eased her features. "It does to me, too."

"When I took the eggs and milk to town on Wednesday, Mr. Clark at the mercantile called possums 'opossums.' All I could think was that made 'em sound like they was Irish. Think he calls porcupines 'oporcupines'?"

Annie's eyes sparkled. "Irish? Oh, Hope, I never thought of it before, but you're right. 'Opossum' is the correct name, but almost no one says it that way. What made him mention possums, anyway?"

"He said a coupla farms were short on eggs. I reckon it's more likely to be coyotes and snakes. That's why I've been askin' Emmy-Lou to help y'all with the baby whilst I gather eggs. I'm afraid she might not see a snake if 'n one was there."

Annie's eyes grew huge. "Merciful heavens! I hadn't thought about that!"

"It ain't my place to say nothin', but whilst we're talking about eggs . . . I know your brother's dearly departed wife loved her Dominiques, but them hens lay brown eggs. It'd be awful nice if 'n he switched over next spring to hens what lay white eggs. Thataway, Emmy-Lou can help out. It's important for her to do as much as she can."

"Why didn't you say so?" a deep voice sounded.

"Oh!" Hope jumped and whirled around to find Mr. Stauffer leaning against the kitchen windowsill. Heart thundering, Hope waggled her finger at him. "You like to scared me straight outta my skin. I reckon y'all got what you got right now, but come next spring, maybe you could send away for some of them railroad-delivered chicks I told y'all about."

"In the meantime," he said, "we can trade hens with some of the other farmers' wives."

"Lena Patterson planned to have a sewing day where we all swapped feed sacks. It'll probably be this next week." Annie shrugged diffidently. "If we say something tomorrow at church, then we can swap chickens at the sewing bee. That is, unless you think it's wrong, talking about business on Sunday."

"I wouldn't count it as business any more than arranging the bee. No one's paying money or making a profit." Jakob stepped back from the window and scowled at Hope. "Don't you ever hesitate to talk to me about Emmy-Lou."

Hope felt Annie tense. Irritated that Jakob hadn't been mindful of his sister's sensitivity, Hope folded her arms across her chest. "Don't you ever go sneakin' up on me or eavesdropping. Serves you right, not likin' what you overheard. You cooked your goose, so go lie in it." She winced. "No, that's not how the saying goes." She thought for a moment. "You made your bed, now go tell lies about it."

Even from the distance between them, Hope saw his smirk. She shook her finger. "You're nothing but a rascal. You got me riled, and now I can't remember—oh, now I do." She straightened up and smoothed her apron. " 'What's sauce for the goose will get up her dander.' "

A boyish grin tilted his mouth. He paused and looked at her through the screen. Even through the mesh, she saw the amused twinkle in his eyes. "Did I get up your dander, Hope?"

She turned to Annie. "I ain't gonna answer that, 'cuz if'n I do, I'm admittin' to being a goose."

Giggles bubbled out of Annie, and Jakob belted out a rich laugh. He took off his summer straw hat and fanned himself. "Geese are silly creatures. You, Hope, would never be a goose."

*Did he mean that as a compliment, or does he think I'm—*Hope covered her eyes for a moment. All of this nonsense was making her head ache. When she looked again, Jakob was studying her as if she needed close watching. "Did y'all want something, or are you up to no good?"

Annie gasped again.

Hope patted her on the arm. "Stop frettin'. That brother of yours is harmless as a well-fed hound. Since you and me're the ones what feed him, he's likely to . . ." Hope looked back at him and forgot what she was going to say. These last days, just being around him sent her into a dither.

"Ask for a carrot," he inserted. "Nicodemus and Josephine deserve a treat. Hattie too."

"You don't have to ask for carrots." Annie bustled over to get them.

"Ja, I do. My boots are filthy. I know better than to step foot in the house right now." He waggled his brows. "Annie, remember the time Mama boxed my ears for that?"

"I'd forgotten."

He chuckled ruefully. "I didn't."

Hope could imagine Jakob as a boy, being scolded and looking sheepish. He'd probably been a handful. "So your ma had some spunk, huh?"

"Ja." Jakob went around to the back porch for the carrots. Though Annie went to hand them over, Jakob called, "Hope?"

What now? She tried to hide her exasperation. Didn't he know she was busy? A few quick steps took her to the door. "What?"

"Mama, she was lively—in many ways, you are much like she was."

His words took her completely off-guard. Hope blinked in surprise. "Y'all couldn't have said nothin' more nicer than that. Judgin' from the son and daughter she reared, I'd say your mama was quite a woman."

Jakob's praise stuck in her mind the rest of the afternoon. She'd already wanted everything to be perfect when she left, but now Hope wanted to do even more. Crazily, though, she felt as if everything took longer and more effort than it ought to.

Annie needed to nurse the baby, so Hope boiled the cheese buttons. As she strained the last ones from the pot, Jakob and Phineas came in. They washed up while Emmy-Lou chattered at them. Jakob took the bowl from Hope. In a low tone, he said, "I need to speak with you later."

She gave him a quizzical look, then realization nearly made her sway from the blow. *He's fixin' to send me away.*

"Tomorrow's Sunday. Don't cook at all. It's too hot to fire up the stove."

"I needed the iron, anyhow." Her voice sounded funny. Strained. She went to the icebox as much to get away and hide her feelings as to grab Emmy-Lou's milk. The blast of cold felt heavenly. As Hope straightened up, the kitchen whirled.

"Hope?" Annie sounded far away.

Staying still for a moment so she'd regain her balance, Hope managed to respond, "Hmmm?" Instead of feeling stable, Hope couldn't quite figure out why the floor kept tilting. *I forgot to get out the milk. What's a-wrong with me?*

"Hope!" Jakob appeared before her. His hands shot out and clasped about her arms. As long as she stared at the uppermost button on his blue work shirt, the whirling sensation ceased—but he didn't have the courtesy to stand still and leave the button in clear view. Instead, he dipped his head and frowned at her. "Are you all right?"

Giving him a perplexed look, she said, "I guess I got me a headache." He let go of her left arm, and she sagged a little at the loss of his support.

Pressing his hand to her forehead, Jakob rasped, "You're hot!"

Hope tried unsuccessfully to bat his hand away. " 'Course I am." He'd just said something about the stove being hot, hadn't he? Maybe if she ate something, she wouldn't feel quite so weak. "Dinner's gettin' cold."

"Phineas." Off to Jakob's left, Annie shoved her baby into the farmhand's arms.

That didn't look right. Hope couldn't figure out why. The way her head was pounding, she couldn't hold a thought. She closed her eyes for just a second, but when she started falling, she couldn't peel them open. Strong arms wrapped around her, lifted her. From a long way off, she heard Jakob. He sounded upset. "Lord, no. Please, God, no."

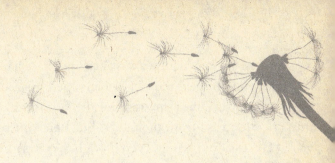

Twenty-Three

"My Marcella, she bakes the best prune cake you ever tasted." Leopold Volkner pushed away from the table and rubbed his stomach. "Ja, Konrad. Just wait 'til next year when I'm married. Come harvesttime, you'll see what a fine cook she is."

Konrad plastered on a smile. Ague had hit with a vengeance. With the fields ripe for harvest and so many men sick, he couldn't do without every last pair of capable hands—which meant he had to feign interest when Volkner boasted endlessly about his fiancée. At least once a day, Volkner pulled out a picture and showed it off like Marcella was a ravishing beauty instead of a fat cow.

Someone said, "It sounds like you found yourself a fine girl. When will you marry?"

"If I had my way, tomorrow."

"Now, Leo." Volkner's mother patted his cheek. "Until the reaping and threshing are all done, you wouldn't have time for a new bride."

"Ja." Konrad raised his voice. "We need to get back to work." He'd already done his fair share of labor at his neighbors'. Back when old man Stauffer was alive, this place had always been the second or third in order to be reaped; regardless of Konrad's maneuvers, his farm was now the last. It rankled him.

Men rose from the tables, but Ben Luft remained seated. He'd slacked all day, even though they were all working shorthanded. *I knew this would happen. I worked hard at his place. He's always been lazy, and now that his fields are done—*

"Ben?" Luft's brother jostled his shoulder.

Ben propped his elbows on either side of his still-full plate and buried his head in his hands. "I tried. I tried, but—"

"He's sick!" Mrs. Volkner backed off. "Take him home."

Facing the loss of two workers, Konrad reacted at once. "He can go lie down. The heat—it's bad today. Rest and water will revive him."

Ben's brother stood him up, braced him, and kneed the bench out of the way. "*Nein.* His wife and children are all sick. I'll get him home."

"That would be best." Leo Volkner made his proclamation as if he were in charge of the day. Deep murmurs of agreement followed.

The men went back to the field and labored. At one point, Leo shot Konrad a grin. "We'll still finish your place by the day's end."

Just barely. "Ja."

"Your wheat—it's fine wheat." Leo looked down at the seeds stuck to his sweaty palm. "Next year will be good for both of us."

Konrad grunted. By exchanging labor with all the other neighbors, he'd come out on the short end of the deal—many hadn't come through for him today. On top of that, since Volkner didn't put in wheat, he'd bartered his labor; his work today cost dearly. Konrad pledged to give him wheat seed for next year's crop. Volkner was no better than that greedy old buzzard of a mother he had.

"Ja, next year should be excellent." Volkner added to the windrow. "We'll have abundant fields, we'll have our wives by our sides, and tasty food on the table."

Folks kept making comments about Annie's absence. Heartily sick of it, Konrad pounced on the opportunity. "After the reaping, I'm going to fetch my wife. You'll keep an eye on things here for me, ja?"

"Certainly. I'll give you a letter to drop off for my Marcella."

Late in the afternoon, Mrs. Volkner and her daughter came out to the field. Work stopped, and the men all drank water and ate sandwiches. It took a few minutes to gulp everything down; then they turned back to the field.

Volkner mused, "I'm thinking to put in some fruit trees. Jakob has peaches. Annie baked tarts for all of us."

Konrad's jaw tightened.

"His wife brought them out to us in a mule cart along with the sandwiches. She made us all eat pickles first—for the salt."

"His wife?" Konrad couldn't believe he'd heard correctly.

"Ja." Volkner's brows scrunched, and his face puckered with concentration. "I didn't think of it until now. How is it that Annie is still there?"

Konrad cleared his throat to buy a moment of time. He scrambled to concoct a plausible reply. "I was surprised that Jakob's wife drove out to the fields. It is good to hear she's up and around. He wrote that she has some"—his voice dropped and he leaned forward—"well . . . *problems*. Until her health gets better, I decided it was best for Annie to stay and mind Jakob's daughter."

Nodding sagely, Volkner said, "Especially with the girl going blind, that makes sense."

"Blind?"

Leo gave him an odd look. "You didn't know?"

"Ja. Of course I did." Konrad quickly recovered. "My Annie wrote all about it. I didn't think they were telling anyone that sad news yet."

Seemingly satisfied with that excuse, Leo started working.

For the rest of the afternoon, anger had Konrad working like a man possessed. Even after the reaper made its final pass and the men all left, he couldn't rest. Jakob had a wife. A wife. He didn't need Annie to watch his brat.

From the first time they met, Jakob acted full of himself—as if he were smarter and better. His brother was the same way. Jakob married and moved away, but his brother was just as bad. Konrad's mouth curled into a sneer of a smile. Bartholomew got just what he deserved the day he'd fallen from the loft, spooked the stallion, and gotten trampled to death.

Konrad sympathized with old man Stauffer and made himself indispensable. Even then, the old man hadn't seen him as more than a hired hand until Konrad resorted to the one ploy he'd held in reserve: After rehearsing until it sounded convincing, he approached the old man with a request to seek Annie's hand. Stauffer gave his blessing, and the marriage ensued.

Pacing inside the empty farmhouse, his emphatic footsteps echoing all around him, Konrad strove to make order of the tumult of thoughts screaming at him. He was married, but he didn't have his wife. Jakob wasn't supposed to have a wife, but he did. And he had Annie.

Volkner had a big mouth. Until now, he'd been so besotted, he'd spoken of nothing but his bride-to-be. Sooner or later, he'd say something about Jakob's bride. *I'll order Annie to tell everyone what I told Volkner—that Jakob's new bride was sickly. And Volkner said the brat was going blind.* That and a sick bride added up to a plausible excuse for Annie's prolonged absence.

Jakob couldn't keep Annie anymore—he had no excuse. Tomorrow was Saturday. Perfect. Konrad would take the train and show up at church Sunday, just as he'd planned. There, he'd reclaim his wife. In fact, he'd insist upon Annie staying in town with him overnight so they could catch the Monday train coming back.

Satisfied with that plan, Konrad stopped pacing.

His satisfaction evaporated. In stark relief to the upstairs, the downstairs was spotless. Annie should have been there to cook and clean for the past seven months—but especially today. A farmer's wife was meant to labor at his side, but cooking for the harvest hands was her greatest responsibility each year. Annie had failed him. Instead, the Volkner women and a bunch of the nosey old biddies had fussed and poked around. The floor gleamed, the furniture had been dusted, and a stupid bouquet of flowers sat on the small parlor table. Konrad knew full well those busybodies gossiped far more than they'd worked, and they'd continue to cluck forever about the way things had been.

It wouldn't happen again. Annie would know her place and stay there; Jakob would keep his distance or regret it. After lighting a kerosene lamp, Konrad shoved the glass chimney back in place. The glass shattered. All at once, he cut and burned his right hand. Vile curses filled the air.

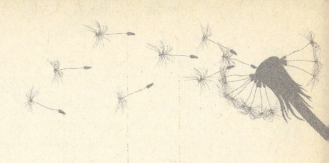

Twenty-Four

It ain't your cookin', Annie." Hope stared at her plate. She'd managed to eat only half of a flapjack and a bite of scrambled eggs. "I'm just not hungry."

"I understand."

Hope didn't have enough energy to get up from the table. She sat there and pulled Jakob's robe around herself for warmth. "I wish y'all woulda gone to church today. You didn't have to stay home with me."

"Nonsense."

Hope absently rubbed her neck. "These here spots just make me look bad off. It's been so long since I took sick, clean forgot about that happenin' whenever I run me a fever."

"We were very worried. We still are—oh, I don't mean that I'm worried about the children. I've told you that, haven't I?"

" 'Bout ten hundred times." Hope skidded her fork around the syrup on the edge of her plate. "Does my heart good, seein' that Emmy-Lou and your little Johnny are healthy as heifers. Wouldn't want nobody to get whatever 'twas that I got, but

291

'specially not the kids. Even if'n they did, they probably wouldn't break out in this silly rash."

"Knowing my brother, he'll ask Velma to drop by on her way home from church to take a look at you. You may as well resign yourself to it." Annie took away the plate and scraped the uneaten food into the swill bucket. In no time at all, she'd washed the dishes.

Johnny let out a series of little squeaks. "The baby's settin' hisself up to sing scales. Best you get him afore he takes a mind to wail out a whole opera."

Annie took her son out of the cradle and nestled him to herself. "I'm so thankful Jakob has that medical book."

"I'm thankful he knows where to look up stuff. It don't make sense to me at all, how they got it in there."

"He practically tore out the pages, searching. At first, we thought you might have measles—but your eyes weren't red and runny. And the rash started right away—but not on your face first. Then Jakob saw the part about fever rashes and read it. We immediately knew that was you. Did you know measles have to be quarantined?"

Footsteps sounded on the back porch. That didn't seem quite right. Jakob always entered through the front door. But that wasn't his walk. Puny as she felt, Hope still knew the sound of his approach. The knob turned without anyone knocking, so it had to be Phineas.

A tall, gaunt blond man stepped into the kitchen uninvited.

Annie let out a loud gasp and backed up a step.

Even if Annie hadn't reacted, Hope would have known who the man was—his eyes were cruel, and the way his mouth tilted into a purposefully nasty excuse for a smile proclaimed him to be Annie's polecat of a husband.

"Annie, you're going home with me now."

Her arms tightened convulsively around her son, and Johnny let out a small wail of protest.

An imperious wave of his hand accompanied Konrad's order. "Give Jakob's wife her brat. You've done more than enough here, and it's past time to go."

Pale as could be, Annie sidled past him and pressed her beloved son into Hope's arms. Her eyes pled with Hope to protect him.

"I'm weak as water." It was no lie. Hope shakily rose to her feet. "I'm going to need help getting upstairs. Please, Annie, carry the baby up for me. I don't want to drop him."

Annie automatically took back her son.

Hope shuffled a few steps, then stopped directly in front of Konrad. "You know that sayin' 'bout 'are you a man or a louse'? Well 'tis plain for me to see which one you are." Her legs started to buckle, and she didn't fight it. Instead, she reached out and grabbed fistsful of his shirt. "Takes a lotta gumption to come in here." For good measure, Hope clung tight and laid her head against his chest. "Thankee. I've been sore sick."

Konrad grabbed her by the wrists and shoved her away. "You've got a rash!" He glowered at Annie. "Did I hear you say something about quarantine?"

Annie bit her lip.

"Jakob's probably gonna show up anytime now. He'll be bringin' a healer with him." Hope paused and chose her words carefully. *God, I don't wanna lie, but I don't want him to hurt Annie.* Bracing herself against the table, Hope dipped her head. "Jakob was reading to Annie about the measles. Last time I saw somebody with the measles, the doc wouldn't let nobody in or outta the house for two solid weeks."

"Two weeks!" The words tore from his chest.

"You're welcome to stay." Hope melted into a chair again. "Fact is, if'n you'd carry me upstairs, I'd be obliged."

"Nein!" Stepping backward, he looked from Hope to Annie. "Give her the brat. You're still coming with me."

Annie nodded slowly, silently. As she approached Hope again, Hope strained to think of a way to safeguard her. A peek at the clock told her church wasn't even half over yet. Jakob wouldn't be coming home for over an hour. "Thankee, Annie, for all your help. Oh no! What's that? You got a spot on your wrist!"

Annie glanced down, then gave Hope a helpless look. "It's nothing."

"That's what I said 'bout mine, too. Mr. Erickson, sir, can you see what I'm a-talkin' bout?" Fear flickered in his eyes. Hope pressed on. "Your wife—she's—Annie, stop covering it and let him see. He can touch your brow to see if'n you've got a fever simmerin'." Hope nudged Annie in his direction. Annie was right—it was nothing more than a large reddish freckle she always had, but her husband probably wouldn't remember it.

Konrad Erickson practically leapt away without sparing even a glance at the spot. "I'll be back for you." He backed out the door. "I'll be back, Annie. You belong to me."

A second after the door slammed shut, Hope reached for Annie's hand and drew her close. "You don't *belong* to him. You don't even belong *with* him. You belong to God, and you belong in this here house."

"He'll come back." Fear thickened Annie's voice.

" 'Course he will. A snake don't change his spots. But we got Almighty God on our side." Hope continued to hold Annie's hand as she sank to the floor. "That's right, Annie. When your knees start a-shakin', that's the bestest time to kneel."

"I don't even know what to pray."

"Let's start with thankin' the Lord for my rash. The Bible says in everything, give thanks. Well, turns out this bothersome rash was God's way of protectin' you today."

In a matter of minutes, Johnny set to bawling. Hope didn't want to leave Annie alone, so she suggested, "How's about us movin' to the parlor? You can suckle your son, and I might be rude and nod off on the settee."

"I'll take you upstairs."

"Three days. I've been stuck in that room for three days. It's a right fine room—don't get me wrong—but I'm fixin' to stay outta it for a while yet."

As she curled up in the parlor, Hope watched Annie draw a shawl over her shoulder. "Reckon you and me could recite our psalm together?"

They started in unison, but Hope strategically let her voice die out when Annie's special verses came up. Afterward, Annie said, "You did that to remind me of God's promise to keep me."

"I did that to remind us both. Far as I can tell, you can't never hear too much of the Lord's words."

Hope didn't want to fall asleep. Annie needed her. She felt herself fading. "It bein' the Lord's Day and us bein' here, why don't we sing a few hymns? Betcha little Johnny'd like that."

"That is a nice idea, but I don't much feel like singing."

"Reckon that's the bestest reason to sing." Hope's voice was unsteady, but she began, "O, for a thousand tongues to sing . . ."

Annie half hummed, half sang the first verse. Her voice cracked on the third stanza. "Jesus, the name that charms our fears—" She laid her head against the back of the rocking chair and started to weep.

Hope pushed herself off the settee and tottered over to her friend. She sang as she sank to the floor by the rocker. " 'Tis life and health and peace.' Didja hear that, Annie? There's power and peace in the name of Jesus. You're ascairt right now." She patted Annie's leg. "But Jakob and Phineas and me—we're gonna pray for God to send a region of angels. No, wait. A lesion of angels . . . That still don't sound right."

"A legion of angels."

"Exactly! See? You're already agreein' with me. When two or more gather and agree in Christ Jesus' name, there's power. Ain't just you and me and little Johnny here. God and a big old legion of His angels are here, too. Good thing Jakob built a big parlor."

Finally, Jakob got home. Just as expected, Velma was with him. She took one look at them and patted Emmy-Lou. "You go upstairs and change out of your Sunday dress."

Once his daughter was out of earshot, Jakob came to the parlor and asked in a somber tone, "What is it?"

"Konrad—he came. He says he's coming back to get me."

"He's wrong." Jakob hunkered down and drew Hope's arm around his neck. "Do you hear me, Annie? He's wrong." As he scooped Hope into his arms, he added, "Konrad doesn't know what he's talking about."

Hope let her head sag on Jakob's strong shoulder. "You couldn't be more right. Konrad don't know nothing." Hope let out a small puff of a laugh. "He thinks you and me're married and Johnny is our baby."

Hope's words abruptly shifted Jakob from wrath to disbelief. "What did you say?"

She yawned, and her head moved ever so slightly to find a more comfortable spot. Lifting her a little, Jakob tilted his jaw to nudge her head closer. Holding her felt . . . right. Just as right as the notion of them being married and having children of their own.

"Konrad—he thought you and Hope were married." Annie clutched her son. "He thinks Johnny is your child. Jakob—he will come back. He said he would. You must promise me that you will keep Johnny. Konrad won't ever know. . . . "

"It won't come to that." Angry with himself for underestimating Konrad, he vowed to set his plan into action as soon as Hope was in bed. "I'm carrying Hope upstairs."

"I'll help tuck her in." Velma waited by the stairs.

Hope fell asleep in the brief moments he held her. Was she that weak, or did she trust him that completely? Jakob pushed aside his selfish musings. He slipped her onto the cot he'd built for her weeks ago, but letting go wasn't easy. He wanted to hold her close and savor how her trust let her rely on him. It took all of his self-discipline to turn loose of her, then step back. *I struggled to let go now. How will I send her away at all? God, give me strength.*

Emmy-Lou's hand slid into his. "Daddy, can you please button my dress?" Without waiting for his reply, she changed her grip to only one of his fingers and twirled like a ballerina to give him her back.

He'd never had trouble buttoning her dresses, but his fingers fumbled.

Annie had ascended the stairs, too. "I'll see to her, Jakob. I'll make Sunday supper, too."

Taking in his sister's tear-ravaged face, he shook his head. "Stay up here and rest with Hope and Johnny."

Bless her soul, Velma waggled her finger at Annie. "He's right. You need to get more shut-eye. I'll feed Emmy-Lou; then she can take her nap, too." Quickly fastening Emmy-Lou's buttons, Velma said, "I'll be down in just a minute. You're going to help me make Sunday supper, so go on downstairs, stand on the stool by the washbowl, and scrub your hands real good."

"Okay!" Blissfully oblivious, his daughter left. Her little feet pattered down the stairs.

"Phineas and I"—Jakob strove to choose his words carefully—"we will talk."

"Good. The sooner, the better." Velma pushed him toward the door. "When I get back to Forsaken, I'm fixin' to tell Big Tim. You can use all the help you can get."

Jakob looked from her to Annie and back. Had Annie told her? Only Annie looked bewildered.

"It wasn't my business, and I didn't poke my nose into it. The day Annie swooned and I told you she was with child, I saw bruises. She had a crop of 'em—all different colors. That only means one thing." The ample cook from Forsaken Ranch turned to Annie and enveloped her in a hug. "As long as you were safe here, I kept my mouth shut. You're in danger, so I'm speaking up. That varmint isn't going to drag you back."

"You knew?" Annie's voice wavered.

Velma gave her a squeeze and stepped back. "Some folks think it's family business. Well, we're family. You're my sister in Christ. It's your man's shame that he thumped on you. He lost any right to have you by his side."

"So." Jakob looked down at Hope. She looked darling all bundled up in his robe. She didn't have one of her own, so he'd loaned her his. "Annie, you will stay up here and take care of Johnny and Hope." He couldn't resist making contact, so he feathered a few golden curls from Hope's temple. "Velma will take care of Emmy-Lou, and Phineas and I—"

"He—" Annie hung her head and bit her lip. "Phineas . . . you are going to tell him?"

"He knows, Annie. He guessed the very same day I brought you here. When Leopold Volkner showed up, Phineas helped keep him away. See? All around you, God has placed people to safeguard you. He'll be faithful. Lie down and rest. Remember the psalm you've claimed? 'He that keepeth thee will not slumber.' You can sleep because Almighty God always watches over you."

"Amen!" Velma declared.

"Huh?" Hope roused and half sat up.

"You go on now." Velma gave him a shove. "Annie and I can take care of her. Hope, I may as well check you out. Glory, gal, this rash must itch like the dickens. We'll use some baking soda—"

"I'm thankful for my rash."

Jakob turned in the doorway at Hope's sleepy comment.

"Scared that coward away, didn't it, Annie? I told him two weeks."

"Two weeks?" Jakob repeated. That kind of time was a huge boon. Hope had bought him two weeks to put his plans into motion. Not only that, she'd have a chance to recover before he sent her away.

"Hope said we'd probably be in quarantine for that long."

Velma chortled softly. "You sure are. Yep. That's what I'm going to tell everyone. Of course I'm sure Big Tim won't pay mind to my edict. Why . . . he'd show up here whenever you want, Jakob. Just to make some plans."

"The sheriff and Pastor Bradle, too—can you arrange that?"

Velma started tugging the belt on Hope's robe. "Easier than bakin' a cake. Now get out of here."

"Okay." Hope started to shrug and wiggle. "What kind?"

Annie tenderly tucked Hope's braid back over her shoulder. "What do you mean, Hope?"

"I'll get out of this and bake the cake."

Annie's eyes widened, and she let out a nervous giggle.

Jakob couldn't help himself. He grinned, too—but at Hope. She'd known exactly what she was saying and doing. He knew it, too, because she winked at him. Hope was some woman . . . and soon, he'd make her his.

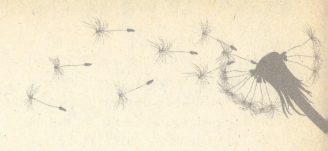

Twenty-Five

Konrad sat with his back against the trunk of the peach tree and watched the farmhouse. Jakob had brought a middle-aged woman home with him, and she left after a little while. Konrad's first impulse was to stop her and seek more information, but he didn't. Waiting would be best. If Annie and her brother were playing him for a fool, they wouldn't be able to keep up the ruse.

A few hours later, three men arrived. Instead of going in the house, they stayed out on the porch with Jakob and the farmhand. The preacher was still wearing his Sunday black suit. A metallic glint from the second man's chest showed him to be the sheriff. The third man—he couldn't possibly be the doctor. Doctors wore suits all the time and spent their time with books. That one was brawny, sun-bronzed, and in jeans.

"No!" Jakob half shouted. "You don't understand!"

A thrill chased up Konrad's spine. It was good to see someone bossing Jakob, telling him things he didn't want to hear. Things he couldn't control. Well, he'd better get used to it. The rest of the conversation rose and fell in rumbles too indistinct for Konrad to overhear.

The sheriff and parson left in about twenty minutes, but the third one stayed behind. He seemed busy at something, but Konrad couldn't tell what until the man nailed up a sign on the porch. The paint was a little runny, but the warning was clear: *Quarantine*.

Konrad stayed out of sight and continued to observe Jakob's farm. Jakob and his farmhand kept exchanging hostile looks. Well, well. The trip here didn't result in his taking Annie home, but Konrad didn't mind so much now. Just witnessing Jakob's being thwarted was worth it all.

It wasn't until sunset that he slinked back to town. The widow woman at the boardinghouse was playing her piano and singing with her little girl. As Konrad started up the stairs to his room, another woman came in. "Mrs. Orion, my husband just told me the Stauffer farm is under quarantine. I wondered if I could depend on you to make some soup."

"Quarantine!"

"Yes. Velma's declared it. I trust her judgment implicitly. Why, when I had the hives, she had Sydney use baking-soda compresses that—well, it's not important, other than it just proved yet again that we're blessed to have someone of Velma's caliber. Anyway, the sheriff is willing to drop off a meal each day."

"It's the least I can do. Would you like it for tonight?"

"No, no. I already have things arranged through Thursday. Would Friday work for you?"

Konrad stomped up the stairs and slammed the door to his room. His wife was minding Jakob's wife and brats, and folks were delivering hot meals to them. In the meantime, he'd go home alone and have to survive on his own cooking for two more weeks. Even on his worst day, Jakob Stauffer still had folks helping him out. Anger had Konrad flexing his fists—but that only made things worse. The cuts and burn stung.

Pouring water from the pitcher over his hand and into the washbasin eased the pain. His left hand was plenty strong enough to handle a full pitcher. He set the pitcher aside and looked at the place where his two last fingers belonged. If anyone noticed the ugly little nubs, he said they'd been lost in a reaper. It was better than confessing he'd gotten caught cheating at cards and paid that horrible price.

Using just his right hand, he splashed the water on his face. A critical look in the mirror told him he ought to pay a visit to the barber—he was long overdue for a haircut, and he'd given up shaving months ago. It saved him a lot of time and trouble—but having the barber trim his beard would make a good impression. If it weren't Sunday, he'd go have it done now. No. He'd wait another week and a half. A slow smile lifted the corners of his mouth. It would be a good sign to everyone back home that he was going to fetch his wife.

He needed Annie home to cook for the threshing. She'd been gone for reaping, but having her there for the threshing would make folks believe everything was fine. And it would be fine. In fact, Annie had missed him. He could tell, because when he'd told her to give Jakob's wife the kid and come to him, she'd obeyed. The old saying proved true: Absence made her heart grow fonder.

Threshing followed anywhere from ten days to five weeks after reaping. Since the wheat had been mostly ripe, it was best to thresh it quickly, else he'd lose yield. Two weeks would be okay. No more than that, though. He'd come back in exactly two weeks. Annie would be expecting him, and she'd be packed and ready. They'd get home on Monday, and he'd arrange to have their farm threshed on Tuesday. No, Wednesday. That way she'd have a day to bake. Volkner made a point of saying how she'd baked for Jakob's harvest hands. Well, folks would talk of how she'd returned and settled right in and done him proud.

Everyone loved it when the thresher arrived—its steam engine could be heard from far away and the loud chugging built up a sense of anticipation. It would be a good welcome for her. The pleasure on Annie's face would put to rest any of his neighbors' suspicions.

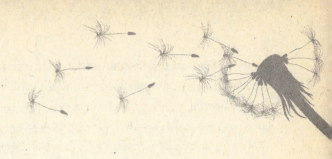

Twenty-Six

"Creighton." Jakob shook his neighbor's hand.

Phineas inhaled deeply. "Something smells good!"

"Ribs. Barbecued them myself." Tim hooked his thumbs in the pockets of his jeans and looked downright smug. "I've got news. Good news. You can scrap your plans."

"Konrad's dead?" Phineas looked delighted.

"No, but almost as good." Tim nudged Jakob. "You gave me great information. It made all the difference. Instead of sending the women away, you're going to be sending Konrad off. Permanently. Let me explain. . . ."

"You can stop hovering. I'm healthy as a mule." Hope gave Jakob a wry look. Annie was in the parlor, nursing Johnny after she'd put Emmy-Lou to bed. A symphony of crickets had lured Hope out to the back porch, but Jakob insisted on escorting her as if she were a tottering old crone.

"What are you making?"

She pulled out her crochet and carefully held up the piece so she wouldn't undo anything. "An apron. I'm almost done."

"It's not very practical. Not very big, either. Are you . . ." Jakob's voice died out, and he clamped his jaw shut.

"It's for Emmy-Lou."

His eyes flashed. "How could you do this? She won't be able to cook by herself."

"No child can. She's good at dumping things in a bowl, stirring, and loves to lick the spoon afterward."

Jakob shook his head slowly. Deep worry lines plowed his forehead. "It's not right to do that to her, Hope. Emmy-Lou must learn that she's different. If you let her think she can do these things, when the time comes that she can't, it will be a bigger disappointment."

They'd danced around this issue more than a few times. *Lord, he's worryin' about his daughter not seein', but he's blind to the truth. Can't you open his eyes?* Hope waited for a moment. Nothing within her warned her to stay silent. *God, I'm takin' that as a sign that it's time to speak my piece.*

"You and me—we're lookin' at it different. You don't want her to have anything that might be taken away later. Me? I think the more she has now, the better she'll be at livin' life to the fullest later. Time might come when she goes blind—but because she knows her colors, you can paint her a picture with words, and she'll see the sunrise anyway."

"That's different than cooking."

"Maybe. Maybe not." Hope leaned toward him. "I was thinking—the measuring spoons and cups. You could use a nail and tap dents on each of 'em so's she'd know which was what. And she'll know by the size of the canisters what's inside. Thataway, she can do quite a bit in the kitchen.

"I was thinkin' on it last night. I don't look at my hands whilst I shell peas or beans. I look at Annie or at the sunset or watch one of the dogs chase Milky. If'n you watch your sis when she rolls out pie dough, you'll see she don't stare at it."

Her boss didn't say anything. Then again, he didn't argue with her. That had to be a good sign.

She let out a small laugh. "As a matter of fact, lookee here. We've been talkin', and I didn't even look down, but my crochet hook's dippin', twistin', and loopin'."

Jakob looked at the piece in her lap.

"Mr. Stauffer, sir—"

"Jakob," he corrected her.

Hope spared him a quick smile. "Jakob, I love your little girl. I think she's the dearest gal God ever made, and I wouldn't never do nothin' to hurt her. You're a man. You don't know what it takes to be a woman. Little girls learn plenty in their tender years. If'n Emmy-Lou learns a heap of things now, she'll be more productive later."

"So this apron—it is a sign to her that she will cook and do handiwork? But that isn't honest."

"Sure it is. No one can do everything. Me? I can't read, and I still have a good life. I have to depend on others—but I reckon that was God's plan."

"The body of believers . . ." he mused. "That is what you're talking about."

She stared at her hook as she continued to work. Though he'd finally understood, Hope didn't feel victorious. She swallowed. "I'll be leavin', but when I do, I wanna have left Emmy-Lou with the stars in her hands, the colors in her mind, and the knowledge that she can still be a happy, worthwhile person."

"You're not leaving!"

Hope hitched her shoulder.

"We have an agreement." His voice came out in a forceful whisper. "You would stay for Annie's sake. Now, more than ever, she needs you."

Relief knotted the hole in her heart just as completely as the crochet thread wound and hooked into place. "I wasn't shore how you felt. While I was ailin', them two weeks after Johnny was born came to a close. Fact is, that night I fell sick, I know you was gonna tell me 'twas time for me to head out."

He gave her an odd look. "In a manner of speaking, perhaps."

Her heart plummeted. *Jakob doesn't want me.* The air burned in her lungs. *I said I wasn't shore how he felt, and he told me. I'm good for Annie. That's all. I'd hoped . . . well, dunno what I expected. I'm bein' silly after bein' under the weather.*

"But you'll stay." He phrased it as a statement, not a question.

Looking down at her crocheting, Hope bit her lip and nodded. "Like you said, we have a pact to help your sis. Long as you feel that me stayin' here protects her from that snake, I'll stay on."

Relief resounded in the gush of his exhalation.

In everything give thanks. I gotta stop thinkin' on myself and see all the good that the Lord's doin'. Hope looked at her boss. He loved his kin with a fierceness and gentleness that touched her. Annie and Emmy-Lou would be okay with him as the head of the home.

"You're needed here, Hope. You're wanted and appreciated, too. I don't know how you think we'll get along without you."

"Don't go countin' your eggs before you lay 'em." She wrinkled her nose. "That sounded silly. Roosters don't lay eggs. Well, don't go a-borrowin' troubles."

"I've got enough as it is. We have five more days before Konrad returns." Jakob shot a look over his shoulder at the house, then scooted his chair a little closer. His voice dropped to a bare murmur. "Tim Creighton has a friend who's an attorney. He's written up a contract I'm going to offer Konrad. I'll sell the farm up north and give him all the money as long as he agrees to leave the country and never contact Annie again."

Taking her cue, she whispered back, "But what's to keep him from takin' the money and going back on his word?" The ball of crochet string started to roll off her lap. She grabbed for it and looked back at Jakob. "I'd sooner trust a rabid coyote."

"He's worse." Still keeping his voice muted, Jakob said, "Often, Konrad has said he wishes he'd stayed in Germany. The money would be enough for him to return there. There is a place called Ellis Island in New York. Very soon, all immigrants will have to come through there. You didn't see Konrad for long, so you might not have noticed, but he's missing fingers." Jakob held up his left hand and wrapped his right fingers around the last two left fingers.

Dreadful as she'd felt, Hope hadn't noticed very much when Konrad had been there. "I don't recollect seeing his hand."

"He's ashamed of it and moves carefully so people won't notice. Even so, the fingers are missing. It never made any difference to me, but now I'm glad those fingers are gone."

Hope looked at him in surprise. "It's not like you to be that way."

Jakob met her gaze without any hesitation. "There are new laws. Anyone with a deformity that might render them less capable of working so they could become a public liability won't be permitted entry to America. Even if Konrad decides to come back, when they'd process him at Ellis Island, they will notice his hand. He could claim he can work well, but there are many places where thieves' fingers or hands are cut off. The immigration law denies entry to anyone suspected of moral turpitude. Either way, he would be sent back to Germany."

Tears filled her eyes. "I hope you're right."

"Annie doesn't know yet. I wanted to tell you first. You give her such comfort and confidence, Hope. When I tell her, I want you there so you can reassure her."

"It's powerful nice of you to say that, but I know what Annie's gonna ask. What if Konrad won't sign the contract?"

"He's greedy. He will."

Setting aside her crocheting, Hope leaned toward him. "Mr. Stauffer . . ."

He leaned in, too. "How many times must I tell you to call me Jakob, Hope?"

She couldn't keep a smile from gracing her lips before becoming solemn once more. "Jakob, I seen the way he looked at your sis. That man ain't gonna be reasonable. He'd double cross the devil if'n he could. Annie's feelin's already jump up and down like a cricket. I don't mean to tell you your business . . . Well, maybe I do. But I don't think y'all ought to tell Annie nothin' 'til it's a done deal and that polecat's halfway 'cross the ocean."

Studying her intently, Jakob said nothing. He compressed his lips for a moment, then nodded. "Ja. I think you're right. You've done so much for my sister, Hope. I'm grateful. She needed you. We all did and still do."

Since the secretive discussion was over, Hope decided to revert back to normal volume—that way Annie wouldn't suspect anything. "It's gone both ways. It's been a pure pleasure workin' for you, and all y'all spoilt me rotten when I took sick."

"We worried about you."

"I 'member you prayin' over me." More than once, dreadful as she'd felt, Hope recalled opening her eyes and seeing Jakob kneeling by her cot. Never before had a man quietly, persistently petitioned heaven on her behalf. Knowing he'd done so touched her deeply. *Maybe that's why I got me these warm feelin's about him.*

"*Ja,* we prayed. Annie and I decided if your fever didn't break soon, we'd cut your hair in hopes of conserving what little life force you had left so you might recover." His gaze raised ever so slightly; then, with just a fingertip, he touched a wisp of hair at her temple. The tenderness of his action made her long to tilt her head and rest into the warmth and strength of his callused palm. Not knowing the flood of feelings his simple, kind gesture triggered, Jakob continued speaking. "I'm glad we didn't have to resort to using Annie's sewing shears. Anything to spare your life would have been worth it, but cutting your hair would be such a shame. Your hair is your crowning glory."

Unsure of how to respond, Hope picked up her crochet hook again. His words pleased her immensely. She'd never really much cared what men thought of her looks. As long as she was clean and modest, that was good enough—but hearing Jakob praise her hair, well, it sent warmth streaking through her heart. *I've gotta get aholt of myself. I'm gonna end up being just like Linette Richardson if'n I don't watch out. Ain't fittin' for a woman to go all moon-eyed over a man just because he treats her well.* She cleared her throat. "Emmy-Lou's hair's got quite a bit of curl to it. Was it like that afore her fever when you cut it?"

It took a full minute or more before Jakob answered, "No. It was straight."

I was rude not to thank him for the compliment, but I don't want him thinkin' I'm setting my cap to reel him in. Onliest thing I'm hookin' is this here apron for his little girl. "Y'all did take fine care of me. Velma came over this mornin' with the sad news of Mr. Vaughn. Such a pity. God must have wanted him awful bad to take him away from a wife and that passel of kids."

"You probably got the fever from him that day you went to town with the eggs and milk. I shouldn't have asked you to pick up chicken feed."

"Nonsense." Hope curled the crochet string around her pinkie. "Plenty of folks have bought feed from his store and not taken sick."

Jakob was silent for a moment. "Knowing he didn't make it makes me even more thankful God spared you."

Hooking the ecru-colored crochet string in and out, in and out was calming. "I reckon God ain't done sendin' me where folks need a helpin' hand."

"He sent you here."

"That He did." *I just don't know when you'll be finished with me and sendin' me on my way.* The thought of eventually leaving dragged at her, so Hope decided to change the topic. "Do y'all think your sis might have five or six little tiny buttons I can put on the back of this?"

"Naomi had a button jar."

Hope glanced over at him. He usually didn't mention his wife. Then again, in the past few weeks, she'd sensed a big shift in him. Grief no longer gave a haunted look to his eyes. Striving to sound casual, she said, "Whenever you got a moment and think on it, I'd appreciate you settin' that jar out. We could use some of the bigger ones to help Emmy-Lou with her countin'."

Jakob chuckled. "Yes, well, I was impressed when she hit twenty-nine, but twenty-ten?"

Hope smiled. "She's such a dear heart."

An unexpected voice quietly intersected their conversation. "Jake . . ."

Hope looked up. "Who calls you Jake?"

"Nobody." He stood and peered into the dim barnyard. A mere breath later, he vaulted over the porch rail and ran.

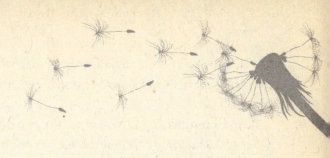

Twenty-Seven

Hope's work dropped to the planks as she dashed after him. "What is it?"

"Phineas." Jakob zigged around the sycamore and to the corner of the barn. By the time Hope reached his side, Jakob had stooped and wrapped Phineas's arm around his shoulders and braced an arm about his waist. "He's hot."

Hope moved to Phineas's other side. "Let's get him to the house. Once he's on the settee, you can come out and fetch his mattress. Would you rather put his bed in the parlor or your office?"

"The office."

"Sorry," Phineas rasped.

☙

Late the next morning, Jakob nudged Hope aside and lifted the sheets from the rinse water. "You stayed up most of the night. Go take a nap."

"Nope. You're a dab hand at a lotta stuff, but I seen you with sheets that one time."

Stubbornly holding on to the sheet, he gave her a withering look that would have made anyone else give in. "Go take a nap, Hope."

"I'm so rested up, I probably won't need to shut my eyes for a whole week." She reached for the sheet. "May as well warn you, Jakob, I'm every bit as stubborn as Hattie."

"Her hat is nicer." Jakob couldn't believe he'd blurted out that insult. "I'm sorry."

"You're sorry you spoke your mind, or are you sorry you like Hattie's hat better?"

Why didn't I keep my big mouth shut? I've hurt her feelings. "Both."

"Seems we got the same taste in hats, then. I like hers better, too. Problem is, I'd have the longest ears and most fattest head in the world if'n her hat fit me. Now gimme that sheet."

"We'll wring it out and hang it up together."

"Many hands make the work right, huh?"

Light. Many hands make the work . . . well, "right" fits the meaning, too. Jakob nodded. "Speaking of hands . . . Phineas isn't going to be in good shape if Konrad comes back even one day early. If I'm not by the house when the sheriff drops off the food, be sure to tell him Phineas is sick."

"Okay." Together they wrung out the rinsed sheet and hung it on the line. As she clipped the last clothespin in place, Hope heaved a sigh. "Jakob, I got me a heavy heart today."

"You do? Why?" He didn't know anyone as buoyant as Hope—but it was good that she felt she could share her burden with him. Even after he'd insulted her one and only hat, she didn't hold it against him.

"Phineas—he's such a good man. And your sister. 'Til last night, I suspected Phineas held a special place in his heart for her. He ain't never said nor done nothin' improper, but I had my suspicions. Last night and today, Annie's hovered over him, and the truth hit me. If'n she wasn't bound in marriage to that worm Konrad, I think her heart would flop straight into Phineas's hands."

"It's not fitting. She's married. Even when Konrad is gone, they are still married."

Hope sighed again. "I know. That's why my heart's heavy. I wisht God woulda done things different. In my head, I know His plan is right; in my heart I wanna jump in and fix things."

"Some things can't be fixed. The best we can pray for is that Konrad will go away and never trouble her again. For her and Johnny to be safe—that's the most important thing."

Though he spoke the right words, Jakob's spirits sank. Annie returned Phineas's affection? How had that happened? When? Sure, they'd been schoolyard friends. But that didn't translate into love. *For Naomi and me, it did.* He shoved aside that thought. Then it hit him: The day he'd told Annie that Linette Richardson had designs on Phineas, Annie fell to pieces. *Lord, I'm like Hope. I want to fix it, but I can't. You work miracles. Can't you do this for my sister and my friend?*

Plenty of chores needed doing. With Phineas ailing, Hope jumped right in and picked up the slack. By sunset, Jakob carried the evening milking to the springhouse and poured it into the De Laval separator. "Jakob, I'll crank that if'n you'll see to gettin' a scuttle or two of coal into the house. I'm needin' more for the stove."

"I'll pour in the other milk can first." After he left her, Jakob filled the scuttle.

Annie had moved the rocking chair from the parlor to just outside the office door. From the shawl over her shoulder, he knew she was nursing Johnny. Sitting on a little stool beside her, Emmy-Lou had a dish towel over her shoulder and her dolly clutched to her chest. "Daddy, me and Auntie Annie are being mommies together."

The sight stopped him in his tracks. Emmy-Lou was copying what she saw all about her—women being wives and mothers. But how would she ever marry and have children if she couldn't see? Even with her strength and eyesight, it had taken all of Hope's stamina to keep up with him that day. No matter how much training Hope gave her, Emmy-Lou wouldn't be able to marry. No man would have her. Each time the thought hit him, his heart clenched.

Annie filled in the silence. "It's fun to play, isn't it?"

Emmy-Lou's curls danced as she nodded. "Uh-huh!"

"How's Phineas?"

Annie leaned a bit to the side and craned to look into the study. "Sleeping. He's been good about drinking for me, so his fever hasn't gotten too bad."

"Daddy, Phineas isn't getting all speckly like Miss Hope did."

"That's good."

Confusion scrunched Emmy-Lou's face. "But you told Hope you liked her spots. Why don't you want Phineas to grow them, too?"

"Hope," he said, knowing his comment would reveal his true feelings to his sister, "Hope is special."

"So is Phineas." As soon as the words left Annie's mouth, she went ruddy.

Ignore it. We will all ignore their feelings; it's the only way to handle this. She didn't catch on to my declaration about Hope. Well, better off she didn't. It's not right to flaunt my love when she'll be denied hers. "Ja, Phineas is special in a different way. We are all special to Jesus."

A smile transformed his daughter's face. "So I'm special, too!"

"Absolutely!"

Annie slid Johnny from beneath her shawl.

"Here. I'll take him." Jakob held his nephew and patted his tiny back. A moment later, Jakob chuckled. "Such a little man, burping already! He's heavier, too, Annie."

"If I don't put supper on the table, he'll be the only one who's full." She rose.

"I thought we all agreed this morning it was too hot and there were too many other matters to attend to. You weren't to cook."

"I haven't. Cold leftover ham and farm cheese. Bread and—"

"Watermelon pickles," Hope added as she came inside. She carried a crock. "We can use the powdered broth and heat it over a kerosene lamp so Phineas has something to fill him and build his strength."

Annie immediately volunteered. "I'll see to that."

Jakob opened his mouth to naysay her, but Hope exclaimed, "Dandy! When you're done heatin' it up, I'll get it into him." Hope breezed over to the sink, but Jakob caught the quick glance she gave him over her shoulder. They'd made a pact to protect Annie from her husband; now they'd work together to protect her from herself.

After washing the supper dishes, Hope took the rocker by the study and crocheted. "Annie, you've been cooped up all day. What say you leave me here with Johnny whilst you, Emmy-Lou, and Jakob go catch yourselves some lightnin' bugs?"

"Can we?" Emmy-Lou jigged as she tugged on her aunt's hand.

"I . . ."

"You bet we will." Jakob swept Emmy-Lou up onto his shoulders. "Annie, fetch a jar, and we'll meet you beneath the sycamore."

Catching fireflies without Hope wasn't even half the fun. The thought went through Jakob's mind again as he opened his bedroom window before retiring. Hope brought delight to even the simplest things. She didn't need to adhere to a schedule to maintain order in the home. Her flexibility allowed spur-of-the moment changes that resolved a plethora of difficult situations.

Jakob crawled into bed and didn't reach for the other pillow. Just when he's stopped hugging it at night, he wasn't sure. Memories of the years he shared with Naomi would warm his heart, but Hope—she filled his life now. The sticky heat of the night wasn't unbearable because his mind swirled with memories of Hope's boundless enthusiasm and love.

Some things didn't need to be regulated by habit; need was more important. Hope understood that. He'd become accustomed to Naomi's well-ordered serenity, but life had changed. Hope honored the customs he held most dear—like prayer after mealtimes. She even went the extra mile and was learning more German. One of her most endearing traits, though, was her spontaneity. No matter what she did, she did it with joy. Her zest for life shone like the brightest star when his life and home had been black as midnight. Her name said it all—Hope.

Early the next morning, Hope woke to the kitchen door shutting and the cows lowing. Johnny was making noises, so she changed his diaper and tucked him next to Annie. "You see to breakfast for this little feller, and I'll take care of the rest of us."

Once downstairs, Hope peeped in on Phineas. He was restless, so she sponged off his face and chest, then coaxed him to drink some apple juice. When she laid his head back onto the pillow, Phineas grimaced.

"Do ya hurt?" she asked.

He closed his eyes. "Do me a favor."

"I'll do anything I can."

After a long moment, Phineas opened his eyes. They were glassy with fever. "Keep Annie away from me as much as you can right now."

Hope didn't pretend not to understand. " 'Kay."

"Honor." Pain laced his voice. "It comes at such a great price."

Hope wiped his brow. "I'll be prayin' for you 'bout that and for your health, too."

She went into the kitchen and immediately lit the stove. After starting coffee, she decided to fix oatmeal for breakfast and to hard-boil a mess of eggs. Some egg salad would be cool and filling later on. Hope put a potful of water to boil on the last burner—she could use that to boil the germs from Phineas's pillowcase and the cloths she'd used to soothe him.

Anything they'd need to cook ought to be done now. Then, she could let the fire in the oven die out so the house wouldn't feel like a sweltering oven all day. Hope whipped up a batch of drop biscuits and started them baking, then quickly prepared Jakob's favorite coffee cake.

He liked slow-cooked beans, too—so she'd been soaking beans and would put the pot in the oven and let them slow cook all day as the embers radiated their heat. Adding spices and a little fat back to the pot, Hope smiled. Jakob would be pleased.

She spied him through the window. Carrying the milk pails, he'd headed for the springhouse. Without being told, he'd know to bring in some milk for the icebox. Even with Phineas sick and Annie being tied up with a newborn, things were getting done. *I knew it from the start—when I saw his hands, I knew Jakob was the most hardest-workin' man I'd ever met.*

Remembering his taciturn reception of her that first morning, Hope smiled to herself. She wouldn't have ever imagined that beneath the stern exterior lay a man of amazing kindness. Jakob wasn't just a man who labored with his hands—he worked to better his heart and mind and soul.

Golden brown drop biscuits came out of the oven and coffee cake went in. The coffee finished perking, so Hope placed the pot on a trivet and decided to brew some tea. Tea would be good for Phineas.

Annie descended the stairs. "I'll go check on—"

"He's restin'. I checked him already, and he's farin' okay. I was just gonna brew some tea."

"Tea would be good for him. I'll do that."

That worked out right nice. "Maybe you could make a lotta tea. Keepin' extra in the springhouse would be good. Your brother—he shore does love a coupla glasses of sweet tea with his lunch."

"Nothing's more refreshing than a glass of tea." Annie headed toward the hook where her apron hung. "What do you have in that pot?"

"Oatmeal."

"Oh." Annie slipped into her apron. The ties on it hung longer down her back now that her belly wasn't huge. "I'll put some rice on. That would be good for Phineas."

"There's a dandy notion. Nothin' much tasted good to me whilst I was sick, but the rice sat well in my belly. When the sheriff came by yesterday with food, he tole me the sickness is spreadin', but most are springin' back after a few days like me."

Annie filled the teakettle. "I can't imagine how Mrs. Vaughn will manage with all of her children."

Hope made a sympathetic sound. "You was busy feedin' little Johnny, so Jakob and me told the sheriff to take the food and help to her instead. We got a good handle on things here."

The kettle clinked down on the stove. "I'm worried."

"Jakob told the sheriff folks were welcome to your eggs and milk. Sheriff said he'd ask Big Tim Creighton to come by to pick 'em up."

"*Sehr gut.* I want to help as much as I can. You were up in the night with Phineas. Today—"

"Best you keep your distance from him, Annie. Johnny needs you to stay healthy. Him gettin' sick from me proves it's catchy. I'm prayin' extra hard that God's gonna keep you and the children and Jakob all well."

Halfway through breakfast, Big Tim arrived. Hope saw to the eggs while Jakob and Tim loaded the milk—then the men stepped off to the side. The low tone of their conversation made it clear they wanted privacy. Just before Tim left, Jakob called over, "Hope, I've asked Tim to pick up chicken feed while he's in town. Do you need anything?"

"We've got what we need. If 'n it ain't too much trouble, Annie's taken a liking to the feed sacks what have them purdy blue curlicues. Four more, and we could stitch her up a dress."

After lunch, Johnny started fussing. Annie went to pick him up. Jakob murmured to Hope, "Thinking to have Annie sew a dress was good—for many reasons."

Hope looked into his oh-so-steady blue eyes. Neither of them listed the reasons, but she knew they were thinking the same things. A wave of sadness swept over her. In a few days, Jakob would deal with Konrad. By then Phineas would be on the mend and Annie had recovered. *I'll be leavin' Jakob—and them all—behind.*

"*Was ist los?* What is—"

"A-wrong?" she translated. "Don't know as I have a real answer to that. More'n anything, so many things are happening, it's hard to get a handle on it all."

"You've been working too hard—especially after being sick." He pressed the backs of his fingers to her forehead.

Even that light contact made her breath hitch. Jakob's eyes narrowed, and Hope babbled, "I'm as jumpy as a cricket on a hot tin roof. Wish Konrad would just show up so's it'd all be over."

Jakob shoved the hand that had touched her into the pocket of his jeans. "In three days, Phineas will be well again. It would be better for Konrad to come then—that would have him see two strong men here."

"Daddy?"

They traded a startled look. They'd been so focused on each other, they'd forgotten Emmy-Lou hadn't gone upstairs for her nap yet. "Ja, *Liebling?*"

"I wanna see Milky and her kitties. Can we go see them?"

Jakob hunkered down. "After your nap, Aunt Annie or Hope might take you if you ask very nicely. Mrs. Orion said Heidi may have a kitten, and Mr. Creighton will take two. Milky is weaning them, so you need to pick which one you want to keep so the others can go to their new homes."

"Heidi's my friend. I'm glad she gets a kitty. And Mrs. Creighton saved me from the dark hole in the ground." Emmy-Lou held up her hand and rubbed her fingers with the opposite hand. "Milky gots five kittens." Her face lit with glee. "Then I getta keep two!"

"No. I told you the day Milky had her litter that you could keep one."

Emmy-Lou's eyes filled with tears, and a few started spilling beneath the frames of her glasses and down her cheeks. "But, Daddy, I wanna keep them. I don't want the other kitty to go away. Everybody always goes away!"

Instinctively, Hope reached out for her, but just before making contact, she recoiled. *She needs her daddy to soothe her, not me. He's gonna keep me around a little while longer, but the time'll come when I'm gonna go away.* Tears filled her own eyes as she inched away.

❧

Jakob woke in the night and lay in his bed, listening. He'd heard something. Having already kicked off the sheet, he rolled out of bed and skimmed into his jeans. The door to the bedroom across the hall was shut. He decided to leave the women and children undisturbed and headed down the stairs.

"Jakob?" Phineas's voice didn't come from the study but from the kitchen. "Is that you?"

"What are you doing up?" The cool planks of the floor felt good as he went toward the sink.

"Getting something to drink. I slept all day, so now I'm wide awake."

Jakob rubbed his eyes with the heels of his hands, then blearily looked at Phineas. "You don't look so good. You shouldn't be up."

Phineas snorted. "Look in the mirror."

"Sweet tea. Hope keeps some in the icebox." Jakob sidestepped and brushed past him.

Hand shooting out to block his way, Phineas rasped, "I know you, Jakob Stauffer. You can't fool me by changing the subject."

He made contact with Jakob and rasped, "You're hot! You've got it, too."

"I'm fine." *I have to be. God, please let me stay strong. So much depends on that.*

"What's goin' on?" Hope's voice preceded her down the stairs.

"Jakob's—"

"Thirsty," he interrupted as he gave Phineas a scowl.

Hope came into view. She'd yanked her green dress over her nightgown. She looked silly. Lumpy. Beautiful. She gave him a sweet smile. "I'll pour all y'all some sweet tea. Phineas, what time's the clock saying?"

"Two-seventeen."

Bobbing her head in acknowledgment, Hope took a pair of glasses from the cupboard. "Then y'all can have willow bark powder." She turned and looked at Jakob. She didn't smile at him, and he decided he'd have to talk to her about that shortcoming. As soon as he quenched his thirst, he would. Hope's head tilted ever so slightly to the right. "You shoulda tole me you was feelin' puny, Jakob Stauffer."

"I'm too ornery to take sick."

Finally she gave him one of her sweet smiles. "You was just afraid if'n you said something, I'd go out to the barn and bring back the McLeans liniment and douse you with it."

He managed nothing more than a grunt at her assertion. If she'd stop swaying from side to side, it would be easier for him to concentrate. That was Jakob's last thought before she pressed the glass into one hand and stood on tiptoe to put the spoon of willow bark powder to his lips.

Two days later, Jakob slumped at the lunch table. He'd managed a poached egg and a few spoons of applesauce. *Lord, strengthen me. Konrad will come tomorrow, and Annie's terrified. I should have sent Hope off with Annie and Emmy-Lou.*

Just how he would have managed that feat escaped him at the moment. Jakob spent most of his waking hours excoriating himself for not setting his plan into motion as soon as Hope had recovered. Now it was too late. *What kind of man am I? I've failed the woman I love, my sister, and my daughter. Johnny, too.*

Upon determining he'd fallen ill, Hope never once rested. She hovered around, sponging him off, coaxing him to sip fluids, fluffing his pillow, and closing the curtains to dim his room so he could sleep. She didn't wear him out with useless chatter, but she tried to cheer him up with little snippets that Emmy-Lou said or verses of encouragement. He knew, though, that while he slept, she was out milking cows and doing the chores he normally did. Such a helpmeet, she'd be—if he could protect her.

Phineas came in late for lunch. He took one look at Jakob and said in a wry voice, "You look like you've been dragged by a horse five miles down a bumpy road."

"Here I was, thinkin' on how Jakob's springin' back faster than me or you did." Hope efficiently set a plate down for the farmhand. "He's ahead by a whole day, gettin' up already."

"You ought to go back to bed, Jakob." Annie bit her lip and looked away.

Of all the times you could have picked, Lord, why strike me down now?

" 'Course he'll go rest." Hope waved her hand toward the parlor. "I recollect longin' to be outta bed. The settee's right comfortable. Whilst you and the little ones nap, Annie, I'll do some ironing. If'n you don't mind too dreadful much, Jakob, maybe you could read a few verses outta the Good Book to me afore you take a snooze."

Even the weight of the Bible in his hands taxed him. Turning the pages, Jakob begged, *Lord, grant me strength. You're the Great Physician. Heal me so I can protect my loved ones and provide for them.*

The solid sound of the wooden brace fitting into the bottom of the ironing board reminded him Hope had asked him to read aloud. "I don't mean no disrespect to the Almighty, ironin' whilst you share His Word with me. Sittin' all still and ladylike comes hard for me. I do better crocheting or mending or ironing."

"My father used to read to my mother while she finished chores. He said 'Idle hands were—"

"—the devil's pig slop.' Mmm-hmm. I've heard that sayin' before, too."

Phineas choked on his food.

"Y'all need some water, Phineas? I hope you're not sufferin' a collapse from being up and around too soon."

He cleared his throat. "Relapse. I'm not having a relapse. Something just—hit me wrong. What are you reading, Jakob?"

"Second Corinthians, twelve." He read aloud and hit the ninth verse. " 'My grace is sufficient for thee: for my strength is made perfect in weakness. Most gladly therefore will I rather glory in my infirmities, that the power of Christ may rest upon me.' "

"Glory, glory, glory. Ain't that the most beautifulest thing you heard all day? Jakob, would y'all mind readin' them last words again?"

Staring at the fragile page of his Bible, Jakob couldn't imagine what he'd read. *How many times have I heard this verse? Heard sermons on it? But this is different.* He read again, testing the words as he said them. *Lord, if in my weakness you're strong, you're especially strong right now.*

"That was very fitting." Phineas rose from the table. "I'll get back to work. If you need . . . help . . . of any kind, just shout."

The ironing board creaked as Hope pressed something. "Gotta tell you, Jakob, God shore takes me by surprise. His Word says Jehovah provides. Well, I was a-tryin' to think of a way to share my special Bible verse with y'all. The one what goes, 'The Lord shall preserve thy goin' out and thy comin' in from this time forth, and even for evermore.' It fit, with you going out to meet with Konrad. But I didn't need to hop into the middle and speak my piece. God done His own work."

"It was nice of you to consider how your favorite verse applied to my life. In Proverbs, it says 'Words aptly spoken are like apples of gold.' "

"Hold it!" Disbelief filled her voice. "Say that again, real slow, will ya?"

He repeated the proverb.

Laughter bubbled out of Hope. "Oh, Jakob, you'll never, ever in all your born days believe what I always thought that verse was. Merciful heavens, I betcha God's a-sittin' in heaven just chucklin' over me botchin' that verse."

He'd never pictured God laughing. The thought intrigued Jakob. "Just what did you think the verse said?"

"Well, you know how when somebody's talkin' mean, folks say they got a viper's tongue? I thunk that verse said, 'words asp-ly,' like a snake— 'are like apples of old.' Like rotten, mealy, apples. Here I was, a-thinkin' it was a warnin' not to speak badly, but it's tellin' us to speak wisely at a good time."

The ironing board continued to creak rhythmically as Jakob laughed softly with Hope. Miserable as he felt physically, she'd cheered him up. Even so, the laughter sapped his energy.

Minutes later, it took every last ounce of his strength just to go upstairs. He'd been too weak to put on his boots, so it simplified falling into bed. It took too much effort to straighten out, so he sprawled across the mattress. Dully staring out the window, he saw a speck on the horizon.

Hope tapped lightly on his open door. "Jakob? I—"

"Look out the window. What do you see?"

She didn't argue with him about the proprieties of a woman being in a man's bedchamber. Instead, she swiftly crossed the room and peered outside. Seconds ticked by. Relief colored her voice as she proclaimed, "It's that feller what's sweet on Katherine Richardson."

Jakob nodded.

Hope approached the bed, grabbed the pillows, and tucked them under his head. She didn't say a thing about his position. "Y'all go on ahead and rest up. Everything's fine."

Lethargy dragged at him. Beneath heavy lids, Jakob watched her leave the room. This time, it wasn't Konrad—but he'd be there anytime now. *And I'm as helpless as Milky's kittens.*

Twenty-Eight

Konrad shivered—more from excitement than from the sweat that trickled down his spine. He'd gone home and stewed about leaving Annie at her brother's. As his anger simmered, a thought took hold. Jakob still owned the family farm, but Annie would inherit it if her brother died. And a woman's possessions rightfully belonged to her husband.

Jakob's farm was first-rate. Bigger. Newer. The house and barn stood strong, and he owned half again as much as the old family farm. With Jakob out of the way, Konrad would sell the old farm. Proclaiming that Jakob's washed-out wife and the brats couldn't possibly work his land, Konrad and Annie would take over Jakob's place.

All it would take was one accident.

After almost two weeks of working out the details, he skulked around the far edge of Jakob's barn. Everything was just as he'd planned. Jakob would come into the barn to do the evening milking. He had not one, but two *milch* cows—proof of Jakob's greed. A farmer had need of only one, but Jakob always had to be better than anyone else.

The hired hand passed by, muttering to himself as he opened the barn door for the cows. From what Konrad saw on the day the household was put in quarantine, the hired hand would mess around in the barn for a while, then leave by the other door and help Annie chase the hens into the coop. That was woman's work, beneath a man's dignity. Once Konrad was in charge, Annie would have to take care of the stupid chickens herself. He'd keep the hired hand busy.

Konrad had arrived at lunchtime today. He'd seen Annie through the kitchen window, even been tortured by the smell of good food wafting toward him. Spurred on by the aroma, he'd vowed this was the last time he'd miss eating his wife's cooking. While everyone at the house ate, Konrad had climbed into the barn's rafters. The pitchfork now hung poised there, ready for him to attach a length of twine that he'd stretch across a spot about two feet inside the barn. Jakob would stride in, trip, and fall directly beneath the pitchfork that the wire triggered.

Meeeoooow. A white she-cat appeared out of nowhere and scared him witless. Stupid thing stropped across his shin and back. Afraid she'd give him away, Konrad cursed under his breath and kicked her. She landed on her feet a few yards away, turned and hissed at him, then walked off in a snit. At least he'd gotten rid of her. Dumb cat could ruin everything.

Heart thundering, muscles jumpy, Konrad eased into the barn and remained in the shadows. He flexed his right hand. The bandana he'd wrapped it with stuck to one of the scabs from his burn. He hadn't let the pain and stiffness hold him back. Squinting at the rafters, he assured himself all was ready, then pulled twine from his pocket.

Tying one end of the twine through a knothole in a board, he indulged in a grin. His plan would work—it boasted all the hallmarks of a successful endeavor. He'd worked out the details, had the essential equipment, and the very simplicity of the trap would give the impression of a freak accident.

If for any reason anyone suspected foul play, no one would ever suspect him. He'd make sure to stop at the train depot in town tomorrow and ask the clerk something just to establish his time of arrival. Better still, he'd go back to that boarding house and charm the widow into allowing him to cut flowers from her garden. He'd arrive at the farmhouse with flowers in his hands for Annie, only to then feign horror at the terrible news regarding Jakob's fatal accident.

His head ached. His whole body felt stiff. Yes, he probably had the same fever that was felling lesser men. Konrad refused to yield to such weakness. Instead, he gritted his teeth and sneaked across to the other side of the barn's doorway. Stretching the twine tight took no time at all; attaching it to the line that went to the pitchfork—that was tricky. His fingers twitched and shook with anticipation. More than once, he had to wipe the palm of his left hand on his jeans to dry it off.

Had he tied the knot securely? The twine seemed to give a little. Maybe he'd better add one more knot. A clove hitch. That was strong. Excitement made him clumsy, but Konrad persevered. Finally satisfied, he slinked back out of the barn.

He ought to leave. Wisdom dictated as much, but Konrad couldn't forego the thrill of victory. He edged away and sat in the shadow cast by the outhouse. Any moment now, Jakob would head toward the barn.

"Jakob!" a woman called.

Konrad's heart thundered. He switched to peek from the other side of the outhouse. He could see the back veranda of the house. Jakob stood on the second step, but his wife reached over and tugged him back toward the house.

Konrad's molars grated. That woman ought to let her husband make the decisions. Well, when Jakob was gone, she'd learn her place.

Let him go do his chores. Let him go. I set up a surprise for him—the last one he'll ever have. Let him go. Konrad watched with growing impatience as that woman yammered at Jakob. His anticipation built. Just a few more minutes, and Jakob would walk into the barn and—

A roar sounded from the barn.

No! Konrad barely kept from shouting his denial. His neck arched back, and he hit his head on the weathered outhouse planks. *No, no, no.*

Jakob shoved Hope toward the house and wheeled toward the steps. The action momentarily robbed him of his balance. Hope was right back beside him, but Phineas ran from the barn. Hope pulled, Phineas pushed, and all three of them wound up in a knot in the kitchen.

Annie stood at the foot of the stairs, her face white. "It's Konrad, isn't it?"

"Someone rigged a trap in the barn." Phineas's fists shook at his sides. "If I'd been walking in instead of leaving, I'd be dead."

"I can't let this happen." Annie sank to the floor and buried her face in her hands. "I'll go."

"Nein!" Jakob went toward the kitchen cabinet.

Behind him, Phineas fell to his knees. "No, Annie. Your verse—it promises God will not suffer your foot to be moved. He will preserve you from evil. I—we will not let you go."

Hope gasped when she saw the shotgun Jakob safely stored on top of the cabinet.

"You all stay in here." Jakob went to the door, raised the shotgun, and fired into the air. He counted to ten and fired the second barrel. By the time he came back inside, Hope was dragging Annie into the pantry. Phineas thundered back down the stairs, Johnny in one arm and Emmy-Lou under the other.

"Hope . . ." Jakob waited until her troubled eyes met his. "No matter what, you keep everyone in the pantry." He knew what had to be done; she would, too, once he reminded her. "We have a pact."

Her shoulders rose as she sucked in a long, steadying breath. "We'll be praying."

"You do that." He shut the pantry door.

"Here." Phineas swiped the shotgun from him and reloaded it. "There might be more traps set. We have to watch each step we take. I'll track—"

"*Nein.*" Jakob fought the unholy urge to seek Konrad out. Until that moment, he'd never understood how one man might kill another. The temptation was enormous. "*Nein.* We wait."

Phineas's eyes bulged. "Wait?!"

"Above all, he wants Annie. If we leave her without protection, we play right into his plan. For now, we must keep watch. God will send help."

"My gun is in the tack room."

"An even better reason to wait." Logical, calm words came from his mouth. Jakob marveled at it, because deep inside, wrath roiled. *I should have suspected Konrad would do something like this. A man who beats his wife won't hesitate to do anything to get his own way.* He looked at Phineas. "If anything should happen to me, I want Hope to stay here and rear Emmy-Lou. Promise me you'll see to that."

"Emmy-Lou's already lost too much." Phineas grabbed the shotgun. "Nothing's going to happen to you."

Thundering hooves approaching foretold help. "God be praised." Jakob went to the door.

Big Tim Creighton and two of his ranch hands were there. So were Asa Bunce and the sheriff. It only took a minute to mention the deadly trap. Jakob started to give orders. "Tim and Gulp, you go east—"

"Hold it." The sheriff scowled. "You're weaving on your feet. You stay to guard the women."

"I—"

"You'll endanger everyone else." Tim stared at him. "Pride could cost someone his life."

It galled Jakob, but he couldn't deny that truth. The men paired up, and the teams fanned out. Though exhaustion pulled at him, Jakob refused to sit down. After shutting the front door and bracing a chair beneath it so no one could enter, he went through the house and out to the back porch.

"Twinkle, twinkle . . ." Very faintly Emmy-Lou's singing seeped into the air. The memory of the night he and Hope spent with his daughter and the fireflies caused Jakob to look toward the sycamore.

A slight movement in its shadow captured his attention.

Anger slammed through Jakob. Konrad must have thought he was out with the other men, so he sidled across the yard and dropped down in the garden. *Crawling on his belly like the snake he is. He comes no closer. Lord, help me stop him.*

Stealthily as possible, Jakob edged to the far side of the porch. He eased himself over the rail and into the soft dirt. The soil muffled his steps as he stalked along the neat rows of vegetables. Rows of pole beans gave him scant coverage. A small rustling warned him that as he'd moved toward Konrad, Konrad had pressed on toward the house. Jakob halted and waited one more second.

∽

A tortured scream rent the air. Even so, Jakob didn't move. He kept his boot firmly planted on Konrad's right wrist, pinning him to the ground. "Here! He's here!"

The lack of struggle worried Jakob. Konrad wasn't one to give up so easily. In fact, he had a pistol strapped to his right thigh and a Bowie knife on the left side of his belt. Images of what he might have done with those weapons lent Jakob strength.

The other men came running. The sheriff had his gun drawn, so Jakob slowly eased his boot from Konrad's wrist. Garbled curses poured from Konrad as the handcuffs snicked into place and Tim divested him of his weapons.

"Phineas, hitch up the buckboard." Jakob cast a look toward the house. "I don't want Annie to see him."

"She won't have to." Tim folded his arms across his chest. "You have eye witnesses that the trap he set was attempted murder. How long will that lock him up, Sheriff?"

"It's up to the judge. Left up to me, I'd vote for vigilante justice about now."

Asa Bunce squinted. "He's got that sickness. Lookit how feverish he is."

"Haul him out of here." Jakob leaned against the garden fence.

"Jakob!" Hope's voice rang through the air. "Are all y'all okay? Do y'all need some help?"

"Stay put in the pantry a little longer. I'll be there in a few minutes."

"Your sis and Emmy-Lou shorely could stand clappin' eyes on you just now." Hope barely paused long enough to take in another breath. "If'n Annie and lil' Johnny cry much more, I'm a-gonna have to start buildin' an ark!"

"An—" Konrad started.

"An ark!" Jakob shouted to drown out the sound of Konrad's shouting Annie's name. In a low tone, he hissed, "Get him out of here."

Unaware of what was transpiring, Hope yelled, "I'm just about as good with a hammer as I am with a fryin' pan!"

The men made a point of laughing loudly as they hauled Konrad away.

Phineas stood by Jakob and rasped, "If you hadn't been sick so you stayed behind, he would have gotten into the house."

"Like that verse in Corinthians I just read—that God's strength is made perfect in our weakness." Jakob raked his hands through his hair. "I never imagined this."

A buckboard arrived in a swirl of dust. Jakob and Phineas went to see who it was. Velma and Sydney Creighton scrambled down before anyone could help them. "Thought you men might need help. Jakob," Velma declared, "you look like death warmed over."

"The prisoner looks worse." The sheriff tapped his foot. "I'd rather have you take a gander at him, Velma. Doc's about as handy as hip pockets on a hog."

Ignoring how Konrad bowed away from her, Velma prodded and poked. She asked him questions, but he barred his teeth and growled at her.

Big Tim grabbed Konrad by the scruff of the neck. "Enough. Velma, he's got the same fever everyone else does."

"Don't think so." Velma inspected beneath the bandana wrapped around Konrad's right hand. "You burnt yourself? What—about two weeks ago?"

Again, he bared his teeth and let out a wounded-sounding snarl.

"Lock jaw. That's what he's got. Tetanus—it's all over in the soil and it likes to plant itself in burns." Velma shook her head. "No way to fix it. Best you make your peace with God, mister."

⁓

The next day, Pastor Bradle rode out to inform Annie that Konrad had died during the night. Annie, still badly shaken, didn't know what to do. Jakob decided he'd accompany the body back to their old town and have it buried there. All things considered, Hope thought Jakob's plan showed great mercy.

Two days later, Jakob hadn't returned. Hope knew he'd be back that day or the next, so she made a special effort to have everything perfect around the house. Once he came home, their pact would be over—they'd protected Annie and seen matters through to the bitter end. Nothing else kept Hope there. It was time for her to leave Gooding.

The pungent smell of ammonia made for a good excuse as to why she kept tearing up, so she washed windows. Emmy-Lou sat on the parlor carpeting and counted buttons. Big, bright buttons contrasted with the milk-glass platter, making it easy for her to see them.

"Someone's coming," Annie said.

Hope rinsed her hands at the kitchen pump. "Looks like Velma."

Velma stopped by to drop off some mail and to see if Phineas could go help unload a shipment meant for the feedstore. Since Mr. Vaughn had passed on, men were pitching in. Phineas left, and Velma answered Hope's and Annie's questions about how other families in the area were faring with the fever.

"I'll go make mercy rounds." Hope straightened her apron. "Velma, you've been nursing everybody. It's my turn."

Velma balked a bit, but she gave in when Hope pointed out Velma needed to get a bit of rest herself so she didn't take sick.

Once Velma left, Annie offered, "I can help."

"Nope." Hope folded her arms across her chest. "Johnny and Emmy-Lou—you and them ain't caught that fever, and I aim to make shore you don't. I'll just go off and see to the neighbors. Come suppertime, I'll be home in time to rustle up some grub. Little Johnny kept you up most of the night. You run on along and take a nap 'long with them kids."

Fifteen minutes later, Hope climbed onto the seat of her mule cart and set Hattie in motion. As they rode out of the barnyard, Hope swallowed the thick ball in her throat. Leaving—today it was just for a trip, but tomorrow, it would be forever.

She passed by the spot where she'd delivered water and peaches and cookies to the harvest hands that first morning. "Hope's agreed to stay here awhile." Jakob's words came back to her. Well, she had stayed awhile, and as soon as he returned, her time was up.

Next came the place in the road where, on her first Sunday, Phineas offered to lend her his Bible. Her inability to read never mattered to Jakob—he'd spent countless hours reading from the Word of God to her. He'd even read about . . . "parturition," she said aloud.

Every fence post she drove past carried with it some memory of life since she'd come to work for Jakob. When had he become so ingrained in her life that every last thought she held revolved around him? Hattie continued to plod along, and when she passed another tree, Hope spied where someone had carved initials inside of a heart on the trunk. "Ain't that sweet, Hattie? I wonder who's in love."

I am.

The words popped into her head and robbed her of her breath.

I've been feelin' funny—sorta antsy and giddy. I thunk 'twas just me frettin' about Annie and Emmy-Lou. Then I thunk bein' weak in the knees was from me gettin' over that fever, but it wasn't. It ain't just me countin' Annie as a dear friend or me thinkin' Emmy-Lou and Johnny are the most cutest kids in the whole, wide world. Them are reasons why I'm sad to be leavin'—but they ain't the real one. I done went and fell in love with Jakob. Lord, have mercy. What am I gonna do?

She pulled into the Smiths' yard. Mandy leaned over the porch railing. "Hey, Gramma! It's Miss Hope! Where's Emmy-Lou?"

"She's helpin' her auntie mind baby Johnny. I heard a bunch of your brothers and sisters are feelin' poorly." Hope climbed down from the cart.

Gramma came over. "How're all the Stauffers?"

"Much better. Thanks for askin'. Heard tell you was sorta busy over here. Thought I'd lend a hand." Hope handed Gramma a crate of eggs.

"Oh my."

"Annie thunk you could use them." She grabbed the pair of pullets she'd brought. Jakob knew his neighbors well and had sent food for harvest; Annie was just as generous. Hope told herself that when she was gone, they'd take good care of one another.

Gramma leaned close. "Daisy's beside herself. The baby's got the fever. To my reckonin', he's past the worst of it, but Daisy hasn't slept for two days."

Annie spent the morning helping with laundry, cooking, and dunking the sick kids in the tub. By the time she left, Daisy had taken a long nap and the baby looked fine. Folks in that household looked a whale of a lot better, but Hope left still every bit as confused as when she arrived. *How did I go and let myself fall in love with a man who's admitted he's been plannin' to send me away? That's the most dumbest thing I ever did. I gotta be careful. I ain't gonna let my feelin's show. Thataway when I leave tomorrow, nobody's gonna get embarrassed.*

The Pattersons and Whites were doing well, so Hope went on to the Richardsons'. A hideous sound from the house warned Hope she'd encounter some kind of catastrophe. Jeb Richardson helped her out of the cart and rasped, "Mama's beside herself. Linette's fever got real high during the night, so we cut off her hair. Now Linette's recovering, but she got a gander of herself in the mirror . . ."

"Merciful heavens." Hope marched into the house, went straight up the stairs, and shouted from the doorway, "Who died?"

She had to repeat herself twice before anyone noticed her. Face blotchy and swollen from crying, Linette shrieked, "Don't look at me!"

"Caterwaulin' like that's bound to make folks take more notice of you." Hope watched Linette fall theatrically across the bed. "If 'n you don't want attention, you're gonna hafta button your lip."

Lottie tugged on Hope's skirt. "I know how to sew buttons. Can I help?"

Laughter blurted out of Marcella, who quickly clamped a hand over her mouth.

"You already have Leo. I won't ever get a man now!" Linette buried her face in the mattress and started weeping again.

Hope jerked her head toward the door, and the other girls gladly escaped. Mrs. Richardson wavered. Hope told her, "I'd take it kindly if 'n you'd shut the door behind you."

Once the door clicked, Hope sat on the bed and tapped Linette on the shoulder. When tapping didn't help, she jostled her. Finally Linette looked at her. "Whatever am I going to do? I'll be an old maid!"

"If'n the onliest reason a man loves you is on account of your hair, he ain't the man you want. 'Sides, if'n your hair was what was supposed to ensnare a feller, then you shoulda caught him by now. Seems to me you're puttin' a lot of store in something that ain't much, after all."

"It's easy for you to say." Linette rolled onto her back. "You have all your beautiful hair."

"You still have your hair, too. It's just shorter, is all. It ain't like you're baldheaded. Didn't I hear Big Tim Creighton whacked off Sydney's hair a while back? Well, it didn't keep him from decidin' to take her as his bride."

Linette still looked ready to plunge back into hysterics.

"Besides, I wanna know what's a-wrong with a gal what ain't got herself hitched." She shook her finger. "But before you answer, you'd best 'member I never got married, neither."

Linette's watery eyes widened.

"That's right. You don't see no weddin' ring on me." Hope held up her bare hand and wiggled her fingers. "I been livin' a good life, helpin' folks and makin' lots of fine friends. The apostle Paul said we're supposed to be content wherever we find ourselves."

"How can I be content when I'm not finding my husband?"

And how am I to be content when I found the one I love, but he doesn't want me?

Linette didn't wait for a reply. "No one understands. Mrs. Whittsley—you know her?"

"She's the white-haired old woman?"

"The one with the cane—not the one with brown-and-white hair who stands out front of the saloon. That one is Widow

O'Toole. Even she's a widow—so once upon a time, a man even fell in love with her!"

"What were you saying about Mrs. Whittsley?" Hope tried to redirect things.

Linette's lower lip trembled. "At a sewing bee last year, right in front of everyone, she pointed that mean old cane of hers at me and said I was wasting away the beautiful days of my youth because I kept worrying about my tomorrows." Tears welled up and spilled down her cheeks. "Less than an hour later she was talking about how she'd had two babies and another on the way by the time she was twenty. I'm going to be twenty-three next month!"

"I gotta year on you. I'm twenty-four." Hope pulled a hanky out of her apron pocket and pressed it into Linette's hand. "But I don't think it's the number of years we got behind us that matter. It ain't even how many lie ahead. It's what we do with each day the Lord gives us."

"Today's awful! My hair's short as a boy's. My sisters are planning their weddings, and I'm going to be miserable and lonely tomorrow just like I am today."

Lord, you sent me here on purpose. You didn't want me to go off tomorrow and pine for what might have been. She squeezed Linette's hand. "You and me—we ain't never gonna find happiness if we expect someone else to bring it. We gotta make our own happiness."

"But . . ." Linette asked in a small voice, "don't you want to be married?"

A few weeks ago, Hope wouldn't have even thought before answering. The question hit her hard, though. *I do want to be married. I want to be Jakob's wife. But he was ready to send me away. He even said so.*

"Someday, if 'n God brings a man along that'll love me deep and true, then I'll be happy to marry up." Hope prayed Linette wouldn't hear the ache in her voice. "But I ain't gonna settle for nothin' less."

ॐ

Jakob pulled the buckboard into the yard and looked around. Everything was eerily quiet. He'd stayed an extra day at the old homestead. Mrs. Volkner and her daughter had come over and helped him pack up many of the things left behind when he'd swept Annie to safety. Annie had always loved Mama's dishes and Grandma's crystal vase, and Jakob was glad to restore those cherished pieces to her.

Then, too, he'd gathered up some things he thought Hope would enjoy. It wouldn't seem right, leaving Naomi's wedding-ring quilt on the bed, so he brought several along—most with a star pattern of some variety. That seemed right.

He'd loaded the cedar chest his grandfather made for his grandmother onto the wagon. The long, lacy infant gown inside—Johnny could wear it for his dedication. Best of all, the chest held the wedding gown both Grandma and Mama had worn. Strangely enough, Annie hadn't worn it—but that was good. It wouldn't upset her when Hope walked down the aisle to him dressed in the yards of billowing white cotton and lace.

Only where was Hope? Where was everyone?

He went into the house. The downstairs was empty. Upstairs, he found Annie and the children all fast asleep. Hope wasn't in the garden or the springhouse. Phineas wasn't in sight, either. Perplexed, Jakob went to the barn. As soon as his eyes adjusted from the bright sunlight to the dim interior, his heart fell to his boots. Hope's cart was missing.

343

When did she leave? Where did she go? He couldn't imagine life without her by his side. Jakob bolted toward the house. He'd awaken Annie and find out where Hope had gone.

In his absence, his daughter had risen from her nap. She sat on the parlor floor, stacking brightly colored buttons and counting to the tune of "Twinkle, Twinkle Little Star." She tilted her head up momentarily, then looked back at her buttons.

Jakob squatted down. "Emmy-Lou, Liebling, where is Miss Hope?"

Emmy-Lou shrugged. "She went away."

Away. Heart thundering and mouth dry, Jakob berated himself for having left without telling Hope he loved her. He'd given her no reason to stay, no indication that her future lay here, on his farm, in his arms.

Logic dictated she'd head north. The farther north one traveled, the later the harvest season. She'd been here so long, the jobs for a cook wouldn't be available until she reached the middle of South Dakota.

"She taked food with her. Auntie Annie told her to take lots."

Instead of finding any comfort in that announcement, alarm jolted through him. She'd gone. Truly up and gone. Not received a single penny or a word of thanks. Hadn't even stayed to say farewell.

"You be a good girl for Aunt Annie. Daddy's going to go find Hope."

He straightened out and strode out of the house. The buckboard would slow him down. He unhitched Nicodemus and didn't bother with a saddle. Jakob mounted up and headed north.

⁂

"Ich liebe dich." Emmy-Lou kissed Hope on the cheek.

"I love you, too, sugar pie." Hope pulled up the cover but didn't want to leave the room yet. This would be her last time to tuck in Jakob's daughter. Everything was settled, and she had no reason to remain at the Stauffers' any longer. One last time, she bent over, inhaled the sweet, indefinable scent of a little girl, pressed a kiss on her forehead, and repeated, "I love you."

Hope lifted her own quilt from her cot and carried it downstairs. She'd cut out the golden star for it after returning from the Richardsons'. Moments later, she sat on the settee in the parlor, taking careful, tiny stitches. The star for the Stauffer family on her quilt—that one would always be her favorite. She'd decided to sew it in the midst of a navy blue spot just because it'd help her recall singing with Jakob and Emmy-Lou that night they'd caught the fireflies.

"Jakob!" Phineas called from outside.

Hope tensed. He'd come home. A low rumble of male conversation, then Jakob's all-too-familiar footsteps sounded on the porch. He came in, cast a long look at her, then turned to clean up at the washstand. "Annie? *Komst.*"

Annie went to her brother. They held a whispered conversation. The speed and volume would have made it difficult to follow, but they spoke in German, too. Hope couldn't understand much more than something about the horse.

Annie sniffled, then went outside.

"I can throw together somethin' for you to eat," Hope started.

"No."

Nervous, Hope swallowed. Doing so didn't dislodge the ball in her throat. "I didn't mean to eavesdrop, but I think you said somethin' 'bout your horse."

"Ja. Nicodemus. He went lame on me again. Phineas and Annie will see to him." Jakob came into the parlor and sat heavily in his favorite chair. He cleared his throat. "Annie said something about you going away."

Hope jerked and barely kept from poking her finger with the needle. "Yup. Like I tole you when I come, I go where God sends me and men need me. You're through the harvest now. You brought in a fine crop, too."

"It wasn't just that."

I know it wasn't. It was a whole lot more. Sorta like this star here—a tiny piece of heaven on earth. She bit the inside of her lip. *Why am I being so fanciful?*

"You know it wasn't just the crop," Jakob repeated.

"The pact. Wasn't that something? God, He come alongside us, and we got Annie through a rough patch. Sad as it makes me to know that varmint Konrad's gonna roast in hell for eternity, I got a peace about Annie bein' safe and maybe someday findin' a scrap of happiness. You and me—we made a fair team."

He hummed a sound of agreement. "There's never been better."

"I finished up that apron for Emmy-Lou. Jakob, she's smart as a quip. Maybe her eyes don't work none too good, but if'n y'all put your minds to it, I think you'll come up with lotsa tricks so's she can lead a full, happy life. The apron—that's my way of sayin' to her that she's a good kitchen helper and needs to do as much as she can to help her auntie." Hope dared to look at him, her eyes begging him to promise he'd let Emmy-Lou do as much for herself as she could.

"Emmy-Lou especially likes cooking with you."

"Ain't that nice of you to say? But she loves her auntie with all her heart. They'll rub along right fine. I put up butter beans for you. I know you're the onliest one what likes 'em, but Annie promised she'll fix 'em for you every now and then."

Lord, I'm blitherin' here. I'm like a clock someone wound extra tight and I'm just tick-tick-tickin' and can't stop myself.

"The only person who ever made butter beans taste half as good as you do was my mother. Annie fixing them won't be the same."

"I'm shore your mama gave her the recipe. Would you be willin' to read to me outta the Good Book whilst I finish sewing? I wanna thankee for doing that most every day. Nothing like hearing the Lord's Word to give a body a gladsome heart." *And right now, my heart's feelin' mighty low.*

God? All the other times you took me from one house and sent me and Hattie on to the next one, it felt like a grand adventure. I'm fixin' to leave in the mornin', and I shorely would take it as a favor if'n you'd give me the grace to leave here with a gladsome heart. If not gladsome, at least . . . settled.

"Hope, I'd like to read to you. In fact, I have a specific passage in mind." He picked up the Bible and shifted in the chair so the lamp wouldn't cast his shadow on the page. " 'I will lift up my eyes unto the hills . . .' "

Her needle froze in midair. He was reading the psalm she and Annie came to love and rely on. He even added emphasis to the verse about not being moved. That had meant so much to Annie. Then he got to the last verse—her own favorite. " 'The Lord shall preserve thy going out and thy coming in from this time forth, and even for evermore.' "

"You couldn't have picked a more better verse in the whole Bible. Thankee, Jakob."

He shut the Bible and set it aside. "There's still some business we need to discuss. We came to an agreement that first evening. Remember?"

At this rate, she wasn't ever going to get that star stitched into place. Hope stabbed the needle into the quilt and folded her hands in her lap. "I remember. Mr. Stauffer—"

"Jakob."

"Jakob, I told you at the start, farmers work hard and don't got much ready cash. The family comes first. Emmy-Lou's spectacles cost a lot and I know you was sendin' money to keep Konrad away. You don't gotta give me one red cent. I'm goin' away a rich woman on account of all the verses and memories I got tucked away in my heart."

"You'll recall we agreed that I'd pay whatever I felt was right."

She wrinkled her nose. "I reckon that sounds like what we decided. 'Twas our other pact that mattered—and with God's help, we done dreadful good at getting Annie through everything." *If'n I keep thinkin' on Annie and Emmy-Lou instead of myself, I can get through this.*

He rose and stuck his hands in his pockets. A few steps one direction, then a few more the other—until he somehow managed to be standing by the settee. He reached down and lifted her hand in his.

Warmth streaked through her, leaving her longing to hold hands with Jakob forever. *I can't be thinkin' like that. Annie. I'll think of her. Annie's gonna feel safe and happy. Any woman would in his hands.*

"I want to renegotiate our agreement. It would involve a different pact altogether."

Hope moistened her lips and stared at him in silence.

"Have you noticed something about that verse of yours? One part always catches me when I hear it. It says 'going out and coming in.' Folks always say 'in and out,' not 'out and in.' Then it hit me why."

He paused, so she half whispered, "Why?"

"Because finally, you'd end up where God wanted you to stay—forevermore. You'd go in, and He'd never call you out from there. Hope, this is that place."

Her chest constricted. Other families invited her to remain with them, but she'd known it was time to leave. *Can it be God's allowin' me to stay here? With Jakob? And Emmy-Lou and Annie and Johnny? Is that why I didn't have a peace in my heart about leavin' tomorrow?*

A thought shot through her mind. Struggling not to sound hurt, she whispered, "But you was gonna send me away. You said so yourself."

"Ja, and it tore me apart inside, knowing it was the only way I could keep you and Annie and the children safe. My plan was to send you to safety, sell the farm, then come claim you."

Her mind whirled. *He wasn't trying to get rid of me? He just wanted to keep us safe?*

He smiled. "In the end, it wasn't my plan that mattered; God's plan prevailed. So tell me, Hope. You don't want to go, do you?" His voice sounded gentle, even coaxing.

A flood of memories washed over her—the kindness in his eyes, the rich timber of his voice as he read to her. His tenderness with Emmy-Lou and Johnny. The tingling warmth when their hands brushed. The inexplicable way that when they were together, she felt completely at ease, yet more alive than she'd ever been. Hope bit her lip and slowly shook her head.

Jakob pulled his other hand from his pocket and went down on his knee. "Hope, I was a broken man and my family was in shreds when you came here. God's used you to restore us, and even beyond that—He's planted seeds of a crop I never thought would grow here again. Seeds of love. I've reminded you that you agreed to accept whatever I want to pay you—and here it is. I'm praying you'll accept it."

He opened his hand. A circle of gold nestled in his palm. "I want to give you my heart, my home, and my name. Hope, please marry me and be my wife."

Suddenly, she understood why she hadn't had a peace about leaving. God hadn't planned on her going away. She'd charged ahead instead of seeking His direction. *I belong here—and not just with Jakob, but to him.*

"Seeds of love? Oh, Jakob, there's no crop better to plant and tend than love." A smile broke across his face, and she realized she was smiling, too. "I'm standin' in a garden that's already flourishing. Somethin' deep down inside me's glowin' like the sunshine—and without a doubt I know it's the love I hold for you. Nothin' would make me happier than to be your wife."

He shoved aside the quilt and pulled her up into his arms. "You once said you were like a dandelion, blowing in the wind. No more. Your days of drifting are over."

"That's okay. Every wish I ever made just came true."

"Me too. Because you'll be mine forevermore." He dipped his head, and his kiss promised a lifetime of joy.

More Laugh-Out-Loud Fun From
Cathy Marie Hake

Ruth Caldwell has always tried to live up to her mother's expectations of what a lady should be...often with less than impressive results. When she's forced to journey west, Ruth hopes she has found a place she'll finally fit in. But her arrival brings about more mayhem than even Ruth is used to.

Letter Perfect by Cathy Marie Hake

Though she alone believes in his innocence, Laney McCain is still devastated by the news of Galen O'Sullivan's shotgun wedding to another woman. As Galen and Laney struggle to surrender their hopes for the future, they come to learn a truly bittersweet lesson on learning to live in God's will and trusting Him.

Bittersweet by Cathy Marie Hake

If You Liked *Forevermore*, Try These Series!

The bustling, energetic city of 1800s Philadelphia is the perfect backdrop for Tracie Peterson's new series, LADIES OF LIBERTY. Follow Mia, Catherine, and Cassie, feisty women of affluence, as they defy the social norms and take unusual careers for the time—reporter, seamstress, personal assistant. But each woman finds herself in over her head and risks losing her family's good-will, her true love—and even her life.

LADIES OF LIBERTY:
A Lady of High Regard, A Lady of Hidden Intent,
A Lady of Secret Devotion
by Tracie Peterson

In the late 1860s, three couples carve out a new life in the wild, untamed Colorado Territory. Each person will be called upon to stand on nothing more than faith, risk what is most dear to them, and turn away from the past in order to detect God's plan for the future. By the time Colorado becomes a state, will they be united by love or defeated by adversity?

FOUNTAIN CREEK CHRONICLES:
Rekindled, Revealed, Remembered
by Tamera Alexander